His Most Italian City

His Most Italian City
by
Margaret Walker

His Most Italian City
Copyright © 2019 Margaret Walker

ISBN-13: 978-1-946409-94-2(Paperback)
ISBN :-978-1-946409-95-9(e-book)

BISAC Subject Headings:
FIC014000FICTION / Historical
FIC032000FICTION / War & Military
FIC047000FICTION / Sea Stories

Our sincere thanks for permission to print the cover art to:
Danijel Frka. Artist
Mr. Oliver Trulei: Owner

Editing: Chris Wozney
The Book Cover Whisperer:
ProfessionalBookCoverDesign.com

Address all correspondence to:
Penmore Press LLC
920 N Javelina Pl
Tucson AZ 85748

Dedication

In memory of

Captain Peter Ferrar

Master Mariner

Australian Merchant Navy

Acknowledgements

The modern military and political history of Italy has been much discussed in my family. My parents-in-law fought with the Italian Partisans north of Turin during World War Two, as did my husband's grandmother. His grandfather fought with the Italian army in the Great War. My own mother, from Istria, worked as an interpreter for the Allied Military Government in Trieste in the years before 1950 when she emigrated to Australia. Whilst her parents took on Italian citizenship after the war, she became Yugoslavian. I was adopted in 1960 and, when I met her in 1989, she referred to herself as Croatian.

The influence of Mussolini on Istria was considerable. I have recorded the experiences of my family. Because I did not grow up with them, I want especially to thank my sister Lynne who, over many years, faithfully recorded every word her mother uttered about growing up in Istria between the wars. From this we were able to put together something resembling a small book of oral history on which this novel is based.

Thanks also to the people of Novigrad/Cittanova for two great holidays and generous help with the family history. My mother didn't come from Novigrad. She was born in Tar, about eight kilometres away, but spent her holidays in Novigrad and visited family there. Her father was born in Trieste in 1886.

I owe a debt of gratitude to the Western Australian Maritime Museum, Freemantle, for fuelling my obsession with submarines, as well as to the Submarine Institute of Australia for their help. I hope they will forgive me for putting literary license before policies and procedures – not always but sometimes.

Lastly, to Michael James of Penmore Press and my editor, Lauren McElroy, many thanks.

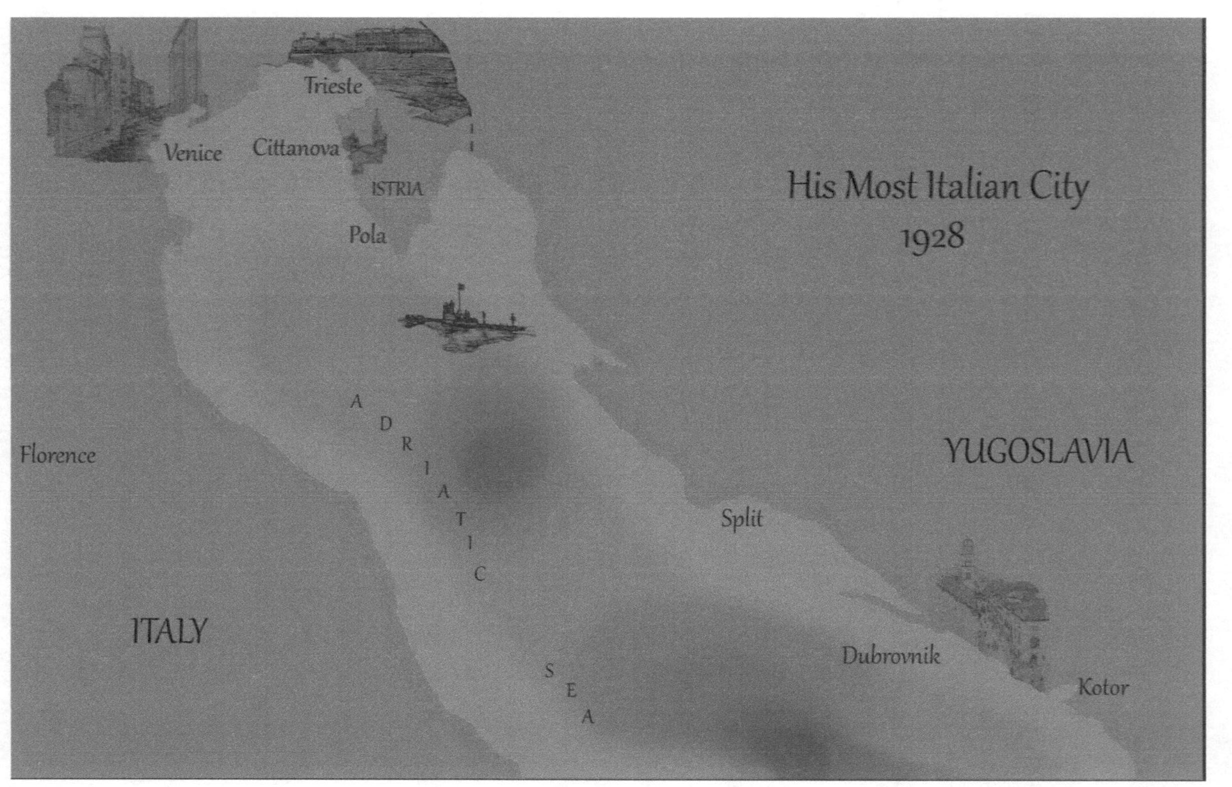

Adriatic Sea

Chapter One

Traveller, if you seek the finest coffee, disembark at Trieste. Back in the days when it was the port of the Austro-Hungarian Empire, people said it resembled a tear weeping from the map of Italy, looking for its motherland. So at the close of the Great War, in a gesture of atavistic compassion, the Allies handed it over without objection, though its proximity to the Kingdom of Serbs, Croats and Slovenes made it the focus of the Fascist Party.

Signor Matteo Brazzi ran a business in this city importing coffee from Brazil and he had an eclectic assortment of other incomes that he preferred not to advertise. When he read in *Il Piccolo,* Trieste's right wing newspaper, that 'holy Italy was rising again in history' he sniffed the winds of change and became a card-carrying Fascist faster than he could down an espresso. Such was the feeling of patriotism in the Italian peninsula.

Signor Brazzi was not particularly patriotic but, like all good businessmen, he put profits first. On the whole, he was quite pleased with the benefits his change of allegiance had brought him in this respect until, one night in April 1928, someone broke the front window of his office and set the timer on an incendiary bomb. An angry young Slovenian thrust the device through the opening in the glass and, as the minutes ticked down to zero, three men hurtled through the sleeping streets to escape by sea.

His Most Italian City

For an instant the city held its breath until an amber flash winked from a quiet street and a sliver of sky below the Old Town reflected a growing apocalypse. To many Triestini, the blaze brought to mind the violent years following the war, when fascism had been working to secure its hold over this most easterly outpost of Italy. In five seconds the handwoven carpet beneath the bomb was smoldering in earnest, in thirty seconds the raw silk curtains from China were well alight and, a mere eight minutes later, Brazzi's exquisitely decorated ground floor, his pride and joy, had been reduced to glowing rubble.

At about the same time, three hours past midnight to be precise, Brazzi tiptoed through his front door so as not to disturb his wife, after an evening of passion with – oh, what was her name? – and, as his office was blazing away, he was experiencing no more disquiet than a difficulty falling asleep on the sofa.

The suggestion of alarm within the city occasioned by the bells and fire trucks, and the not unpleasant aroma of burnt natural fabrics, wafted away in the background while he, flat on his back, found he was quite unable to roll over without his one-piece underwear either strangling his groin or boring a ridge into his shoulders, and the wool itched like chicken pox. It was supposedly the latest fashion: 'Tailor-made from pure Australian merino, manufactured in Manchester for the pleasure of the discerning gentleman.' He had bought it when he still believed what was written on the label, only to discover – in the small hours – how uncomfortable it was to sleep in.

Finally, he cursed the offending undergarment for the circus act it was and fell asleep from sheer exhaustion, with the underwear half on and half off, clutching a bundle of blankets to his chest to keep out the spring chill.

At the terse knock on the door he swore as the wool wrapped itself around his trunk, and he lurched from the sofa with the dignity of a performing bear. Dignity had not been high on his list of priorities when he'd gone to sleep. He opened the door.

There on his threshold stood a red-faced sergeant with cinders in his eyebrows who conveyed the terrible tidings in a measured monotone while Brazzi's uncomprehending eyes roamed the sitting room. Only the rumpled blankets on the sofa disturbed its understated pretentions.

'Who did it?' he at last managed to gasp.

'Perhaps you have enemies, Signor Brazzi?' suggested the sergeant.

'Me?' Brazzi blushed quickly. 'Enemies?'

Yet even as he said it his eyes were becoming resigned.

'So the perpetrators may be known to you?' the policeman asked.

Brazzi shook his head and exhaled fitfully. Though the policeman's lungs were full of fine ash particles, he kept his breathing calmly under control. Before the light from the shaded bulb the dawn retreated and the waning night pressed in on the room. The policeman observed Brazzi shrewdly, for it seemed to him that he looked as isolated as if he were alone in the universe. Fleeing from him into the bedroom, Brazzi re-emerged half-robed along with a dark-haired woman bleary with sleep who struggled to assist him into the arms of a dressing gown. Brazzi waved her away and she shot him a hurt look but remained where she was.

'We chased the perpetrators to one of the piers beyond the building of the Port Authority,' added the officer quickly to spare himself embarrassment and to emphasize the efficiency of the police force. 'Where they escaped by boat.'

'By boat?'

'A slim boat, signore. Our officers fired at it but it disappeared into the darkness off the end of the pier. One minute it was there, the next it was gone.'

'What do you mean, the next it was gone?' Brazzi clutched at a love bite on his neck. 'What boat doesn't leave a wake?'

'We heard the shots hit the cabin, signore. That is all.'

'And then it disappeared?'

'The port was very dark.'

His Most Italian City

And the seascape of Trieste a broad black abyss. Brazzi riveted a trembling thumb upside down into his mouth until his bottom teeth hammered away at the nail.

It couldn't be him, surely. Not after all this time.

'You seem upset, signore,' observed the officer.

'The bombing has upset me, naturally.'

The officer inclined his head. '*Si*, signore, naturally.'

'Matteo,' begged the woman, 'please tell me what this is all about.'

The sofa, the blankets and their implications of adultery had relegated the pretty little wife to a dispossessed expression of concern in her own home. She looked fragile and swollen about the breasts and the officer, who had four children himself, wondered if she was pregnant. *Busy man*, he thought.

'Go back to bed, Angelica!' Brazzi shoved the thumb behind his back. 'Sergeant, how do the police propose to hunt down the perpetrators of this crime?'

'The perpetrators would be wild Slovenian youths with a grudge against Italians,' the policeman said with a shrug. 'Given the number of Slovenes in this city, it usually is. Don't worry, Signor Brazzi. There is no longer an emperor and there is no longer an empire. Austria can't protect the Slovenes in Trieste any more.

'By the way...' – he paused with a hand on the door – 'I loved your last article in *Il Piccolo*, *"Trieste è la città Italianissima"*. Great title. It is the most Italian city now.'

Brazzi drew himself up to his full height. With his hat on he'd be nearly up to the man's forehead.

'Flatter me some other time!' he stuttered. 'What about my safety?'

'Your safety?' The cool brow creased. 'Of course you are safe from the Slovenians, signore. We'll get them. You must be aware of Italian ravages on their property? I have seen your name repeatedly in the newspapers and I assumed you were helping.'

'Yes, yes. I help when they ask me.'

'Often?'

'When they ask. As I said.'

'Then you don't have confidence that Mussolini can protect you in the same way? The perpetrators of this crime will be locked up in the San Marco prison in Venice with the rest of their agitators, signore, or sent to Sardinia. Or they'll be hung.'

He opened the door, but Brazzi restrained him.

'You said *three men* were seen running towards a pier? It may be that your officers could identify *one* of them.'

The officer regarded him.

'One in particular?'

'Yes,' mumbled Brazzi. '*No*, but can't a better description be found than "three men"?'

'Two ran faster than the third.'

'And who was the third?'

'I told you, signore, at this stage we don't know.'

The officer departed, leaving Brazzi rolling in hopelessness, as if a time tunnel had opened at his feet and was leading him backwards. Just when the past had seemed closed. He began to dress, but the drawn out process, which usually gave him so much pleasure, had been spoiled and now he watched himself adjusting his silk tie in his mirror with all the enjoyment of a cat in the rain.

The clock on the mantelpiece read half past five. He couldn't eat, but to calm his nerves he had smoked two cigarettes and woken up the dozing Angelica to percolate him an espresso. Now he stood, in a brittle temper, looking out the window of their apartment onto the waterfront, waiting for the sun to rise so that he could go down and inspect the damage. In the vague pre-dawn a cargo ship approached the harbor from across the Gulf of Trieste and a squat dredger raced behind it towards the Old Port. Even though it was so early the passenger piers had finished with the first

His Most Italian City

morning's traffic and the Audace pier extended, as empty as a wilderness, far out into the water, with only two small coastal steamers and a police launch tied to three of its many cleats. A long, long pier strolling back in towards the city and at its end the massive bulk of the Austrian commercial buildings that the empire didn't need any more.

He watched as the first sunbeams struck the harbor, polishing the dusky gray water and bringing it to life. He imagined without excitement passengers travelling across the gulf to Venice or down the Istrian coast, while he watched the flags rise on Government House and heard the bells ringing for early Mass, until there was nothing else for it but to go down and see what remained of his office.

The first sign of the fire was the water lying in puddles on the footpath and trundling down the gutter. Coming towards him from the building itself floated fragrant ashes, behind them the harsh reek of oil and varnish. A truck parked in the street had caught fire and there were, in addition, wafts of smoke from its scorched tires. Aside from several blackened windows in the offices directly opposite and above his own, the damage did not extend beyond the ground floor of his building, and Brazzi stood observing the destruction of beauty with the taut face of a trainer who has just lost his prize racehorse.

Ten meters away, beyond his charred desk and the skeleton of its chair, a detective and a young constable probed the still smoldering ruins.

'Does anyone know where they came from?' Brazzi shouted to the detective. 'From the harbor? From the docks?'

The man stumbled across a blackened floor while wood paneling transformed to charcoal crumbled in his path.

'No one heard them come in.' The crisp bass voice implied it was all in a day's work.

The morning breeze squeezed between the old imperial buildings, seeking space. Finding none, it trickled away through Brazzi's broken windows. Such a solid place, Trieste.

'An entire harbor and no witnesses! How it that possible?'

'We've made enquires up and down the sea front.' The detective sounded bored. Better investigate an assault on the government than a small-time operator like Brazzi. 'Planning has gone into this. This is not the work of impulsive young men, Signor Brazzi.'

'But this morning the sergeant said wild young Slovenians…'

The detective interrupted him.

'We found the remains of an incendiary bomb inside with a timer attached to the detonator,' he stated brusquely, as if he had no time for Brazzi's protests, as indeed he hadn't. 'This has been planted by someone with military knowledge. They didn't just smash the window and hurl in petrol.'

'So what now?'

'A lot rests on you,' said the detective. 'Signore.'

There it was again, that significant pause and its relationship to Brazzi. This man in his shop-bought suit and pedestrian tie was implying that Brazzi knew more than he was letting on.

'No one I work with is in the armed forces,' Brazzi insisted regally.

The detective examined a tiny flake of ash soiling his cheap lapel – clearly he didn't believe him – and checked his wristwatch.

'Then perhaps someone you used to know.' A tram rattled down the hill and the milkman hurried past with his horse and cart and a glance at the destruction. The city was waking up. The interview was over. 'When a crime scene presents with excess passion or a degree of unwarranted care and foresight, Signor Brazzi, the explanation is always found close to home.'

Brazzi evacuated his devastated premises like an army in flight and began pacing up and down the Piazza Unità, to the waterfront and back, until he was wheezing and dizzy and couldn't pace any more. The clock on the Town Hall dragged its hands towards the hour. Not yet eight o'clock! Even time had turned against him. He realized that he had started looking back over his shoulder, so utterly had the police convinced him that the perpetrators were people he knew, to whom he had an accountability. Truly, he had come to believe it himself, as if he had constructed a desperate plot against himself and put one man at its head. Like a self-fulfilling prophecy. A warped revenge.

Yes, that's exactly what it would be. It was interesting, also, that, by a division just as diabolical, he seemed to have reduced the three men to one. Not perpetrators, perpetrator. Men who made money always had enemies, but Brazzi could not explain his conviction that it was this one enemy in particular. The police had said that he left by sea? So? Trieste was a seaport, no surprise there. All the observation had really done was jog his memory of a man he would rather forget and the heartache he had forgotten with him. *Had* he forgotten it? Well, he had loved and lost, so perhaps he hadn't quite, and those days when he might have been redeemed were behind him. So the desperate soul-searching continued without resolve, until finally it was nine o'clock and the commencement of the business day. Without further delay he headed towards the offices of the Fascist Party, where he hoped someone might help him without the subtle intimation that it was all his own fault.

*****

Francesco Giunta, Mussolini's right-hand man, rose to greet him from behind a roll-top desk so beautiful that Brazzi, even in his agitated state, felt tempted to make an offer for it. Yet it was the office of a military man and well ordered even so. An ink well, a quill, three nibs and a blotter were arranged upon the desk beside writing paper and envelopes, and labeled files waited neatly in chronological order on a bookshelf beneath the window. Framed upon the wall was a map of northern Italy, proudly swelled along its eastern borders by the Slav-filled territories acquired from Austria since the war.

Margaret Walker

Within the present government, Giunta had a well-deserved reputation as a superb organizer. He had read the preliminary police report on the attack on Brazzi's premises and now stood eyeing the elegantly tailored coffee merchant trembling in front him, before straightening his mouth and commencing a grave discourse on the danger of the Slavic races to Italian purity.

'And now you, signore,' he concluded, 'have seen the atrocities of these barbarian Balkan criminals for yourself.'

'Good,' blundered Brazzi before recollecting himself. Such a slip would not shift the limelight from him. 'Though it has not yet been proven that the bombing was the work of the Slovenes.'

'The Slovenes in Trieste are antagonistic towards Italy, Signor Brazzi. The Party has been very pleased with your actions against them on our behalf, but perhaps you are not aware of the scale of the Slavic threat in the territories redeemed by Italy?'

'Like Trieste?' blurted Brazzi.

'Trieste was always Italian, Signor Brazzi.' It was just possible to detect menace in the evenness of the reply. 'I was referring to Istria. We could possibly have an opening there for an honorable fascist. How would you like to serve il Duce in Istria?'

'You mean to integrate its Slovenes and Croats into Italian society?'

'Assimilate, signore, not integrate.'

'But I haven't decided to leave, Signor Giunta,' gabbled Brazzi with a weak smile. Seeking help from Francesco Giunta might have been a fundamental error. 'Not entirely. I am a loyal Italian and I love Trieste. In fact, I would state without qualification that I am a city man. This bombing has unnerved me… What I was hoping for from the Party was reassurance … Yes, "reassurance" is entirely the word I was looking for.'

From beyond the window he heard the splash of a fountain, the squeals of local children playing in its water.

His Most Italian City

'I require a man on the ground,' Giunta went on while Brazzi backed against the door. 'Begin by changing surnames so that they sound Italian. I don't anticipate you will have any problems; in every Slavic name there is an Italian root.'

Certainly Giunta possessed an attractive degree of hubris, though Brazzi hesitated to call him narcissistic. He watched as Giunta smoothed an erudite finger from the arch of one temple down the side of his nose. Licking his lips would have been just as effective, and Brazzi wondered what sort of woman was waiting for him at home and her expectations when he walked through the front door.

Maybe he *should* get away for a while? Perhaps if he went somewhere where his name wasn't written on his door, nothing worse would happen to him. He would be running away, yes, but would he phrase it in quite those terms? A short break… Business interests?

And then his eyes fell on the police report lying on the desk. Giunta hadn't even bothered to conceal it. 'Destruction of commercial premises. Perpetrator known to victim. Wasteful employment of the police.' Unstated: a public nuisance. And below the words he saw a list that included several of his associates known to police, but not the one name he was thinking of.

They were trying to get rid of him.

'I'm happy to see you have no objections, Signor Brazzi,' observed Giunta, nonchalantly raising his quill.

He didn't take the trouble to look up and acknowledge Brazzi's mounting panic. He dipped his quill in the ink well. He was writing, he mentioned with the vagueness of his disinterest, to fellow soldier Giuseppe Monfalcon in Cittanova, a popular tourist resort of the old empire, to say that he was appointing Matteo Brazzi to be the fascist mayor of the town and his representative in eradicating any residual Slavic culture in the area.

'You will have the help of the Prefect of Pola,' concluded Giunta as he blotted the letter. 'And I know you can rely on him. Hand this to my secretary as you leave.'

Brazzi was amazed he didn't ask him to post it on his way home.

*****

He opened his front door to noises of commotion coming from the bathroom. From the random flaps and thuds, he thought at first that a bird had flown in through the open window and was unable to get out. One flap had scarcely started when the next thud began, and when he went to investigate, swearing a little under his breath, Angelica stumbled out, one hand clutched rigidly to her abdomen, her face convulsed with crying.

Wearily, he confronted her.

'What is it, Angelica?'

'Matteo,' she moaned, 'I'm bleeding. Again.'

Not right now. He couldn't manage anything else, now. He stormed over to the new telephone on the hall table, hoisted it up in front of her, then brutally slammed it back down.

'Telephone your mother!' he snapped.

Then he remembered the inlaid wood. Ah, what had he done? Abandoning his wife to her inglorious howling upon the tiles, he examined the surface of the small table, relieved to see that the intricate pattern had survived his tantrum undamaged. He dusted it down, then carefully replaced the telephone.

*****

Capitano Giuseppe Monfalcon was accustomed to being feared. It was a leftover from his involvement in the Great War and he couldn't shake the attitude. As an officer of the Arditi, the elite Italian forces, he had waged bitter trench warfare on the Southern Alps against the soldiers of Austria and Hungary. He was brave, as he had had to be, for they had given him the most risky assignments, though he had never been the fine specimen of Italian man expected of that daring force. He carried his shoulders too far forward, in the attitude of a bulldog, his face was puckered at the edges through conspicuous valor, and he did not have the firm mouth expected of heroes. But something of the physical prowess of the Arditi lingered in the bearing that still suggested he was about to leap into a trench with a dagger between his teeth.

Teresa Urizio was terrified of him. He reminded her of a vulture. He had the height and the stoop, and seemed just as omnipresent when seen from below.

'I have had a letter from the Party in Trieste,' he had explained, looming over Teresa while she struggled to gather herself together – he was offering her a job, after all – 'requiring me to employ a cook and a maid for one of their members, whom they are sending us. And you are a good cook and gregarious, Signora Urizio.'

'Thank you,' answered Teresa, 'but there are dozens of other women like me in Cittanova.'

'You speak Italian and they don't.'

'I learned a bit from the tourists, Signor Monfalcon, that's all.'

'Nevertheless, I feel that you would be the ideal fascist welcoming party.'

'What's fascist?' quavered Teresa.

'We are all fascists,' beamed Monfalcon. Her fear was very pleasing. 'Mussolini says that if you are Italian, you're a fascist.'

This had Teresa stumped but she remembered her manners.

'Would you thank Signor Mussolini for me?' she replied politely. 'I've only just got used to being Italian.'

Monfalcon patted her on the shoulder, even though Teresa was older than he was.

'Urizio is an Italian name.'

'But my father was Vellovich,' explained Teresa. 'And you still haven't told me what fascist means, Signor Monfalcon.'

'A fascist is someone who looks after Italy, Signora Urizio.'

Margaret Walker

'Well, I don't know whether I can do that, but I can cook. So when do I start?'

'When the boat gets in, signora. If you would kindly meet Signor and Signora Brazzi when they come in on the steamer from Trieste on Monday week.'

*****

When, two weeks after the bombing, Matteo Brazzi left his beloved Trieste to sail south down the Istrian coast to Cittanova he succumbed to a misery as grand as Trieste's architecture. His delicate nose was upset to be loaded onto an elderly, grubby, single-funneled coastal steamer along with farmers in old clothes who smelled of manure. He became seasick the instant the *San Carlo* pulled out from the pier. He clutched the rail, gagging and wheezing like the asthmatic albatross he was, and, as the boat met the swell of the open sea, he experienced an existential urge to remove his shoes and socks and baptize his feet in the holy water he was leaving. Signor Brazzi vowed he would never again be seen unclothed by a member of the police force, or the public, so he bravely resisted this longing though it broke his heart to do so.

The four-hour trip was extended to five when a wretched woman fell in whilst attempting to board one of the smaller craft that came out from the shore to meet the boat. To general applause, the ship's mate dived from the bow to rescue her, though it was clear to Signor Brazzi that she had done it on purpose and didn't deserve the attention. Indeed, he could scarcely credit her conceit when he was perishing at the hands of a coastal steamer, and the sight of dolphins dancing merrily down the coast only made it worse. He finally became aware that his misery was about to end when the *San Carlo* sounded its siren and turned in towards a sheltered, west-facing cove where a town of red-roofed houses, a campanile and a multitude of parks beckoned to him across the final stretch of water.

At the end of a broad pier that swept in towards the town, a large two-masted sailing ship had docked, and the steamer pulled around it to a square expanse of wharf forty meters further along, where an eager crowd awaited it. The arrival of the pottering old vessel was clearly a highly anticipated event, and Signor Brazzi observed with distaste a squad of barefoot little boys poking barge poles into the water, plump housewives wearing headscarves instead of hats, and working men with their sleeves rolled up and cigarettes hanging from their lips, all shouting and waving in greeting. But he also noticed how the sea encroached upon the town until it lapped the rock it was built on, and how its houses sheltered in the sole safe wedge that remained.

In a querulous mood, he brushed the legacy of his travelling companions from his coat and escorted his wife down the gangway. To their right he saw a row of tall houses and seawalls; to the left, fishing vessels, fishing tackle and fishing nets.

'Angelica,' he announced, 'we will stay away from the fish!'

Angelica Brazzi did as she was told, for her husband had an aversion to seafood. She had dressed that morning, for his benefit, in a lovely coat of fine red wool, with a cloche hat and gloves to match, and had vamped her naturally sultry eyes (which he liked), and now she observed his response to the crowd with unease.

'Perhaps we shouldn't move *too far* away, Matteo?' she whispered. 'Didn't Signor Monfalcon write that we were being met?'

But the jubilance of the throng surged up and overflowed into the sunshine, and just who might be meeting them was not clear, so they eased further down the wharf, passing, as they did so, three cats, a dog, and a seagull as big as a turkey. From the high prow of a fishing vessel the bird opened its beak, threw back its head and squawked purposefully at them.

Angelica shrieked, and her husband started as if he'd been struck. At once a woman in her middle years hurried up to the bird and shooed it away. Behind her, a dour man watched in silence with one hand in his pocket and the other resting on the head of a donkey hitched to a small cart.

'What was wrong with that bird?' demanded Brazzi.

'With the seagull, signore?' panted the woman.

'Is that what you call it?'

'He won't hurt you. He's just saying *buon giorno!*'

She inspected the couple with undisguised delight and smoothed the front of her dress.

'Signor and Signora Brazzi! For a moment I was wondering how I'd find you!' she exclaimed in barely passable Italian muddled up with dialect. 'Then Emilio said, "That's them, Teresa!" and I said, "What a beautiful coat his wife is wearing! You don't see coats like that here!"'

Brazzi struggled to understand her. His small moustache bristled and the woman anxiously tightened her headscarf. She had little experience of bristling moustaches.

'Signor Monfalcon sent us to welcome you,' she proffered tentatively. 'I'm Teresa Urizio and this is my husband, Emilio.'

'But could not Signor Monfalcon have come himself?' enquired Brazzi.

Teresa hesitated, either because she didn't want to answer the question or because Signor Brazzi had spoken in perfect Italian.

'Signor Monfalcon doesn't like crowds,' she said.

She let the explanation hang in the air and signaled to a seaman who was unloading luggage from the deck.

'Now, the house we have prepared for you is on the other side of the piazza. I will be your cook and Signor Monfalcon has organized a girl to help you around your new house. If you would kindly walk with me, Emilio will collect your boxes.' She cast a sharp eye over Angelica in such a way that Brazzi could not fail to notice. 'You're very pale, signora.'

Yes, Brazzi knew she was pale and he knew why, but she *would* hobble along bravely by his side. They'd have to wiggle through these old buildings to get to the piazza – he could see no direct route – and she wasn't good at wiggling today. He felt annoyed, all of a sudden, that Angelica seemed to elicit concern from everyone who saw them together.

Teresa held out a consoling hand and Brazzi wanted to slap it.

'Cittanova should be just the place for you, signora,' she continued warily. She withdrew the hand. 'The ladies here are so friendly. Do you like fish? I know a thousand ways to prepare it.'

'Fish?' snapped Brazzi so crossly that his wife was embarrassed. 'One method will suffice, served infrequently.'

'Poor Matteo,' explained Angelica to Teresa, 'he was so sick on the boat.'

The women were already confidential – a very bad sign – and so they set off towards the piazza and the pretty town floated passed them.

Time and chance had divided its proud Venetian walls until only segments remained as a reminder that, like Brazzi, Cittanova had once required protection against an enemy from the sea. An ancient duomo extended into the clustered piazza and by its side stood a modern campanile with a bronze saint crowning its peak, to defend the town from Turks, waves, and all slim boats that were there one minute and gone the next.

Brazzi regarded it morosely.

'Here is the sea again, Signora Urizio! You have led us around in a circle!'

'Indeed, I haven't, Signor Brazzi!' protested Teresa. 'It's just not a very big town.'

On they walked, to an alley of weathered limestone houses and, for a third time, there was the sea like a grim assassin, grinding its knife on the rocks below the Venetian lookout.

This was the end. Brazzi's valor, hastily constructed from thin air that morning, departed to its afterlife. The long day declined and his heart of paper sunk into its purple limbo. By the time Signor Urizio and his donkey lumbered along with their boxes, he had succumbed to nervous oblivion in a modest, salmon-colored Istrian house.

Angelica regarded him on the sofa, marveling at how vulnerable he looked. Such vulnerability as she had so often hoped for. Since the afternoon was cooling, she took off the red coat and laid it over his legs to warm him.

Teresa touched the soft wool with the tip of one finger.

'That's the loveliest coat I've ever seen,' she whispered.

'Do you like it?' Angelica plucked wanly at a leaf that clung to the hem. 'Matteo bought it for me so that it would match his.'

'And did you mind that?'

'Oh, dear Matteo,' explained Angelica, blushing, 'I didn't want to hurt his feelings.'

Teresa left without a word, which was unusual.

As her departing footsteps fell silent Angelica whispered, 'Matteo, do you think this is where I'll finally have my baby?'

Matteo didn't hear her. Angelica brushed her lips softly across his forehead and he murmured something that might have been her name.

Chapter Two

Silvana saw a monster in the sea the night that Nono changed his name. She connected the two events with more guile than the average eight-year-old because one was improbable and the other unlikely; thus they were linked by their unnatural existences. Everyone said she was too young to be so pragmatic.

The Bora was blowing that night, too. The vicious northeasterly shrieked through the chimneys of Cittanova. Beneath, a solid roar of wind charged across the port and collided with the squat lighthouse, sending spray high into the heavens. The broad half-moon of protected water that looked so safe in daylight spread wide its stone arms by night and, within their black embrace, the monster glided briefly through the flickering beam and back into the darkness, sending a thrill up Silvana's spine, a thrill partly of curiosity and partly of pleasant terror.

Silvana noticed that the monster's head seemed ringed by a halo of mist and that its tail was a white cauldron. Black water swept across its flanks and the wind annihilated any sound it might have made, drawing her into the unearthly scene with such fascination that, had the Bora ceased to blow, she would not have realized.

She pulled the shutters tightly together. Collecting her one precious candle, she stole a glance behind her in the hope that the monster might not rattle the shutters with a view to invasion. One could never tell with monsters and so a rearguard action was always advisable. Holding her candle high, she made her way down the narrow stairs to inform her family of the threat. The flame flickered nervously into the shadows and she had nearly reached the bottom when she heard the raised voices of her grandparents and her uncle, Zio Lin. The note of anger in the well-loved voices made her stop and pay close attention. All thoughts of monsters flew from her head.

'That's outrageous!' she heard Nona gasp. 'At his age.'

What has Nono done? wondered Silvana.

'They can't make him!'

Silvana relaxed her grip on the railing. Well, it wasn't Nono's fault at least. She listened to the dulcet reply of her uncle. He had lived in Florence for eight years and had taught biology at its university. In those years he had picked up the pure, more musical Italian of that city in contrast to the Venetian dialect that her grandparents spoke. Tonight he spoke Venetian with the accents of Florence.

'They can, unfortunately.'

Her uncle paused and Silvana took advantage of this opportunity to poke her nose from the hall into the kitchen, with her candle almost spluttering onto her skin.

'What are you talking about?' she demanded.

'Nono is changing his name!' answered Nona.

Not her lovely Nono, surely, moping at the table as if he'd done something wrong, the inevitable cigarette slanting from one hand. The fingers on his free hand meditatively tapped the table. Above it rose his snowy hair and Imperial moustache, which, though still dark, did not effectively hide his grimace. She wondered with a brief surge of concern if Nona and Nono had had an argument, but though Nona was strict she was not cranky. She disapproved of Nono smoking in bed, that was all. With her hair in a silvery bun and wearing a blouse just as white, she paced beside her husband, their heads for once at the same level, for Nono, when standing, towered over his tiny wife and even over his moderately-sized son. After a lifetime of trying he still could not find enough room to fold his long legs beneath the table, and rumor had it that the wood had shrunk to spite him.

Silvana felt sorry for Nono. He was trapped.

'Nono can change his name!' she declared. 'People call him by different names all the time!'

But Nona only said, 'Put that candle down, Silvana, before you burn your fingers.'

So Silvana placed the candle on the table, slopping the melted wax in its holder onto the scrubbed wood, and recited rebelliously, 'Zan, Giovanni, Zvane, Johannes! Venetian, Italian, Croatian, German!'

'I like Zan,' mumbled Nono while he could.

'Though you must agree, Popà,' said his son, 'that you are a polyglot.'

'Istria's the polyglot, Giovanni, not me.' He stubbed out his cigarette into Silvana's solidifying wax. 'But I am not changing my Christian name, Silvana. The government in Italy wants to change my surname.'

'Micatovich?' exclaimed Silvana. 'Change it to what?'

'Di Micheli,' he replied. 'Like Zio Lin.'

'But Di Micheli sounds silly!'

'Yes, trivial, isn't it?'

He pursed his lips, and the family nodded. It would take just such a crisis to ruffle his balmy temperament.

'I think it's a name for a small person,' declared Silvana stoutly.

'Not for me?'

'No, you're too big.'

'Well said, Silvana, but is your Italian better than mine? Can you read the letter that explains why they are doing it?'

He handed her a sheet of typed paper.

'The twenty-ninth of November nineteen twenty-eight,' read Silvana before continuing slowly in Italian. '*Il controscritto cognome di*

Micatovich è stato corretto a quello di Di Micheli con decreto del Prefetto di Pola.'

'*Corretto!*' wailed Nona. '*Corretto!* Of all the rudeness.'

'I don't know what it means.'

Her grandfather patted Silvana's curly head fondly.

'Picked up German from the tourists but can't speak Italian,' he laughed. '*Corretto* means "corrected," Silvana. It reads "the surname Micatovich has been *corrected* to that of Di Micheli."'

'Well done, Zan,' said Nona.

It is said that sarcasm is wasted on children, and it didn't work on Silvana because her grandmother was not generally sarcastic in front of her.

'So what?' said Silvana.

Zan nodded.

'That's a safe attitude to have, Silvana, and your last name might be spared because Zambon is Venetian. It's the Slavic ones they're changing.'

'Why?'

'Because Mussolini doesn't like them.'

'Who?'

'The prime minister.'

'Why?'

'He's a Fascist.'

'He's a *what?*'

'I don't really know,' confessed Zan. 'We'll ask Zio Lin, shall we?'

He looked hopefully at his son, but Nona exploded, 'Silvana! You would talk the legs off an iron pot! Zan, she is too young to understand and you're only encouraging her.'

'Sorry,' said Zan, 'but she's cleverer than I am, Maria.' Actually, they all were.

So Maria demanded of her son, 'Can't they leave us in peace, Giovanni?'

His Most Italian City

Giovanni had been leaning against the chimney, watching the sparks fly upwards. He watched his bewildered father, his tiny irate mother and felt the warmth murmuring towards him from the brick behind.

'We're the meat in the sandwich, Mama,' he replied. 'Caught between Yugoslavia and Italy, and Italy's problem is that it thinks it's the Roman Empire.' He puffed dismissively into the chimney. At once a bouquet of sparks blossomed upon the bricks. 'In any case, poets are the Caesars these days.'

'Poets, Giovanni?' asked his father.

'Bloodthirsty poets!'

'Stop teasing.'

'I'm not teasing. Italian poets *are* bloodthirsty.'

'Well, I'm terrible at poetry anyway.'

'Then you should write! Write to the stable governments that Italy admires so much, like the British. Remind them how much the world owes Italy, in a lengthy display of colorful whining.'

'Zio Lin!' exclaimed his niece. 'Why are you all laughing?'

'We're laughing, Silvana,' – how did one explain this to an eight year old? – 'because Mussolini says he will make Italy great again but he doesn't know anything about politics or how to run a country.'

'That's not why you're laughing.'

'There!' concluded her uncle, relieved of his burden. 'You're a clever little thing. I think Mussolini's learning on the job, so let's just say he would *like* to make Italy great again, and everyone seems to agree with him. Or rather, he agrees with them, and both parties are working together these days, as far as I can tell.'

It was all too much. Such an extravagant conversation did not suit simple men. Zan rolled another cigarette carefully between his fingers and thumb then licked it with a sideways swipe of his tongue. He stood up until he was his full huge height and attempted to light the cigarette from the candelabra that hung from the ceiling. No one else was tall enough to do this and it was some compensation for his lack of native wit. The remainder of the ceiling drifted off into a rounded square of imagined corners like an old calendar with flourishes for compass points. Silvana could just make them out if she peered closely, and any spiders undercover in the faraway recesses would have no trouble at all being fruitful and multiplying unless Paulina, who came each day to help, happened to be in a vengeful mood.

They used oil to light the candelabra but it brightened the room ineffectively and people would look up hoping for revelation only to see the smoke wisp skywards like a specter, frightening the old beams in the roof. Sometimes they said, 'Look, it's a ghost!' but to Silvana, ghosts performed the same function as sea monsters, an entertaining interlude until the right explanation turned up. She strained her neck and observed wisps of smoke, thinking that some of them looked like her monster but others didn't. This one here, for instance, with the head that rose out of the water.

'Excuse me,' she began, while her grandfather planned his approach.

'You're going to set your hair alight, Popà,' said Giovanni.

'Not tonight.'

Zan stood on his toes and placed the cigarette at the edge of the flame.

'I saw a monster in the port, Nono.'

Zan inhaled.

'Got it!'

'It was off the breakwater.'

'Couldn't you have used matches, Popà?'

'I needed to see if I could do it.'

'Good for you. Now you have.'

Silvana tried again.

'Excuse me, Nono. I saw a monster moving from the breakwater to the pier.'

His Most Italian City

Zan settled back into his chair, emitted a grouchy puff, then whistled to Gilda who wandered across from her bed by the stove wagging her tail.

'I wish that king of theirs had never let Mussolini form a government,' he informed the dog. 'Then they mightn't have changed my name.'

'But I saw a *monster*, Nono.'

'Why "monster," darling?'

'Because it had a big head and a long black body and a white tail.'

'Did it breathe fire?'

Zan chuckled at Gilda who regarded him with canine bewilderment then went back to bed.

Silvana gave up.

'The king didn't let Mussolini form a government, Popà. He invited him.'

'Why, Giovanni? Does he feel that Mussolini will help Italy?'

'I don't think he knew what else to do. The people are behind Mussolini.'

'He's popular?'

'Oh, very. The glorious nation of Italy is leading the world into a new era of peace, didn't you know?' Giovanni dropped his voice to a whisper.

'The walls don't have ears, Giovanni,' said his father.

'Not yet, they don't. The root of the problem lies in Italy's conviction that such a nation deserves an empire. Britain, in particular, will back Italy as harmless if it serves British interests.'

'And is Italy harmless?'

'They promised us more freedom than we had under Austria, so what do you think?'

Maria put horrified hands to her face.

'I think they're changing our name!' she cried, completely forgetting Silvana, listening inquisitively to every word.

'Correcting our name, you observe.'

'Why are they correcting it, Zio Lin?'

'Because we can't spell, Silvana, evidently.'

'I wish you were my school teacher.'

'She's not cynical.'

Although, frankly, thought Giovanni, *Mussolini might be cynical if we corrected his name to Musolovich.*

Standing thoughtfully by the old brick stove beneath the varnished glow of the lamp, Giovanni's profile had the severity of a formal photograph: the good brown suit, stiff collar and tie, the high forehead and full lips that might at some dreadful moment part to pour forth anatomical terms in Latin and Greek and a tome of homework. This profile would soften with age and, later on in life, he would not appear so formidably academic. But, for now, it was only when you looked twice that you detected the tender eye that had dedicated itself to the nurture of young minds. On this dark and blustery evening it seemed that it was dedicated to one young mind in particular.

Every child deserves a Zio Lin, thought Silvana, and he wasn't formal to her, this lovely uncle who took such a delight in words. One day he might even tell her what 'cynical' meant.

'I've heard within the university, Mama,' he went on, 'that Mussolini expects Europe to hand Italy its empire on a plate. It can't achieve the empire it believes it deserves in the manner it thinks it should.'

'What's an empire, Zio Lin?'

'It's a tongue twister, Silvana.'

Maria adjusted her corset, which had risen up during her brief outburst. Soothing her blouse down upon her bosom, she asked Giovanni to stop talking politics in front of The Child because she wouldn't understand and it would only upset her.

Giovanni gave an Italian shrug – all those years in Florence.

'She looks pretty keen to me.'

So Maria turned to her granddaughter and said sharply, 'Bed, Silvana!'

'But I'm interested.'

His Most Italian City

'Look at the time!'

'It's only nine o'clock.'

'Way past your bedtime.'

'But…'

'Off!'

Silvana was experienced enough to know when the game was up, so she launched straight into her bedtime routine, in which everyone had their assigned roles.

'Good night, Nona.'

'I'll be up soon with your hot water bottle, Silvana.'

'Good night, Nono.'

'Sleep tight, darling.'

'I love you, Zio Lin.'

'*Anch'io ti amo*, clever girl.'

Then Silvana lit the stub of her candle and retraced her way upstairs to see if the monster was still there.

*****

'Micatovich corrected to Di Micheli by the decree of the Prefect of Pola; property owner, aged 71. Rusich corrected to Rossi; fisherman, aged 69. Cocianzich corrected to Cociani; fisherman, aged 69. Knez corrected to Nessi, fisherman aged 69. Rukavino corrected to Roccavini; farmer, aged 68. Glavich corrected to Glavi; fisherman, aged 68. Cattunar corrected to Cattonaro; fisherman, aged 67. Cemerich corrected to Cerneri; fisherman aged 65. Valentich corrected to Valenti; farmer, age 65. Cicitanovich corrected to Civitani; carpenter, aged 64.'

The fat man with the blunt fingers poked the leather-bound register of *Battezzati* – baptisms.

'Here it is again, Micatovich corrected to Michelato; farmer, aged 64. Whoever makes these names up has forgotten he's already called his cousin Di Micheli.'

'Are you finished?' Monfalcon's croak emerged like that of a toad calling through a fog, muffled by the brim of his hat. He was backlit by a candle on the table and shrouded within a rancid suit of clothes.

'Nearly, Giuseppe. Gregorovich corrected to Gregori. Simonovich corrected to Simeoni. Stoinich corrected to Stoini. Valkovich corrected to Valconi. Krall corrected to Cralli. Naprioloich corrected to Naperotti.'

Andrea Morato put the book down and stretched for relief. Too fat. Really, too fat.

'The Prefect of Pola has been busy,' he remarked.

'How many more are there?'

'That's just a handful of the old men. I haven't even started on the youngsters.'

'The population of Cittanova is one and a half thousand and there are another thousand in the countryside. Is that all the men over sixty?'

'As far as I can tell.'

Morato handed the book to Matteo Brazzi, who was sitting beside him and eyeing his drink with the neat concern of a bank clerk. Across the table from Brazzi sat Giuseppe Monfalcon and the corpulent Morato – Greed and Gluttony – between them an unprepossessing bottle of something amorphous they were trying to force down Brazzi's throat. He sniffed the light brown liquid in his glass – as sickly sweet as an overblown rose, with behind it the stricture of turpentine – and gagged.

'Something the matter?' asked Morato.

'What's this?'

'Walnut brandy. Guiseppe made it.'

Brazzi flapped the book shut irritably and pushed his glass away.

'The City of Trieste doesn't serve real brandy anymore?'

'Humor him, Matteo, and drink it. You can go back to Trieste if you don't like walnut brandy.'

'I'm not going back to Trieste. I came to Istria for Angelica's health.'

His Most Italian City

'You came to Istria to hide your secrets, my friend,' snorted Monfalcon. 'And your wife's suffering from your roving eye. What has she got, syphilis?'

Brazzi shifted uncomfortably.

'Look, that's the lot, Giuseppe, the men in the baptismal register that you've just heard.'

'The prefect has quite a job to go, then.'

'Not really. He just went through and scribbled "corrected" next to each name. I could have done that.'

Brazzi had not come to this meeting with high hopes of financial gain, and the furious night beyond the window depressed him. His continuing sobriety depressed him. He stole a wary glance towards the broad port but all he saw was the glass clattering in its weathered window frame, the cobwebs in the corners. He sat back in his chair with the foreboding of a bull at an abattoir. He had failed and Monfalcon was watching him. He was sharpening his blade.

Monfalcon believed fervently in the destiny of Italy and it had once been his ambition to be sacrificed on her altar. What he had sacrificed instead were two fingers, the result of an accident with a grenade, and he was unable to hide the scar running the length of his lifeline, which looked to the civilian world as if he had shot himself to evade military service. Doomed to survive the War while other Arditi were martyred around him, he had loped into this town where no one knew him with the accusation of cowardice hanging from the end of one arm. He was mutilated, frustrated, but he was no coward, and he drowned the poisoned thought.

In drink, did they ask? All his soldiers drank. A libation to the beauty of violence whose fire cauterized negotiation, understanding and all weakening influences. Yes, though the armistice had been declared for a decade, the idea of slaughter to strengthen and sanctify the Italian nation still had appeal. It was a religious idea, he considered, sacred violence: a phrase he had coined himself though he was not a poet and not romantic according to the current Italian vogue for flamboyant atrocities.

He downed his shot glass and belched charnel fumes across the table at Brazzi.

'You're not yourself tonight, Matteo. What are you looking at?'

'Nothing!' Brazzi spat at the angry lips. Nerves, guilt, fear. The reactions of a schoolboy.

He took a second glance at the window, knowing the suspicious eyes would follow the action, knowing it was too black to see what he was looking for. And here was Morato, reopening the gilded register which he seemed to think would be their salvation: Morato, the proprietor of the hotel and an agreeable man, but not above making a quick profit.

'To business, gentleman!' he said. 'Now this Micatovich – this Di Micheli – the oldest landowner. How much has the prefect suggested for him to ignore this decree about his surname?'

'One hundred thousand lire, or ten thousand per month in installments,' answered Monfalcon.

'Has he, indeed, the greedy bastard! You've missed your true calling, Brazzi.'

'Yes, I expect I should thank Mussolini for opening up new possibilities,' Brazzi replied vaguely. A silvery fog had begun to obscure the lower glass. 'Dim old Zan wouldn't understand anyway.'

It was clear that in a very short while the bottom pane would be obscured from the outside and, from within by the heavy condensation of their breath. He shuffled in his chair and bumped the candle.

Monfalcon watched its light flow over the table and drench Brazzi's tense features in golden waves.

'Dim old Zan is quite wealthy,' he responded.

'Then what about the son?' interrupted Morato. 'Will he inherit?'

'He teaches in Italy,' muttered Brazzi.

His Most Italian City

'We *are* in Italy.' Monfalcon suddenly turned upon him. 'Why are you looking out that window?'

'I'm not.'

'You're lying.' It was remarkable the sneer the soldier could convey while scarcely raising his voice. 'You've done it three times in the last quarter hour. The hotel should be paid for the privilege – "This famous window! It has an extraordinary view. Signor Matteo Brazzi has glanced from it three times! Yes, three, signore and signori. *Viva l'Italia! Viva la libertà!*" That's how we will make money. We will sell Brazzi's window for its view, which he swears is magnificent.'

Brazzi assumed an air of gaiety.

'*Credere, obbedire, combattere!*' he sang.

'Yes, you can be fascist enough when it suits you.'

Morato sighed.

'We'll be poor, not fascist, Giuseppe, unless we ruffle a few feathers.'

'Extortion won't help you,' said Brazzi. 'This is not the city. Someone's house burns down, they're stoic. You put on your black shirt and tell them the fascists that did it are protecting the rights of the landowners. This Micatovich, he *is* a landowner – he will galvanize his friends and they'll rebuild the house. He'll pay for it. It's too small a community for us to profit from the political situation.'

To mask his disgust Monfalcon agitated his shot glass and barked, 'Drink, drink, drink!'

And shall I bow to the inevitable? wondered Brazzi. *Perish at the hands of a home brew and spend eternity in Cittanova?*

He disposed of the poison as bidden, immediately afterwards turning quite red in the face.

'Faugh!!' he gagged, spitting it out.

They sniggered at him, Morato chuckling and chortling above his many chins and Monfalcon's glee temporarily enlivening the void of his dead face. He paused between breaths and, just as it seemed that he would stop breathing forever, he suddenly retrieved the bottle of brandy and thrust it across the table.

'Go ahead, Brazzi, embalm yourself. It mightn't cure syphilis but at least you won't rot.'

What was there to do? Stay and listen to the wind? Marvel at the fury of the waves? He hated the port tonight, where his doom brooded over its dark waters, the desolate pier and the gray sky. A wooden barrel on the pier broke free of its ropes. It gyrated across the base of the pier and splashed heavily into the port. Brazzi's heart leapt into his throat. Oblivious to the glances from Morato and Monfalcon, he rose and, carefully descending the stairs, opened the back door a fraction.

Immediately he was plastered against the doorframe by the force of the wind. He hung on with one hand, easing himself the single pace to the corner of the building, and peered into the port while his hair streamed into his eyes and half-blinded him. Horse's tails shot across the water meters from his feet and the beam from the lighthouse was fractured by seismic spouts: sulfur and magnesium. He gulped the cold tang, the freezing vapor, felt it invade his nostrils and searched – all to no avail, for the pavement at his feet was deserted. He peered to the right, then to the left, then right again up the entire eighty meters of the pier, at first unable to see anything. And when he squinted through the buffeting gale the reason was clear: the harbor light at its end was out. Brazzi shoved back his hair and looked a second time, unsure that the furious gusts tormenting land and sea hadn't simply obscured the harbor light's glow, which would gleam again at any minute. He was certain that the kerosene lamp had been operating when he arrived. Now its absence leant the wild night a sinister overtone. And could it just be possible that a low object sat beside the pier? – for he thought he saw the furious water breaking into white caps at the waterline. And what was that image of reprisal, bowed low by wind, stretching its arms towards him?

His Most Italian City

He began to apologize, but the words came out like the blather of a frightened child.

'I'm sorry. I've said I'm sorry. How many times do you want to hear me say it?'

But he saw that the arms were wind and the head flecks of twisted foam, the whole thing an illusion of the storm. The wind wailed and the sea tossed but his view from the doorway was empty; the pier swept away like the embracing arm it was and disappeared into the darkness.

Brazzi closed the door. He leaned against the wood, caught his breath, calmed his heart and let the silence wash over him; then he climbed the stairs and resumed his seat, staggering a little, not entirely the suave mayor.

Morato gaped at Brazzi's face. 'Everything all right, Matteo?'

Brazzi brushed his hair back across his head. 'The harbor light's gone out,' he said.

Monfalcon scratched his ear. 'Is that all? Some fool forgot to fill it.'

*****

Giovanni let himself out into the back lane and was immediately enveloped by the wind. He pulled his collar up around his ears to shield them from the gusts that whistled down the old street like a call to arms. For a while he perched on the single step, observing the warm glow from the three-story houses that ran down the lane. In their homely security the occupants were unaware of the forces that were vying with each other to change them. Then, lowering his head, he stepped out into the semi-shelter provided by the houses, turned into the Corso and marched straight to the end, feeling the gale increase in fury as he entered the unsheltered piazza. The campanile chimed the half hour as he hurried past and he scarcely heard its flat peal above the wind. He ran into the public garden, where trees threw heavy shadows across his path, descended the stairs two at a time and paused to gaze across the churning port at the point where the Bora ploughed head-on into the breakwater.

The distressing conversation with his parents had gone on for half an hour after Silvana had been banished to bed. They had lived too long beneath the paternalistic arm of the Hapsburgs and naively assumed that Istria would be governed with the same unruffled egalitarianism under fascist Italy. But Mussolini had slipped easily into the role of prime minister, a euphemistic term to describe the leader of a nation that since its unification had struggled with democracy. His aim, Giovanni knew, was a state bent to his will, and to acquire it he had astutely exploited the unstable, uncertain politics of his country, waiting until the opportune time then accepting with hypocritical humility the king's offer to form a government. With that, the Fascist dictatorship had begun in earnest. Italian nationalism, from which it had sprung, considered Italy to be the heir of the Caesars – in short, that the territories held by ancient Rome were rightfully Italian. Not to be outdone in appropriation, nationalists threw in what they called an ethical claim to the lands encompassing the Venetian Republic, styling themselves the heirs of the Renaissance and thus of any modern region that could be interpreted to be Italian, by language, geography or choice. That they should have viewed themselves so loftily even before the war was laughable, except that no one was laughing. Now they staked their land claims in forceful terms internationally and were angry when their demands were not met.

Giovanni braced himself and strode onto the breakwater. Furious surf crashed across the broad walk of flat stones and he heard its hollow boom beneath the boulders, whose razor-sharp edges pointed south towards the sea. All he had to do was lose his footing or be in the wrong place before a wave that was bigger than he was and he would plummet head first into the black water and be broken upon the rocks. He knew that his behavior was foolish, but by then he was too disturbed to care.

His Most Italian City

Three hundred meters across the water lay the pier, the second stone arm encircling the port, where the steamer from Trieste that cruised down the Istrian coast disgorged its load of seasick passengers. He could identify it only by the harbor light upon its pedestal at the furthest end.

Lost in his thoughts, Giovanni was forced to jump to one side as a wave went thundering over the breakwater, splashing high into the air, obliterating completely his view of the pier. Even the harbor light was no longer visible and, as the tumult cleared, the path where it lay remained black.

That's odd, he thought, since everything along this coast was built to withstand the weather.

But he marched on until he reached the lighthouse where his courage finally failed him. He huddled in the shelter of its small doorway while two terrific crashes battered the structure, then he ran back to the garden at the edge of the breakwater, where he brushed the worst of the water from his clothes behind a pine tree. A second small flight of stairs ran from the garden down one side of the mediaeval city wall. Giovanni jumped quickly down them to the rocky port beach and crept cautiously the hundred meters back to his father's house, with the tide lapping at his boots. The house shared its walls with the houses on either side but was taller by a whole floor and, at the very top where its roof protruded, the two tiny windows of Silvana's bedroom peeped out like curious eyes looking over a hedge. One more step, through the door in the sea wall, and he would be home.

But here he lingered, strangely calmed by his hike through the tumult and unwilling to relinquish that peace by returning home. To his left were the rocks that marked the start of the pier, and glancing above them he saw the detached two-story hotel, City of Trieste, placed to take advantage of the trade from the coastal steamer. Above its wide front door, to the right, a candle blinked from a window.

Giovanni remained watching, imagining the warm sanctuary within and, for that single minute, sensed an odd out-of-body experience, as if he had been transported into the restfulness of the room. On every side of him swirled the angry night, the shrieking gale, the waves hurling themselves to infinity and, in their midst, that small calm light into whose world he had been drawn.

Reluctantly he turned to leave and, as he did so, he received a crushing blow across the back of the neck so that, believing himself alone, he wondered that he had not seen the wave coming. He staggered into the tide and fell across the boulders supporting the pier, slicing gashes into his shoulder and thigh before striking his head on a rock below the waterline and losing consciousness.

Five minutes later, as the curved arc from the lantern swept across the port, Silvana, watching from her window, saw a black head sluice through the angry water and disappear behind the lighthouse. There *was* a monster in the sea.

Chapter Three

Silvana's mother had been born imperious. A happy stroke of nature had blessed her from the cradle with such an autocratic glare that she gave the impression of looking down on people even when they were taller than she was. With hard work and the right attitude, she had improved upon her aptitude for superiority so that her petite frame became the equal and more of anyone who opposed her will. She was well dressed from the minute she slipped her dainty feet from her bed into silk slippers each morning, enjoying the better things in life, which first her father and then her husband had provided, and she derived much pleasure from the receding opulence of the old Austrian Empire into which she had been born and the fashionable Italian Istria in which she now lived. She felt no grief for the replacement of her family name with a mock-up Italian substitute. Rather the reverse. She was delighted.

Shopping, beauty parlors, dinners and parties were her life. She never grew tired of them and looked forward with the thrill of a small child at a birthday party to whatever materialistic excursion the fates threw her way. It was perverse, therefore, that her only child was large, robust, clumsy, short-sighted, dismally unhappy anywhere near materialism and would rather kick a ball with the local boys than exploit the lovely money she had been born into. Really, it was infuriating.

Silvana was forever crashing into the furniture, twisting her ankles, breaking heritage chairs, apologizing when she saw her mother's furious and dismayed face. Incarcerated in frilly dresses, she trailed after her parent through the salons and cafés of Trieste like a sad clown, longing to be somewhere else. She had a habit of walking directly in front of her mother so that that lady must either tread on her heels or tell her continuously – in that irritated voice she seemed to have adopted since the day she was born – not to do it.

In short, by the time Silvana was five it was obvious that mother and daughter did not get on and that the nightmares Silvana had begun to suffer from would only get worse on further acquaintance. At that point Silvana went to live with her grandparents, whom she adored and with whom – as Zan also had the odd moments of inadvertently falling over things – she felt in good company. The house was too old and sturdy to worry about its clumsy inhabitants. It had taken a few knocks in its time. In addition, Maria's distress over the assaults to the furniture had never approached the same degree as her daughter's. Over the years of attack, first by her husband and now by her granddaughter, she had learned to turn a blind eye to the damage and hire a carpenter for the repairs.

The morning following the Bora, Maria threw open the shutters over the port, overjoyed to see a calm, pale morning with the promise of later radiance, so typical of the Adriatic in winter. The myriad tiny troughs on the expanse of the port mottled its surface in leaf green and emerald, and from the wave's crests sparkled a host of diamonds. Maria breathed deeply and was grateful for its loveliness. The one thing that detracted from her pleasure was the lack of her son's boots by the front door as she passed it on her way down. That and the unwelcome memory half obscured by sleep that she had not heard him come in. Maria slept the light sleep of the elderly, but it was just possible that he had tripped carefully up the stairs with his boots in his hands to avoid waking her. He had, after all, left home fifteen years ago and she could not treat him like a child, even though he was her child.

Very soon Zan came up behind her, rubbing his hands in anticipation of breakfast and, following him, was Silvana, dressed for school.

'Giovanni did not come home last night,' announced Maria by way of greeting.

'Oh,' remarked her husband without interest.

'His boots are not by the front door.'

She heaved the percolator onto the stove, reflecting that the coffee was getting heavier every year.

'Perhaps he's forgiven that girl who broke his heart and it's all had a happy ending,' answered Zan mischievously. 'What was her name?'

'Shh!' hissed Maria. 'Not in front of the…'

'Which girl?' interrupted Silvana, all bright eyes and curiosity.

'Never you mind,' Maria replied firmly, at which Silvana stuck out her bottom lip and sulked. To Zan Maria continued, 'He went out.'

'Yes, I know,' replied Zan, addressing his bread and cheese. 'Giovanni left home too long ago for you to continue to worry about him, Maria.'

Maria returned to the coffee, bubbling smoothly now that her tired old hands were no longer at the helm.

'He might have told me where he was going.' She thumped the cups onto the bench, which was the only mutiny she could manage these days. 'Out for a walk when the Bora's blowing, indeed! And he *will* go onto the breakwater! Young men!' she fumed, long past the days of risk-taking herself. She thrust a pot of cherry marmalade at Silvana.

Silvana began to spread the rich jam on her bread and was just considering the pleasant picture of her uncle pursuing his political diatribe when the picture of the black head dissolving into the raging sea rose before her eyes and the significance of what she'd seen assumed a terrible reality.

'Oh, Nona! Oh, Nono!' she burst out, the knife in her hand. 'Zio Lin was eaten by a sea monster! I saw it last night and I tried to tell you, but you wouldn't listen.'

Then she started to cry.

'Don't be silly, Silvana!' sighed Maria. 'Sea monsters, indeed! That's not like you.'

And, as Silvana continued to weep, Maria took the knife and completed the spreading of the marmalade.

'Zio Lin will be at Gilda's, you'll see,' soothed Zan.

'Gilda's the dog,' replied Maria.

'*She* is also Gilda.'

'Aha! So you did know her name, after all.' Maria clicked her tongue at her husband, but a cloud had passed over the morning sun and the kitchen was plunged into shadow. 'Now stop crying, Silvana. We'll send Nono down to get him. Zan?'

'When I've finished my breakfast!' declared Zan.

'And be discreet, for goodness sake.'

'Didn't you know I am the soul of discretion?'

'No, I didn't know that.'

Only marginally reassured, Silvana followed her grandfather's example, then added as an afterthought, 'I did see a sea monster, though, Nono. A black one.'

'Monsters are usually green, my love.'

Silvana considered this seriously.

'No, Nono, it was black – or, I think it was. I couldn't see well because it was too dark.'

Since Silvana was a practical child, when Zan's diplomacy had failed, her grandparents did not continue the attempt at persuasion. As breakfast concluded with no sign of their son, they began to accept that, if Silvana had said the monster was black, it probably was, although they did not believe the two things were related.

His Most Italian City

After breakfast Zan tied a rope to Gilda's collar and, having walked Silvana to school, he continued on to Gilda's home on a street off the piazza, where the dog barked merrily in greeting and the young lady replied modestly to his enquiries, saying that, no, she had not seen Giovanni. Unfortunately.

So Zan led the dog through the groves of oak and pine and into the gardens at the commencement of the breakwater, hoping to get some feel for where Giovanni might have decided to go when the Bora was blowing so fiercely that he could have barely stood upright. Here he met Antonio, one of the local fishermen, sitting cross-legged upon the irregular paving stones, fixing his net with a needle.

Antonio had been fishing the waters around Citttanova since he was nine. Today he was dressed in the height of fashionable disregard for a fisherman – two shirts for warmth but no coat, despite the cold. The sleeves of the first could be seen beneath the second and it gave Antonio the reflective air of having dressed to impress, which was not true.

'Sit,' said Zan to Gilda.

Gilda sat. Zan removed his hat.

'Good day to you, Antonio,' he began respectfully.

'And to you, Sior Micatovich,' replied Antonio, pausing to look up from his mending.

'A peaceful morning.'

'*Si*, sior. No tourists.'

'Winter is much quieter here than summer,' agreed Zan.

'Since the war, sior, the Italians and the Austrians hate each other, and the Germans are tight with their money.'

'But are the fish still biting, Antonio?'

'The fish are still biting, sior.'

'I'm very glad to hear it.'

The pleasantries over, Zan coughed and said, faltering slightly, 'I wonder, since your trade keeps you so near the sea, whether… either last night or this morning… whether…'

'*Si*, sior?' enquired Antonio helpfully.

'Whether you have seen my son?' blurted Zan at last.

Antonio regarded his net as if he hoped it might answer for him.

'Sadly, no, sior,' he murmured.

'He went for a walk about half-past nine last night. And I dare say he has not gone far, being thirty-two and well able to look out for himself.'

'And may I ask, Sior Micatovich,' said Antonio, 'why you are searching for him? Young men…' He shrugged. Everyone knew young men. Yet, he considered, thirty-two was not that young.

'Well,' hesitated Zan, a little abashed by the confession he was about to make, 'my granddaughter – you know, little Silvana who lives with Maria and me – said he was – forgive me, Antonio – eaten by a sea monster – a black one, not a green one.'

The nice old gentleman is more muddled than usual, thought Antonio, though he did not believe that he should be the one to point this out. So, to Zan's startling piece of information he admitted mildly, 'Children will go saying these things.'

'Not Silvana,' said Zan. 'She was very upset and Giovanni hasn't returned.' He stared out over the water until struck by a sudden reflection.

'Why are you doing your repairs here, Antonio? Isn't your boat over in the *mandracio*?' The protected inner harbor around the shore to the east.

'*Si*, sior,' replied Antonio, biting off the twine. 'My cousin arrives today from Pola and I am waiting for the steamer. From here I can see her first as she pokes her smoky nose around the point and, if I get tired of waiting, I can admire the town.'

'Ah, yes, good idea, indeed. But if you can see the steamer from here, you could also see a sea monster,' persisted Zan stubbornly. 'They'd be about the same size, wouldn't they?'

His Most Italian City

Antonio frowned and rolled up his twine.

'If you say so, sior.'

'But I suppose that no one would come here on a night like last night looking for sea monsters?'

'Probably not,' agreed Antonio.

'Ah, well… that's a shame.'

'But Bruno might have been here anyway,' Antonio suggested quickly, noting Zan's dismay.

'Ah, Bruno!' answered Zan. Here was some hope. 'Do you think so?'

'Bruno loves the wind, Sior Micatovich. It calms him down.'

'Then thank you for your help, Antonio,' cried Zan quickly, retrieving his hat and giving Gilda's rope a tug. 'Thank you!'

'I hope you find him, sior.'

In such a small community as Cittanova, misfortunes were accepted as part of life and shared accordingly. Bruno was one such misfortune, an overlarge boy of eighteen, an afterthought when his parents had been in the buffer zone of their reproductive years and their offspring had numbered just one short of a dozen. Bruno, although he made the full complement, had been more trouble than the other eleven combined. He himself did not seem to realize this, a blessing, surely. From the day he was transferred from the womb to the crib he had been a difficult baby, crying for unaccountable reasons and unable to be comforted. A late walker, a late talker, blank-faced in all the emotional turmoil of his family except his own, he ate the same food every day and screamed at any variation. Happy alone, yet never lonely, he wandered the streets of Cittanova absorbed by a single crack in a wall or a pattern in the sand. He had no regular work but could occasionally be hired for heavy labor by farmers outside the town. Unmoved as he was by most human emotions, he was nevertheless known to be fascinated by the Bora and when it blew roamed between the *mandracio* and the port with a look of wild delight on his stolid features.

Zan knew that if anyone had seen Silvana's monster it would be Bruno. But when he knocked at the door of the Munda house on the shore of the *mandracio*, with Gilda panting beside him, Euphemia, Bruno's mother, confessed that she hadn't seen her son since breakfast and he had not said anything about black sea monsters when he'd come in the night before. She volunteered that, even as they spoke Bruno was heading out on the road to Buie to fulfill a request from the Picolich family to rebuild a retaining wall, although Euphemia fancied Bruno would spend the day pushing the wheelbarrow. She would send him to the Micatovich house, she added, when he came home.

'When might that be?' Zan asked.

'Well, you know Bruno.'

Euphemia shrugged, Zan bowed and Gilda wagged her tail.

Chapter Four

Giovanni awoke in a coffin, to a tiny sawing noise like bone scraped upon wood. In the gradual awareness of consciousness, he did not immediately realize where he was or how he had gotten there. He did not open his eyes. He did not move. He lay oblivious to sensation. If this were death, then he was not initially alarmed.

But consciousness, like the thief who steals in the night, cast its rapacious eyes his way, and under its gaze he sensed a measure of concern about his dark, closeted environment. His hands lay still, two dead weights upon his chest. His feet he could not feel at all. His resuscitation had achieved particularity in some points and obliteration in others, so that his legs remained paralyzed even as in his fingers he detected the faintest tingling, which quickened over the minutes and forged a path towards his wrists. He wriggled one finger, then another. Some sensation returned to his palms, his wrists, and his forearms and, with that knowledge, he discovered that his hands were tied – and wasn't that odd if this were death?

But there went his brain again and he couldn't stop it, sailing over the horizon and into sleep once more. This time he dreamed that the gate in the sea wall opened to him of its own accord. The roof of the high old house reposed in shadow but, as he watched, the dawn forged a path across the ridge cap and at once the tiles lit up like autumn leaves. With the sparkling new day the Bora had ceased and Giovanni saw his father waving a greeting from the kitchen window. Relief coursed through him as he realized that everything was all right, after all. He smiled and waved back, but a distracted look had crossed the old man's face and from inside Giovanni heard the dog bark. His father peered down and said, 'There you are, Gilda! We were so worried.' Then he turned to Giovanni. 'Nice to meet you. A pity you have to go, but I have something for you.' He grappled within the room, pulled out a poker from the range and began to scrape it against the windowsill. Though it looked far away, it sounded very close and Giovanni was unable to resolve the paradox. Scrape, scrape, scrape.

I've got to get out of this dream, he thought. He shook his bound hands and stretched them upward.

Immediately they collided with a low lid and, when he shot out his left elbow, it hit wood. Oh, God. Quickly he rolled his head to the right and realized that, barely beyond his ear, there was a void. Yet, even as he welcomed it, such a cascade of dizziness overcame him that he was forced to lie back and let it pass. He waited in the cozy prickle of his wet wool suit until he detected wounds burning in his thigh and shoulder, a throbbing neck and a roaring headache from that crash onto the rocks – now he remembered what had happened. He'd suffered an injury outside his home and here he was, lying fully clothed in a coffin with three sides. It all made sense! That noise that scraped and slid, as muted as a shovel into a grave, as persistent as a funeral bell. That sweating stink that sank into his lungs like corruption. Like a carcass that was returning to the earth.

Surely I have not been left alone with the dead!

Still too frightened to open his eyes, he eventually realized that he felt warm. If he were buried he would be cold, would he not? Vaguely, out of the fug in his brain, he perceived a rushing sound and a sense of movement. Perhaps it might even be that the walls vibrated and, very distantly… Could he hear an engine churning out a monotonous clunk?

Slowly and methodically, Giovanni forced himself to breathe in time with its rhythm, and imagined at each pulse the blood rushing through the wound in his thigh and on, to his knee. As he breathed he felt his calf, then his ankle and finally he imagined that life was returning to his feet, encased in wet socks and boots – and tied also!

At last it was that clunk piercing his skull, that persistent scraping and the odd combination of warmth and moving cold that persuaded his eyes to tremble apart. He unglued one eyelid and through the lashes saw a faint amber, trembling against one wall.

It's not a grave, he marveled, *for what grave ever throbbed and glowed? Therefore, I have not been buried alive. If there is a mechanical source of sound and a light source, it means that men are behind the creation of this sphere.*

This calmed him somewhat while, in his more hopeful frame of mind, the overwhelmingly putrid smell – even though it was still there – now seemed tinged with something sharper. Something he had smelled from time to time along the thoroughfares of Florence and even on the farms of rural Istria: diesel. That smell at last convinced him. He opened both eyes completely and now he could tell that he was certainly in a machine of some sort that, with its throbbing pistons and dim lights, seemed to him like an industrial Dante's inferno.

He strained his neck into the void and looked around. To the far left of his vision he saw a passage branching off towards the source of the light, so narrow that there was space for only one man to pass. To his right was blackness. Above him, beyond the confines of his niche ran pipes, and the low ceiling along which they lay seemed no higher than he was. The shadowy, shrunken room pressed in on him: a rank, suffocating, claustrophobic enclosure. For a moment, the discovery of diesel had quieted him, but now Giovanni, biology teacher, nature lover, felt the rise of panic.

He heaved himself up until his head brushed the board above him and by the clotted light flickering against the hem of his trousers he observed a large rat filing its front teeth on his boot – scrape, scrape, scrape. With a gasp of horror, he kicked his legs until his knees slammed into the wood above him.

'*Va via!*' he yelled. 'Go away!'

The rat plunged from its perch and disappeared. He heard its claws scrabbling for purchase on the floor below him.

Heavy steps sounded from down the disappearing passage and suddenly it seemed that five or six men stood directly in front of him, with more behind whom he couldn't clearly see. With their arrival, the source of the stench was immediately obvious. Unwashed bodies, diesel, human waste, the glorious stench of young manhood, decayed dinners, and the rat. The whole lot had accumulated in the slim bunk upon which he had been laid, which they had probably all slept in. Even the metal ceiling with its dimly outlined pipes seemed to reflect and intensify it, and the walls pressed it in upon him like a dark cocoon.

The men themselves did not seem to flinch under the sour reek, but the years spent among the Florentines had honed Giovanni's natural fastidiousness. The smell was so overpowering he felt barely able to breathe. As much as he tried, he could not stop wrinkling his nose in disgust.

Rather than look offended the men laughed.

'You're in a pig boat,' said one, a huge man, older than Giovanni and twice as heavy, who had to stoop to avoid knocking his crown on the ceiling.

He spoke the rough Italian Giovanni had heard on the docks of Trieste, and his human words, the laughter and the attention, broke the spell.

His Most Italian City

Giovanni calmed down, realized he could breathe, took a gulp of air. The tiny room expanded.

He examined the remaining men. They were all young except one. At a quick reckoning they might have been much the same age as his students, some smooth-cheeked, others on the verge of manhood, overgrown and resolute. All of them were curious about him rather than wary, knocking against each other in the small space, their back row digested by the gloom.

The exception stood with his arms folded across his chest and his eyes focused on Giovanni with the direct stare of authority.

'What's a pig boat?' Giovanni asked him because under such scrutiny it seemed scarcely permissible to ask anybody else.

'No room to wash in a submarine,' replied the man.

Nobody spoke. Giovanni didn't speak either. Silly, really, not to talk, but it couldn't be helped. It was as if he had relinquished control of himself, and his claustrophobia dissipated as he was held to attention by the man with the commanding eyes.

Giovanni peered out from his prison. The man seemed to be of medium height but stocky, with a strong upper body, dark hazel irises, a short sparsely graying beard and hair of the same salt and pepper. Though the floor shifted with the movement of the boat, he maintained an experienced stillness and, if anything else were necessary to proclaim his profession of seaman, above blue military trousers he wore a loose, collared shirt like the fishermen of Cittanova. Nevertheless, Giovanni had the impression that he would look exactly the same whatever he wore because his mere presence demanded one's attention so much that it would render any clothes unremarkable.

Even as Giovanni lay prone before him something in the tremor of the boat caught the man's attention. His eyes lost their fixed gaze.

As they released Giovanni, his former panic abruptly returned.

'Let me out!' he cried, for he felt that the ceiling was falling on him and the walls were contracting. 'I can't breathe. Please, let me out!'

He twisted his legs violently towards the weakly lit corridor and only succeeded in tilting halfway off the bunk when the weight of his dead feet and wet boots dragged him into a sodden pile on the floor. At the level of his eyes stood a dozen pairs of sea boots ornamented in a paisley pattern of mold in white, green and orange.

The captain – for what other term could be used to describe him? – growled some command to the men crammed so tightly into the miniature room that their shoulders rubbed together, and one, producing a sailor's knife, cut the ropes tying Giovanni's wrists and ankles. Then he retreated, as shy as a child, without assisting him further. The huge man who had first addressed him scowled at the sailor, shoved two meaty hands under Giovanni's arms and hoisted him to his feet.

Giovanni swayed weakly, clutching his spinning head until he overbalanced backwards and hit his shoulder on another shelved bed stacked above the one on which he had been lying. Three bunks lay on top of one another almost to the ceiling, which he could have brushed with his head by standing on his toes.

'Thank you.' He looked down. 'Where's the rat?'

'Plenty more where he came from.'

'In a submarine?'

There was no reply, either from the crew or from their intimidating leader, though Giovanni sensed that the young men were waiting for the man to speak first. He began to feel as restrained as one of his students. Any hope he might have had of striking up a conversation in this foreign world seemed destined to be disappointed. He tried again.

'Is this the navy?'

The captain seemed to find this entertaining and his closed manner softened enough to permit a restrained amusement.

'For you we'll term it the People's Navy.'

His Most Italian City

'The People's Navy? You're a patriot? A pirate? A spy? Yet you speak Italian. What does that make you?'

'We choose to speak to you in the Italian of the Austrian docks. That's all you need to know.'

'Then you come from Trieste? I thought the submarine base was at Pola.'

'That's where he stole it from,' countered the huge man.

'Don't shoot us in the foot, Zorko, any more than you have already,' returned the captain while the slightest indication of emotion entered his voice. It may have been frustration but Giovanni could equally have called it anger. 'Let's say I borrowed a submarine for the occasion.'

A ripple of mirth spread through the men.

'What occasion?'

From the rear Giovanni observed a knuckle pushed into a palm accompanied by a muted sound like surf on a beach, a parody of an explosion which required little interpretation. A wind of fear raised the hairs at the back of his neck. They were all watching him, standing before them in his suit and tie, twisting his wrists like a nervous secretary and biting his lip. A shudder knotted his shoulder blades, an urge to gulp the fetid air instead of breathe it, and with it came a compulsion to talk. As he gained momentum Giovanni realized that he sounded like a man devoted to his family, who rarely had the occasion to be anything but neatly dressed and whose temperate wit was appreciated in academic circles. Which was what he was.

'You stole a submarine? That's innovative and, if the consequences don't bother you, I have no problem with it but, if it was me, I would consider them first. And could you tell me why I'm here, please? I'm no threat to you. My parents were upset because the government changed their name. Did you know that? My father is seventy-one. What's the point at his age?' He swiped a rim of perspiration from his top lip. In a second, the hot prickle returned. 'So I told them I'd just step out for half an hour to clear my brain, and they'll be wondering where I am. Do you want money? I'm only a teacher. I don't have any. I work in Florence. I was visiting my family. Do you think you could take me home or drop me off somewhere convenient? I promise I won't say anything incriminating and I don't mind a walk.'

'You're Italian?'

'No. I told you. I was visiting my family.'

The group regarded this wordlessly while a wave of recrimination seemed to pass through them. After the minutes of restrained silence, the younger crew commenced speaking rapidly amongst themselves in a language Giovanni didn't understand but recognized as Slavic. Clearly they were discussing him and not looking very happy about it.

The captain stood listening while they argued and interrupted each other, and the set of his jaw tightened with the emotion Giovanni had earlier detected until the sides of his mouth strained like a dam about to burst. At length he slammed his hand hard against the pipes above him and swore in the same language his crew were using.

The chatter abruptly stopped. The captain rounded on Giovanni.

'Name!'

'Giovanni Di…..um, Micatovich.'

'A teacher in Florence?' broke in Zorko. 'That's not your real name.'

'I just said the government changed it,' insisted Giovanni. 'But it is my real name. I studied in Graz when Istria was Austrian. I fought for Austria during the War, not Italy, but now Istria's Italian I have to find work here – in that language. I've taught in Florence for eight years.' He rushed a breath. 'And, anyway, what's wrong with being Italian?'

Zorko spat on the floor in front of him.

'Fascist,' he said.

'Fascist? I'm not a fascist!'

'You look Italian.'

His Most Italian City

'But I'm Istrian! My name is Micatovich, with a 'k'. My mother's name was Matjašić. Very Slavic,' he insisted with more confidence than he felt. 'I'm on your side.'

Zorko leered close with his enormous dirty face. 'And which side is that?'

'Well, weren't you speaking in a Slavic language just then?'

'Yes, and which one was it?'

When Giovanni stumbled for an answer, the captain nodded to his crew.

'You see?'

'We can't let you go now,' added Zorko. 'You know too much.'

'I don't know too much!' cried Giovanni. 'I don't know anything except that I'm sure I'm here by mistake.'

The captain refolded his arms across his chest.

'Yes, you may be,' he acknowledged, ending cryptically, 'It would be wise not to be so well dressed next time.'

'Or the same height,' Zorko chimed in.

'You're impatient, Zorko.'

'It was dark,' remonstrated that man.

And, thought Giovanni absurdly, *someone as big as you has no need of language to get your point across. I'm half your size and look how prone I am to illogical speech in desperate situations.*

'I really must escape this dreadful machine,' he explained out loud while they squabbled tersely and the walls lurched in on him. 'Point me to the exit, if you please, right now.'

The captain seemed not to be one for debating for he welcomed Giovanni's prim request in order to turn away from his quarrelsome companion. He asked pertinently, 'Can you swim?'

'Please...'

'We're halfway down the coast, Giovanni Micatovich. Until I work out what to do with you, you're stuck here.'

Giovanni tried once more.

'I need to get away from the rat.'

'Yes, so do we.' He turned to leave. He was losing interest. 'The best thing for those who don't like confined spaces,' he observed in passing, 'is to look down, not up.'

'And then you'll see that rat as well,' Zorko said with a wink.

The captain allowed the younger men to go out before him, the courtesy of rank forbidden by the cramped enclosure. Then, with that rolling walk that seamen acquire from keeping their balance in rough seas, he finally retreated back down the narrow maze until his shoulders dissolved into the gloom.

With his departure hopelessness settled upon Giovanni. He sat down on the bed and stared at his boots, pulled at his trousers where the damp fabric clung to his skin, loosened his tie. He discovered that he had lost a cuff link, so he checked and removed the other one, laying it as carefully as a treasure in the deepest pocket of his trousers lest he lose it as well and by so doing unwittingly deposit a little part of himself in this tomb. He hoped that he had lost the first cuff link in the water by his father's house where it would be free. The thought quickened a note of nostalgia in him and a faint smile washed a little of the sadness from his face. It dropped swiftly away and, as he watched its descent, there, *en queue,* was the rat. Its wicked little eyes had been watching him from its small corner the whole time.

He leapt up and stumbled after the men.

'Wait!' he cried. 'Don't leave me here!'

But he was overtaken by further dizziness and such a surge of nausea that he had to stop, holding his head in his hands, breathing harshly, fighting the urge to vomit. One of the young men noticed. Shaking his head and clicking his tongue as if he were Giovanni's mother, he put a hand beneath his arm and guided him back to the bunk, laid his head on the pillow and waited until he settled. Then he handed Giovanni a wrench.

His Most Italian City

'If the rat worries you,' he said kindly, 'belt him with this.'

54

Chapter Five

Zan and Gilda set off out of town on the road to Buie. The looming city walls reflected the morning sun as they strolled passed and, even as Zan assured his tired legs that he wouldn't take them too far, north of the dusty street he spied Bruno in a small family vineyard consisting of two rows of pruned grape vines with a fig tree at either end. (It was true that few detectives save Zan could have achieved this. From his great height he had looked over a wall tall enough to be shielded from shorter prying eyes.) As he approached the open door through the wall he saw that the boy, who was seated upon the ground, was absorbed in making patterns between the vines with the dead leaves and twigs he had dug out of the mulch. Each pattern was exactly the same: a small shriveled leaf, a pencil-like twig, a walnut-sized pile of compost and a medium leaf that had decayed to a skeleton.

While Gilda sniffed the mulch, Zan sat down on an old horse trough to one side of the plot, took off his hat and mopped beads of cold perspiration from above his eyes with his handkerchief. Then he rose and extended his hand.

'Good morning, Bruno.'

Bruno took the hand without replying, dropping his own hand limply down before returning to his patterns.

His Most Italian City

'How are you?'

'Good,' replied Bruno because Euphemia had taught him to.

'Are you going to help the Picolich's?'

'Yes.'

'So are you off now, Bruno? I think it won't take you long. Only half an hour.'

'Yes,' replied Bruno and added another twig to his leaf.

Though Bruno was unable to conduct a conversation and rarely initiated requests, he could recite information he had picked up from others with commendable skills of repetition, but rarely did so when asked. Rather, it seemed when he was muttering that he was amusing himself, and this often proved to be the case. On a good day, however, he would respond 'yes' and 'no' to questions; on a bad day, 'yes' and 'no' to the same question.

'Were you on the pier last night, Bruno?' asked Zan.

'Yes.'

'Ah, good. You were on the pier.'

'No.'

'Did you see Giovanni on the pier?'

'Yes.'

'Did you see him come home?'

'See him come home,' repeated Bruno.

'Do you know where he is?'

'See him come home.'

'Do you know where he is?'

'Home,' said Bruno without raising his head.

Thoroughly dismissed, Zan nevertheless felt he had a duty of care to at least see Bruno on the road to employment before he went home himself. It did not occur to him until later that one of Bruno's seven surviving brothers and sisters could have done the job equally well.

'Let's go to the Picolich's!' he announced, and when nothing happened he tried, 'Off we go!' A further nothing.

'Oh, dear,' said Zan.

He sat back down on the trough while images of Bruno making patterns in the mulch until kingdom come worried the sad old life from his brain. No work, no money and winter nearly upon them. What would his poor mother do? Zan determined that on his way home he would stop by and pay Euphemia a day's wage in recompense for his inability to rouse her son to manual labor. With this in mind, he tried one more time, projecting into his voice so much mild authority that he barely recognized himself.

'Stand up!' And to his astonishment Bruno stood. Considerably encouraged, Zan continued in the same tone, 'Walk to the Picolich farm!' And Bruno did as he was commanded. Just to make sure, Zan watched him go for five minutes, until Bruno's rounded shoulders disappeared beyond the blurred edges of his vision. Then he collected Gilda and went home himself.

Upon his arrival, he found Maria furiously dusting the hall clock, the stairs and the picture frames that sat around the hallway.

'Isn't Paulina here to do that for you?' said Zan. 'I haven't forgotten to pay her this week.'

'Paulina is not worried like I am!' Maria barked back, raising a soft cloud of dust from the underbelly of the old clock. The dust settled peacefully onto the floor, where she attacked it again.

'Stop this, Maria,' protested her husband, apprehending the duster and holding it a meter above her head. 'You'll wear yourself out.' He looked about him. 'Where is Paulina, by the way? Doesn't she go home at two? You'll leave her with nothing to do and you won't bring Giovanni home any faster.'

Maria glared at him before subsiding somewhat.

'I sent Paulina to the markets, so I could worry alone.'

His Most Italian City

'And where is Silvana?'

'At school, Zan.'

'Yes, of course,' mumbled Zan humbly. 'I took her there myself.'

Maria collapsed heavily onto the bench set against the wall, suddenly too tired even to raise her head.

'What did Gilda say?' she asked.

'Nothing.' Zan plunked himself down beside his wife and rolled a cigarette. 'And I asked Antonio Cecatti who was down at the port waiting for the steamer, but he hadn't seen anything either. The only clue we have so far is Silvana's sea monster.'

'Oh, for goodness sake!'

'Yet you have to agree such a pronouncement is unlike her. It is *not* like her to say she has seen something when she hasn't. I can't ever remembered her doing it.' He rummaged through the contents of his pockets looking for a match, finally finding a squashed box containing just two, one of which, with a bit of effort and a lot of the patience that came naturally to him, he managed to light. He inhaled two puffs of his cigarette then exhaled a long cloud of fragrant smoke into the dim hallway.

'But a sea monster!'

'Until Giovanni walks through that door,' puffed Zan, 'it's the only clue we have. A little later I will enquire of the fishermen in the *mandracio*. One of them may have been out last night. And Bruno may have been, too. I have just tried to speak with him – with little result. He's at work today – or, I hope he is – but I'm sure if he says anything to Euphemia she will send him up here to tell us.'

Maria fixed her jaw into such an attitude of suffering that it set her back teeth together.

'Don't break that set like you broke the last one. Bruno's harmless.'

'He's not twice your size!'

'You don't have to let him in. Just listen to what he says if he comes. I doubt whether he'll answer any of your questions. He hasn't answered any of mine. Maybe you can prompt him by telling him what Silvana saw. He's probably the only person in Cittanova who won't laugh at you.'

And when Maria still looked unconvinced Zan said, 'I'll probably be back by then.'

'Ha, ha. Very funny.'

'I don't know when Bruno's coming, either, Maria, but I'll be back for lunch and Euphemia is reliable. She will send him if he has any information.'

Chapter Six

The new day had relinquished the torments of last night without a struggle. Matteo Brazzi was fairly purring with the sunshine and fair weather. Intimidation? Let him try! Yield? Never.

His seven month's sojourn in Cittanova had proved to be a sanctuary that he could not have foreseen, and any more letters summoning him to covert showdowns under cover of darkness would be treated with the contempt they deserved. It had read:

Meet me at ten o'clock at the inlet.

How preposterous!

Indeed, Brazzi was fast transforming into such a carefree country gentleman that his old friends might scarcely have recognized him. For the benefit of his new friends he had remodeled his exile to resemble a decision he had made himself, and so happy was he in the pure air, amongst wholesome rural morals, that he even gave up smoking and was considerate towards his wife. Under his thoughtfulness, Angelica recovered her health and spirits, and quickly made friends who proved more than sympathetic to her history of repeated miscarriages. She took an interest in the house and the slim garden by its side, and spent long hours in the kitchen nattering away to Teresa, picking up the local dialect.

Teresa had proved a capable housekeeper but served little for lunch except pasta and, as she had threatened, cooked dinners swarming with fish. On Monday they ate bream, on Tuesday cod cooked the Pola way, and sea bass cooked the Gologori way on Wednesday. On Thursday they ate sausages, then oven-baked grouper on Friday, mackerel with anchovies on Saturday (that's a joke, *non è vero?*), prawns in sauce for Sunday dinner and back to bream on Mondays, for Teresa cooked to a strict routine.

'Could there be any benefits associated with a diet containing quite so much seafood?' enquired Signor Brazzi.

'Angelo Podigornich is ninety-seven and still has all his teeth, signore,' replied Teresa smartly.

Here was evidence of an unforeseen nature and he apologized, naturally, explaining to Teresa that quite honestly he hadn't taken much notice of the fishing vessels that left the *mandracio* every morning. He promised to observe them more closely next time he passed the Adriatic.

As for the cultural cleansing required by the Fascist Party, Brazzi had quickly discovered that Cittanova's inhabitants were too much taken up with the struggles of earning a living to create divisions within a community that had been regional for over a thousand years. He had attempted to convert the old men sipping homemade wine in shady corners who offered him a glass but showed little curiosity. Farmers, who lived by the seasons and were stoically fatalistic about every dreadful event that would have had him racing home to whine to the amenable Angelica, proved equally impossible to arouse. And since taking up arms in the cause of Italy was something he had preached about but never actually done, when soldiers who had fought for Austria refused to talk to him he remained unconcerned.

At all these obstacles Signor Brazzi smiled with relief and, as the hills of Istria rolled towards the sea through aqua mists and olive groves, he was forced to review his fascist future lest he be accused of enjoying life without Mussolini. He still longed for his darling Trieste but as he could not stay there, he had regretfully decided, Trieste must come to Cittanova. He would do what he knew: sell coffee.

So he opened a café on the ground floor of a building in the piazza owned by three elderly sisters and called it the *Caffè Fascisti*, a tactful suggestion of the political party he allegedly represented. He decorated its interiors in Art Nouveau style and, beneath weeping nymphs and garlanded Dianas, festooned his tables with fascist propaganda: newspapers, pamphlets and artwork. Perhaps, suggested his wife, he could direct the reading material towards women? Women can't vote, replied Brazzi, who afterwards relented and added a small bookshelf of French *Vogue* and *Home Fashion* for Angelica and Teresa.

And thus it came to pass that, as the Italian flag flew proudly in the Piazza Umberto I, Signor Matteo Brazzi became the proprietor of the *Caffè Fascisti* and reported back to his colleagues in Trieste that the fascist creed was alive and well in Cittanova. Aside from that pleasant fiction, he found that he was enjoying being what he had always wanted to be although where he had least expected – a prosperous businessman in a tourist resort. And when his landladies descended for coffee, as they did at least twice a day, he found that he could play the part devoid of subterfuge.

'*Buon giorno*, Fräulein Müller! And to your sister, fräulein, and *buono giorno* to you as well Frau Winkler! You're looking so lovely this morning, ladies! How that hat becomes you, fräulein! If I may adjust that rose to its full perfection. There! Excellent! They are wearing them turned out this season.'

Fräulein Müller the elder giggled girlishly and tried not to blush as Brazzi bent her silk flower to the declared angle, though Fräulein Müller the younger blushed for her, and Frau Winkler, recently widowed, did not change color at all. The three elderly ladies curtsied to Signor Brazzi the way they had been taught in the Old Empire and reclined gracefully at their favorite table, ready for their morning coffee and Linzer Torte. They were dressed for an earlier age in white skirts and white silk blouses and, as if the Great War had never ended, the youngest sister still wore the black armband she had donned for her lover. Even when he had fallen fighting gloriously for Austria on the Serbian front she had been middle-aged. On the embroidered silk it sat as incommodiously as a chimney sweep at a wedding. She had never recovered from her loss and, even though they had been too old to start a family, she had looked forward to the marriage with the zest of the young. She always wore the small rose-gold ring with the single ruby that he had given her as if at any moment he might return to claim her hand. Her elder sister had never had a lover and still bore the hopeful expectancy of the faded virgin, while her eldest sister, Frau Winkler, mourning her husband, kept herself to herself with Teutonic efficiency. She could be partial to Signor Brazzi's charms when the weather was warmer but today she pulled her shawl close and barely managed a smile.

'But your café is delightful, signore!' beamed the middle sister. 'How happy we have been since we rented you the shop below us. It was a very good decision, was it not, Lena?'

The youngest sister returned a fond acknowledgement.

'Yes, indeed, Louisa. There was a similar café here when I was a child and our parents brought us from Vienna on vacation. So many Austrians came here then, you know.'

'But we still get our fair share,' replied Brazzi.

'That's reassuring! But then your cakes are so delicious. Give our compliments to your cook.'

'Teresa is an excellent cook, but you have lived here…?'

'Twenty years just the two of us, and dear Brigitta joined us after Easter.'

'So you would know Teresa, surely?'

The women regarded each other with puzzled faces.

His Most Italian City

'We don't get out very much, signore. And the local dialect…' They shrugged delicately to make their point. 'Just German and Italian for us.'

'Teresa knows some Italian,' Brazzi pointed out.

'Ah, yes, but where did she learn to speak it?'

'From the tourists, I believe.'

The elder Fräulein Müller tittered daintily, smearing lipstick on her dentures. 'To learn the *proper* Italian one needs to go to Italy. Don't you agree, signore?'

'Cittanova *is* in Italy now, fräulein.'

The sisters appeared startled.

'Is it?'

Then they exhaled with relief and fluttered their eyelashes as if they realized he was joking.

'You are so funny, Signor Brazzi! Well, do assure the excellent Teresa how much we admire her cakes and inform her, if you would be so kind, that to learn Italian one must go to Italy.'

Thoroughly comforted, the sisters completed their morning repast then headed back upstairs to disassemble their toilette and spend the two hours until luncheon recovering from the effort. By then they would be back, their costumes completely changed, ready to enjoy their lunch.

In their absence Brazzi served other customers and hung a patriotic placard, decorated in line with the rest of the café. The elder Fräulein Müller (the talkative one) paused before alighting once more at the table with her sisters and read:

DEVOTION TO ITALY

Istria is Italian: conquered by the Romans, settled by the Venetians whose arches, whose language, whose great Lion of St. Mark itself bear witness to the improvements wrought by Italy. This educated community has long established itself along this pleasant coast. Further inland the civilizing effect of Italian culture has not yet penetrated. These rocky acreages are tilled by Slav peasants, Croats and Slovenes, who are undergoing a process of improvement until they can count themselves blessed to be called Italian – a benevolent assimilation. Along the coast these Slavs are employed as servants to the Italian households in the hope that they might profit by association.

Let us recall the Pax Romana, the peace of Rome that so benefitted its conquered lands by allowing barbarians to become citizens and benefit by virtue of Italian civilization until even St. Paul declared, 'I am a Roman citizen!'

Slavs who have settled in Italian Istria are privileged to breathe the same air as Dante, Giotto, Da Vinci, Verdi and the sainted Italian Jerome who gave the Bible to the Western Empire.

Istria was Italian! Istria is Italian! Istria will always be Italian!

The Caffè Fascisti supports the redemption of the Dalmatian coast and its islands for Italy, admired by the world, supported by the Allies, repressed by Austria no longer.

Viva l'Italia!

'Oh, that *is* lovely, signore,' purred Fräulein Müller, a thoughtful finger on her chin. 'You are trying to educate us. Although my sisters and I *are* Austrian, so perhaps if you were to say those nice things without blaming the dear Hapsburgs entirely for Italy's repression…' she drifted off suggestively so as to emphasize her point, and Brazzi had the feeling she often drifted off in that manner and was practiced at it.

'Of course, fräulein!' he exclaimed with as much horror at his indiscretion as he could conjure. He, too, had been practicing. 'I shall attend to it the instant we close today. Forgive me.' He had no intention of changing the words and was fairly confident that Fräulein Müller would take his word for the document's correction without reading it a second time.

So he fed and watered the old ladies once again, farewelled them up the stairs, in their nimbus of lily of the valley and Chantilly lace so evocative of an age that had passed. Being among them seemed to Brazzi like entering an old shop that had long ago closed its doors only to reopen at the urging of memory. The other customers presently enjoying the high quality of his coffee required no more care than his politeness – Brazzi did not pay rent to them – and, with the exit of his landladies, he could relax and reflect on how well things, on the whole, were going for him.

As Mayor of Cittanova he had the government on his side, the prefect of Pola and the small king of Italy, so much smaller since he had met Mussolini, poor man. In a world where presentation meant everything and monarchs were still painted as though they were about to ride into battle, no one looked impressive when they were only one hundred and fifty three centimeters tall. Signor Brazzi felt extremely sorry for the man. He could not escape himself. The second he appeared in public his height was the first thing anybody noticed and it was even whispered that the enlisting height for the army had been dropped to accommodate him.

But the best part was yet to come. The king's wife, Elena of Montenegro, towered thirty centimeters above her husband and when the two of them were brave enough to appear together in public it was only the consideration of the cost of the jewels on her dress that distracted citizens from mocking such an absurdly matched couple. Brazzi knew it was cruel to persecute a man for something he had no control over, but happily he was not accustomed to combatting his baser instincts and gave up the struggle without a fight.

Not being that tall himself, he had learned early in life that it was more than possible for a man to tower above his tallest opponents through sheer force of will. But he would not attempt it without charm, although Brazzi's charm often resembled the weather. He remained comfortably upholstered by the adage, true in his case, that clothes made the man, and he was a giant in terms of the particularity of his attire. Before walking out his front door every morning he made sure his shoes were so shiny they reflected the sun. He insisted on black socks, never a clock pattern or checks. His slicked-back hair gleamed with brilliantine beneath his Milanese felt hat, his suit was freshly pressed and he wore a white silk rose prominently in his buttonhole. He always kissed his dear wife on the cheek one too many times for the sake of the neighbors. In short, he dotted all his Italian's 'i's and crossed its 't's, and made sure everybody knew it.

In such a small town his position as mayor was only an honorary one but, fortunately for his finances, Matteo Brazzi had his fingers in a lot of pies. And that really had been the issue with that shabby little meeting last night. That nasty bully Monfalcon and the fat slug Morato criticizing his city sensibilities in one breath and milking him with the next! For safety financially ambitious networkers like Brazzi functioned independently and pursued an eclectic range of incomes: a parcel of land here, a few tenants there, presents for services rendered, post-war profiteering, contraband, the odd bribe astutely invested, with extortion – only if absolutely necessary, when funds were running low – and tax evasion, naturally, cruising artlessly along beneath the rest. In these days of fascism he had a lot of things to protect or, to put it in more practical terms, too many sources of income to lose.

With a fond smile over his shoulder at his customers he opened his door, heard the pleasant trill of the bell above the entrance and stepped into the piazza beyond, pulling his jacket a little closer for warmth. The pines in the park to his left stretched their branches towards the campanile as if they were grasping for it; from the sea beyond he smelt the salt tang, heard its soft murmur. A little ramble along the shoreline to blow the coffee out of his system would be just the thing, although when could it ever be said of a Triestino that he had had too much coffee?

His Most Italian City

Brazzi had composed his epistle about the superiority of Italians over Slavs in a whimsical mood and had placed it on his café wall because he knew he had official backing. Though it had no doubt come as a relief to many in power when Mussolini had declared "We can easily sacrifice 500,000 barbaric Slavs for 50,000 Italians," Brazzi did not share Mussolini's view that Slavs were subhuman compared with Italians, because he did not care. He merely kept the racist attitude up his sleeve as a handy panacea. Like all Italian nationalists, il Duce craved Slavic territory and had been dismayed when the Treaty of Versailles had not accorded Dalmatian territory to Italy but handed it instead to the newly formed Yugoslavia, a grubby amalgamation of the working class, as Brazzi viewed it, getting grubbier as it moved inland and away from Italian coastal territory. He always thought of the Dalmatian coast as Italian – anything prettily charming should be Italian. Surely everybody realized that?

But there was nothing charming about fascism, and therein lay the faults with its system. Although creatively truculent, Brazzi was unadventurous and he did not aspire to fascist violence. Unlike Monfalcon and the students who swelled the fascist ranks, he did not glorify war. Brazzi was given instead to public bouts of nationalistic rhetoric, which were as impressive as a night at the opera and achieved as much. Too congenitally lazy to applaud Mussolini wholeheartedly, he did not hesitate to exploit those elements of society – the socialists, the rural workers, the journalists and others – who had turned fascist out of fear while the police stood by and did nothing. If dirty work had to be done in the cause of fascism he would rather make it easy for someone else to do it, then take the credit if he could. He had not lived long in Cittanova and did not want its people to learn that he had already taken plenty of credit for the suppression of Slavic culture elsewhere in Istria. He felt completely justified in prohibiting the use of Slavic languages in public and in names, and allowing the obliteration of Slovenian and Croatian street signs and the closure of schools run by those ethnic groups – in summary, forbidding anything Slavic to muddy a town that was now Italian. The benefits were twofold: this policy kept the spotlight off him, and was the key to staying alive and profitable. One only had to murmur against Mussolini for him to change from posturer to predator.

But it was all such an effort! Signor Brazzi strolled languidly from the Piazza Umberto I, formerly the Piazza Grande, renamed after the second king of Italy, to its continuation of Queen Elena Street, formerly Port Road, renamed after the current queen (the tall consort of the short king). Then he turned left into the Corso Victor Emanuele, formerly Grand Street, renamed after the man himself. And thus were commemorated two of the three kings of Italy and one of its queens. Cittanova was too small, really, for such heavy-handed Italian patriotism. A shame it didn't have more thoroughfares, or Italy more kings.

The Corso wound smoothly through the houses and businesses that lined it, continuing almost as far as the port, where it performed a little dogleg to the left and entered the port near the City of Trieste. To the right of that hotel lay the shore, also renamed, this time after Nazario Sauro, the mariner lauded by Italy as a martyr and hanged by Austria as a traitor. Brazzi recalled the fuss at the renaming of this stretch, now happily subsided, because in Cittanova people had better things to do than take on the establishment. Signor Brazzi could be reasonable when it suited him and his reason told him that this had been an overly provocative act by the new government. Men might accept the naming of streets after kings and queens, who were often viewed as apolitical and charitably inclined. Indeed, Queen Elena was noted for her generosity. But naming this shore after an Italian nationalist, born in Istria, known for his anti-Slav sentiments, who had supported the Italians against Austria, was entirely another thing in Cittanova, where memories of the benign Austrian rule had not yet faded and so many young men had donned the Imperial uniform. It made Brazzi's job harder, and he really felt that Mussolini could have waited a little longer to rename this shore. But it was a statement that typified the fascist motto *Me Ne Frego* – I don't give a damn – which had been the essence of Mussolini ever since his March on Rome six years previously. Signor Brazzi had not taken part in that march because he didn't like black shirts. He only wore white ones.

Here Brazzi stopped to watch the fishermen sorting mackerel, anchovies and the big blue tuna to sell in the markets. They had tied their small barques to the quay along the *mandracio* and, with their wives, were presently on their knees chatting amicably in Venetian with the odd expression from another language thrown in. Their backs were bent low over the wooden trays and Brazzi caught the strong aroma of fish, saw behind them the Adriatic glistening in the morning sunshine and the green shore stretching to the point of Carpignano.

He turned from the waterfront and virtually collided with the corrected Signor Di Micheli who had appeared suddenly from the lane in which his house stood. The old man appeared troubled and Signor Brazzi, quite unlike his normal self, was moved to enquire about his health and family.

'*Buon giorno*, Signor Di Micheli!' he chirped cheerily.

Zan winced.

'Micatovich, please, Signor Brazzi.'

'No, no, no, Signor Di Micheli.' The mayor flourished an educational digit. 'One must acclimatize oneself to the new regime here in Cittanova.'

'Then Sior Micatovich has not had the pleasure of meeting Signor Di Micheli,' protested Zan lamely.

'Allow me to introduce him.'

This mayor picks an inconvenient time to play games, thought Zan.

He was so preoccupied that his words, when he answered, became trapped in the tension of his jaw. It made him mumble and the mumbling might have embarrassed him had he been in a mood to care.

'You haven't lived long. I mean, lived here long... um... Signor di Brazzi.'

'You have had an order from the Prefect of Pola,' answered Brazzi, rather sternly in view of Zan's obvious confusion. 'And it is my duty to see it enforced.'

'Which order?' blurted Zan. 'Oh, the one about the name! Are you going to force me to use it?'

'Force is an ugly word. I prefer introduce.'

'I don't understand. You want us to use only Italian? We don't speak just one language here and lots of men have Slavic surnames. Why, my son was even called Zvane when he was little. That's a Croatian nickname for Giovanni.'

Brazzi looked distressed.

'Why, there aren't many actual Slavs here, are there? I thought they'd all be servants or something.'

'My wife had a Slavic name,' explained Zan. 'She came from a town near the Austrian border, a long way north of Cittanova.'

'How odd!'

'And where there's one Slav there may be more. Istria under Austria was a polyglot, as my son said… only last night...'

The phrase faded away and, although its sadness was obvious to him, Brazzi allowed a trace of hardness to enter his voice.

'Istria is Italian now, as it should be!' Then he whacked Zan on the back as a father might a son and continued more equitably, 'Come, come, signore! Let us talk of more pleasant things.'

Zan groaned inwardly. Varying your days between reprimanding your citizens and meaningless small talk came with the job of being mayor, evidently, and the wretched man seemed determined to prolong the conversation.

'It has turned into a magnificent day after the Bora, has it not?'

'Yes,' said Zan.

'I thought I had bid farewell to the Bora with Trieste but the whole coast is cursed with it.'

'I stay inside when it's windy.'

'That is the sensible option, of course. Do you go very often to Trieste?'

'No.'

'I expect you can get all you need in Cittanova.'

'We don't need much these days.'

'My wife is enjoying the town.'

'It's a nice place.'

'Have you been here long?'

'My family has lived here for several hundred years.'

'Indeed? Then you know a great deal about the town's history.'

'Not really.'

'But you must remember it before the campanile was built.'

'Yes.'

'How very interesting! What did it look like?'

'A lot flatter.'

'Yes, yes, I suppose that is to be expected.' He paused as if only now remembering his former surprise. 'Did you say what brought your wife here?'

'She ran away from home,' said Zan. 'Her father was a drunk.'

He lost his focus. Scarcely aware that the mayor still meandered by his side, he searched the horizon and thought only of his son. Though it seemed ridiculous to be unnecessarily concerned about a thirty-two-year-old who had lived away from home for over a decade, Silvana's sea monster returned to him and he felt the first stirring of anxiety stick in his chest just below his breastbone. It wriggled and squirmed and would not be eradicated by common sense. How could Giovanni have simply vanished without a trace? Was this even what had occurred? Perhaps, having been rejected by Gilda – and it had always been Zan's understanding that Gilda was the reason behind his son's continued bachelorhood – there was another girlfriend Zan did not know about and

Giovanni was, at this moment, waking up in her plump and pleasing arms after a night of passion when time, as reckoned by his parents, had ceased to be.

Although it was nearly lunchtime one or two boats were still entering the *mandracio*, catching the light breeze in their single sail, their nets strung up in their bows by a pole. In some cases the sails were eight meters high and it always amazed Zan, no sailor himself, how the boats did not tip over in the strong winds. A group of women chattered amicably on the wall along the shore of the *mandracio*. As each boat came in, they hailed and waved, passing comments to one another in slight nudges and laughs as they compared the number of boxes of freshly caught fish stacked on the bows. One, folding a net that lay upon her knee, ran down to examine a catch, relieved at another safe homecoming. Seamen and their families had good reason to be superstitious about the treacherous sea, as everyone knew but, nevertheless, Zan wondered how to introduce his theme of Silvana's sea monster to the happy families before him in a way that might attract their interest without insulting them. How many sea monsters could they have been expected to see recently in local waters?

He continued his walk with the mayor in an uneasy silence.

'I do not usually see you in the *mandracchio* at this hour,' Brazzi began in his best Italian.

'*Mandracio*,' corrected Zan.

'Pardon?'

'You said man-dra-ki-o. We say *man-dra-cho*. Three syllables, not four.'

'You confuse me, Signor Di Micheli,' blustered Brazzi, rather angry that the old man should imply that he was ignorant after Brazzi had insisted on conformity. 'You had a Slavic name, you speak Venetian, but frankly this town looks Italian to me.'

'This is who I am and this is where I live,' responded Zan simply. 'Micatovich is Croatian and *mandracio* is Venetian. Now, if you'll excuse me, Signor Brazzi, I have come here to speak to the fishermen who may have been near the port last night.' He hesitated. 'My granddaughter insists she saw a sea monster out past the end of the pier under the beam from the lighthouse.'

Was it his imagination or did the mayor lose his flushed face and grow a shade paler?

'How old is your granddaughter?'

'Silvana is eight.'

'Well, children, you know...' Brazzi affected unconcern.

'Yes, that's what Maria and I thought, but my son, Giovanni, was walking in that area last night – Bora and all, very foolish of him – and he has not come home.'

'Dear me.' The mayor stopped and assumed a thoughtful pose. 'He grew up here? He has friends? Maybe he is with one of them?'

'I hope so,' said Zan. 'But I couldn't help wondering what Silvana saw. Imagining monsters is not like her. She was quite upset about it. How to phrase my question to the fishermen so as not to insult their intelligence is my problem, you see.'

'Oh, I don't think you need concern yourself on that score,' returned Brazzi. 'If they're illiterate they're probably Slavs. And I'm sorry about your wife. Try not to let her origins concern you. She should be pleased that Micatovich has been corrected for her. It was originally Italian, you know.'

He wrinkled his nose at the townsfolk working peaceably along the shore. *Which smelled worse, the fishermen or their fish?* Then he shrugged Zan a dismissal and walked off, leaving the old man staring open-mouthed after him.

*****

It had never occurred to Matteo Brazzi that Signor Di Micheli had been born before the unification of Italy, in a geographical region that had been Celtic, Greek, Roman, Slavic, Venetian, Austrian and Italian in turn.

Nations came and went and nationalism meant little to the old man, living from birth in his one small windy corner of the world. Indeed, he did not seem to espouse nationalism at all.

Now Brazzi, by contrast, embraced nationalism as one of the great innovations of his age. The flowery belligerence of its language had proved quite wonderfully stimulating to his indolent nature. Where else but Italy could violence be glorified by poets? Italy, the great martyr among nations – thank you, Pascoli – downtrodden no more! Nationalism had gone to his head, intolerance had transported him, and he despised Austria for allowing such a racial free-for-all within its old empire for so long. It made his job that much harder when one felt resistance to a new order that had contributed so greatly to his ego.

And on that lofty note, he'd just better sort out the little matter of the harbor light while he was here. Find out what had really gone on last night. Employing more than his usual haste, Brazzi made his way as fast as his polished shoes would allow him around the corner of the customs house and the old Venetian toll box, skirted the back of the City of Trieste, noting that the hotel no longer seemed the sinister meeting place of last night but almost respectable. In the distance he saw a large steamer heading towards the town from the south, smoke pouring from her funnel and trailing high over the water behind. Already travellers and friends were hurrying down the pier as she reduced speed, her two masts empty and from the high bow an anchor hung below the bridge. Over the port and starboard sides two small lifeboats hung from davits, and her decks were crowded with the travellers that could never fit into them. He watched as the mate hurled a rope to another man waiting on the wharf, who secured its bow to a cleat and did the same with a second rope at the stern. Then the railing was opened, a gangway pushed out and a great human mixture swarmed onto the wharf, into the arms of the excited people waiting to greet them. Amongst the crowd, an old man wearing two shirts but no coat fondly embraced his cousin.

His Most Italian City

Ports the world over attracted people, mused Brazzi, observing the throng. They had a life of their own that dictated the mood of the nation. What should I look at? Where should I commune with my heart? The port, of course, which drew all things to itself. Where the buildings faced the water without question the shore became the hub of the town and greetings took as great a place in the collective subconscious as Turkish pirates and Venetian merchant vessels had.

Brazzi strolled in as nonchalant a manner as he could towards the happy scene, his eye firmly fixed on the harbor lamp about four meters away from the steamer. An unfortunate optical illusion made it seem that he could idly pass and check the fuel in the lamp with a single glance, but the pedestal on which it was placed grew exponentially as he approached, until he realized it was at least twice his height. The actual lamp was only accessible by a slender ladder which would certainly have spoiled his clothes had he tried to scale it. Added to that, it was protected by a crow's nest of thick metal. The sight of their mayor, with his stern fascist agenda, climbing to the top would undoubtedly undermine his credibility. Thwarted in his ambition, he waited a further ten minutes, until the steamer had finished disembarking its passengers and the wharf was beginning to clear, before his eyes alighted upon a small boy watching him curiously.

'Can you climb?' enquired Brazzi in his best schoolmaster's voice.

'*Si*, sior,' answered the child, a bright-eyed little fellow of about seven. 'There's no one in Cittanova who can climb better than me.'

Brazzi struggled with his incomprehensible dialect.

'Ah, good,' he at length replied. He flipped a five-lire coin in front of the child, who grabbed at it unsuccessfully. 'This is for you *if* you can tell me how much kerosene is in that lamp. Do you understand?'

'*Si*, sior.'

And, like a monkey, the boy sprung up the ladder, hoisted himself to the top, peered at the glass with his face hanging over the crow's nest and returned, jumping back onto the ground, all in under a minute.

Brazzi watched him without displaying the slightest envy for his own vanished youth, spent firmly on the ground.

'Well?'

'The lamp is half full, sior, perhaps a bit more.'

Brazzi tossed him the coin and the child ran away. One flat chime from the campanile proclaimed the hour.

The day that had started its ascent with such promise had been overshadowed by a brooding forecast and a bank of clouds was building in the south. Brazzi felt the breeze picking up. A hat went flying off a head and a sea gull cried harshly from the shore. He lost his focus so that the comings and goings, the chatter of the crowd faded from his perception and he felt isolated and alone.

Monfalcon had been wrong about the harbor lamp the previous evening even as Brazzi had only seen what he wanted to see. Some fool had not forgotten to replenish the lamp. A vessel had docked at the far end of the pier. An eight-year-old claimed to have seen a sea monster. Those last two observations, one mechanical and the other paranormal, were nevertheless not too hard to interpret, although a child that age should know a ship when she saw one. So what exactly had she seen? If he were being honest, he knew exactly what she'd seen and it was an accurate description. But, adding in Signor Di Micheli's missing son, he had no idea as yet how to connect all four events. In all likelihood the man would arrive home in the course of the day. But still… but still…

Meet me at ten o'clock at the inlet.

Where the pier began, hidden at the base of the old wall, protected by the tide.

The letter had been unsigned. And he hadn't needed to sign it; his handwriting, the thick quill, his assertive downward stroke and robust letters, all were unmistakable. He hadn't bothered to disguise them. He didn't care. He was taunting Brazzi for his impotence because he knew he couldn't fight back. Matteo Brazzi with his elegant copper-plate. Not so elegant now that his hands were shaking. But, you see, Brazzi was not such an innocent, after all. All along he had suspected the perpetrator, and now he knew.

Ten o'clock at the inlet. Under normal circumstances Brazzi would never have succumbed to such a preposterous proposal. What was he, a smuggler? Cigarettes, cocaine? Those days were behind him. Even tax evasion was more difficult away from the city. Bullying, extortion and bribery in a small community? Possible, but not recommended. These days Brazzi only involved himself in government-sanctioned crime. He was grateful to Mussolini for easing his livelihood in that respect.

Yes, the letter had been blunt but it had not been the first communication. The instant he had opened that parcel delivered to Angelica at the café in September and seen what it contained, he knew that his days of peace were over.

He's found me.

A hard rock had plummeted from his throat to his stomach and stayed there.

Brazzi, who was somewhat naive when it came to covering his own tracks, had peered at the metal tin wrapped in tissue paper and had not initially understood what it meant. At first it had seemed innocuous enough: a large can of soup with a handle. And then he saw what looked like a jovial little hat on the top.

He had stood there with a hand on his belly, feeling sick. He had a vague notion that he should know what the hat was but he hesitated to put his thoughts into words, so dreadful they seemed. A detonator? A fuze? Cautiously, he sniffed beneath it. A taut metallic scent. He shook the can. He peered inside. It seemed empty but he couldn't see past the jaunty angle of the brim.

Margaret Walker

All at once he had had a horrible vision of being mocked and he had thrust open the top drawer in the café's kitchen, searching for a knife, and determinately levered the detonator until it hung by a single wire from the top of the can.

'There!' he cried at the vision. 'It's dead. You can't hurt me anymore.'

He smoothed his waistcoat over his shirt, adjusted his tie, and carefully surveyed the creases in his trousers to make sure they were straight, and felt better. But the grim specter would not go away, and neither would that hot prickle behind his eyes.

'Go on, laugh!' he exclaimed furiously wiping away the tears. 'And I hope you've learned to dress better!'

How had he found him? Newspapers? Telegraph? Word of mouth? Impossible. Who knew he was here? The Party secretary? Angelica's parents? The waterside workers who loaded his boxes onto the ferry? The children hanging off the wharves at Trieste? The fish?

So he had gone home distressed, and only at some later stage, when the night shadows from the acacia tree in the garden shivered the bedroom with gray and Angelica slept beside him dreaming of babies, had he begun to appreciate the audacity of his enemy.

Chapter Seven

Giovanni had lapsed into a state of controlled panic.

He had been unable to prevent himself losing consciousness again after the rat incident, and had woken an indefinite time later with no sign of the offending rodent, concluding that it was off pursuing its nefarious activities in another part of the vessel. He did not desire the company of the strange group he found himself with but neither did he relish solitude. While he'd slept, the bunks above and below him had filled with men, and three hammocks, also occupied, had been strung across the small space. Hot bodies and warm breath had produced condensation that bubbled visibly upon most surfaces, coalesced into rivulets and showered downwards sporadically, angling to the left or right as the boat rolled. Two of the men in the hammocks had covered their faces with oilcloths.

Giovanni thought briefly of remaining in what now resembled a campsite in a wet cave before deciding that men awake and silent were better company than men asleep. Scattered remnants of young male disorder lay around him: bunched-up socks, a crust of bread, a rind of cured meat, a water bottle in a canvas sack, a pair of discarded boots, a flat wicker basket designed to slot into a shelf, a balaclava and a thick cabled jumper whose intricacy of design bore witness to a patient parent and a warm hearth far from here. The boat chugged along with the same noise, smell and confinement he might have expected within the engine room of a coastal steamer and, feeling marginally better than he had earlier, he peeled himself from his bed and cautiously made his way through the narrow corridor, swaying with the roll of the vessel, supporting himself by placing his hands before him on the walls.

Scarcely had he left than he ran into a solid metal wall with a large round hole, through which he had to bend over double before at length unfolding into another space – he could not call it a room – lit by a single electric bulb strung in a cage from the ceiling. The space seemed to him like a narrow railway carriage with the blinds down and, though swarming in broad pipes and snaking cables, it had a higher ceiling than the sleeping quarters. Beside two spoked wheels, like a bicycle without a seat, a slender youth with buck teeth stood as patiently as though he had nothing with which to concern himself but to await orders. *He might be about to milk the cows*, thought Giovanni, observing the young man's bovine tranquility, before upbraiding himself for his lack of charity.

'What is this?' he asked.

'The control room,' answered the boy.

'What do you do here?'

'I'm the apprentice electrician. I stay until I'm relieved.'

'May I sit down?'

He nodded, so Giovanni carefully arranged himself on the dampish deck plating, with a watchful eye on the bewildering tangle of ironwork surrounding him.

The control room resembled an automobile where body, muffler, exhaust and every moving part had been dismantled and reassembled into an area half the size, squashed and suffocating, for a complex network of pipes stretched over every available surface except the floor, even up into the arched roof. It was much hotter than the crew's quarters and, through a further small curved door passing through a metal wall above him, he heard the booming rhythmic knock of the diesel engines from which the heat originated. Without windows the heat was unable to escape and the gloomy atmosphere had become very close, like summer without the sun. From time to time a young face flitted across the opening and another man, as youthful as his compatriot, seemed to busy himself at what might have been something electrical at the far end. Above him sprawled a structure like the many-headed hydra, its flanks mounted with dozens of wheels of all sizes, from fungus-sized buds to bloated gargoyles to enormous enteric flowers. In the turgid gloom, the complex and intimidating monstrosity loomed over Giovanni. Less and less easily could he call to mind the world he thought he belonged to, for he would never before have called a machine intimidating.

Under his arms and up into his groin his skin itched from being encased in his wet woolen suit – the crew worked only in trousers and shirts with the sleeves rolled up.

It'd be better to take my jacket off like them, he decided. *Roll my sleeves up. Florence wouldn't approve, but does Florence matter?*

And he was just about to do that when an uncomfortable little voice whispered to him that by doing so he was condoning this situation. It would be best, his homunculus went on, if he did all he could to preserve the person he believed himself to be. So the boat stank with the odor of unwashed men and he just sat and sweated and added to it: sweat, diesel, urine, bile, rotten egg gas. To top it all off, they pitched and rolled in the swell and he was starting to feel seasick.

But worse, far worse than the stink, the machinery and his deteriorating self-perception was the need to leave this enclosure immediately: to escape the lowering ceiling and forge his way up to the sky. With the claustrophobia arose the conviction that there were not two people squashed into this iron cupboard but three. The third, an intangible menace, had arisen as he'd sloughed off his unconsciousness. Down the brief passage it had accompanied him, through the bulkhead and into the control room, and now it settled above his head, threatening and malevolent. By devious means it attacked his heart which began to thud wildly within his chest. Then it strangled his breathing. The weak tungsten globe fading in the clutch of its wire cage seemed like the last sliver of twilight and, as night closed in, the presence focused itself upon him. He felt as if he were travelling along a tunnel searching for daylight, with this awful phantom clinging to his back, and, at each moment, he anticipated the approach of the sunshine that would subdue it. But he saw no end to the tunnel. And no sun. And so the fear and the panic proliferated. It was distressing to think that he, a product of a comfortable home and a good education, had been reduced so rapidly to this desperation. The presence hovered just beyond his recognition so that he was unable to name it, but when he closed his eyes he saw its face melting like ice in a flame.

Eventually he managed to control himself just enough to develop some distraction strategies while a dozen or more drops of warm condensation rained down upon him. First he said the Lord's Prayer and the Gloria, then he recited his times tables in his head from one to twenty. That took him ten minutes, seventeen, eighteen and nineteen being the challenging ones. Next he reviewed his knowledge of biological classification systems which forced him to recall his Latin and Greek, and that moved his thoughts on to Epicurean philosophy which he hoped to emulate by living modestly and learning about the natural world. Finally with the engines pounding in his ears he listed the dukes of Savoy, the kings of Italy, the emperors of Austria, thirteen of his favorite Italian wines and the church's calendar from Advent to Pentecost.

If the men coming and going beside him paid him no attention in the meantime, as little did he notice them, and gradually he derived the reassuring notion that he might not be a prisoner at all. No one had in so many words stated the terms of his captivity and it looked like, as their leader had said, they were still working out what to do with him.

So he cleared his throat and addressed the control room electrician as moderately as he might have done before a biology class with his fingers spaced before him on the lectern. Only the topic fell short.

His Most Italian City

'How do I get out of here?'

The young man seemed surprised to be spoken to a second time, and his teeth protruded a little further from his mouth, but he answered Giovanni's polite request agreeably enough.

'Up there,' and pointed to an aluminum ladder sliding into the room, which Giovanni had been too absorbed with itemizing Italian wines to notice.

He shifted so that he could see what it led to, a heavy round object with a wheel, apparently sitting on the ceiling.

'The door? The lid?'

'It's a hatch.'

'Oh yes, I see.' Giovanni examined it through the humid murk. 'It looks shut.'

'We can open it. It's not secured.'

'Then why don't you?'

'Well,' began the boy, before pausing in order to give his reply some placid consideration. (*He has certainly come from a farm*, decided Giovanni. *He has milked the cows and now he is explaining the features of his new tractor.*) 'We're not very big and we roll a lot, that's all, especially when the sea's up. You don't want too much water getting into a submarine.'

'Aren't they like ships?'

'No, no.' He shook his head. 'We're not a ship. No superstructure. And a funny shape. Bit unstable.'

Dreadful things and dire warnings.

'Are we going to sink?' gasped Giovanni.

'No,' the boy answered, mildly startled at the alarm in Giovanni's voice. He frowned before returning to the patient mode of explanation in which he was clearly more comfortable. 'I don't think so. But Captain doesn't want water in the circuitry or the batteries.'

But Giovanni was already surrounded by water. Water draining in unseen cavities towards a slurp-gulp, slurp-gulp repeater that could only be a pump. Water chopping on the hull. Water in his hair, water on the walls and water in his dreams. In fact, water everywhere.

'It does seem rather wet in here to me.'

Through the boy's reserve came just the hint of a sly smile.

'We're not bailing the bilges yet. *That* would be wet.'

'Ah, yes. Yes, I'm sure it would be. Thank you, um... what's your name?'

'Anton.'

'And my name's Giovanni. How are you, Anton?'

'Good,' mumbled the boy.

'Well, you see, Anton,' explained Giovanni, struggling not to sound desperate, 'I don't like being shut in. I would feel better if the hatch was opened a little.'

Anton seemed unsure how to answer and, though it was no use pretending the young man was part of one of his classes, Giovanni smiled to show that his reasoning was on the right track. The boy seemed pleased.

'Well,' he said, clearly relieved to feel that he had finally helped, 'Captain might leave this one open for you if the sea were not so high... or if we were at war or something.'

'What difference would war make?'

'You'd probably want to get down quickly.' He nodded as if he were agreeing with himself. 'There's also another hatch below the bridge, above the helm in the tower, but you've got to leave that one open for the diesels to breathe.'

Giovanni had not understood a word of this and he was beginning to see that any attempt to ask the boy to repeat himself would only end in more confusion. He gathered that the hatch was going to stay shut. Reflecting bleakly that teachers were doomed to consider duty of care in any and all circumstances, he commented in his attentive classroom manner, 'You sound like you're really interested in submarines.'

'Yes,' agreed Anton. 'They are interesting.'

This enterprising exchange was interrupted when a sudden shower of water tumbled into the control room, followed by a blast of cold salt air and a perfect ray of sunshine that played upon the floor at their feet. With a cry of joy, Giovanni grasped at it like a drowning man at a rope until the captain jumped down into the room from the middle rung of the ladder and shut the hatch behind him, cutting off the light.

As if the earth had shifted in its orbit, the atmosphere in the cramped room immediately tightened. Anton squared his shoulders, a face from the engine room checked to see if he were wanted, and even Giovanni sat up straighter. In his hand the captain held a sextant that he rested on the floor with a dull steel thud. Then he gave Anton some directions and presently the buck-toothed electrician disappeared into the crew's quarters.

Giovanni waited alone on the lifeless floor. He had felt some companionship with the young man, and the sunbeam had heartened him. Now he sensed only a profound loss, and lurching back towards him inched that dark fear.

'Please, please, could you leave that hatch open?' he begged.

'Not in these seas,' said the man.

'But not much water would get in if you opened it a little.'

'Not now.'

'But I could climb that ladder and you could close it behind me.'

'There's no room on the bridge at the moment.'

'You don't understand… I'm frightened. I'm so lonely.'

Given the tasks he had at hand, the captain allowed a look to cross his face that was midway between incredulity and annoyance. In its muted tone, Giovanni suspected that there may have been a time when he comforted small children but right now he'd forgotten how to do that. So he made an incorrect assumption and instead of soothing he said, 'If you want to go up I can take you before sunset, after this watch.'

'Sunset!' lamented Giovanni. 'I'm never going to get out of here! How long till sunset?' He scrutinized his wrist watch, scrunched his eyes up, and managed only to look like a myopic clod. His academic colleagues would not have recognized him. Either through his dip in the salt water or because he had not wound it last night, the timing mechanism of the watch had stopped at three o'clock. He tapped it, fiddled with the winder, frowned at the hands. Why wasn't it working?

The captain realized that it was broken but was not sure why Giovanni was looking prehistoric. 'The sun sets at half past four,' he said. 'This watch ends at three.'

'What time is it now?'

'It's gone midday.'

Giovanni sank back upon his soggy floor plate. Two drips landed on his forehead and ran down his nose.

'I'll just amuse myself until then,' he volunteered miserably. 'If you've no objections.'

Irony was not what the captain expected to hear. From his crew he expected, 'yes, Captain' or 'no, Captain.' He let out a terse sigh, as if he had been pumping up tires all morning and finally they were all filled. The last heave. He faced Giovanni as if he'd had enough of pumping.

'What do you want?'

'I want you to open that hatch.'

So the man heaved himself halfway up the ladder and shoved open the recalcitrant hatch. With finality. Don't ask me again.

'Thank you,' said Giovanni.

The sun hovered just over the meridian. Giovanni couldn't see it but it announced its presence by softening the silver of the aluminum rungs leading down from the world above, though it lacked the angle to dapple them. He thought that if he lay flat on the floor beneath the open hatch he might just have a chance to see it before it dipped westward. Only a fine mist was seeping down the cold tower. So he rested his head upon the slimy floor, positioned himself beneath the tower and scanned hopefully. Almost immediately he was hit in the face by a jet of water – a big *whoosh* as if from a blowhole – that cut him like a blast from a fire hose. Dripping wet, he shuffled along the floor plates into a safer position and watched the ladder change color as the vessel rolled. Back, gray, and forth, silver, back and forth, gray and silver, back and forth, gray and silver. As if launched from the hands of demented bailers, random showers started to spray the floor plates below the tower and soon Giovanni was aware of a substantial slosh of bilge water below him that until now he had noticed as no more than the purring of a tide. In response to the sound, he kept his eyes on the ladder as if it were a lifcline, despite the deluge further drenching him, so that he wished, bizarrely, that he had brought his umbrella.

One thing, though, salt water smelled clean. In the midst of Giovanni's bath, the captain glanced up reproachfully but said nothing and after a moment more under the waterfall, Giovanni retreated to what he was coming to think of as his scullery. And the hatch stayed open.

He was getting his head together now, but the loss of control and his panic had been outside his experience and he remembered how they had possessed him. Here he was learning what fears prowled around the outskirts of his world.

Above him the captain inspected a book and scribbled some figures with a pencil on a scrap of paper inserted between the pages. He transferred the result of his sums to what Giovanni assumed was a log, and placed both book and log on a flat iron surface adjacent to the phalanx of wheels. Next, he commenced scrutinizing a sea chart. Occasionally he tapped the pencil on his teeth or angled the chart away to protect it from getting wet, but he did not talk to himself, or belch, or fart or yawn. He did not even stretch. He seemed the most physically composed person

Giovanni had seen for some time and he commenced observation of the captain.

For I have nothing else to do, he mused. *And it is astonishing how one's discernment is sharpened by captivity, monotony and the desperation to hold fear at arm's length.*

The dark hazel eyes turned upon the chart did not invite conversation; rather, they were focused on the task. Even the captain's breathing in the stale air was regular, and seemed under his control. If he had thoughts to share, then within himself they would stay until he felt inclined to share them. Nevertheless, Giovanni passed the time formulating possible scenarios based on the man's physical features combined with what he already knew.

He has stolen a submarine, Giovanni decided, *because he wishes to approach by stealth. Therefore his actions reinforce the traditional criticism of submarines as being ungentlemanly. Opposed to this is the observation that he has the loyalty of his crew. They are quite pleasant, except that big fat one whose one redeeming feature seems to be his loyalty to his captain. The boy by the wheels could have been tense, but he wasn't, and that other motherly man was almost kind. Not something one expects from terrorists.*

He actually carries a sextant. He must be a pirate! Kind as his crew may be, I don't know anyone who carries sextants except pirates, and people who kidnap biology teachers on the high seas are obviously pirates. It suits me to call him captain because an adventure story is the only scenario I can summon under the circumstances. He would be Captain Under the Water or Captain Unscrupulous or Capitano Sotto Voce, or something along those lines. This pirate captain, then, is only a little taller than I am, and a moderate height must be an advantage in a confined space. His face is tanned but not thickened by sun exposure, like fishermen, and his hair is plastered to his scalp with salt spray. I can smell the salt and his shirt is wet. It has welded to his skin, becoming the color of dried bone. Through it I can see him breathing in and out, as shallow as a fish. His chest is defined by his wet shirt, rather broad, and he has gills, certainly. (Giovanni spent some minutes determining how gills might develop from human respiration.)

He is considerably older than his crew, perhaps twice as old, maybe more. One would expect a man of that age to have settled down to a desk job and not be gallivanting around the Adriatic badly dressed and bearded. Something in his past has rendered him an outlaw, or, more likely, somebody has done something to him. I wonder what it is?

He squinted his eyes towards the face that until now he had only wanted to elude.

There's nothing more tantalizing than a man with a past, but how do you read a face that is unreadable? How do you discover his story? No one here is going to tell me because I am just part of the background. I have no purpose but to frame the purposeful. I cannot be found because I was never lost.

A single drop of condensation hung poised on the sextant's telescope until it fell imperceptibly onto the measuring arc below.

That drop is my insignificance, mused Giovanni. *Nobody wants me at all.*

So he continued to watch the captain with the same detached curiosity, as if they were moving in separate worlds, until the man completed his navigating and again approached the ladder and Giovanni comprehended that he was about to disappear and take with him the answers to his questions. Worse, he might close the hatch. He shook himself from his reverie, reached out and tapped the man on the calf. He turned around. Giovanni looked up.

'Excuse me. Where are we going?'

'Back,' the captain passed a grimy hand through his beard. 'To do what we should have done when we picked *you* up.'

'Home?' Hope sprung in his heart. 'When? I mean, where are we now?'

'South coast. Just off the shipping lanes.'

'You mean…'

'Not far away.' He shot Giovanni a malicious grin. 'Does that please you?'

The phrasing of this curt remark did not tally with his appearance.

He certainly has a past, concluded Giovanni to himself. *Something has brought him to this, for in other circumstances he has been clean shaven and better dressed. He has come from a different world.*

'You're educated?'

'Less educated than you,' the captain answered shrewdly.

'I'm only a teacher.'

'You teach in Italy but you're not Italian. Enlighten me: what gives Italy the right to suppress another race? Education or a treaty drawn up by foreigners?'

Giovanni was struck by the inconsistency between his words and his looks.

'Who are you to ask me this?'

The man began to reply then apparently thought better of it.

'Just curious,' he said.

'I don't think you'd go to all this trouble over a treaty.'

'I might.'

'Well, I wouldn't,' replied Giovanni. 'I know treaties are not fair. Allies betray each other. People who were once neighbors are now enemies. That's what happens after a war. It's a shame.'

'You've got a comfortable view.'

'Yes, that's true. I have fitted in, but I had little choice.'

Giovanni's interest had been sparked and he felt determined, now he finally had a conversation established, that he would not let the subject go and meekly resume the role of prisoner. He pushed himself up on one elbow. 'Referring to your earlier comment, I would like to know what it is you think you should have done.'

The resting head turned slightly.

'When?'

'When you picked me up. You said,' he persisted, '"what we should have done when we picked *you* up." You can only be looking for the person I was mistaken for.'

The captain paused. In the set of his jaw and the stillness that veiled his gaze, Giovanni knew, as if by second sight, that he nursed a hurt that differed as much from a grudge as a tree did from a splinter.

I was right! he thought, allowing himself some modest triumph.

That certainty quickened his emotional antennae. People said he was soft but his answer to this would have been that the natural sympathy that he possessed in abundance would not permit him to either deliberately hurt another person or stand by unmoved when he could help. It particularly pleased him, as well, that his instincts had been correct, and, as if the man were one of his pupils with a personal problem, he forged ahead when he should have held back.

'You are, aren't you?'

He moved his body forward into an attitude of compassion.

'Whatever's happened in your past,' he pursued gently, 'is none of my business, but I'm happy to listen.'

Now he had laid down the gauntlet. He had probed the man's life like a seer. He had looked into his heart and seen its secrets. In his professional opinion, the time for revelation had arrived.

But the ploy could not have been more obvious if he had asked him to relate his story and offered support, and, too late, Giovanni realized his mistake. The captain's composure disintegrated in front of him. Horror swept his face as he battled the rush of emotions Giovanni had provoked. His hands clenched by his side, the firm mouth warped and, for an instant, such a mask of penetrating regret obscured his features that Giovanni forgot his own troubles in his surprise. And, just as quickly, it was gone, replaced by anger, shame at a moment of weakness, and, with it, the desire of the wounded to wound.

In a second he had sloughed off the moment as if it were a pretense. He was in control again and his indifference was more terrifying than his anger.

He snapped his fingers. 'Zorko!'

Zorko's huge mass at once squeezed in through the engine room hatch, scraping his big ear. He'd had it pressed to the engine room bulkhead the whole time and he'd been looking forward to this.

The captain jerked his head at the conning tower.

'Throw him overboard.'

The giant commenced pacing forward. As Giovanni struggled to his feet and backed away, Zorko grasped one of his shoulders and shoved it into the ladder.

'Up!' he barked.

Giovanni noticed little things then: the sunbeam had come back and, in the patch of seawater on the floor, a rainbow was shining on its scum of diesel. The frosty winter air swarmed into the high narrow opening like a gale through a tunnel, sweeping out the stench and the dead rankness, filling the steel hull with hope. But he could see nothing save the ladder leading up to the world he had loved and feel only a terrible sadness at leaving it. He shut his eyes. Somewhere very close were his parents, frantically wondering what had become of him. Close were the green hills, the parks of oak and pine, the fishermen sorting their catch, the blue waters of the bay, the grand and overarching sky. Giovanni stared numbly at the first rung, unable to move, wiping away the tears that would not stop.

When he saw him weep, Zorko slapped him on the back as if he were the presenter at a boxing tournament, leered familiarly into his face and said, 'You're not navy material, we regret, but have you tried the army?'

His Most Italian City

Then he roared so heartily at his own joke that at length he was forced to wipe his eyes with a sleeve smudged with oil, until he imagined he resembled the pistons he had just been lubricating. This notion caused him to laugh with even greater gusto and, as he returned to the engine room, his snorts were drowned out by the diesels, but only just.

The captain remained, watching Giovanni, pensive and grim, while something akin to gratification flickered across his features.

'Nearly got what you wanted. And you'd better hope that we don't run into any ships because, the minute I see something, we're diving. You won't like that.'

Back he went up the ladder, the hatch closed behind him and the end of Giovanni's bid for freedom was like its beginning: the walls, the stink and the gloom.

A hollow shudder rocked his soul. He seemed lost in a moonless night upon a black ocean, alone but for the mournful cry of a sea bird and the clang of a warning bell laid upon a rock. Only that old fear to keep him company. Then grief surged in and its wave broke at the crest, snatching him away, sweeping him on towards the beach. Left alone on the swell, his unpleasant familiar drifted out to sea. And there was some sort of peace without it. Giovanni sat down and abandoned himself to sleep.

Chapter Eight

At any one time there were four men on the bridge and each was given a quarter of the ocean to watch. In fine weather a watch ran for four hours. Today the sun was unobscured by cloud as it reached the highest point in the sky and at midday the captain had been able to measure the angle between it and the horizon, and then, from his almanacs and charts, calculate their position at sea.

The commercial shipping lanes to the ports of Trieste and Venice were well out to sea and, with the forced postponement of his objective, he had sailed slowly southwest, out of sight of land. Unless they saw a cargo or passenger ship and were forced to dive, which he thought was unlikely, they would in any event perform their daily practice dive, then, under cover of darkness, position themselves directly west of Cittanova and steer straight into the old port. Then the only point at which the boat could be identified would be the small sweep of white light beneath the lighthouse that it was not possible to avoid. He noted the increasing wind and the build-up of clouds on the southern horizon. By the late evening he knew that this south wind, though not as violent as the Bora, would nevertheless be blowing hard enough to whip the swell into surf and send it pummeling over the town's breakwater from the opposite direction.

The captain only knew one way of speaking to anybody and that was the direct way. He had told Giovanni that there was no room on the bridge and, with five of them on the small platform, there wasn't. He would return to Cittanova, as he had also said and, this time, he would require the assistance of the local man and his local knowledge. It was equally true that he had no time for reflection, but the conversation in the control room had disturbed him and, uncharacteristically upon the crowded bridge, he found himself seeking comfort.

As always the sea was glad to see him. As the small submarine pitched into the next trough, it leapt towards him, caught the sun in its foam and crashed jubilantly into the tower. He leaned right over because he wanted to be part of it. A great wash coursed across his face and through his eyes. It ran in rivulets down his chest and he heard its hiss as it washed across the deck and was sucked back into the sea. As the minutes passed he was absorbed into its rhythm and became increasingly unaware of the four men standing beside him. They took no notice. They had sometimes, but not often, seen him like this before.

Mesmerized, he continued to watch, until the perpetual motion became the thing by which he defined himself. In and out, in and out; the sea swept in like the nights he dreamed of her, and out as each morning drew her back into sleep.

Many times when he saw the color of her hair in his dreams, and that front tooth that overlapped its companion as she smiled, he tried to hold onto her. The loose hairs brushed her forehead. He smelled the sweet breath of her kiss; hers was the voice he heard. She was never able to keep it in the lower register. Somehow it would rise up, no matter what she did, and make her sound like an excited teenager.

She was always deprecating it.

'But I like your voice,' he said, reaching out to her. 'Keep talking to me.'

But he couldn't hold onto her.

'I love you!' he called, yet still she left him every morning. He had thought that his sleep was kind, but what it gave him it took back again.

Yet it was his sleep, in the end, and no one else's, and one day he would follow her into what belonged to him. It was not as if it was a journey into the unknown, and death was not something to be feared, only like going to sleep at the end of a long day.

He remembered how she used to come and sit at the end of his bath and tease him when he got home from the sea.

'You're doing a very poor job, Commander!' she'd say as he washed the grime from his body in front of her. 'You've missed a spot.'

'Where?' he'd ask.

'Oh, there,' she would reply idly, wearing next to nothing. 'And there.' Pulling the pins from her hair one by one. 'And there, where I can't quite see.' Pointing directly over him until she nearly fell in. 'Right *there*.'

Until quite soon there were more immediate things on his mind than being clean. But he, of all people, should not have looked at the bathroom floor afterwards, as if he were surprised to see water.

'Now look what you've done!' she chided. They were both sloshing. 'What a mess!'

She knew what to say to him. She was no wallflower.

'You shouldn't tease,' he answered.

But why hadn't she worn the orange chemise? His favorite. He preferred its feel on his skin to the thin blue one she was wearing, and she had disappeared just as he'd been gearing up for the next round.

'Hoy, wait! Where are you going?'

'To get changed. Look at me, I'm all wet.'

'You should have worn the orange one.'

'It's apricot.'

'Apricot?'

He stationed himself across the door so that she tried to get out and gave up. But sometimes words are more effective than force.

'It's apricot,' she said with determination. 'Not orange.'

His Most Italian City

He still wouldn't budge: breadth of chest, wet hair and beard together blocking the door.

'I'll change. You shave,' she told him.

'Later,' he said. 'What's the rush?'

'You look like Poseidon.'

She ducked under his arm and he chased her down the hall while she threw him a muffled joke about being overpowered by a sea god. Into the shaded, narrow bedroom she plummeted, and then he was on top of her.

'I take it back,' she said, struggling and laughing. 'Let me go.'

'Put the apricot one on.'

'Get off me, you Greek thug, and I will.'

He rolled into the dip in the middle of the mattress. A spring pricked his shoulder and he shoved a pillow into it, smelling feathers, lavender and, somewhere to the side, warm wool. Varnish flaked aromatically from the bedstead, and he rested his arms above his head and watched her.

She could be a recalcitrant angel, he thought, as she rummaged through her underwear drawer in the wet chemise, for the thin silk accentuated every curve of her body and her thick dark hair created a halo of soft static around her head. Because she was tall for a woman, almost as tall as he was, she resembled the angel Gabriel more than a cherub. Her beauty was further defined by an almost perfectly symmetrical face, which always seemed to be turned his way, features as crisp as the first snowflake and a neck as graceful as a swan's. Like him, she was intelligent in a capable way and possessed, moreover, the skill of piercing his mind and soul like no one he had ever met.

But he'd lived too long amongst men to worry about covering up, and she was never discomfited or looked away. She liked men.

'Keep searching,' he said. 'We'll wait.'

'One of you is not waiting.'

Once there were children on the scene, they tried different ways of solving the problem of finding time for each other. On shore leave, towards the end of the war, when their daughter was five and their son was two, he had tried the old soldiers' trick of throwing colored sprinkles on the lawn, then rushing into the bedroom.

'Off you go, kids,' he'd announced, like a commander calling from the bridge. 'Pick them up!'

'How long will that take them?' she asked, closing the door.

'Probably not as long as we need.'

And, sure enough, shortly afterward came the tiny knock, and a shy voice, 'Mama?'

The little boy was too young to understand and his daughter, as articulate as her mother, was not impressed. She stoutly informed him that 'You put sprinkles on cakes, not on the grass'. As he couldn't tell her what their purpose was on this occasion, he was forced to agree.

So her mother took the children that first night, and he had come to expect the four of them waving from the pier when his boat came in, all dressed in their best clothes. Nataša held his son in her arms, waving his little hand for him while the toddler wondered at the excitement of the crowd and the bearded stranger walking towards him who looked a little like his father. His daughter, more prosaic, told him he smelled, and when he kissed her she complained that his beard was prickly.

'Can I kiss Mummy?'

'You can kiss Mummy when you've had a bath,' she answered seriously.

'Then I'll go home and have one.'

So in the interests of family unity her mother would leave with the children in one direction and he'd go home with Nataša in the other.

Chapter Nine

In the early afternoon the gossips had gone home to have lunch and every table of the two rows in the Caffè Fascisti was empty except one. On this reposed the remains of the morning's Linzer Torte before its three occupants: Brazzi, the corpulent Morato and the pathologically famished Monfalcon. Morato, having over-eaten at lunch time, was idly reducing the criss-cross pastry to a snail trail of jam blobs and almond crumbs. Brazzi had consumed a delicate slice and was arranging his knife and fork as neatly upon his plate as was necessary to remind himself of the city. Monfalcon's slice lay untouched before him. All three had forgotten the cream, though, some time earlier that day, Emilio Urizio had whipped it into shape for Teresa and didn't care whether it was eaten or not.

Brazzi was never exactly clear when Monfalcon had usurped his role as mayor of Cittanova or why this afternoon the café seemed to have become his unofficial council chambers. Any meeting with Monfalcon was ultimately about money. And fascism. One came with the other. They were his consuming obsessions.

'The order from Pola about the school came last month,' said Monfalcon, his eyes down as if he were flipping through an agenda, 'and you haven't done it yet?'

'Gospoda Radin has been teaching here for a long time, Giuseppe,' Brazzi answered. 'She has a reputation for militancy. She won't like it.'

'Her opinion on the matter is entirely superfluous. Anything Slavic ended in these towns in 1918. What is she doing in Cittanova in 1928 using "gospođa"?'

'"Gospođa" is Croatian for "signora,"' explained Brazzi.

'Yes, I know that.'

'She came from Zagreb in 1890.'

'Well, she can go back to Zagreb *right now* if she can't use "*signora*." What is she, sixty? A working woman is an embarrassment to her husband, let alone one of that age. You can solve all your problems by getting rid of her.'

Monfalcon smoothed his sour hat over his pickled head. Like most of his clothes, the hat had taken up permanent residence.

At moments like this Brazzi positively panted to return to the city. So much for the clean air of the country – Monfalcon smelled like a jar of sauerkraut on one side of him and Morato, all sugar and cinnamon, was on the other. He sniffed the cologne on his handkerchief and considered that there must be more pleasant ways of making a dishonest living. The hour with Monfalcon in particular was turning his stomach. The creeping decay of the man, the alcohol abuse that was its cause and his general lack of hygiene.

'I can't account for your reluctance, Matteo.' Monfalcon farted and Brazzi averted his head. 'You're not even being asked to close the wretched institution. All the teacher has to do is use "signora," not "gospođa." Oh, and Italianize her surname. Stick a vowel on the end of it. Inform her that Radin was once Radini. That her name is merely being returned to the original Italian. Organize for it to be erased from the board outside the school and substitute the new one. Leave her no option.'

Gloomily Brazzi wondered if the cause of self service was worth all this unpleasantness. Monfalcon evidently thought so. But Matteo Brazzi, who had adopted *dolce far niente* as his motto many years ago and was still faithful to its dictum, was quite upset that Fascist doctrine did not agree. It *was* sweet to do nothing and, if anything was whining for attention, far better to let the plebs handle it and for Brazzi to rest his feet on the proceeds. If nothing eventuated, fine. At least he hadn't expended his own reserves on something that was doomed to fail.

And was that Italian skepticism? Yes... No... The jury was still out.

Brazzi, in his more literary moods, often contemplated the source of *dolce far niente* and found himself thinking it must certainly have originated before fascism and Mussolini's empire fantasy put so much pressure on one coffee merchant of medium height and low energy levels. Certainly it had little to do with lazing away long afternoons basking in the proceeds of profiteering that took care of itself. Tax evasion, to cite one example. Contraband, now there was another. He'd had ample opportunity to conceal his laziness in the city, but here, where everybody – except the three imperial relics he rented from – knew everybody else's business, he had as much chance of concealment as a dog in a henhouse.

'Matteo!'

'Yes?'

At the angry summons, Brazzi roused himself. He leaned an elbow on the counter and feigned interest.

'How many Slovenian schools have you closed in Trieste, Matteo?'

'Well I, personally, or the government?'

'Just answer the question!'

'I can't give you a precise number, Giuseppe.' Brazzi circled his other hand in the air. 'Four hundred and eighty-eight Slavic schools have been closed throughout the whole of the new Italian territories – that's over the ten-year period from the end of the war, of course, and not all were Slovenian – some were Croatian. But I supervised the closing of some schools that spoke Slovenian in Trieste, and a few sporting clubs... I also made suggestions about changing street signs, and, eh, wrote one or two items for the popular press and signed whatever the Party wanted. The secretary did most of the heavy work, though I tried to take the credit for it.'

'Heavy work?'

'Slovenian banks, law courts, libraries… and so on… gelato bars, fruit shops. '

'Who burned their books?'

'Someone else lit that pyre, and I didn't ignite any intellectuals either.'

'Don't get sarcastic with me. You just did as you were told and you don't really care. They hardly ask you to do anything here and this is your response!'

Across the table, Morato, who had squeezed his stuffed brown suit onto one of Brazzi's delicate chairs, now sat tinkling his fingers on the table, thoroughly enjoying Brazzi's tedium and Monfalcon's efforts to shatter it.

'They ought to get you to change the names on the tombstones at Saint Agatha's cemetery,' Morato chuckled. 'Battle the dead as well as the living.'

'I have heard that postulated,' mused Monfalcon.

'Battling Signora Radin *is* like battling the dead,' complained Brazzi.

'She is Slavic, Matteo,' returned Monfalcon bluntly. 'Slavs are an inferior race. They are barbaric. Mussolini has said so and his words must commence the fascist liturgy in these border territories.'

'In any case,' pursued Morato, 'Slavs should be pleased to be Italian. We're doing them a favor by closing their schools. Italians are the dominant race, superior in all ways. The *civilized* descendants of the Romans.'

Brazzi reclined artistically against the counter, or perhaps one could say he adopted a rehearsed slump.

'Italy's obsession with its Roman empire is exhausting me,' he sighed. 'My life would be so much easier if they'd never had one.'

His Most Italian City

'I don't need a history lecture,' spat Monfalcon. The phlegm caught in his throat, sinking to a pool behind his sternum. 'Tell me again what Di Micheli told you this morning about his son.'

Brazzi fingered the latest edition of *Il Piccolo*, the right-wing newspaper from Trieste, copies of which he kept in a pile by the cash register for the eager country proselytes he had hoped would batter down his door for copies. He knew better by now.

'All Signor Di Micheli knows is that his son has disappeared and his granddaughter says he was eaten by a sea monster.'

'*A what?!!*' roared the two men.

'My reaction entirely,' lied Brazzi.

'I tell you, Matteo,' gloated Monfalcon contemptuously, gushing methane across the table. 'I don't believe you now and I swear I never will. You're a city man and you're keeping your city secrets. You've never divulged why you're really in Cittanova and I smell a rat like your ship's sinking. You don't try to adjust to life in the country, standing before me with your smart suit and a silk rose in your buttonhole which no one here would wear because roses don't bloom in winter. You think milk comes from a bull, you oil your moustache instead of your pasta, you don't know one end of a fish from the other and you're a hopeless Fascist!'

'I run a nice café.'

'The Caffè Fascisti? Caffè Lip Service!' He cast his jaundiced eyes down Brazzi's placard *Devotion to Italy* on the wall. 'That's new. Who wrote it?'

'I did.'

'Well, it's a start, but it'll hardly turn the mood of the nation. Did you fight in the war?'

'No.'

'And it shows. You're fifty years out of date. Your language is not aggressive enough. You have to tell them what you want them to believe. That a patriotic Italy is an aggressive Italy. That these lands are Italian and we are justified in suppressing any other races who live in them. You must get people excited about the cleansing attributes of violence, not romantic drivel.' Monfalcon emphasized each sentence with a reflective pause and a slight decline of his chin towards his audience to leave them in no doubt as to the importance of what he was saying. 'To give you one example – and this will help you, Brazzi – establishing the Italian-ness of Trieste was a priority for the Arditi. Italy's involvement in the war had secured the city for us the year before but more work needed to be done.'

'The war didn't go far enough?'

Monfalcon shook his head. 'Not so close to Yugoslavia. The Armistice didn't finish the job, and our attacks on socialists and the Slavic media in Trieste were aimed at impressing the need for a final victory. No nation worthy of its name can be kind to its enemies, for such charity would weaken it.'

After he had been demobilized Monfalcon had spent some time in Trieste where the mood of the city excited him. This was the place to live, where the geographical position fostered in the Fascists a hatred of all who were not purely Italian! Austria to the north, Yugoslavia to the east – what better city in which to proclaim an Italian empire! Monfalcon had been stimulated as he could not have been anywhere else in the new nation. If only he could have stayed!

'War will give us our empire,' he went on eagerly.

'Another war?'

'If Italy was a single fighting unit, if we believed in self-sacrifice – for Italy, then yes, it would. The rest of Italy could learn from Trieste. It set the tone for Italian nationalism in – and this is the best example – the attack on the Narodni Dom the following year.'

'You attacked the Slovenian National Hall?'

'Of course. What's the problem with that?'

'Look at his face,' laughed Morato. 'He's delicate.'

His Most Italian City

'Reserved occupation.' Monfalcon gave such a casual flick of his mutilated hand that Brazzi thought its two remaining fingers would fly off and leave him with none. 'I didn't engineer it, Brazzi, that was Giunta, but I went when he asked me.

'It was a new building. Only ten years old at the start of the war. State-of-the-art, so they said. The Slovenians must have sensed the growing tension in the city with the Italians, yet they built it anyway. That can only have been a provocative act and they can't have been surprised when it was attacked. That ugly business in Split was merely the excuse Giunta had been waiting for. "Now is the time, Italians!" he cried. "Attack the cowards and the spies for the salvation of Italy!" We had overwhelming numbers. Very soon the building was one ball of flame. Then the designer turned Fascist after the attack. How do you like that? We didn't know whether to laugh or cheer when we heard.

'You were in Trieste in 1920, Brazzi. Did you go to watch?' Monfalcon swiveled in his chair. Saw only Brazzi's blotched face, his distressed eyes. 'What's the matter? You look like you've seen a ghost.'

'Of course, I *saw* it,' answered Brazzi quietly. 'It was visible from all over the city. I had other reasons for not being there that night, that's all.'

Morato laughed.

'Who was she?'

'*Shut up!*' snapped Brazzi so sharply that both men stared.

'It *was* a woman,' agreed Monfalcon.

He shuffled a hand into his trousers and from their subterranean depths removed a battered fountain pen. 'Now, we are in a position to re-word your *Devotion to Italy* for you.'

He turned over one of Brazzi's elegantly printed menus and began scribbling on the back, talking as he went.

'Istria is Italian (you got that right) regardless of race or language. The Slavs who live there now are the most direct *threat* to Istria (or you could use "scourge" or "pestilence," Brazzi). There have been other threats, like

Austria and Napoleon, but Slavs are the worst. Why? Because Slavs are barbaric and Italians are civilized. How? Slavs are polluting Italian purity in Istria. What can be done about this? Eradication, preferably. Emigration, hopefully. Forced Italianization only as a backup. No, don't say "forced," say "corrected." Anything good about a Slav is there because it was originally Italian, or Roman, or Venetian, which are all the same thing. While they remain Croats or Slovenes opposed to the Italian nation, they are guilty of biting the hand that feeds them.

'There!' He handed the menu to Brazzi. 'Put *that* on your wall.'

'I'll go out of business!'

'Coffee will always sell.'

'You know nothing about coffee.'

He stroked his new espresso machine. The captain of the steamer had complained that it all took up too much space in his hold. Too many delicate chairs, too much fine china, too much fuss for hassled seamen. What was he doing opening a high-class café so far from Trieste, anyway?

'Philistine,' thought Brazzi unhappily. 'I hope you get an ulcer.'

He could do with some comfort right now. The beautiful machine was the very latest in espresso technology from La Pavoni of Milan, bought shiny and conceited in contrast to how he felt. Crystallized lactose from the morning's customers encrusted the steam outlet; he smelled the sweet scent of milk. Taking the damp cloth from beneath the counter he wiped it down, giving the shoot a defiant sweep for the sake of the two men watching him.

A few desultory crumbs from Teresa's torte decorated several tablecloths and he heard that good lady herself in the kitchen washing the cups, saucers and plates before heading home to prepare his dinner. The aroma of coffee wafted through the afternoon peace. Above the lace curtain covering the lower half of the window Brazzi could see that the piazza was deserted save for a couple of the inevitable cats hurrying home beneath the descending winter sun. He was used to cats. Trieste was full of them and a similar plethora was found in other Istrian towns.

And all the while the same thought weighed upon his mind: *He'll be back.*

His relief at the deserted pier of last night had not outlived the discoveries of the morning. He had trodden his cautious way home through the gale, sheltering temporarily behind buildings before rushing out again into the Bora, then sheltering once more. One took one's life in one's hands along this coast and Trieste had been just as bad. Brazzi had seen laden carts turned over, men struggling to keep their feet, veiled ladies gripping onto railings and lamp posts, trusting in concrete to save them.

Despondently he let his thoughts run on. First the bombing in Trieste, then that queer metal tin through the mail. No message, nothing. But the unwritten words were as clear as crystal, unsigned but clearly identifiable for all that. Who else would send him a bomb? And if it hadn't been for that letter, he would have been nowhere near the pier last night.

His thoughts returned to that morning in Trieste, a mere seven months ago.

Terrible, terrible… It had been just terrible. And wasn't it typical of the devious iconoclast to destroy something beautiful? His lovely office. The delight of his leisure hours. The deep mahogany furniture, the thick-pile carpet, curtains of raw silk from China. Gone. All gone. Angelica, bearing her usual injured face, claimed it was the shock that brought about her fourth miscarriage later that day, and he had sincerely hoped it was.

Brazzi exhaled a sigh of distraught memory so loud that Monfalcon and Morato looked at him as if, in his silence, his thoughts had turned into words. Desolation, burnt out National Halls, and his most crushing fear: that his heart was on public display. That all his life he'd had one chance at real love and he'd blown it. Now the whole world could see that there had never been anything in his heart but himself.

Margaret Walker

✳✳✳✳✳

From the kitchen Teresa listened with one ear to the cups and saucers and with the other to the conversation from the café. When Monfalcon had initially approached her about the position with Signor Brazzi Teresa had been flattered, naturally, relieved to be able to work when Emilio could not. Even though his back was better now and he had returned to the mechanic's, Teresa was happy to continue cooking for the Brazzi's as much of the money went to help her son, whose farm, which he ran for his father-in-law, was struggling after a poor harvest, and he was weary of fishing to supplement his income. Besides, Teresa had taken a liking to that drooping little wife of Signor Brazzi who would be so much happier if only he'd give her a house full of children.

She strained her ears towards the trio but they had averted their heads and were speaking in hushed tones. Signor Brazzi didn't appear overjoyed at their presence, observed Teresa sharply. She watched him wipe down that magnificent espresso machine of his with abbreviated swipes before Signor Monfalcon's attitude of disgust. *Nasty man*, she thought. *I wish he'd go back to wherever he came from and leave us in peace.* What was so wrong with a quality café in a small country town, anyway? Teresa had never seen a shop so beautifully renovated. The neglected lower floor that had belonged for so long to those three old Austrian women had scarcely seen a duster until Signor Brazzi came to town, and now it looked fit for royalty. The man had taste, she'd give him that.

She felt a sharp prick of dislike for Monfalcon, watching his jaundiced eyes imagining money, like a cash register. You could bet the crook had his hands in something underhand, as usual. Teresa plopped the last cup on the sink and wrenched out the plug.

✳✳✳✳✳

His Most Italian City

'All right. Stop it! I've had enough of you, you and your wretched machine! So let me get this straight: Zan's highbrow offspring has disappeared from the face of the planet and the old fool would rather believe an eight-year-old than the likely truth, that Giovanni is not the pure virgin he thought he was and is shacked up in some pleasant attic with a fisherman's daughter.'

'I don't think Signor Di Micheli is that naïve, Giuseppe,' said Brazzi.

'And that family was always very close,' broke in Morato. 'Giovanni was never wild, even when he was young and still playing with the other boys. Before they sent him away to school. He really ought to be home by now.'

Brazzi slumped into his seat.

'That was the impression I had when I spoke with him this morning,' he said without enthusiasm. 'That the son had gone for a walk when the Bora was blowing and hadn't come back; and the situation had gone on too long for romantic attachments.'

'He probably fell in.'

They sat considering this in silence until an evil blush turned Monfalcon's yellow chin the color of bile.

'We should send the family a demand for money!' he exclaimed glowingly, ebullient at his own brilliance. 'Before his body washes up on the shore.'

Brazzi gasped.

'On what pretext?' Making money from shady business deals was one thing, profiting from his neighbor's distress was quite another.

'Who cares what pretext? Make one up. It doesn't have to be logical, merely believable. And lucrative. People will pay anything if they're desperate enough.'

Morato creaked his bulk across Brazzi's delicate chair and gave the matter some thought, observing Brazzi's discomfort with the pleasure of a dog at the butcher's. He wound his watch, a synchronous habit he employed when deep in consideration.

'Giuseppe may be nearer the truth than he knows, Matteo,' he reflected. 'Men disappear in Rome all the time these days. You don't want to cross Mussolini. This son will turn up in his own good time and, mark me, there'll be a lesson in it for all anti-Fascists.'

'You mean someone's killed him?'

'How should I know?' demanded Monfalcon with a burst of spittle. 'This is the not the capital, after all. The reality will disappoint, no doubt, but we need to act quickly if he's only drowned, or we'll miss out on the cash.'

Brazzi waved a finger in his face. 'I won't have any part of this!'

Monfalcon grabbed the digit and thrust it so far into Brazzi's mouth that he thought he would eat it.

'Gone off money, Brazzi?' he gloated. 'You think you deserve to be so self-righteous? The trouble with this town is that they really don't know about your crimes committed in the name of Fascism. Living on their scenic coast, so sentimental about Italy. If I told them what Italy means to a Slovene these days they mightn't be so keen to be Italian. In fact, I think I might do that, and wouldn't it make you look good?'

Brazzi blanched. 'I didn't kill and I didn't burn.'

'That's right, you're too old and too scared. You left the violence to the young men.' Monfalcon hammered his fist on the table. 'I have a job for you, Matteo Brazzi. If you can write that sentimental drivel on your wall, you can write this, too. Fix a sum, let's say two hundred thousand lire, and word it appropriately. Let me see… ' He whistled through a gap in his lower teeth. 'Make it look as if Giovanni's got himself mixed up in some student protest. With a deadly result.' He laughed malevolently. 'As if… even if the family pays up, they'll lynch him anyway. There! Say that! Put the wind under their sails.'

'I won't write that. That's cruel.'

His Most Italian City

Guiseppe Monfalcon yanked at his frayed cuffs, at the mutilated hand, purplish, dead. Hate welled up in him.

'Don't come griping to me! Don't tell me what it's like to be branded a coward. At least you deserve it, Brazzi from the Big City. I can't help looking at your pale perfumed face and concluding that there's something you're not telling us.'

Under the onslaught Morato had lost his agreeability. His tight suit looked like it had suddenly got tighter. Brazzi chewed his lip and tried to stop his restless eyes from giving him away. He felt no compassion for Monfalcon and his rant against the fate that war had dealt him, for he had no interest in disabilities. So Monfalcon was bitter, so what?

He'll be back. He'll be back. Brazzi had his own obsession. Well, he expected he was almost resigned to it. What could be worse? But what would he look like after eight years? *Would I even recognize him? Now that's a thought. How do I know he's not here already? Could that be him, stalking along the shadowed wall of the duomo?* Brazzi stiffened, squinted over the top of the lace curtain. He didn't remember him as being that tall or ever wearing a hat, but still. The wind whispered to him from the belfry, made suggestions, warped his memory. Then the furtive figure slipped beyond his sight, melted into the shade and disappeared into the public garden, to be lost among the trees.

Why leave me in peace for eight years and then bomb me? Why pursue me to Cittanova? Why? Brazzi chewed his lips. Had he searched every town over seven months until he reached Cittanova? *No, that makes no sense. Inefficient. Not his style.*

Brazzi, lacking the patience of a detective, could not have done it himself, therefore he assumed that no one else could. Another mistake among so many.

From under the counter he extracted his receipt book and ripped a blank page from the end, on which he scribbled a bare sentence with a pencil. He passed it across the table, watching as Monfalcon's beady eyes skimmed the taut phrasing.

'I don't know what you need money for,' Brazzi observed coldly. 'You won't survive long enough to spend it if you shrivel any further.'

'"If you want to see your son alive,"' read Monfalcon, 'be at the front of the piazza at midnight with two hundred thousand lire in cash."' The last two words were underlined. 'A bit clichéd. All right, have it your own way, but add, "We're watching you. Be there or your granddaughter will be next."'

'Di Micheli won't believe that, and you're only adding unnecessary drama.'

'Then change "midnight." The directives came, short and sharp. 'Say "half past ten." That sounds more like a partisan than a novelist. And change "piazza" to "pier." We don't want an audience. And offer to go with him. I'll get some local urchin to steal the money and, by the time he realizes his son's not there, it'll be too late.'

But I can't be at the pier again tonight – Brazzi chewed a manicured fingernail – *because he'll be back. He'll be back. I know he'll be back.*

'I can't go to the pier tonight.'

'Why not?'

'I'm not going!'

'You'll do as I tell you.'

'Go yourself!' Brazzi retorted. 'Or send Morato. Not me.'

Monfalcon reached into his pocket and, from its depths, extracted an army pistol. From the wear patterns on the grip, it was plain it had seen some service, and the effect this artifact had on his disagreeable features was remarkable. They softened until he looked almost human. Somewhere back in the nineteenth century his father had reared him on the notion that the lost centuries of invasion and subjugation Italy had suffered were merely an itinerant episode in history, that the military disaster that defined modern Italy could be put out to pasture and the poor regions once again rejoice in their empire. The old metal gun seemed to him to be the embodiment of this exciting idea, of what Italy could become, that, if polished, it would reflect *Roma Invicta*. Monfalcon stroked the gun fondly and Morato beamed at him with such hearty encouragement that he cocked the trigger and pointed the barrel directly at Brazzi's heart. Brazzi blanched in horror and Morato laughed.

'You and your old pistol!' Morato exclaimed.

'But he's going to shoot me!' squealed Brazzi.

'Then you won't have to go to the pier, will you? Is it loaded, Giuseppe?'

Without changing his position Monfalcon pulled the trigger. A dull click. Gunpowder fluffed onto Brazzi's white silk rose and Brazzi collapsed across the counter.

'It's not loaded, but he's dead anyway,' observed the soldier.

'He fainted, Giuseppe.' Morato patted Brazzi's flaccid cheek. 'Matteo, Matteo! Wake up!'

Brazzi groaned, stirred and crumpled into a chair while Monfalcon resurrected three tarnished bullets from his pocket and shoved them into the pistol's barrel.

'Now it's loaded.' He swished the weapon in the air patriotically, pointing around the cafe. '*Avanti!*' he trumpeted.

'Ho, ho, ho!' roared Morato, a jolly fellow who appreciated the macabre.

The writing was on the wall. This was the first time Brazzi had ever thought of himself as mortal.

'It's half past two,' announced Monfalcon. 'You have eight hours, Matteo, to reconsider your position.'

'I'll go,' whispered Brazzi.

'Good, well, that's settled!' responded Monfalcon briskly. 'A shame you couldn't have acquiesced so quickly in Trieste.'

He blew the barrel free of gunpowder but, before he slipped it back into his pocket, he regarded it for an instant, as if he were its doting mother and in its achievements he saw his youth reflected. Again Brazzi noticed the curious softening of his face.

Then suddenly Monfalcon said, 'You think about yourself too much, Matteo, and it is making you unhappy. Think about Italy instead. She rallies behind Mussolini because devotion to our motherland overrides all other considerations.'

Chapter Ten

Nataša had not held with revenge.

'Vengeance solves nothing,' she'd told him when he'd seethed with fury after two Italians sank the *Jugoslavija* in Pola Harbor in 1918, killing the captain and four hundred sailors; two men from an unstable country struggling with its national inferiority complex, as jealous over the new kingdom of Slavs as children over a ball. This was what he hated, that he felt an enemy motivated by self-pity was not an enemy worth fighting. Instead, it was the school bully who, when ego let him down, discovered that bigotry and violence were a legitimate back up.

'Be patient, Stefan.' Be patient. How sensible. 'These things won't make Italy great.'

'Patient!' he had stormed back. 'What for? Italy's been agitating against us for forty years and who's come to help?'

But it was the loss of Pola and Rijeka that upset him more than anything, even more than Trieste.

'The best ports,' he lamented.

Given to Italy, which didn't need more ports, given by foreign powers who didn't care and who believed, in the sort of inimical statesmanship that destroys lives in an afternoon and then goes home to dinner, that humanity inhabited the earth according to a set order of races: British and American at the top, followed by a selection of European powers, then Slavs at the bottom. Italy escaped censure by virtue of the partiality generated by its history and culture, unrelated to its present political problems. Old empires like Austria-Hungary with their policies of racial autonomy were viewed as outmoded by the intellectual sweep of nationalism and racism, its brutal progeny.

Racism? In Trieste? Half his friends had come from mixed marriages. Austrian and Italian, Slovene and Venetian, Croatian, Jewish. Not so long ago racism would have been unimaginable.

Though Trieste wasn't Venice. Nothing to write home about, really: sturdy middle-Europe cradled in its gulf, its eyes looking towards the sea, where its money came from. A nice train trip from Venice. The world had mostly bypassed it until Vienna needed a port. The occasional visitor had even commented that they couldn't remember much about Trieste once their visit was over. But to him it had represented true multiculturalism, that gift of the Hapsburgs whose memory was running away faster than he could chase it. He had loved its relaxed human bustle, the merging of its myriad languages, the open door it had seemed for all nationalities, creeds and cultures: Italian, German, Jewish, Greek as well as his own Slovenian, Trieste's largest ethnic minority, who had lived there for a thousand years.

With the onslaught of nationalism all that was changing. Now perched precipitously at the eastern edge of Italy, it had never been The Most Italian city, as the fascists claimed – *La Città Italianissima* – but the port of the empire of the Hapsburgs, for goods destined for all parts of Europe, whose reason for being lay in materialism, not nationalism. But in such a city, poised at the crossroads of Italian ethnicity and Slav, foreign policy that supported Italian nationalism against the local Slovene culture could only lead to trouble.

Even in those early days it was Nataša who realized that a dictator could only take over a weak country and that Mussolini, if he was able to eventually form a government, would have the support of a poor and shell-shocked nation, whose soldiers returning from the Great War hadn't understood what they had fought for. A people who had no experience of central government and just wanted to get on with their lives, believing that Mussolini could provide it because he said so, who were happy to listen to his highly cultured language and didn't mind that he was short on detail. But she made one mistake. Even as she reassured him that it would all calm down and Slovenes and Italians could continue to live in harmony in Trieste as they had always done, the drive to remodel the city went on apace.

The former Austrian coast had been parceled out between Italy and the new nation of Yugoslavia, and once its navy disappeared, his career collapsed with it. Italy wouldn't have a Slav in the Regia Marina, even if he'd wanted to join it, and, like other seamen, he had picked up work on the docks, tinkering unsatisfactorily with tugs and ferries to make ends meet.

'I need to get back to sea,' he said.

'I know you do.'

She'd been so lovely about it. Afterwards, that was what he remembered most, how understanding, how amenable, like a mother as well as a lover, so that he felt she nurtured the whole of him. And they had discussed it; well, she had discussed it. She had been the loquacious one. He only ever said what he needed to say.

Stefan had first gone to sea when he was fifteen, in the earliest years of the twentieth century. Until he'd lost himself in its limitlessness, the immensity of its age and, like a story without end, had listened to it and allowed it to mold him, he had scarcely known who he was. As he grew into manhood he came to believe that only on its swell could he find his true self and, when he had first met Nataša, the equation was complete. With her and the sea, he had become himself. At the naval base at Pola he'd heard the story of Jason and the Argonauts and how they'd founded the city after their escape up the Danube – the Ister, as it was then known – with the Golden Fleece, calling it Polai, the City of Refuge. But it was the sea that became his refuge. Nataša had laughed at him then, telling him she hadn't known he was a poet, and one day she might wean him off the sea like she'd weaned the babies from her breast.

He had always been mechanically minded and when he'd volunteered for submarine duty, when Austria was first experimenting with them as a weapon of war, it suited him to multi-function, for a submarine commander had to be his own engineer, navigator, mechanic and fireman. And in the end, the submarines were the real reason why he wasn't with her when she needed him.

In the old empire, Trieste had been the trading and embarkation port of Vienna. Pola was the naval base and, in the last days of the war, when it was clear that they were losing, the Emperor had given the entire Austro-Hungarian fleet to the newly proclaimed State of Slovenes, Croats and Serbs – what some were already calling Yugoslavia – who, between them, held the Dalmatian coast. So far so good, but, when the new state was proclaimed, none of the entente powers, neither Britain nor France nor Russia, replied to the proclamation and in 1918 the remaining eighteen Austro-Hungarian submarines that had survived the war were handed over to the winners. Yugoslavia requested them all, but the fate of the boats could not be determined by the whim of the losers but by the Allied Powers at the Paris Peace Conference. When the Allies rejected the Yugoslav request, the Slavic states reduced the eighteen to a modest four. Not even this was allowed. Six submarines were given to France as war reparations and the remaining twelve to Italy, which issued orders to scrap them. The entire twelve, and all they had wanted was four!

By 1920 there were eight submarines in Pola Harbor, the one harbor in the world he knew like the back of his hand, and that was when he got his crazy idea.

Even Zorko, with him from his earliest days at sea, had told him he was mad.

'You'll never get away with it.'

'You watch me,' he'd said.

His Most Italian City

Nataša had understood when he told her 'I have to go.'

'I understand.'

'I'll be back soon.'

She'd stood silently querying him, that half-loving, half-exasperated look she had when she would have rather told him not to take the risks he did but knew him too well to chide. During the war years he had once or twice wondered if she feared he would not return from a mission. He himself had felt no fear and it was not so much because there was nothing to be afraid of but because, once the hour was upon him, fear had no place in his instructions. Each problem encountered was a problem to be solved, nothing more.

'Are you going to tell me what you're doing?' she asked, hands on her hips.

'I'm going to Pola to steal a submarine.'

'Stefan, you're joking!' The hands flew up. 'I thought you wanted to have a last look.'

'When have I ever been sentimental?'

She had been dressed that day in a light summer frock of white lawn, to take Evie to school and then Luka to the gardens. The hem and three quarter sleeves were trimmed with *broderie anglaise* and in the hot July weather she had bound her daughter's hair, thick like her own, in two plaits with green ribbons. Luka had worn a plain white shirt and light trousers and didn't want to wear his hat.

'Daddy won't wear his hat, either,' sighed Nataša. 'Put your hat on, Luka.'

She pinned on her own straw hat. The hatpin in her mouth muffled her speech and its pearl end emerged from between her teeth.

'By the way, I saw Matej the other day.'

'Banich?' he asked without interest. Nataša slammed the pin through her brim, freeing her tongue. Luka was still rejecting his. Stefan began playing a game with the small boater, and when it ended up on the floor, he put it on his own head. Luka laughed at him. 'Still up to his old tricks?' he added.

'He got married. To Angelica Cerocchi.' Nataša lowered her voice. 'And he says she was expecting at the time. Only at the time, actually, because poor Angelica miscarried.'

'Ha!' he responded. 'So he finally got caught. Well, marriage should keep him out of mischief.'

'He's not that bad, Stefan.'

'Tell that to the people he's swindled.'

'Anyway,' Nataša went on, fiddling with the heavy hair that, hidden by the hat, was falling from its pins at the back of her head. 'He said he's going to change his name to Brazzi.'

Stefan grunted.

'Apparently for the sake of his business and for the government it has to be Italian. He says he'll never get on now, with the other one.'

'So it's all about getting on, is it?'

'That's just the way it's going here,' she replied. 'And he said he's not bothered about the switch. He's just being loyal to the city.'

'Banich's loyalty is to the same place it's always been. Himself.'

Her forehead wrinkled in a sad little frown, except that she didn't seem sad, and the sudden puzzlement caught his attention. He thought at first that her corset was too tight and that that was the cause – a passing distress ladies often seemed to feel before mysteriously carrying on. Was it something in their layers of clothing or the cycles of their bodies? He'd never quite figured it out.

'What's the matter?' he asked.

'Well, I suppose I shouldn't be worried, but there was one other thing.' She was stalling, and then he saw it again, that confusion, like words that couldn't find their way out of a maze.

His Most Italian City

'Matej has joined the Fascist Party.' She watched the sides of his mouth tighten, his characteristic indication of emotion. 'What could that mean, Stefan?'

'It means he's scared,' he said with disgust.

'Of being Slovenian?'

'That or losing money.'

'But I've heard that lots of people have joined the Fascist Party,' she insisted. 'And changed their name. Not just Matej. Perhaps that means it's not as bad as we think?'

He saw that she was trying to convince herself. He turned her face to his. 'They're scared, too. Are you?'

'No!' she insisted stoutly. Then, 'Yes. I am a little.'

'Would you leave?'

And she'd looked out from the side window across the harbor to the Southern Alps, over the dresser, the vase of roses, her sewing box, the children's toys. As he watched, her eyes had softened; it was as if she saw something that he couldn't, and even then he had had a fleeting sense of her departure. A lonely wind from the sea.

He was a sailor and sailors were notoriously superstitious, but he shrugged it off as he did all those premonitions. And she smiled dreamily, still looking out the window and said, 'Could that be snow on those peaks so far away?'

'In July?' he returned.

She laughed, a slight, sad acknowledgement of the separation he sensed, and he was concerned enough to say, 'The merchant ships come in that way. I'll ask them.'

But last winter, when she'd looked from the seafront – almost too far to see with the naked eye – she had often said, 'Stefan, that's snow!'

He remembered now how happy she'd been the previous winter and his brief disquiet vanished. He knew she'd never been to the Southern Alps. He was going to take her there. It was one of those things he had planned: after the war, when the children were a little older, when he got a steady job. One delay after another. For now it remained the faraway place she saw each morning across the harbor in Trieste, whose gleaming peaks she imagined, like a fairy story.

That morning, waiting in the hall with his family, he had watched her gazing out across the busy port, over the people coming and going, over the train, over the ships, over the pier, to the silent majesty that called her.

'Leave our home?' she asked.

'We'll move to Yugoslavia,' he said quickly. 'The new navy will need officers. I'll have work.'

'Very well, Stefan.'

He saw her hesitancy, her eyes watching the children. She was thinking they should get out before she felt pushed to decide.

'If Banich has joined the Fascist Party, Nataša,' he said, perhaps more forcefully than he intended, 'it means this city is changing. We can't wait around to watch that happen.'

And he was no philosopher to argue with this man he'd known from his youth – who remembered how welcoming Trieste had once been – about standing up for what was right instead of what would protect him and his interests. He could picture Banich now with his smooth manners and his slick reassurances, a man who had dressed fashionably when they were both so young that Stefan had thought fashion was only for women. A fashionable man, now what was that? One who hadn't fought in the war, who had never worn a uniform, now proclaiming to honest citizens how to fight in the name of intolerance.

'You think he's intolerant?' she asked.

'I think he's self-serving, and intolerance works for him. That's the only reason someone like Banich could be dangerous.'

And that was a lot of words for him, so he'd kissed her on the nape of the neck where her heavy hair cushioned his cheek and he caught her scent of lavender and rose like a hidden garden. Evie pulled a face, so he did it again.

'Can I give you a kiss, too?' he asked her.

'Nooo....'

'Then can you give me a kiss? I've had a bath.'

She'd given the matter much grave thought and the minutes ticked away, and just when he thought he was going to miss out she put her arms around him and he bent down for her to kiss him on the cheek. Then they all walked out together, Nataša with the children to the school and he to work at the docks.

The humidity hit them once on the street. A tram came rattling past, full of businessmen sweltering in wool suits and ladies in summer frocks above layers of cool cotton lingerie who nevertheless looked hot. Stefan, as usual, wore the same ensemble he did around the calendar, shirt and trousers, and could easily be spotted on a city street as the only man without a hat. From his fingers dripped Luka's discarded sunhat and, at Nataša's frown, he placed it on the small head beside him and gave it a pat.

'Wear your hat, Stefan,' she chided. 'Set him a good example.'

'I'm not wearing a boater,' he grumbled.

They parted at the corner where the tram tracks ran down towards the waterfront.

'I shouldn't be much more than a week. I'll be off early tomorrow. I'll send you a telegram when I'm on my way home.'

'The Pahors are coming to town,' she said. 'You'll just miss them.'

'Where are they staying?'

'In the Narodni Dom this time. That sister they always stayed with has left the city. The trouble here was getting to her. I think the Arditi attacks here last year were the last straw. First Milan, then Trieste.'

'We're going, too,' Stefan told her. 'As soon as I get back.'

'You don't think it will all settle down?'

'I don't want you to stay and find out.'

The Narodni Dom, the National Hall of the Slovene community in Trieste, was a multipurpose building only sixteen years old, built at the northern end of the city where the bulk of the city's Slovenian population lived. As well as apartments, the six-story complex housed cafés and restaurants, a theatre, a gymnasium and an art gallery, and was the hub of Slovenian social life, a symbol of their culture. Stefan and Nataša often went there to meet friends, and even took the children there to eat. They had passed it that morning, admired its soaring front windows and its decorative brickwork.

'But I've heard,' said Nataša, 'that the government is going to excavate beneath the Old Town for Roman ruins. To prove to the world that Trieste is Italian.'

'I hope someone warned the Romans,' he said. 'They mightn't have welcomed the comparison. Give the Pahors my best. I'm sorry I'll miss them.'

As she merged into the crowd he had stood watching her white dress, her arms, her shoulders, the soft triangle of neck he had kissed, her hands holding her children. The small hat beside her bobbed up and down, weaving in and out of the crowd until it, too, disappeared.

And so that last day came to its swift finale, and he didn't notice how time seemed determined to end it, how it was possible for something so cherished to be rushed to its conclusion. Later, when she was gone and the regrets began, he had reviewed every hour and found that each one had been filled with insignificant things, bombastic trivialities that, like the children, competed for his attention and achieved nothing but taking away the time he should have spent with her. If only he could have seen the future, he would never have been so careless. Then, before he realized, the long shadows of evening had crept across the city and he had looked behind him and seen their advance without concern because he hadn't perceived the parting they foretold. And when he'd left home just after four thirty the next morning, Nataša was asleep and he didn't like to wake her, so he headed out the door and gave no more thought to Banich or fascism or the peril hovering so closely above their heads.

Chapter Eleven

Brazzi's letter was sealed and given without explanation to the innocent Teresa to give to one of the urchins who roamed the piazza and the docks and were willing, for a coin, to help the smart mayor, the fat hotel proprietor and their ominous companion.

Zan greeted the faint knock with his customary rising ritual. He expressed surprise. He removed his spectacles. He rose ponderously to his feet, exhaled and brushed the ash from his waistcoat. Then he slowly descended the steps to the door, opened it and looked down. He had looked up on only one occasion in the last half century, when the carpenter Maria had hired to fix the railing on the stairs – he had broken it – arrived bearing a two-meter length of oak to which a red rag had been affixed at the top for safety.

The boy standing almost literally at his feet was so small that, for an instant, he couldn't make him out over the slight rise of his elderly tummy. But the more he looked – yes, he was sure – there stood a child before his door, with a letter in his hands.

'Is school finished already?' Zan asked him curiously, considering that Silvana should be home in that case.

'Here,' pouted the child, a grimy little fellow wearing short pants in the cold weather, a sweater with holes at the elbow and over-large shoes that he seemed to have borrowed for the occasion. He shoved the envelope into the hand the old man held at his side.

His Most Italian City

'What's this?' asked Zan who looked at his hand as if he were surprised to see it on the end of his arm.

'Here,' repeated the boy.

'Thank you,' said Zan, still puzzled. At the last minute he recollected himself. 'Wait a minute.'

He trudged up to the kitchen and from a shelf produced a jar of boiled sweets. Back down he went.

'There you go!' he said brightly.

The child quickly extracted a handful of the colored sweets from the jar, muttered his thanks and took off back to the docks.

Without closing the door, Zan examined the envelope at arm's length. He sighed and rubbed his eyes. He would have to find the spectacles he had taken off. Now, where had he put them? Oh, yes, beside the chair. He swung the door shut behind him and rumbled up the stairs, located the spectacles and folded them around his ears, finally opening the single sheet of paper inside and flattening it out. The room faced east and the narrow Fish Shop Lane below it had lost the light as the wintry sun passed across to the west of the town. Zan held the paper to the window and strained to read the small, cramped writing.

'Signor Di Micheli,' he thought he read, 'if you want to see your son alive, be at the end of the pier tonight at half past ten. Bring two hundred thousand lire in cash.'

'Ah…' breathed Zan while a heavy warmth attacked his stomach and formed a bath of tingling acid that pushed downwards into his loins. 'Ah, dear me.'

The lane slept in the afternoon hush. All around him the town was quiet. The fishermen had sorted their catch and gone home, housewives had finished their shopping in the markets. Lunch had been eaten and the evening meal was yet to be prepared. The children had not returned from school. No footsteps passed, no sound was heard. All alone, Zan sat and re-read the brief letter, hoping that it referred to someone else.

When he had finished and the heat from the initial shock had dispersed, he leaned exhausted against the window and gave way to cold despair. Yesterday, he thought, Giovanni and Silvana and Maria and I, we were all here. Yesterday. And since yesterday: no boots at the door, a bed that hasn't been slept in, no breakfast, no lunch. And what has today brought? A black sea monster, and Brazzi, something about Brazzi and the monster he could not recall. Zan, the picture of domestic altruism who, save for the rabbits he shot for dinner, had endeavored to coexist with all of God's creatures who crossed his path and to be on good terms with all. But he had never warmed to Brazzi, and trying to find the connection between Brazzi and Silvana's sea monster meant investigating a personality he would rather ignore.

With the revelation of the letter he held in his hands he would now have to explain to Silvana that she had been mistaken. Evil men and not a creature from the sea had apprehended Giovanni, for money, something Zan's family had always had so much of that he rarely gave it any thought. To desire money, to commit evil with the prospect of gain was abhorrent to him. And it didn't seem right to tell Silvana that she was wrong when she was not an inventive child. She had not conceived something that didn't exist, so what *had* she seen? It seemed to Zan that in their lust for wealth the writers of the letter he held in his hand had tarnished his granddaughter as well as his son.

He didn't want to worry Maria, but there was nothing else he could do. On unsteady feet, his hands shaking a little, he found his wife talking to Paulina in the kitchen, exactly where they had been when he had taken the jar of sweets from the shelf.

'Who wanted a sweet?' asked Maria. She stopped short on seeing his face. 'What's the matter, Zan?'

Zan crumpled onto a chair at the table; the piece of paper fell from his hand.

'What's this?' She picked it up.

'No, no!' cried Zan, too late.

Like her granddaughter, Maria was short-sighted. She had no need of her husband's fumbling glasses routine. In a stroke the letter was read, digested and dispatched.

'Giovanni…' she murmured. She staggered.

Paulina, a burly woman of firmly stated opinions, quickly sat Maria down beside her husband and scanned the cruel words.

'Of all the nerve,' she exclaimed hotly. 'To threaten you like that!'

'Now, Paulina,' Zan said, raising a warning hand, 'you mustn't repeat any of this. But who could it be from?'

'Whoever it is, is up to no good!' declared Paulina, bustling around Maria in a consoling fashion.

They kept the stove alight all day in the cold months. Paulina moved the heavy iron kettle onto the hot burner, stirred the charcoal beneath and laid out the ingredients for mint tea.

'For you, too, sior?' she asked.

'No, thank you, Paulina.' Zan reached for his hat and overcoat. 'Maria, I must talk to Romano. He'll know what to do.'

'Shouldn't we tell the constable?'

'Romano first. Then the bank manager, then the constable, then…'

'Sior, it's too much for you,' Paulina protested, struggling to keep the excitement from her voice.

It was true that such an adventure had never crossed her path and, within the confines of the stewardship entrusted to her, she intended to defend her small world with all the skills that world had provided: decency, candor and a good sweeping arm.

'Let me get the tea for Siora Maria, then I'll go with you.'

'Thank you, Paulina, no,' returned Zan (and he was too distracted to notice her disappointment). 'If you would just make the tea. I hope I won't be long. Not a word, remember!'

'Of course not, sior!'

Margaret Walker

So Paulina made the tea and went home, swearing her husband and son to secrecy. The son told his wife, who promised not to repeat it but was so shocked that she passed the dreadful news on to her neighbor. The neighbor repeated it in hushed tones to the grocer who only told the customers who he knew would keep the Micatovich's secret. Luckily, they realized at once that the wisest course of action was to inform anyone who might have laid eyes on Giovanni since he'd arrived home from Florence. And so it was that in under two hours most of Cittanova had become incensed up to an inflammatory point, even though the day was declining and tempers usually cooled towards evening.

*****

Matteo Brazzi stood at the curve of the Corso Victor Emanuele from where he could observe the Micatovich house. So this is what he had to do to survive now, perch himself on an arctic corner of a medieval maze? He had been informed at the museum that Cittanova had once been an island and, quite honestly, that's what it felt like this afternoon: he couldn't get off and he couldn't swim. How could things have possibly come to this? Brazzi searched his conscience – he had to find it first – for the pride that had come before his fall, the slip down the slope to perdition. He wasn't a bad man, was he? He hadn't killed anyone. All he'd ever done was place his own interests first. What was wrong with that? Now here he was, not with one persecutor to worry about but two and, standing alone in the frigid street, the perverse notion occurred to him that whilst serving one of them he could be protected from the other. Monfalcon could just whip out that pistol of his and shoot him. Good.

He had seen the boy deliver his letter, imagined the anxious scene within even as he shivered, and was rewarded for his chilblains when he saw Signor Di Micheli step from his door into the lane and hurry in the direction of the piazza. Trouble had caused the old gentleman to become neglectful and he had put his hat on backwards, a slip which he only seemed to realize after some minutes of walking. Brazzi watched him remove it only to put it on backwards again and continue the way he had been going.

Brazzi pulled his overcoat more tightly around him, chewed his teeth to stop them from chattering and lend himself instead the comfortable appearance of having warmly lounged away the early afternoon in his café. He cautiously followed Signor Di Micheli down the Corso, then shot left down School Lane. Forgetting how much he hated exercise he next ran around the small block of trees, houses and gardens blooming with cabbages to greet Signor Di Micheli as he was about to enter the piazza, where he almost knocked him over for the second time that day.

'Sior Brazzi,' mumbled Zan vaguely, in his plight forgetting to speak Italian, 'you've been running.'

'Asthma,' wheezed Brazzi. And it was true, though he had not had the uncomfortable wheezing nor the suggestion of a dizzy head since the boat trip from Trieste. 'The cold has affected me. I've been in my warm café most of the day.'

In the three hours since Brazzi had last seen him the signore appeared to have aged ten years and, for a moment, he almost forgot himself enough to be moved by compassion. The slight pouches beneath the brown eyes had descended like the twilight and their skin had taken on the fragility of tissue paper. His hands trembled. He breathed with his mouth hanging open, as if he could no longer see the point in closing it. His eyes were rheumy and the lower lids had sunk into shallow pools of tears.

'Are you all right, signore?'

'Yes, no, that is, I am going to see my son-in-law. To ask him what to do.'

'To do?'

'I can't explain right now, sior. I must speak to Romano.'

Brazzi creased his brow. 'Are you sure you'll make it? You don't look very well.' He reached up a hand and clasped the old man below the shoulder. 'Why don't you sit down in my café and I'll make you some coffee? You are nearly there, you know. It's quite providential.'

And steering Signor Di Micheli with the same hand, he directed him across the piazza.

'Stop!' begged Zan, for events were taking on a feverish quality and, like a stain, he wanted to wipe off Brazzi's hand, but the man held him in a determined grip.

'Only for a moment, signore, and see if you don't feel better afterwards.'

There, muddled Zan desperately, *he's got something in mind!* And to Zan's mind it had to involve Silvana and the sea monster because that had been the moment this morning when the mayor had lost his slippery self-possession. Silvana and the sea monster and Brazzi. Yes! But what was it? What was it? Why, for once, could he not have been as bright as the rest of his family? Silvana was such a clever little girl, too, always jumping up in class and yelling out the answer. Who beat the boys? Silvana. But who got the lowest marks for behavior? Guess who? Well, she always found obeying rules hard, mused Zan, and for an instant his face folded indulgently. Not like her mother – obeyed every rule in the etiquette book and look what it had gotten her, a diametrically opposed progeny.

But his heart had commenced palpitating in his chest. The disturbed circuitry sent shocks of giddiness into his brain so that soon he felt he must either sit down or fall down. They were walking and he couldn't resist, hurried along by the one man he didn't want to be with, as if the encounter had been planned and Brazzi was lying in saying that he had been inside all day. *That's it!* realized Zan. *He's a liar. He was lying about the sea monster this morning! He has made me doubt Silvana when* he knows *what the monster was.* Zan reached for the words so that he could pull them down in front of his eyes before they escaped. Then, just as it all made sense, he became so light-headed that the inevitable happened and he forgot the whole thing. The uncomfortable sensation of relying on the strength of a man who was so much smaller – and whose soul Zan was sure was twisted – brought the rambling walk to a halt and Zan simply could not form the phrases to be rude to his tormenter. By the time they struggled off again, he could see no end to it and simply needed to sit down.

The inevitable cats watched them, perched upon balconies and under shutters, eyeing the unequal procession that was like an ant dragging a biscuit. Cats beneath Venetian palaces and cats on floral lintels. Cats on three-story roofs and cats roaming stone alleys. Cats on wells and cats behind window boxes. Cats behind shutters and cats in kitchen gardens. Cats in fishing boats asleep in the nets and cats among the bells in the campanile, admiring the view of local waters.

After what seemed like a marathon but was in reality less than fifty meters, they crossed the piazza. At the far end soared the campanile, to its right waited the ancient duomo and, beyond it, the sea. Zan wished to escape to its freedom but the hand beneath his shoulder was steering him through a half-wooden door that had above it a piece of fine filet lace. Zan thought how much Maria would like that lace even as he was dropped onto a delicate chair of curved dark wood – upon which one was expected to sit up straight and be a gentleman, he reflected dismally. With a wheeze of relief, Brazzi had flitted like a shadow from above him and the door slammed shut. Its bell tinkled once and was abruptly silenced, and the two offended felines who had taken up residence on the step strutted away with their tails held high.

Zan looked around him. No doubt about it, Brazzi was a talented liar. Whatever his intentions in bringing Zan here, the room indeed was comfortable compared to the frosty piazza, the sea – to which he had looked so longingly – shut out by the firm hand of taste and elegance. Within, all was hushed. From the kitchen wafted the sharp bitterness of grated chocolate. Above it coffee grounds, essences of almond and lemon and some comforting sensory deception as well that aroused the memory of companionable meals, that drew one in and suppressed the desire to leave. Zan felt his heart ease.

Only one corner of the café was still occupied. A silhouette in the shadows. With the disturbance of Zan's arrival he would surely soon realize his tardiness, drain the last dregs from his cup, rise and depart with a courteous apology.

'Sior Brazzi,' groaned Zan from his chair, 'thank you for your consideration, but I really do need to see my son-in-law.'

'As Signor Brazzi has been so considerate, ought you not to oblige him?'

Zan squinted at the speaker and saw that the silhouette had moved. It was indeed a man, but of an age made indeterminate by neglect and the abuse of alcohol. He saw a profile turn from the dusky corner into the light. Oily hair protruded from beneath a hat greasy at the front through much wear, liver spots stained the hands and the man's nose was crossed by tiny veins. From beneath his chin hung bags of skin like sheets drying in the sun and, although this ruin was out of place within the exquisite interior, Zan saw that Brazzi knew who the real master was.

'Sior Monfalcon!' he blurted.

Unable to rise, he tipped his hat then laid it upon a table as elegant as the chair it accompanied. '*El me scuxa.* I didn't recognize you.' Then, regretting his rudeness, he added, 'Over there in the corner.'

'Which language are you using, signore?'

'Um… the normal one.'

'Then let me hear you say my name in Italian, if you please.'

'Signor Monfalcon!' exclaimed Zan unsteadily. 'That's what I said, sior. I said, "Signor Monfalcon."'

Now he had said it three times.

'Don't forget.'

'I didn't forget.'

'Now, please have a cup of coffee, Signor Di Michele.'

His Most Italian City

'I don't want any coffee,' said Zan.

'Have a cup of coffee, Signor Di Michele!' Monfalcon flashed a hand at Brazzi.

Sullenly, Brazzi thumped the steam lever of his coffee machine. Morato had withdrawn to the safety of his hotel and was nowhere to be seen, abandoning Brazzi to play Monfalcon's game in front of Signor Di Michele. Brazzi dashed a shining espresso in front of the old man, who looked so overwrought that he was more likely to fall off his chair than drink the coffee.

'Drink!' commanded Monfalcon.

The coffee was boiling hot and had been made without sugar. Zan sipped and choked. The muscles at the back of his throat stiffened and the coffee pooled there. It left a bitter taste on his tongue while a drop lay poised on his lower lip.

'Stop!' ordered Monfalcon. 'Must we sit here all day and watch you dribble? Get up and come here!'

'But…'

Monfalcon clapped his hands. 'Signor Brazzi is a busy man. You're keeping him waiting.'

Zan's initial reaction to such rudeness was shock and a notion that he was being interrogated. Was he at school, perhaps? Though his recollections of school had faded to a fear of Latin, the rebuke from Monfalcon had awakened darker memories he thought he had forgotten: rows of hard wooden seats, high windows and ink wells, and a master in a black gown and mortar board extracting puzzled shame from the lanky youth whose brain never quite matched the size of his body.

He studied the plush room anxiously. Two rows of tables ran along both sides, each covered by a white cloth, with a menu of vellum in the center, ornamented with vines and trellises and discreetly naked maidens. At the top of the menu was the Italian flag, beneath it the name, *Caffè*

Fascisti. Below, two painted children assured one another, "Mussolini is always right."

And he didn't know a great deal about Mussolini, did he? He hoped they would not ask him questions he was unable to answer. Wary of giving Monfalcon a further avenue for offense, he accomplished the difficult crossing from one row to the other until he sat across the table from the man. There he waited with his knees together, the hem of his trousers sliding up his ankles and his bulky knuckles agitating the hat on his lap, as if they were playing a game of jacks. Monfalcon's lifeless eyes watched him. Zan saw the light filtering through the curtains flicker onto the yellow sclera where he could have sworn there was nothing but decay. It was like passing time in a tomb.

'You didn't finish your coffee. Go back and get it,' ordered Monfalcon, clapping his hands like bones. 'Do we have to wait all day?'

'What have I done this time?' muttered Zan under his breath.

Too weary to move his protesting legs yet again, he dragged his chair across the floor and retrieved the cup. Half the contents slopped into the saucer and a brown surf washed out upon the pristine cloth. Zan knew that even should he survive Monfalcon, the stain would accuse him. It sat there staring at him. Paulina, perhaps, would be able to remove it but not without a conspiratorial glance at Maria. Clumsy.

Monfalcon looked at the stain, and Zan looked at it, and then he looked somewhere else, while the mountain of accusation became harder and harder to scale. Stupid old Zan.

'I'll get Paulina to…'

'I'm sure Signor Brazzi can manage.' Monfalcon arranged his crotch on the hard wooden seat, then, glowering, he began, 'Where were you going?'

'To see my son-in-law.'

'Why?'

'A private matter, signore.'

His Most Italian City

'Hardly private in a small town like Cittanova. Didn't think you were so naïve.'

'I'm not naïve.'

Monfalcon smiled patronizingly while Brazzi hovered by the counter.

'What were you doing just now?'

'I have said…'

Monfalcon slammed his hand on the table.

'What were you doing?!!' he roared while those horrible eyes rotated into his head and even Brazzi jumped.

'I received a letter… It's personal… It's nothing.'

'Show me the letter.'

Zan fumbled around in his coat pocket and produced the squashed sheet that he rested on top of the coffee stain with the air of disgrace of a small boy caught with his hand in the biscuit tin. Brazzi rescued it from the spilt espresso and Monfalcon feasted on the words like a vulture.

'Dear me,' he sighed. 'So Giovanni's gone missing, has he?'

The two men shook their heads but Monfalcon shook his harder.

'Signor Morato knew Giovanni.' The head was still shaking. Its feigned sympathy made the ugly face uglier. 'Such a bright little boy. So much promise. Playing in the port with the other kids. Row a boat out, swamp it for fun and swim back laughing. Those boys are hauling fish with their fathers now and Giovanni's moved on to better things. You must be very proud of him, Signor Di Micheli, working for Italy.'

'Giovanni's not working for Italy,' Zan responded. 'The government wouldn't accept his Austrian qualifications. He's just teaching, but he'll never be allowed to rise any higher.'

'All for the best, signore. All for the state.' Monfalcon had assumed a rather artless way of imposing his views. He patted his hands airily before him to suggest his point but the knobbly skin looked like pancakes ready to turn and the sudden lull was false. 'Italy wants peace and quiet, work and calm. Violence is only the necessity to which it has been driven.'

Then his face grew grave and he uttered those terrible words, 'When did you last see your son alive?'

Yesterday, before the sun rose on a world without him.

'Don't reflect too long, signore. Desperate men pen letters like this.'

'I don't understand,' whispered Zan.

'Yet it is easy enough. Your son has lived in Florence for… how long?'

'Since nineteen twenty.'

Monfalcon tapped his jaw.

'A portentous year for Italian and Slav relations, wouldn't you say?'

'I wouldn't know.'

'No, I didn't think you would. Yet you can hardly have remained unmoved by the violence in Trieste that year.'

'I had heard a little of it, but we didn't think such violence between neighbors would happen in Cittanova.'

'It was happening up and down the Dalmatian coast.'

'Not here.'

Brazzi looked at the perplexed old face and wanted to call him stubborn. But there was just a possibility that Signor Di Micheli was telling the truth, that he didn't distinguish between races. That he even, heaven forbid, had never made the distinction in his mind. An old fashioned gentleman who had asked little of his long life except a loving home to return to every evening, who had a kind word for everyone and, when push came to shove, genuinely believed that men and women of different races could get on as they always had, if only they tried. Brazzi, along with Mussolini, believed that race was a feeling, not a reality, a popular sentiment amongst opportunists.

'You paid no attention,' concluded Monfalcon.

'I don't read the newspapers a great deal,' Zan confessed. 'I never talk about politics.'

'You're blind, old man! Your son, to be blunt, has worked for eight years in an Italian university. Lots of young students are fascists. Did you know that? You didn't, did you, because you never talk about politics! Fah! These same young men, some of whom are more than likely students of your son, have fought for fascism.'

'Giovanni is not a fascist.'

'But he may be a socialist? Our policy is to smash the heads of socialists.'

'I don't think he's a socialist.'

Monfalcon leaned across the tablecloth, elbowing the half-empty coffee cup out of the way, and leered into Zan's soft jowls, the puzzled visage, the quaint bow tie and nostalgic moustache.

'Are you sure?'

'Well, yes, Signor Monfalcon,' he mumbled, 'I'm his father.'

'Though I warrant Giovanni's got more ham on his pizza. You haven't studied yourself, signore? You haven't worked? If I recall, you look after the property you've inherited. You shoot game. You're a good shot, I've heard. Well, they're useful skills, I'm certain.'

Monfalcon's tone had become paternalistic and it was possible to see that he had not looked dead all his life.

'How often does Giovanni come home?'

'A few times a year.'

'So you're telling me that an Italian teacher who has crossed the path of hundreds of intelligent young men over a period of eight years, many of whom are honored to call themselves fascists, has somehow maintained his detachment to such a degree that he doesn't even understand the forces that are reshaping Italy, much less act upon them?'

'Giovanni is Istrian.'

'*Italian!!*' Monfalcon thumped the table. 'Istria is naturally Italian! Fascism only redeemed what Austria suppressed.'

'Never mind about that, Monfalcon,' Brazzi interrupted quickly. 'Let's keep to the point.'

'The point *is*, Brazzi, that Signor Di Micheli doesn't seem to know his son very well at all, or his recent activities, which have instigated this letter. Wouldn't you agree?'

Brazzi pursed his lips, which seemed an acceptable acknowledgement.

'We'd like to help you,' offered Monfalcon kindly.

Brazzi realized that Monfalcon's kindness was a joke, but to Zan it was no laughing matter. He searched for his glasses, for it seemed to him that to see the face of his inquisitor clearly would free him, but when he at long last found them in the pocket of his waistcoat it was only to discover how hard it was to see the features that accused him. Hidden beneath the hat, obscured by shadow. Unknowable.

'I just want to find my son,' he begged. *My cherished son.* Although it was only mid-afternoon, already night seemed to be falling. 'What are you suggesting?'

'We are suggesting, signore, that you are the victim of an extortion attempt for the return of your son. Even you should understand that. We further propose that that son has been targeted because of something he knows, some plans by an anti-Fascist group – anti-Italian, probably socialist – that has come to his notice within the university. This letter that has been sent to you is an indication of that. Il Duce does not argue with those who oppose him, he destroys them. If I were to tell you the fate of the men who have crossed him, then maybe you wouldn't treat the situation so lightly. You wouldn't sit here drinking coffee when Giovanni's life hangs in the balance.'

To which Zan had nothing to say but looked longingly at the door, which he hoped might open for him of its own accord.

'Romano would know what to do,' he murmured.

'The surveyor?' Monfalcon made no attempt to hide his scorn. 'Then naturally you should have asked him first.'

'I should have… this morning. I should not have waited.'

His Most Italian City

Now the seed had been sown and from it emerged the black root of self-doubt. Monfalcon was right and Zan was wrong. This had all been his fault. Shame would pursue him rightfully – for he had sinned – and he could see no way of escaping it. A creak on the floorboards above him reminded him of the Fräuleins Müller whose peaceful existence he had also disturbed. He wished the men in front of him would at least ease his anxiety by using his real name.

'Yes, Signor Di Micheli and I spoke about the disappearance on the Riva Nazario Sauro several hours ago,' recalled Brazzi.

'Then I am surprised, signore,' scoffed Monfalcon, 'that you have taken this long to act. What have you done since? Waited for your son to walk through the front door?'

And were they not the very words Zan had used to Maria only this morning? A terrible knot strangled his heart. He struggled to his feet.

'I need to go! I need to go!'

Below him Monfalcon's eyes were shining. He'd had such a good time.

'Wait, signore!' he cried as Zan stumbled towards the door. 'You haven't paid for the coffee!'

Zan threw a handful of coins behind him and groped blindly for his letter. Staggering, scarcely aware of where he was going, he left the café without picking his feet up and tripped down the step into the piazza. From inside he heard Brazzi's sudden hoot of laughter.

Monfalcon watched Zan go and his smile collapsed into a satisfied sneer.

'Well, you finally thawed out. Now follow him! Talk to this son-in-law. Make sure they know where to be and when.'

Chapter Twelve

Cold. Twilight decaying. Night closing in. The Val di Torre is iron-red earth, aqua sea and limestone; above it are woods and meadows, a patchwork of olive trees and vines. The fields have been tilled and await the Christmas wheat, for tomorrow will be December, the turn of the season, and already the leaves brushed by his feet are past golden. They are shriveled and brown, falling fast. His road is narrow, strewn with gravel. Bushes on either side caress him. The air is still and smells of pine.

He has walked up along the hiking trails because he wants to see Cittanova again. This need has grown like an ache in his heart and he knows, as one does when traversing the landscape of dreams, that his desire will forever elude him. This vision he longs for.

But suddenly it is here, the town that grows into the sea like a rose from the fertile coast, and the sheer kindness that has permitted him to see it humbles him, diverts his attention from himself. Though three sides are sea-bound, the fourth narrows to an eastern promontory through which runs the road he needs to get home. And look! Here is the patient donkey waiting for him, tied to a tree by the trail. The oxen are yoked to the cart. It's time to go home.

Beneath the tiles his mother will be storing green pomegranates before the snow comes, washing the snails in brine, frying onions for risotto. He sees her from his hill, writing with a finger on the frosty window. She has left him a message and he has to read it. But he is distracted by the hunt for the tiny, fragrant wild strawberries that hide under the leaves. And even though the harvest is over and frost is on the vines and he knows it's too late for strawberries he is compelled to look. And while he is looking he loses the road home. The donkey has gone. The oxen have left without him and, as he searches for them, he hears a bell.

'Wait!' he calls to his mother. The bell intrudes into his dream, louder and louder. It triggers an urgent need and he begins to run. 'Wait for me!'

But she turns away lovingly and says, 'Where I'm going you can't follow.'

Her writing melts. The vision disappears. The town is gone.

Giovanni wakes up and his face is bathed in tears. He forgets where he is, searches around him without recognition.

'Diving stations!' he hears.

Men are running. There is no room to run, yet he hears their urgent footfalls. Activity is all around him.

A clutch is pulled, diesel gives way to electricity.

He looks up and sees the wheels in the hydra, each man standing at his position – broad shoulders, strong arms. He hears air hissing up into the sky to which he no longer has access. The worrisome shriek fills his ears. It escapes and he longs to follow it. But the moment is gone and from below he hears water roaring in.

'Planes down five.'

The captain's voice is steady but the sea has developed a human impatience now that it is no longer held back. It thunders into the main tanks saddled to the boat's sides. It seeks every crevice to inhabit. It is impetuous and greedy. The tanks fill and he hears the pitch lower as it satisfies itself.

Water is in Giovanni's world, water inside and water out. It is his recurring nightmare of being overtaken by the torrent. He is sealed in a pressurized container and his ears hurt. In his chest he feels a sick lump which blocks his breathing. It clamps his racing heart. He shudders at the anticipation of what he knows is happening. He trembles. He grows pale. For he finds himself and all around him sinking down like a hand pressed forward into a pond. The water closes over it.

Now the noises from the boat frighten him. Its hull groans under pressure from a greater force. Its ribs and rivets complain and the floor that had seemed so solid rocks beneath his feet and slides away. Foam from the stinking bilge water and its diesel slime rises up through the floor plates. As he tries to hang on, Giovanni slips on the slimy floor, overbalances into a lurching forest of pipes, conduits and wheels and puts his hand out to avoid falling over. Immediately he receives an electric shock, pulls the tingling arm away and rubs it until he can use it once more, only to fall forward again into a set of four gauges whose dials tremble in the dim light, as if frightened by the dubious stability of the boat.

For it is too far down at the bow.

'Andrej, correct your trim.'

In so vast a sea the small submarine does not willingly obey the laws of physics. As they work to balance it an intense young man behind a perplexing collection of wheeled valves on the wall forgets the hair falling into his eyes, the sweat running from his brow, and obeys the captain without question. He selects which wheels to use and his hands revolve them confidently, but an anxious look betrays him.

'Zorko, Danilo, Joče, move aft. Full ahead.'

The huge man and, behind him, two large boys emerge through a bulkhead and carry their mass up the slope toward the stern while the speed of the boat is increased. Very gradually the alarming angle resolves, the forces of buoyancy and gravity agree with each other once again, the bow resumes its slighter downward angle and the boat stabilizes. Faces express relief. Everyone breathes more easily.

'Good work. Make your depth thirty meters.'

His Most Italian City

Zorko, Danilo and Joče, their duty as emergency ballast accomplished, return to the engine room and, beyond it, the electric control room, treading warily so as not to upset the trim.

As they descend, a hand supports the stumbling Giovanni and hustles him forward, back to the noisome bunks where he sees the wet blankets, touches the wet walls, sits on the wet floor. Above him is the sound of water churning, which fades so slowly that it seems it must surely have disappeared even as he still hears it. Now he is in a solemn, noiseless world. His heart, which clamored to be released, has drifted away on the ebb tide. There are no longer any voices, no throbbing of engines, no rushing of water. For all these things have ceased.

Chapter Thirteen

To Silvana's mother, looking her best meant that she ruled the household. Romano Zambon, born in Trieste, qualified Austrian surveyor, failed to see the connection between clothes and autocracy that seemed so obvious to her. Dolores Micatovich managed to carry off the pretension with no higher education than finishing school, for which her husband blamed all subsequent domestic disputes.

In 1925, during a rough patch in the marriage – he wanted a son, she didn't – she had sent him a postcard of them as a newly married couple posing outside the Western façade of the duomo in Florence. Despite all her friends wearing the white skirt and blouse popular in 1919, Dolores had donned an embroidered dress hot off the loom and quite a long way above her ankles, loosely belted at the waist. To this she had added black silk stockings, high heeled shoes with expansive bows, and gloves, with a hat, or rather a turban-like arrangement that raised the diaphanous fabric skywards at the same time plunging it over one shoulder like a waterfall. Romano had never found the words to describe it. By the day of the photograph, he had gotten over his wedding night jitters and stood modestly beside his bride in a plain brown suit with matching felt hat, stiff collar and formal black tie, black shoes and a walking stick.

On the back of this postcard Dolores had written:

His Most Italian City

'Romano! Ricorda le dolci ore piene d'ebbrezza trascorse in questa bella città e in grazia della felicità che t'ho dato in quel tempo si buono, vogliami ancora bene e perdonami – Dolores.'

Which, translated, read:

'Romano! Remember the sweet hours of euphoria spent in this beautiful city, and because of the divine happiness that I gave you in that wonderful time, love me still and forgive me.
– Dolores.'

'I gave you' was the important phrase here, not 'you gave me.' Today there were certain issues that needed to be sorted out along similar lines of control.

'Romano, your canaries have made a mess on the floor. Again. Where is the maid?'

Romano tut-tutted dolefully at the sad yellow birds in their enclosure.

'The maid is walking Silvana home from school to your mother's house.'

'If that school had more than a single girl the maid wouldn't have to. She could be here cleaning the floor.' Dolores inspected her fingernails. 'And how is the dear little nuisance?'

'Well, the last time I saw her.'

'Excellent. I have always said that babies should be born at eight. She should be almost bearable someday soon. Did you notice she's grown again? She's almost as tall as I am now.'

'I believe I did notice that.'

'That child grows like a weed! She has more arms and legs than a bunch of celery.'

'Your mother *will* feed her.' Romano, who was as fond of his daughter as he was allowed, was looking out the window.

'Stop admiring the view and consider the furniture. If it wasn't for the canaries this room would be spotless.'

'If you wore your glasses you could admire the view.'

'Glasses don't suit me,' snapped his wife as if that settled the matter. 'Can we return to your canaries? How do you account for the state of the floor when there is glass halfway up the cage?'

'They're birds. They flew.'

'You should curb that sarcastic tongue, Romano, when you address your wife.'

'It was not sarcasm, Dolores, merely an observation.'

This tête-à-tête was interrupted by a knock at the door before Dolores could descend once more into cultivated criticism and Romano into misinterpreted sarcasm. Romano opened it to find his gigantic father-in-law diminishing on the doorstep faster than a snowflake in the sun.

'Heavens, Zan!' he exclaimed. 'You look dreadful. Come in! Come in out of the cold.'

'Popà!' shrieked Dolores, abandoning the canaries and quickly taking his arm to help him up the step to avert an imminent collapse. 'Here, sit down.'

She assisted him into the hall and across into the well-furnished room they had just left, where the flapping canaries were still as defecatory as ever, but the room was warm and not so ostentatious as to be unwelcoming. There Zan sank into an armchair, shaking his head from side to side, one hand on his chest to arrest his labored breathing, the other searching for the tobacco pouch that he had forgotten at home.

'Are you all right?'

A large tear trailed down one side of Zan's face, circumnavigated his moustache and plopped onto his tweed lapel. Dolores hastily dabbed at it with a lace handkerchief then stroked his poor cheek where another was threatening to descend.

'Popà, what on earth has happened?'

His Most Italian City

'Giovanni's gone!' wept Zan, the simple words so obscured by grief that Romano, standing by, could scarcely understand them.

'Gone? Gone back to Florence?'

'He went for a walk last night and didn't come home. And look, Romano, look!' Zan wobbled the coffee-stained ransom demand over his head at his son-in-law. 'What should I do?'

Romano took the piece of paper from Zan's trembling hand but, before he could read it, they were interrupted by a second knock of a rather more decisive nature than the first. Romano returned to the door to find a man in a very smart suit, felt hat and tailored overcoat, well-shined shoes, a white silk rose in his buttonhole, not overly tall and with a correspondingly small moustache, smiling at them engagingly.

'Matteo Brazzi,' pronounced this fashionable display, removing his hat to Romano. 'Signore.'

Romano bowed, Zan's letter still in his hand. Dolores had risen at this new interruption, to stand beside him.

'The new mayor,' murmured Romano, his mind elsewhere.

'I am honored to be.' Brazzi cringed at his own ingratiating goodness. *I am taking after the cats,* he thought. With a deep breath, he raised Dolores's hand to his lips.

'Signora.'

'Maria Dolorosa Di Micheli Zambon,' returned Dolores, thrilling to the barest brush of his moustache upon her skin. 'How do you do?'

'I am well, signora, but I'm afraid I cannot say the same for your father.'

'You brought my father here?' exclaimed Dolores. 'How kind of you. I regret that we are leaving you standing in the cold. I didn't see you and I can't offer you refreshments. As you see...' She gestured towards the warm sitting room where Zan's long legs protruded into the doorframe. 'Perhaps some other time?'

Brazzi carefully considered his answer to this. Installed as the Fascist mayor only seven months before, he was not well known in Cittanova and he was aware that he was not well liked in some quarters, either. The aversion did not concern him. This afternoon he was on a mission and his wells of charm needed to be directed to the purpose at hand. He'd get nothing out of seducing a married woman in front of her husband and father, much as he'd like to try.

Dolores looked closer to thirty than forty. Small, slim, dark-haired, beautifully dressed in a dropped-waist frock with a skirt of handkerchief points and matching coat straight from the racks of some Paris designer. It may have fallen in step with Dolores's dictum to 'Always look one's best' but to Brazzi it seemed rather wasted on a chilly afternoon in a fishing village.

Permitting himself a constrained sigh, he determined to remain strict. He was here on Fascist business, or at least what passed for it in his survival kit.

'I am happy to hear you use your Italian surname, signora.'

Dolores replied in delighted tones – she had been thoroughly drilled in obsequiousness at finishing school, 'Having a brother in Florence, you know.'

'Yes, indeed. Very fortunate. I fear your father may not embrace it with such enthusiasm.'

'My father is old, signore. He may need some encouragement. Now, if you'll excuse me…' She turned away from him and Brazzi regarded the sway of her hips and the pert tilt of her posterior for a moment too long as she knelt again before her father.

'As you are the mayor,' demanded Romano – he was not impressed by Brazzi's charm, nor did he appreciate the subtle summation the man was giving his wife – 'perhaps you could tell me what could be the purpose of forcing one old man to change his name? He can't pass it on. He has a single granddaughter and his only son is unmarried.'

His Most Italian City

'It has to be seen that these border territories are Italian, signore.'

'Then I hope your government has inherited the Hapsburg empire's knack of peaceful cohabitation along with its lands, Signor Brazzi.'

'These lands are Italian and Mussolini doesn't believe in peace where it threatens Italy's empire. You've not heard Mussolini yourself? He's a very good speaker and a proficient journalist.'

'Both jobs that lack integrity,' commented Romano drily. 'But to reply to your question, I *have* heard him. My father had a profitable hat shop in Trieste, signore, which he established with his brother. We were there, in the shop, when I heard the crowds cheering Mussolini in 1920.'

'Yes, he's very popular in Trieste and elsewhere in Italy, of course. He tells the masses what they want to hear.'

Romano winced. 'And what is it that the Italian people want to hear?'

'That he is going to make Italy great again, naturally.'

Romano liked Italian culture and history but he didn't trust Italians. He understood that Italian political ideology was driven by its decadent, northern intellectuals, fascinated by force, violence and death. He felt that after a long history of invasion and settlement by occupying powers many ordinary Italians had become suspicious of anyone outside their walled communities, just as they had when the city-states Florence, Milan, Venice, Pisa, Genoa, Sienna, Ferrara, Verona and Mantua spent the Renaissance battling each other incessantly on land and sea. With that degree of local animosity, one scarcely needed foreign invaders.

'Mussolini came from nowhere,' he replied to Brazzi, 'and has no experience holding the reins of government.'

'He has made the trains run on time.'

'Trains,' replied Romano, 'are not much use in Cittanova.'

Brazzi cleared his throat.

'You can be fully confident in Mussolini, Signor Zambon. It is your class, the bourgeoisie, that he has sworn to protect.'

Romano had vulnerable eyes (which his wife exploited), and a mop of curls that suffered from the prevailing fashion for long straight fringes. The locks would not remain oiled back in the same manner as Brazzi's but sprang above those eyes as if he were in vaudeville. It was anything but what he felt.

'In two years, Signor Brazzi,' he replied keeping those eyes upon the intruder, 'my daughter will turn ten. At that time, she will have completed the highest grade in the school here in Cittanova. She will need to go to Trieste to further her education and I will need to work there. Your government has the power to deny me my choice of employment because my qualifications are not Italian. As we speak, they are trying to employ me in other parts of Italy, away from my family. This is how Mussolini has protected me.

'Now, you come upon us in the middle of a crisis and I will have to find some other time to discuss politics. As it was you who brought my father-in-law home, would you mind informing me of the circumstances?'

Brazzi gathered himself together.

'That letter...' – he eyed it carefully – '...that you are holding in your hand...'

'I haven't had a chance to look at it yet.'

Brazzi stepped back while Romano scanned the words then abruptly looked up.

'You know something about this?' he demanded.

'Only that I came upon Signor Di Micheli in the piazza in the state in which you see him.'

'I have never seen my father-in-law in this state.'

Brazzi ignored him.

'The situation seems to be, signore, that a demand for money has been made, on which Giovanni's safe return depends. I would strongly advise following the directions in the letter. On the pier tonight...'

His Most Italian City

'Two hundred thousand lire!' Romano interrupted angrily. 'Where is he expected to find that by close of business? Do you know who wrote this?'

'I don't believe the letter is signed.'

'Then you've read it! Did Zan allow you to do that?'

'We'll ask him…'

'No, you won't!' Romano stepped out into the street, shutting the front door so firmly behind him that Brazzi was forced to either follow him or be hit by the wood. Immediately they stood out in the chilled lane where houses shadowed them on either side. Two small children chasing a ball through the dust eyed them curiously until hustled inside by their mother.

Romano faced Brazzi squarely and spoke in level tones.

'I don't think you brought Zan home at all, Signor Brazzi. I think you followed him here. Now, if you have any further information, you may tell me, otherwise I must ask you to leave.'

*****

Failure in triplicate. How could such a situation be aptly described? Critical. Assaulted on all fronts. And Signor Brazzi could bet that that thoroughly upstanding citizen who had just kicked him out would go straight to the police. Now there was no escape except by water, from which his nemesis was coming. He could feel it in his bones. Perhaps he could pay him off? Yes, that's what he would do. How much had he at his disposal this late in the day? That little emergency stash in the safe beneath the counter? He'd just nip back to the café and get it. Or would he? Would that carcass still be there? Damn the man, was he a permanent fixture? Brazzi hurried the short distance back to the piazza and looked carefully around the corner. Yes, there was that ghoulish concavity moldering away next to his beautiful espresso machine! And if he asked when he was leaving Monfalcon would at once deduce his reason to be rid of him. *Where's the money?* How could someone be so moribund yet so observant? He'd end up handing over his precious hoard to the horrible man. All he needed to do was to pull out that gun again. And he would. Then if Brazzi neglected to do his duty on the pier tonight, Monfalcon would shoot him anyway. Not long for this world, he would nevertheless ensure that Brazzi predeceased him.

Unhappy! Signor Brazzi was so unhappy!

What about Angelica? *Who? Oh, her.* Well, needs must and the crisis before him which (let him be totally honest) he had seen coming, was upon him. *Forget her.* He trailed through his options. There was only one car in the town. One! Who could he bribe to drive him? But, even had there been more than one car, the roads were not made for transport. Rutted, graveled, pot-holed. No wonder the same people had lived here for centuries. Some divine comedy was clearly acting to keep the roads useless and the population static. Well, let the heavens laugh at him. He would accomplish the impossible even it meant another steamer. They would all expect him to return north to Trieste, but what if he went south to Pola? There, at least, was a railway line; he could get back to Trieste the long way. He would retrieve the money, pack a bag and get Morato to put him up for the night. Pay him to keep quiet, then lay low until the morning steamer.

Brazzi waited in a dreary huddle in the cold shade of the lane for a further half hour until he was able to gather up sufficient courage to look again. Then he tiptoed into the piazza, slunk along the buildings heading seaward and cautiously peered into the cafe. In the same corner, in the same posture, slouched Monfalcon's decrepit figure. Asleep. Brazzi cursed his luck. He'd be there all night now. There was no telling when the eyelids might stir and the corpse would arise. Cautiously, Brazzi removed his hat and, muffling the bell with it, eased the door open a bare fraction with his other hand. Then he pulled the small brass key to the safe from his pocket, crouched down and tip toed across the meter and a half to the counter.

'Have you come to confess?'

His Most Italian City

Brazzi's heart leapt into his throat. It beat so rapidly that he could barely breathe. He hastily shoved the key into his pocket. Monfalcon's head lay upon his wrist and in his hand he clutched his pistol.

He did not even look up but continued in a muffled voice, 'Tell me everything, Matteo, and I could guarantee you absolution, if I chose. How did you get on with old Zan? Do you have some good news to tell me?' He began to roll the pistol around in his palm. Brazzi noticed how it slipped heavily into the gap created by his absent fingers.

'Put that thing down!' he cried. 'You're scaring me.'

Monfalcon did not even look up.

'You should be scared, Matteo,' he said, marking out patterns on the tablecloth with the barrel. 'I send you out on a simple errand and I can tell by the look on your face that you've failed.' He suddenly cocked the pistol and aimed it directly between Brazzi's eyes. 'I wonder why you've decided to come back just now. If I were you I would have gone straight home and packed for a rapid exit, and yet you've returned – and with a key in your hand. Not too many guesses what a key's for with a man like you.'

Brazzi inched around the decorated walls towards the door, clutching his hat. Everywhere he went the pistol followed him.

'If I know you,' deliberated Monfalcon, 'and I know you very well, I would say that the key is for money. You're looking after your own interests, as always. In fact, I've always wondered which of those interests brought you to Cittanova.'

'Giunta didn't tell you?'

'Perhaps he expected you would,' responded Monfalcon. 'And you wouldn't have told him the whole truth. Not you.'

'If I tell you everything will you let me go?' begged Brazzi.

'I don't know. But I'll certainly kill you if you don't. You've betrayed Mussolini. You deserve to die.'

'I had to leave Trieste because I was the victim of terrorism,' declared Brazzi, expelling gallons of wounded pride. 'Somebody bombed my office.'

To his dismay, Monfalcon didn't put down the gun.

'*You?*' He gaped as if the astonishing confession had caused him instead to forget it. 'Who would bomb *you*?' For someone so congenitally ill-disposed, the news seemed invigorating. Monfalcon actually smiled. 'That was a waste of resources.'

'He didn't think so,' said Brazzi.

Monfalcon's eyes widened.

'Then you know who did it?' He rested his chin on one hand and raised his eyes from beneath the brim of his hat so as to better study this marvel. 'But I wouldn't term it terrorism to attack someone like you. Just consider,' he meditated, 'the planning, risk and co-ordination involved in an attack on a city.' He stopped suddenly. 'Day or night?'

'Night,' said Brazzi.

'Did they catch him?'

Brazzi shook his head.

'Well, well, well,' pondered Monfalcon to himself. 'No witnesses? A clean getaway. I like his style. So you ran away? That's just like you. And you've been acting very strangely lately. Quite the country gentleman, but now suddenly paranoid. What does that tell me?'

'It tells you nothing!' barked Brazzi.

'Oh yes, it does. It tells me that you're worried enough to come back here needing money before tomorrow. That you plan to disappear before the bank opens. I wonder if the two events are connected…' The brim of his hat framed Monfalcon's eyes almost whimsically, instead of hiding them like an old punter reading the racing guide.

'I'm in quite a receptive mood this afternoon, Matteo,' he continued. 'I like a good mystery. I think I'm going to amuse myself by finding out what happened to you.'

His Most Italian City

He tapped a little rhythm with his feet and it struck Brazzi, as it grated on his nerves, that he had never seen the man actually stand on them. If he had, he would have noticed that Monfalcon, despite his withered form, had enough height remaining to compliment his military bearing. Brazzi was not very tall and, as they continued their standoff, like a mouse before a cat, there was only a head between them.

'First,' announced Monfalcon in a methodical manner, 'why would someone bomb you? Would they bomb you for the offences against the Slavs you took credit for but didn't do? For a few florid newspaper articles you wrote? No. Or perhaps it was in retaliation for one of those four hundred and eighty-eight schools someone else closed for you? The attacks you didn't take part in? The ethnic cleansing you only said you carried out. The war you avoided. The propaganda you weren't interested in, except to serve yourself. And now here you are, running a café that is fascist in name only. All along, you see, you have been using fascism to protect yourself from fascism! First point established!'

'I wouldn't be the first man to do that,' Brazzi retorted.

'No, and most of them came to as poor an end as you will. Second – and I still haven't answered my question – there's something else going on here, and there's only one thing you're notable for, my friend, aside from a love of money. So who was she? His wife? His girlfriend? His daughter? Someone who resents you has seen an opportunity for revenge and taken it. I must say, Matteo, you have risen in my estimation. You must have really pissed him off.'

He adjusted his clothes, tucking his shirt into his trousers and smoothing his moth-eaten waistcoat over the top, as if he was suddenly aware that his appearance and Brazzi's did not invite comparison.

'Are you going to tell me what you did to him?'

'I didn't do anything.'

'You're lying.'

It was clear to Brazzi that he should never have come to this town where his actions were so transparent. He shifted his weight from one foot to the other. How he hated feeling afraid! How he resented these times, when he seemed to live in an atmosphere of fear. Fear had followed him here from Trieste. Fear of fascist violence. Fear of revenge. Fear of discovery. Fear had spoiled everything he enjoyed. Beauty, desire and sensuality. It had made a mockery of money. For how could you enjoy these when you lived in fear?

And now here he was again, frightened in front of this cunning soldier.

'He's coming back,' he bleated.

'How do you know he's coming back? And where is he coming back to?'

'Here! Di Micheli's son didn't disappear by accident. A foreign vessel was seen in the port by his granddaughter *at the same time*.'

'You said the child saw a monster.'

'Yes, I know what I said!' Brazzi snapped fretfully, nerves like fine china. 'I should have been there last night. He was on it. He wanted me to meet him. But I wasn't in the port. I was in the hotel with you and now this son's gone missing. So I'm telling you, I know he's coming back for *me*.'

'Where is the son?'

'I don't know! He's involved somehow.'

'You knew and you still wrote that phony ransom note, without telling me?'

'Who cares!' wailed Brazzi, and he looked like such a bewildered wreck that Monfalcon started to laugh.

Laughter and Monfalcon not being on familiar terms, very soon he was so overcome that he didn't care about anything. He dropped the gun from his three-fingered hand. It hit the edge of the table and landed on the floor.

'No ransom, no money?' Monfalcon wiped his eyes. 'Hand me my gun. I'm going to shoot you.'

The pistol lay between them on the parquet floor. Unwilling to infect himself with the man's touch, Brazzi kicked it gingerly out of reach. Monfalcon laughed harder.

'Better clean that shoe, Matteo Brazzi!'

Brazzi's voice cracked. An ocean of pathos overwhelmed him.

'*I hate you!*' he shrieked. 'I hope you die laughing!'

His Most Italian City

Monfalcon shrugged.

'Maybe I will, maybe I won't, or maybe I'll just shoot you right now.' He held up two fingers.

'Bang!' he said.

Signor Matteo Brazzi fled then. Out through the door, right down the Via Belvedere and left into the Via Pestrini, scuttling like a displaced crab, seeking the side street wherein his house lay. Somewhere along that tortured trail he discovered that he had left his heart behind and, by the time he felt the hollow in his chest and placed his hand upon the gap left by the living organ, it was too late to return and retrieve it, and nowhere for it to fit. Sheer self-protective panic had rushed in to fill the void.

Monfalcon sat in the Caffè Fascisti resting his heaving chest. When he felt secure enough, he levered himself heavily from his seat, coughed hoarsely, picked up his gun and left.

*****

After Brazzi had gone and even the soft tread of his expensive shoes had died away down the street, Zan dried his eyes and searched the pretty face of his daughter, who was kneeling in front of him.

'What are we going to do?'

'Nothing.' Romano had re-entered the room. 'I smell a rat. That mayor knows much more than he's letting on.'

'But what about Giovanni?'

'Giovanni's no fool, Zan. He'll turn up. In my opinion Brazzi has preyed upon you. I don't believe he knows where Giovanni is any more than we do.'

Zan related to his son-in-law every outrage that had taken place in that café, starting with the dreadful cup of coffee.

Romano nodded.

'Yes, it's money they want, but what crime can remain hidden in a town this size? Mark me, somebody knows something. Nobody disappears in Cittanova without a witness.'

Chapter Fourteen

Bruno was talking to himself.

'That's him. See Giovanni on the pier. No, it's not. Quiet, quiet.' Here followed a string of *sotto voce* mutterings and several clicks of his tongue. 'Who's there? Walk to the Picolich farm, Bruno. I've got him. I think it won't take you long. You were on the pier. Stand up! That's him. Are you going to help the Picolichs, Zorko? Only half an hour. Help the Picolichs. Help the Picolichs. Heavy when wet. Giovanni on the pier. Only half an hour. Off now, Bruno. Good boy. See him on the pier. Hurry, Zorko. You were on the pier. Giovanni's on the pier. Do you know where he is? Giovanni's on the pier, Zorko. Stand up! Walk to the Picolichs. Off now, Bruno! *Good boy, Bruno!!*'

This last was exclaimed loudly after which Bruno lowered his voice and went right back to the beginning. The impression was that he was repeating voices as he had heard them, using the original nuances. He never became emotionally involved himself and the whole show was similar to an actor rehearsing his lines fifty times before a mirror.

The Picolichs, father and son, spent several perplexed minutes listening to Bruno's echolalia, which he had kept up in a steady stream for an hour now in an absorbed, dispassionate manner. He even talked as he waited for them to load the wheelbarrow and then commenced pushing it to the side of the house and the retaining wall that they had been securing. Eventually they shrugged their shoulders. Everyone knew Bruno. It was not possible to give a reason for the strange repeated words. It was just something he did.

'See Giovanni on the pier. On the pier. Quiet, quiet, Giovanni's on the pier. Do you know where he is? Heavy when wet, Zorko. Are you going to help the Picolichs? Slow astern. Are you off now? Stand up, Bruno!'

Martin Picolich laid aside his shovel as Bruno, still muttering, wandered away with the wheelbarrow to the wall marked by a straight line of string.

'Who do you think he's on about?' he asked his son, a scrawny young man a couple of years younger than Bruno with twice as much hair as his father but half his brawn.

'Giovanni?'

'Giovanni who?'

'Dunno.'

'Who was the other one?'

'Zorko?'

'I don't think we know any Zorkos.'

Martin paused to observe Bruno unload his wheelbarrow and tap its base carefully to make sure that all the dirt was gone – Bruno would have been very anxious had the dirt, by friction, gravity or plain ill will, neglected to deposit itself on the pile where he had been told it had to go.

In the course of the day, over an open range in the kitchen of the stone farmhouse Siora Picolich cooked two meals heavy enough to satisfy the appetites of three men laboring in cold weather. Bruno ate potato polenta for lunch and, when his work was done, would eat sausages served with sauerkraut.

Martin Picolich waited for Bruno to clean his polenta bowl with a chunk of bread, then said to his wife, 'Know any Giovannis?'

'Every third man,' she returned.

'Zorkos?'

'No.'

'Any Giovannis on the pier?'

'No.' She kicked at a loose piece of charcoal that had fallen from the fire then, covering her hands with a cloth, she lifted the cast iron pot from its hook, placed it on the ground and commenced scraping the remains of the polenta from its base to give to the pigs.

Martin sat for a further minute in the dusky air watching the smoke rise up the chimney, then he slapped his thigh and stood up, followed by his son. Bruno glanced reluctantly at the warm fireplace before heading out into the afternoon chill.

About an hour and a half later, his wife hurried out of the house and across the yard towards them with a flushed face.

'Giovanni Micatovich!' she exclaimed to her husband.

'Haven't seen him for a while,' commented Martin, shifting his shovel from one hand to the other.

'He's missing! And his poor old father has had a demand for money for his return.'

'Which idiot told you that?' Martin reproved her.

'No idiot. Gospođa Radin, the teacher. Not her exactly. Goran's just in from school and told me now. And you were asking about Giovannis.'

Martin considered how foolish he wanted to look in front of his wife, so he grunted and went back to work but, after considering the matter for an hour or so, he put down the lump of limestone he was fitting into the new retaining wall.

'You,' he ordered his son. 'Go back into town with Bruno after dinner and pay his mother for today's work. Then you can tell her what he said.'

'I'll be too tired,' complained the boy.

Martin clipped him over the ear.

'Stop whining,' he said, 'and do as you're told.'

Chapter Fifteen

Nothing could persuade Giovanni to lie once more upon those stinking bunks, so he was sitting on the floor with his knees up and his head down when one of the crew entered, sat down beside him and, to his great surprise, began to rub his back at the spot of tension between his hunched shoulder blades. Strong hands moved up and down his spine with practiced ease, stopping wherever they found a tight muscle. Sick, stunned by the experience of being buried under water, and unable to rouse himself to arrest the strange gesture, Giovanni allowed the hands to relax the knotted muscles in his back and neck. After five minutes of activity that apparently pleased him the man stopped, asking with more cheerfulness than Giovanni expected, 'Better?'

'Yes… thank you.' He looked around him as if only now realizing how quiet it was. 'Why have the engines stopped?'

'They haven't stopped,' said the man. 'When we dive we're electric. Run on batteries. Much quieter. The diesel's only for the surface.'

He spoke without suspicion and in his overt kindliness Giovanni recognized the man who had returned to help him and had handed him the wrench to deal with the unfortunate rat.

'I'm Mirko,' he said. He held out a hand, explaining modestly, 'My mother was a nurse.'

Giovanni shook the proffered hand. 'That's great.'

Mirko gave Giovanni's unhappy face a further diagnostic glance. Apparently not satisfied, he suggested, 'I could massage your feet if you like.'

'Why?' asked Giovanni suspiciously.

'Just a precaution. Not so long ago we had a fellow in that we had to hit on the head.' He was a cheerful young man. He told his tale conversationally and, in other circumstances, Giovanni might have found him amusing. 'He went completely to pieces. Couldn't handle being shut in and cracked up in a rather spectacular way. Before we knew it, Zorko had clobbered him. That shut him up but he wasn't quite the same afterwards. Dribbled a bit. We'd hate that to happen to you.'

'Who was he?'

'A journalist.'

'What was his name?'

'You wouldn't know him,' he remarked dismissively, 'unless you belonged to the Fascist Party in Trieste.'

He handed Giovanni a mug of water. A scum of diesel floated on the top.

'Sorry.'

His sincerity was touching and Giovanni risked a delicate sip.

'Are you hungry?'

'No. I just want to get out.'

'Why?' said Mirko. 'It's nice and quiet down here. I like it. No rolling. No seasickness. Then again, I don't get seasick,' he boasted. 'We can't stay down for that long anyway and we're not far below periscope depth. Captain will go and have a look soon. If the coast is clear he'll blow our tanks and up we go.' He made a swishing movement with one hand.

'Blow your tanks up?'

'Blow the water out of the ballast tanks with compressed air. There's a lot you need to learn about submarines, Giovanni Micatovich.'

His Most Italian City

He was quite young and spoke with enthusiasm. He had straight brown hair, brown eyes and a forehead above them as high as Giovanni's but broader, for Giovanni was like his mother and his oval face had a tender look, particularly when he was in a loving mood. It reminded his family of his childhood. Mirko looked much sturdier. He had the strong hands and shoulders associated with seamen. His face, which in other circumstances could appear just as loving as Giovanni's, now had a higher cause in mind and his features expressed solidarity with it.

He seemed very starry-eyed about his captain.

'He's not a bad man, Giovanni, just got a lot to be angry about.' And opening a wooden hatch diagonally opposite the bunks he drew out a packet of cigarettes and a box of matches.

Giovanni gasped.

'You're not going to smoke in here, surely?'

Mirko shrugged. 'He'll open the hatch later and let it all out.'

The match flared in the cramped room that was lit only by an electric lamp hooked to the low ceiling, and in its compressed, reeking space Giovanni discovered the pungent smell of burning tobacco acting on his nerves like an antiseptic.

But when Mirko offered him the packet he drew one out and hesitated.

'I don't often smoke.'

'You look like you need one.'

Mirko lay back, inhaled with satisfaction and with the subtle pity of the young regarded Giovanni, still forlornly well dressed. Under the scrutiny Giovanni undid his collar button and slid both collar and tie into his pocket. He picked up the matchbox and lit his cigarette.

'How old are you?'

'Nineteen.'

'You're not afraid – down here – after what went wrong earlier?'

'Nothing went wrong. Submarines can be hard to balance, that's all. Captain sent the three biggest men aft because they're so heavy. Once' –

he leaned forward eagerly – 'and this is the best story, Giovanni – we *all* had to move aft. That was last year when we got the new submarine. We were sinking so steeply that things were rolling down the aisle. In a heavy sea these boats want to flip on their nose or their ass, and sometimes they do anyway. Today Andrej trimmed her quickly – he's got a good feel for it – and Captain picked her speed up. It worked, but that other time we were trimming her most of the day. Up, down, up, down. We've improved since then,' he explained to the floor.

'Trimming?'

'Moving water around the smaller ballast tanks. That's what half of those wheels are for.'

'I think I'll stay on dry land.'

'No. This is an awesome experience. Most of the guys I went to sea with are stuck on coastal patrol or slaving away on the docks. Anyway, Captain'll surface as soon as the cargo ship's gone. Open the hatch, see the sky again, eh?'

'What cargo ship?'

'Dunno.' Mirko flicked ash into the chemical-saturated atmosphere in a way that made Giovanni shudder. 'Some poor bastard outside the shipping lanes. Captain wasn't happy about it. Got a lot on his mind. But we're in Italian waters, so better safe than sorry.'

From within the boat Giovanni heard a joke in a foreign tongue, a whispered response, and the faintest hum of a motor, all quickly followed by the wary silence of this strange world.

Water deadens all sound, he thought, *yet sound passes easily through water.*

A contradiction, surely.

'You hear that?' said Mirko. 'The ship's gone.'

'I don't hear anything.'

'You would if there was a ship near us.'

His Most Italian City

Giovanni sat wordlessly. At the end of his fingers two centimeters of ash hung from the tip of his cigarette, black, and as fragile as sunburned skin about to peel. Neglected, the ash fell onto the damp floor and quickly coagulated into gray porridge. He watched as more of the white paper began to be consumed and the red glow from its interior coaxed him to finish it.

'Why is your captain angry?'

Mirko gaped at him.

'Where have you been the last decade, Giovanni? Oh, yes, Italy, haven't you? Well, if you'd raised your eyes above your wine glass you might have noticed what was going on in Istria away from your lovely Venetian coastline. Mussolini treats all Slavs in Istria as subhuman because that's what he thinks we are. There is nothing Slavic here now thanks to him: no culture, no churches, no schools, no banks, no newspapers, no courts, but there's plenty of state-supported violence. It's a really fabulous place for Slovenes and Croats to live, I can tell you.'

He took a piercing draw on his cigarette and subsided back against the wall.

'I'm sorry, Mirko,' replied Giovanni who, being naturally sympathetic, didn't have to try very hard. 'I didn't know.'

'Didn't know what?'

'Well, the newspapers are Fascist-run. You know, we don't get a lot of factual reporting. I had heard rumors within the university, but then I work in Florence, not Trieste. I think, in answer to your question, that within the bulk of Italy it's not generally known.'

'Nothing?'

'Well...'

And when Giovanni faltered to construct the standard pacifying reply, Mirko continued angrily, 'So we're fighting our guts out without an audience, is that it? Istria's Italian, apparently, but Italians know nothing about it. Lovely, charming Italy! Typical. You go back and you tell them this from me: that *their* fascist thugs want to exterminate us. That *their* police let them because racism is state-sanctioned in Italy. They've even closed our sports clubs. Well, you know what that means, don't you?' He paused for effect and when Giovanni looked at him blankly he exploded, *'It means no soccer, and how would you like that?!'*

'You like soccer?'

'I love soccer!' cried Mirko. 'I was a forward before I joined the navy. The best goal scorer on our team. Fascism has ruined my life, Giovanni! No soccer! I hate Italians!'

'Not all Italians are fascists, Mirko.'

'Mussolini says they are.'

Giovanni recalled only a fortnight since having a similar conversation with another nineteen-year-old, one of his students, who always wore black shirts to lectures. Well, he was used to young men and it was hard to get out of his habit of the reasoned response he thought this situation called for. He leaned forward and spoke with his trademark tone of commitment. Did he detect suspicion as Mirko turned his face away? He went on anyway.

'Look, I don't like Mussolini either. I don't agree with his actions or trust his motives, but plenty of Italians do. They love it when he tells them that Libya is Italian and Dalmatia is Italian, and some new Italian aggression in Africa or Albania will give Italy the empire it deserves. Then he says that your country is Italian, too.'

The low ceiling seethed with condensation. Mirko flicked a couple of drips from his hair.

'Do you hear what I'm saying?' persisted Giovanni.

'Yeah, I hear you. You sound just like a teacher. You understand it, so you're going to ride it out. Have another cigarette, Giovanni. You might even blow the boat up this time and wouldn't that would make your life a bit more exciting?' His face cracked from ear to ear but, behind it, his smoldering sense of injustice shifted him on his orbit and lent to his engaging grin the suggestion that he might be more than merely a good-natured young man. 'I've got a good idea! You're smoking, you're dirty and you need a shave. Why don't you join us?'

Giovanni drew on his cigarette and exhaled cheerlessly. 'I've already been rejected. I just want to go home.'

'Oh, he's going to let you go,' returned Mirko, still with that dichotomous smile.

'Your captain? Well, I wish he'd told me.'

'He's holding onto you because he needs some help with this guy he's after. Banich. The man Zorko thought you resembled. Do you know him?'

'Banich?' Giovanni wracked his brain. 'No.'

'You might know him as Brazzi.'

'Ah, him! Yes, I've heard of him. He's the mayor, or what passes for one.'

'What do you know about him?'

'Nothing. I don't live there anymore.'

'You don't know where he lives?'

'Not really – somewhere at the southern end of town. Behind the piazza.'

Mirko bent forward. 'Listen, I'll tell Captain that you do know, all right? Give you time to think before he puts you on the spot.'

'I really don't know, Mirko. I'll have to ask someone. Why does he want him?'

'He's a traitor,' replied Mirko simply. 'He's not Italian. He's a Slovene like us, but he's a self-serving opportunist. A petty criminal. He backs any team, whatever their politics because what he really wants is money. He and the captain grew up together in Trieste, went to the same school, spoke the same mix of languages that we all do in this part of the world. Well, during the war Banich applauded Italy swapping sides for land because he'll swap sides, too. Whatever's best for him. He'd be happy enough to stay Slovenian if it made him rich safely. After Trieste became

Italian in 1919 he changed his name to Brazzi and quickly became involved in the propaganda against Slovenes in that city.

'It became rabidly fascist. Too many German speakers. Too many Slavs. You want to know why the captain is angry? Banich has personally had a hand in enforcing the use of the Italian language in anything public: trams, trains, the courts, the post offices, newspapers. The German and Slovenian languages are forbidden. Our culture is being eradicated – with force, with burning. Banich had even begun to close down Slovenian schools and infiltrate Slovenian churches.

'He stood back and allowed the violence that was occurring against his own people, but the worst thing is that in his heart he doesn't care. The use of force to annihilate his cultural identity, witnessing the suffering it caused, meant nothing to him as long as he protected his own interests.'

Mirko puffed smoke out the side of his face, jerkily, like an engine. 'Now, if I tell you this, what will it cost me? Will it stay with you?'

'Don't tell me if it worries you.'

But suddenly Mirko's mood brightened.

'You know what?' he said, smiling. 'You've got an honest face. I think I will. One night, earlier this year, we took this old sub up to Trieste and bombed his office. Andrej planted the bomb. He's even angrier than the captain. The entire place went up. So this Banich, too much of a coward to put his own life at risk, packs up his family and leaves. Ha, ha! And he's so guileless that we find him, and here we are!'

'What do you want him for?'

'You think resistance groups finance themselves?' Mirko shrugged as if money was an arbitrary notion. 'We need funds. Well, who doesn't? So, when the captain discovered that his old school acquaintance, having abandoned the city of his birth, was biding his time in Cittanova, he sends him this incendiary device he nicked from stores. "Remember me?" Sick, isn't it? Then he follows it up with a letter about last night and arranges a time to meet. At ten o'clock in the evening at the inlet below the hotel, exactly where we found you. The Bora ruined everything and I think that Banich, being a coward, simply chickened out.'

'So this was a kidnapping? To extort his family for money?'

Mirko nodded. 'Exactly. Captain says he's rich, and so agreeable that it's possible even his wife is unaware of the full extent of his crimes. She'll pay to get him back. Even you would find him charming if you met him. It's how he worms his way so easily into new territory. He's made himself popular, I'll bet.'

'In some quarters,' mused Giovanni. 'Your story sounds plausible, Mirko, but it doesn't tally. All this trouble. There're other ways of getting money. And you know what? It's not what I sense about your captain, either. He wouldn't go to this amount of risk at his age, just for money. He must be forty. Money is a young man's stunt, Mirko. Your captain's got some personal motive.' Bolstered by his earlier experience, he added, 'In fact, I'm sure he has.'

Though Mirko was clever, he couldn't prevent an uncomfortable blush from staining his cheeks.

'Zorko told me,' he whispered.

'Something to do with Banich?'

Mirko nodded.

'What happened?'

'I can't tell you.'

'Well then, can you tell me who your captain is?'

'I can't give out his name, but he was in the Austrian navy during the war. Learned about submarines in Pola. This is an Austrian vessel, one of the ones given to the Italians by the victors after the war. He nicked it from under their noses.'

Mirko looked up at Giovanni and this time his eyes were shining.

'I'm proud to serve him,' he said. 'You think he's brusque and rough. That's what you see. Well, you're wrong. I would follow him anywhere.

Trieste, they say now, is pure Italian. "But what is pure Italian?" Captain asks us. I don't know. "It's an idea," he says.

'Mussolini says that to be Italian you only have to feel Italian. That's Banich, you see. He feels Italian, therefore he is.

'Italy is thirty times bigger than Slovenia – and growing, if this is all you need to do to be Italian. This huge fascist nation forbids a handful of Slovenians from being Slovenian. It's petty. It's childish. But Italians respond to it because some fanatical joker gets up on a box and turns this "pure Italy" into a romantic idea.'

In the dimness he dropped his voice. 'What we want is what we had: our identity, our language. You haven't heard of TIGR? Not living your high life down in Florence, I don't expect you have. TIGR is the only organized anti-fascist resistance group in Europe.' His face shone with pride. 'Everyone hates them but only *we* are doing something about it.'

'What does…?'

'Trieste, Istria, Gorica and Rijeka – it's an acronym for the places we come from.'

'You're partisans? But this is partly personal.'

'It doesn't matter. Banich fulfills all the requirements and many of us who collaborate with TIGR are military personnel.' Mirko drummed his fingers on the floor and counted time, and when he raised his head his tones had stiffened into a more militant voice. 'You haven't been entirely honest with us, Giovanni. You told us your name was Micatovich. They wouldn't let you use that name in Florence. So what are you, Italian or Croatian?'

'Well, until a few years ago I was Austrian.'

'And now?'

'Now I'm called Di Micheli.'

'So you're one of Mussolini's feel-good Italians?'

'No! I couldn't refuse the name if I wanted a job.'

His Most Italian City

'You played it safe? You allowed some clown of a clerk to erase your identity with the stroke of a pen. Well, it's your life, I suppose, but I don't want people accusing me of capitulation.'

'I didn't capitulate!'

The conversation had become heated. Ears listened in from beyond the bunks, Giovanni was sure of it. He drew a careful breath.

'Look, I'll talk to you, Mirko, but you must try not to threaten me. The way I see it is this: Istria was given to Italy after the war by Britain, France and America because the Italians asked for it, and to reward it for fighting on their side. Now that Istria's Italian they're not going to get involved in how Italy governs it.'

'Governs it?' cried Mirko. 'Italy's only had it for ten years and look at the mess it's made.'

'My parents haven't complained.'

'Cittanova hasn't complained, you mean? Of course they haven't, they're pro-Italian.'

'I don't know that my parents are pro-Italian, Mirko.'

'But being Italian makes them feel safe, you're saying?'

'Not necessarily.'

'But Micatovich is a Slavic name!'

'Yes, and my mother's was Matjašić if you want to know.'

'Yet you seem Italian.'

'I work there.'

'You work in Italy.' Mirko slammed his fist and demanded, 'How can Istria be Italian when Istrians don't speak the language?'

'Well, it is – evidently. And Italy is not prepared to grant minorities language rights.'

'But Slavic languages are the majority in Istria.'

'In the hinterland, yes, but down the coast we speak Venetian, although there used to be some Croatian in our churches before Italy occupied us.'

'So you're the voice of reason, are you?'

'No.'

'Yes, you are! You think we should sit back and take it.'

'No! I'm only saying that Italy is very nationalistic and nationalists believe that minorities are a threat.'

'A threat to what?'

'To racial purity. That idea you were talking about.'

Giovanni was too sick and tired to go on. And he had no reserves for comprehending, not then. So he said, 'You're passionate, Mirko, I understand.'

Wrong thing to say. Giovanni registered repugnance in the young eyes before him and then the immediate exclusion of passion, as if Giovanni had soiled it. Mirko became detached and reasoned, an advocate for his cause.

'You understand? Oh, really? And from what position do you understand, exactly? Maturity comes with age, is that what you're saying? You're going to win this argument because you're older than me and what I feel must be an inexperienced appraisal? Or what I'm doing is illegal? And in your eyes any law is important, even a bad law? So are you going to hurl your wise advice at me, Giovanni? "Dictators fall. Good will triumph. What would your mother say?" You, with your nice home and your nice job. I'm happy for you.'

The comfortable lack of distance between them that had fostered their camaraderie had become a gulf Giovanni felt it was impossible to bridge and he realized he had made a second mistake that day. Neither his textbook liturgy nor his generalized compassion translated to an understanding of the effect of the actions of Fascist Italy on a small, unprotected ethnic group. Nor could he suggest to Mirko the likely end of his resistance movement against an enemy with such huge reserves of manpower. What chance did they have? But did he have the right to classify Mirko's decision as youthful folly when confronted by such an oppressor as Mussolini? He recalled the effect of last night's letter on his mother. "*Corretto*." Your name has been corrected. Odd choice of word. Why not use '*cambiato*'? Say 'changed' because changed was what the government had done. Instead they had chosen to write 'corrected' because this philosophy that pouted and intimidated needed to declare its moral superiority. You're wrong, we're right. We have corrected you.

Before him, Mirko shifted his weight, rested his face in his hands. The heat from the boat had sweated half circles under his arms upon the heavy cotton of his shirt and glued it to his back in wet ridges, like sand hills after the rain. Emotion had disconnected his face so that it seemed that he held in his hands not his eyes and his lips but the burden of his race and the anguish in his heart, and for a moment Giovanni forgot how young Mirko was. How unfair of Mussolini to place this burden on the shoulders of youth, who would invariably feel the injustice more intensely because they could see it more clearly. That was the thing with young people, their perception had not yet been compromised.

'You're gentle, Giovanni,' Mirko said.

From down the narrow corridor they heard the captain give a command. Quickly Mirko squashed his cigarette into the floor and rose to leave.

'What did he say?' Giovanni asked.

'He's surfacing. He said "First watch, stand by." I have to go.'

Giovanni put out a hand.

'Mirko?'

'Yes?'

'Why didn't you leave me when you realized I wasn't Banich?'

'Your bad luck. We were just about to when we were observed by a man near the pier and it was far too dangerous to let him recognize that you had been with us.'

'I wonder who it was.'

'An absent sort of guy, heavy, ungainly. Just moping around.'

'Bruno!'

'You know him? Then we were right to take you.'

'No, no, no!' Giovanni shook his head. 'You were not right at all. And poor Bruno is handicapped, although you weren't to know it. Now you could stay here and tell me the whole story.'

'I've already told you what I know.'

'No, you haven't, Mirko. Your captain waits nearly a decade then suddenly ups and responds aggressively to a rumor. He doesn't look like that sort of fool to me.'

'You're right,' said Mirko. 'He's not.'

He vanished.

Giovanni did not watch him go. He was aware that they were moving between worlds. He heard a hiss and felt the boat rise to the surface. In its construction, which had been strained, right spheres were restored. Then came the sudden release of pressure and his ear drums popped. A burst of fresh air and light. Activity. Men were climbing.

He moved into the control room, squeezed himself next to a pipe. He stood and watched, and was ignored, which pleased him. He noticed that the slim circle of light below the conning tower had aged and the day was declining. He was waiting.

Chapter Sixteen

When Silvana arrived home from school that troubled day and the maid left to clean up after Romano's canaries, she found her grandmother on her knees in the warm kitchen, a rosary in her hands and a cup of mint tea grown cold on the table. Next to her waited Gilda, her big brown eyes brimming with canine sympathy. Paulina had prepared the evening meal before leaving, and a fish casserole rested beside the stove.

'Is Zio Lin home?' asked Silvana anxiously.

Maria shook her head, rose heavily to her feet and took Silvana's hand. From the window they stood and watched the colors of the port intensify as the sun declined, the stone turning to gold, the water to dinted bronze. Over the horizon a surging bank of clouds thrust sunbeams into the sky, and above it single nimble tuft seemed about to hurry across the water, as if to whisper to Maria the location of her son.

How to describe the clouds? By desire, by destination, or by the will of man?

'This cloud,' Maria told Silvana, 'is a king in a faraway kingdom. He is returning home from fighting dragons with Saint George. He has brought back the wealth of Arabia and has loved many beautiful women. That gray one is the portal to the underworld, and this one that looks like a church on a hill is for men who go down to the sea in ships.

'But this one over here – yes, that large white one – that is the kingdom of heaven, and if you look carefully you can see an angel in the cloud. He's a very busy angel. He has to hold the gates open for Saint Peter, so he hasn't much time. You must be quick. Do you see him? No, that was just his silk robe fluttering.'

As Silvana looked very closely her grandmother sat up straight all of a sudden, like a cat. 'Oops! You missed him!'

'No, Nona. He's gone because he had a lot of work to do.'

Nona nodded wisely.

'Yes, you're right. He has gone to find Zio Lin.'

It was half past three and the air was filled with the close of the day. The night could not be stopped now, nor its sorrows with it. Above the port, the bright azure sky began to darken and the day drew in to an early winter evening. To the north of the pier, beyond the chapel of Saint Anthony, a single row of tall pines had been left beside the shore. The grass beneath them glowed intensely green and a path wound through them like a fairy tale towards the regular lines of olive trees behind.

'Perhaps he is walking home along the path. Perhaps he is walking home upon the water.'

Maria closed the shutters, sealing off the clouds, the pines, the path and their stories. Immediately the kitchen darkened. She drew out a taper and opened the stove, exposing the warm red interior. From its glowing embers she lit the taper and, with it, a few of the oil lamps in the candelabra to lift the gloom from the room. Silvana watched the oil flicker and the flame grow, shooting the suggestion of light into the shadows, differentiating between the seen and the unseen. Just enough to question the darkness.

From its recess beneath the twin marble basins set in their wooden scullery table, Maria drew out Gilda's bowl and set it on the floor. As Gilda watched with hungry eyes, the squeak of the door into the lane distracted her. She heard a trip up the steps, and the unmistakable stumbling entry of Zan – Zan stooping to fold himself into his chair under the table, spying his tobacco pouch and reaching for it eagerly. Silvana saw her grandmother raise her eyes hopefully when she realized that there were other steps behind him, only to register disappointment upon seeing that it was not her son. She glanced instead at her son-in-law with aching eyes.

'Hello, Romano. It's kind of you to come.'

Silvana's father always entered a room as if he meant to be there for her. They shared the identical brown curls, the same practical observation, and one day they would even be the same height. Immediately he sent her that fond, proud look she loved.

'How's my girl?'

'Good, Popà.'

'No sign of Zio Lin?' he asked her.

'No.'

Romano addressed Maria. 'We spoke to the constable on our way over. He doesn't believe that letter Zan received any more than I do. He asked the usual questions: Who could have anything against Giovanni? Against us? And so forth. We don't see crime like this here: implausible crime, threats, ransom demands. What he suggests is that we go out with Zan at the time specified, but he doubts anyone will turn up. Not even Signor Brazzi.'

'But where is Giovanni?'

'In the monster!' insisted Silvana.

'Monster, Silvana?' demanded her father, turning his surveyor's eye keenly upon his daughter. 'You're not such a silly girl as to say things like that.'

'The monster was something I *saw*, Popà. Something black in the water.'

'Moving?'

'From the breakwater to the pier.'

'Fast or slow?'

'Slow.'

'Was it a boat?'

'I couldn't see a deck.'

'Why did you call it a monster?'

'Because it had a big head sticking up.'

'And you're sure about the deck?'

'I think water was on it.'

'So it was sinking?'

'No, it wasn't.'

Many an eight-year-old would have quailed under Romano's logical bombardment, but Silvana loved speaking this way with her father and only grew more confident as she waited expectantly for the next question.

'The port is too dark to see so much, Silvana.'

'Yes, Popà. I only saw the head as it passed the lighthouse.'

'And when it crossed to the pier?'

'Only the white bit out the back.'

'The wake?'

'I think so.'

'Was it a submarine?'

'Yes, Popà. It might have been.'

'Ahh…' Maria put her hand to her mouth and Romano smiled at his daughter.

'That's my girl!'

'When have you ever seen a submarine, Silvana?' demanded her grandmother.

'In the newspaper, Nona,' replied Silvana precisely.

'Nono doesn't buy the newspaper.'

'It was at the markets.'

'Well, I never!'

'And I would have told you it was a submarine last night but it was too dark to see it properly.'

His Most Italian City

'Do you know,' – Zan, having lit his cigarette had commenced his methodical process of calming down – 'I told Signor Brazzi about Silvana's monster this morning. He looked upset – or was I imagining it?'

'Doesn't seem so now,' answered Romano.

'I wouldn't have expected him to look so upset, that was all.'

'He knows what's going on, that's why.' He headed for the door. 'Ransom demands! That man would exploit his own mother for profit. You try and get some rest. I'll be back with Dolores about eight.'

They ate early so that Maria could lie down, but the fish casserole was the latest disaster of that day. It had too many bones, an indication of Paulina's distress or perhaps her excitement. Five o'clock found them carefully picking their way up the fish spine when an affronted bark aroused them to the knowledge that Gilda had not yet been fed.

'I was distracted,' groaned Maria.

'I forgot,' said Zan.

So Silvana waited until her grandmother's back was turned and gave Gilda the casserole dish. Gilda finished it off and got a bone caught in her throat.

'Would you like some more, Zan?' asked Maria, who had been too tired to notice.

Zan surveyed the empty dish on the floor without concern.

'It's all gone,' he said. He fed the gagging dog a piece of bread. Gilda wagged her tail.

'I fed her,' said Silvana.

'Why did you give her that fish?' demanded Maria.

'You hadn't fed her.'

'The bones will get caught in her throat.'

'They did get caught, Nona.'

So Maria gave Gilda another piece of bread. Gilda wagged her tail.

'I gave her bread already,' explained Zan.

'You shouldn't have given the dog our dinner, Silvana.'

'No one else was eating it.'

Zan said, 'Look at poor Gilda. She's still hungry.' Gilda wagged her tail. 'Put the bones in the compost and let Gilda lick the plates.'

'*I'll* wash the plates,' frowned Maria, rising. 'Silvana, get a tea towel.'

'Mamalina says the kitchen sink is not our place,' replied Silvana.

'Your mother's not here now.'

So Silvana got a tea towel.

Later, when Maria had retired to close her eyes and pretend to sleep, Silvana and Zan sat alone in the kitchen by the warmth of the stove. As Zan slowly smoked, his pouch of tobacco diminished until it grew as thin as the block of chocolate Romano had once brought Silvana from Trieste. For a long while he didn't speak and Silvana, who had not been privy to events, sensed hidden feelings in the darkness that swirled around the old house and crippled the usual repartee between them.

At length Zan lit a further cigarette and said, 'Politics is a dirty game, Silvana. But don't tell Nona I said that. She's more polite than I am.'

'It's not rude to say "dirty", Nono.'

'No, of course not, darling.'

He patted his knee. 'When you were very small I would bounce you on my knee and you would say, "I want a cuddle without arms."' He coughed apologetically. 'But I had to cuddle you or you would have fallen off.'

'I still don't like cuddles with arms, Nono.'

'Well, you always were a practical little girl. Now, listen carefully because I'm going to tell you something important. Our name, Micatovich, means "son of Michael." It's the name of an island a long way down the coast of Dalmatia. Or perhaps it was a town.'

'Which was it, an island or a town?'

'I don't know because I was only your age when my grandfather told me, and when I looked for the island on the map I couldn't find it, but that's what I was told. There is a synagogue at Dubrovnik, in that area, so I have often wondered if our name was Jewish. You see, the priest told me that Micah and Michael mean 'who is like God' in Hebrew. Jews weren't allowed to own land a long time ago and I thought that, when the family came to Istria, they might have disguised it as Micatovich so that they could buy land. At that time Venice permitted people from their southern territories to move north to the coast of Istria to repopulate these towns which had been almost wiped out by the plague. And we've been here ever since; that was well over three hundred years ago.

'Now, Zio Lin and I are both Giovanni but, when he was small, he was often called Zvane, which is a local name for the same thing. He went off to Graz in Austria to study biology but, you see, he was born here in Istria and, almost as soon as he finished, Istria became Italian and the Italians won't recognize his Austrian qualifications. So, although he can teach at their university he can't be promoted any higher and he can't work there under the name Micatovich because it sounds Slavic. And Mussolini doesn't like that. So Zvane Micatovich has become Giovanni Di Micheli.'

'And where is he?'

'I don't know. We must try to find your submarine.'

Chapter Seventeen

Trieste, July 1920

During his years at sea Stefan had seen a lot of ports and, although not naturally romantic, apart from his love of the sea, he fondly believed that his home port was the best and busiest in the world. Trieste was either busy in the sheer number of vessels, the variety of those vessels or the crowds of people that sailed on them. The Piazza Unità, flanked by solid cliffs of ornate Austrian architecture, directly faced the port, and ships of all kinds lay open to the busy eyes of the merchants, the ponderous gaze of the government and the bright vision of its citizens, who knew wherein the wealth of their town lay. On any given day a customs official, a titled lady, a businessman, a shopkeeper or a seaman could pause in the piazza and count fishing boats, water taxis, coastal steamers, cargo ships, naval vessels, tugs, pilot boats, coastguard cutters, schooners, dredgers, row boats and dinghies, all packed, loaded and ready for business. He loved it.

After the sultry clouds of the previous days, Trieste, even in the rosy pre-dawn, promised a perfect summer day to come. Already nudging five o'clock, the last of the night was hastening away in the west, the sky was clear, and the stars faded as the first sunbeam launched itself above the hills behind the town. With the briny morning breeze ruffling his hair and the cries of the seagulls in his ears, Stefan strode briskly past Central Station and along the connecting Corso to the harbor. An early steam train chugged along the quay, and he passed behind its wagons and sprang across the tracks, continuing along the paved shoreline and onto the broad Audace Pier.

There he found Zorko, big, dark and unhappy. By the dejected angle of his shoulders and the bulging rucksack he had flung onto the pavement like a compost heap, Stefan could tell he was already worrying about what might be in store for him.

'You took your time.'

'It won't go without me.' And with that confident joke, he exchanged such an air of jubilance for Zorko's gloom that Zorko could have sworn they were off on a boys-own adventure. 'Did you get the tickets?'

They both rummaged around in their pockets for tickets and wallets.

'Blood brothers!' said Stefan, slamming his money into Zorko's fist.

'Whatever it takes,' replied Zorko, handing over a ticket. 'I hope.'

Two large steamers waited on the south side of the pier. They headed towards the second one, slowly puffing out black fumes. Below, in the shadows, the water lapped the vessel's hull and at the gangway stood a sleepy seaman. Though it was so early, the boat was full to overflowing with excited passengers caught up in the anticipation of departure. Children waved, ladies clutched small hands and broad-brimmed hats, men stood soberly by. The scent of coffee hung in the air.

The pier itself smelled of diesel and coal smoke, of salt and sweat and fish, and above it all the heady mixture of fresh air and foul that marks the beginning of a sea voyage. Stefan pushed eagerly through the mass of people on the deck with Zorko grunting behind him, as far forward as they could go, and leaned over the bow rail until he could see the anchors hanging down like nostrils. Almost immediately the steamer gave a blast from its siren, accompanied by an ear-splitting hiss of steam, reversed from the pier and swung its bow to starboard.

Stefan leaned right over as the steamer picked up speed, watching the bow cut the green water.

'This is the best bit,' he said. 'I like this bit.'

'Yeah, so do your kids.'

Once out of the harbor, the steamer would hug the coast for most of its five hundred-kilometer trip to Split, which was as far as this one went. It called first at Parenzo then their destination of Pola on the Istrian south coast, where it would spend the night. On the second day there would be a further stop at Dalmatian Zara and another night at Sebenico. Not until the morning of the third day would the steamer arrive at Split.

By the time the first afternoon was on the wane, the weary vessel had reached the entrance to Pola Harbor and commenced the five-kilometer journey to the docks along the winding shoreline. The magnificent Roman amphitheater that dominated the town and its vast harbor was so large that it could be seen from out at sea. As sunset approached, the coarse white marble of its construction began to assume that mellowed agelessness of ancient buildings that have counted so many centuries that time itself becomes a variable in their equations.

The bridge to the Katarina Naval Base and dockyards neatly divided the commercial and military ports. Its base rose up towards the Austrian fortress, and the amphitheater looked out onto the commercial port. Of the eight Austro-Hungarian submarines, four had already been dismantled and sold for scrap. The remaining four small coastal boats lay moored side by side along the shore to the south of the bridge, and Stefan thought that if ever human sentiments could be transposed onto inanimate objects it was now. Abandoned to their fate, rusty and awaiting execution, bobbed a U-1 and a U-2, both American-designed and built here at Pola, along with a U-21, a Danish boat, and at the end a U-27, which had been designed by the Germans.

'That's our one,' he said.

'Why that one?'

'Because it's at the end.'

'I remember the U-27.'

His Most Italian City

'A great submarine. She'll do.'

Stefan was friends with the Italian harbor master, whom Zorko remembered from the docks of Trieste in its Austrian days, those happy times when the sea united them and flags failed to divide. A burly fellow, he looked like an archetypical seaman. Hair sprouted everywhere except his head and his hat hovered over it like a seagull. Its brim shaded the fine spray of veins on his nose and he wore multiple chins with the ease of long acquaintance.

Zorko watched Stefan enter a small office on the shore of the commercial port and when, an hour and twenty minutes later, he emerged – more than a little tipsy and with a satisfied smile on his face – he came back to Zorko, who was waiting hungrily on the quay. When Zorko begged for an explanation, Stefan said that would have to wait.

Zorko was somewhat peeved and justifiably sulked, for had he not given up a week of his time on this mad pursuit?

'Very well, then,' said Stefan, 'the military states that the sentence for theft of their property, of wrongful appropriation or larceny, causing the capture or disruption of a service ship and providing the enemy – that's us – with material assistance, if it can be proven that the property belonged to the person or business…'

'You're drunk.'

'And I haven't even stolen it yet!'

'All right,' demanded Zorko, 'what did he say?'

'Not a lot after all he'd consumed.'

But Zorko's stomach was rumbling audibly by now and, in response to the internal clamor, Stefan added, 'He said to come back when the boat's operational.'

'So can we eat now?'

They trudged off and ate in a *ristorante* in the winding back street of the Old Town, then, across the paving stones, found two beds in a cheap *pensione* – which smelled like the spaghetti they'd just eaten – and slept the sleep of the saved.

*****

Nature, on the whole, had not intended Zorko to be a submariner. His father swore he had been conceived on the wrong side of the blanket for he had the head of a Gypsy violinist his father had once seen perform in Budapest, as round as the moon. Too tall, too fat, impatient in word and deed, he also had a troubling tendency to acquire jock itch from the humid conditions inside submarines and had scratched holes in both sides of his fly. His wife, who might have cured him of this condition, had left him years ago for an accountant, but he had such an intuitive feel for boats that over his years in the navy his repair success rate had acquired a mystical quality. Captains often asked him what was wrong with their vessels because, although Zorko was a mechanic, not an engineer, he was an expert diagnostician and could fix anything from a four-stroke engine to electrical wiring, to valves and plumbing. He was a living, breathing mechanical barometer. People said he could smell trouble.

In theory he foresaw no complications in simply steering a thirty-seven-meter boat with two diesel engines out of a harbor. They could easily accomplish that. Although they couldn't dive, because that would require the batteries to be charged, and the extra men they didn't have, and sufficient depth of ocean and compressed air to surface… and… and – he was going to stop right now before he talked himself out of this – there were still plenty of things that could go wrong.

The rudder might be jammed, the propellers could be out of alignment. Diesel was a good lubricating fuel for marine engines and it didn't produce explosive vapors. A diesel engine would potter along contentedly under most of life's tribulations, but when had this one last been used and how corroded had the parts of the engine become in the meantime? And speaking of diesel, said Zorko to himself, where were they going to find enough to get them as far as Split, a day and a half away? Then, in what condition were the batteries? Had they leaked sulfuric acid? With such a leak and the presence of salt water there was a real risk of chlorine gas forming in the submarine, and everyone who had been in a trench during the war knew what that did.

Then, how watertight was the boat? Because submarines sat so low in the water, they easily became swamped. As well, they possessed a number of features passing through the pressure hull that could potentially lead to flooding and sinking: the torpedo tubes, the fore and aft hatches, the propeller shafts and the conning tower hatch, the periscope fittings, open valves that should have been closed, flanges passing through the outer casing, and the main air induction vents that supplied oxygen to the diesel engines. The bilges might already be flooded with water, and were the pumps operating? Even the primitive toilet, when it worked, could potentially flood the boat. There was so much potential for disaster that no one in his right mind would do it.

Zorko considered the electrical engine room and the chances of a fire in the circuitry from a salt-water leak. Maybe they would be safer if he disconnected the batteries? But without electricity the compass wouldn't work. A magnetic compass couldn't be used within the iron pressure hull so submarines were fitted with a gyro compass instead, in the control room below the tower. Well, he expected they knew this coast well enough to steer by dead reckoning.

For two days he had sat with Stefan atop an ancient box tomb in a park watching through binoculars the comings and goings of the port, separated from the four submarines by a cast iron fence and a road. To the right along the fence a gate permitted entry to the shore. Ferries, tugs and cargo ships went in and out from the commercial docks like clockwork, but the military side of the harbor that had seen so much activity during the war seemed melancholy by comparison.

By the commencement of the second afternoon, as the midday sun baked the town and gobbled up the remaining shade, he was still sitting

there, so engrossed by the tempting blue water that it was all he could do
not to throw himself in fully clothed. Along the road an ice cream vendor
plied his wares in a striped shirt and boater: a small cart, mothers in
straight white dresses, children at their skirts, a volley of hats. Zorko
watched Stefan stare single-mindedly at the end submarine while the
dripping sweat blurred his vision and he was tormented by the scent of
vanilla.

'If you stare at that thing much longer it's going to leave without you.'

'Better that than being scrapped,' Stefan returned.

His unrestrained fringe resting in a brindled block over his eyes lent
him the look of a far-sighted eagle. Since marriage he had worn it longer,
according to fashion, but not even Nataša could get him to oil it back like
other men. Zorko knew, by his fixed gaze, that Stefan was recreating,
centimeter by centimeter, the interior of the vessel he intended to steal
and, by so doing, was reliving every mission he had fought, every dive,
every attack he had survived, every enemy vessel he had sent to the
bottom.

'What did you sink?'

'One British warship and a Japanese destroyer. Eight merchant vessels:
four Greek, three Italian and one French.'

'Do you want an ice cream?'

Stefan raised his eyes from his obsession and frowned mutely at
Zorko.

'I'm hot,' the mechanic explained.

So finally Stefan stood up, crossed his arms and said, 'No one's gone
near it.'

But he didn't say anything else, particularly the question Zorko had
been most anxious to ask: Have you thought this through? Because by this
stage, hungry and on the boil, Zorko had thought himself out of any
heroics.

He jerked a hand up and down the back of his neck.

'Yeah, so what?' he muttered.

But he visited the ice cream vendor and had a swim and finally, on the third night after their arrival, they crept down to the quay.

They found the entry gate padlocked, so Stefan gave Zorko a leg up over the spiked iron fence and jumped over after him, and then they clambered across the decks of the first three boats until they reached the last one. The broad harbor waited expectantly. Not a breeze ruffled its surface. To the west lay the winding exit to the sea, to the east rose the serene crescent of a new moon. On the shore in between, the ancient amphitheater reared upwards into an ocean of stars.

The small submarine floated gently, its deck flat and unremarkable. Equidistant between the bow and the stern the conning tower loomed like a dark shed over a meter high. Above it a horse-shoe-shaped barrier formed the bridge. The head of the periscope rose about another meter further above and on the bridge itself was situated the first of the three steering positions.

Stefan climbed up and over the railing, knelt behind the bridge and made a few investigative tugs of the wheel that opened the top hatch into the tower.

'Hoy!'

'What?'

'Hold it!' urged Zorko. 'You don't know what's been going on down there. Look away while I raise it.'

He dumped his rucksack on the deck, climbed up and with some difficulty ground the stiff wheel anticlockwise, easing it with a creak of hinges until it opened to reveal a hole, impenetrably black and smelling of cold dank iron.

'That's one down.'

Stefan lowered himself inside and felt the first rungs of the ladder. Zorko lit the hurricane lamp under cover of the bridge and handed it down to him, then descended himself until he was standing around the lower hatch that passed through the pressure hull. Here he cast around him with closed eyes, then squatted down and cautiously laid his ear on the hatch, then one squat palm, and ran a finger around the seam.

'This one's going to blow.' He gestured impatiently. 'Turn around and hang onto the ladder. Better still, get right out.'

Unwilling to miss the excitement, Stefan stepped into the tower helm and turned around as Zorko struggled with the second wheel. Finally they heard a low jeer like the displeasure of an audience and, without further warning, the entire hatch blew open in a crescendo of putrid air, an eruption roaring up from below with the sound of an express train approaching in a tunnel. The gale of pressurized air caught Stefan up the back of his legs and lifted him off his feet, tore his shirt from his trousers and wrapped it around his head, along with two pages of newsprint. Accompanying the blast was a cloud of fungal spores, several withered rodents, an oily rag and a boot that shot up and splashed into the water. Spray sprinkled the hull and the lamp blew out. The hatch rocked back on its hinges and slammed shut.

Zorko yanked it open. He re-lit the lamp and passed it across, but already Stefan was lowering himself into the control room.

'Are you coming?'

Convinced he would regret this, Zorko retrieved his rucksack and squeezed his belly into the hull. He bumped down the few rungs of ladder and toppled onto Stefan, who was already standing on the floor plates and squinting into the gloom. A dense fog, yellowy-white and foul, had formed between the dank walls. Because it had been created by the release of pressure, it did not swarm like a wind-driven cloud but sat dead upon the floor. Shrouded in its motionless embrace, the iron room seemed as still as a mortuary, save for the water gently rocking the hull.

'I hate it when it does this,' moaned Zorko. 'I can't see a thing!'

But beside him, Stefan's eyes shone bright with adventure.

'It's been waiting for us.'

His Most Italian City

The warm outside air stayed up and the cold air waited below, and gradually a draft formed, uniting the two, twisting at the fog until it shivered and began to disperse. Zorko waded through it and emerged facing the forest of wheeled valve handles. He flicked a switch and to their amazement the single electric lamp shone brightly above their heads.

'There's still some charge in the batteries!' Zorko tapped the fuel gauge, watching it tremble briefly before returning to rest. 'Fuel zero, naturally. What are we going to do?'

'There's a whole harbor out there full of diesel. We'll think of something.'

They switched the light off and returned to the struggling lamp, then squeezed through a gaping bulkhead and into the diesel engine room. Zorko planted a brawny hand above the hatch, wallowing up to his thighs in stinking fog as the pistons of the port and starboard engines, each with four cylinders, rose nearly to the ceiling along both sides of the small room. They reflected the glow of the lamp and withdrew back and forth into the fog like disembodied spirits.

Zorko hit his head on a bank of gauges and swore. He stepped along the aisle separating the engines, imagining only with difficulty the proud history of this boat, the most successful of all the empire's submarines, now so derelict that she might have been an artifact in a museum nobody visited. He regarded the warning lights, the motionless dials for pressure and temperature set on the walls, the pumps, clutches and compressors, the daunting complexity of her design; so much squeezed so precisely into the tiny room, like a doll's house designed by an engineer. But the smells of diesel and lubricating oil that he would have expected were overlaid instead with the citrus tang of salted rust. He ran his fingers down one cylinder and raised them smeared with rancid oil and droplets of condensation.

His face smoldered in the dappled lamplight.

'These haven't been used for a while.'

From his rucksack he extracted a crow bar a meter long and shoved it between the teeth of the flywheel of the port engine. When there was no response he leaned back and, hitching both hands together, thrust down again. A hog-like grunt. Still nothing. He repeated the attempt with its starboard companion. The pistons ground reluctantly up and down.

'That port engine.' He tightened a nut holding down a piston head. 'Perhaps water in the cylinders? Can't compress water. Need to replace the heads. Take the caps off. Oil the cylinders. See that?' He scraped a thick layer of salt encrusting the cylinders and along the crankshaft. 'Got to get rid of that.'

'But will they work?'

Zorko tickled his bristles. 'Not very complicated, a diesel engine. Yeah, they'll work, but for how long? Bit worried about that port one. White metal gone to the bottom of the camshaft? What do you think? Should we disassemble the bearings? That's a lot of work. Then you've got to grease all the moveable parts. Pumps, propellers, hydroplanes.'

'We're not using the hydroplanes.'

'Though you could dive at the entrance. Thirty meters?'

'Thirty-five. We won't have to, though.'

'How will you get her out of the harbor if you don't dive?'

'Talk to my friend the harbor master.'

'Why is he your friend?'

Stefan tapped the ceiling.

'He owes me one. You remember those three Italian merchant vessels I sunk? Well, one of them was his and I didn't sink it. He was a collier and, when we inspected his cargo, he was carrying food as well, so I let him go.' A rueful memory inflated his cheeks. 'Luka and Evie had the measles.'

'Agh!' spat Zorko. 'You're getting soft.'

'Not soft.'

'Not soft, just married.'

His Most Italian City

'Married eight years!'

'And Nataša let you come? What did you tell her?'

'I told her the truth.'

'If you've been reduced to that, there's no hope for you. So are you friends with anyone else? Because we need another two men to sail her to Split.'

'I don't have another two men. You worry too much, Zorko.'

'Your problem, Commander Pirjevec, is that you don't worry at all.'

'No, I am worried,' he admitted. 'About Trieste. I've decided: when I get back we're leaving.'

*****

In the end, Zorko had only to disassemble three pistons in the port engine and give the remaining pistons a thorough oiling until the crowbar could move them smoothly. While they worked, Stefan counted the nights he had been away. Two, plus one to get in and a final two to get her operational. One night to escape and another to reach the port of Split in Dalmatia, where he hoped to get support to sail her to the fleet base in the Bay of Kotor. Seven nights and two more to get back. More than he had told Nataša.

But as dawn broke over the harbor on the last day they found themselves with little left to do except grease the wheel and the rudder, and nothing to think about except the crime itself. Early in the afternoon they caught sight of the bunker barge. It was just finishing the refueling of a naval vessel close to the commercial port and would soon commence on a tug moored within hailing distance of the small line of submarines.

Stefan pushed himself off the tomb.

'Where are you going?' demanded Zorco.

'There's our fuel.'

Zorko's mouth went slack.

'You're not actually going to ask them? They won't know you're a commander. If you wore your hat you might at least look like one!'

'Attitude, Zorko,' he reprimanded.

Brushing down his shirt and assuming his best official countenance, he strode across the road and through the open gate as if he owned it, then approached the long flat vessel moored beside the tug. Two men were arranging long rubber tubes from the barge.

'*Senta!*' he shouted in Italian and, when one of them looked up, he called him over. '*Vieni qua!* Are we next?'

The larger man, a tanned colossus, waved irritably at Stefan then took his time investigating the hail. Eventually he stomped across and leaned from the stern of the barge, eyeballing Stefan uncertainly, not at all sure how the brisk man on the quay with the direct gaze ought to be addressed.

'Haven't seen you here before,' he replied carefully.

'No, I'm long gone,' confessed Stefan truthfully, acknowledging the man with the briefest of military salutes.

Hastily assuming culpability for tiredness and hot weather, the man corrected his wilting demeanor, returned the salute and enquired respectfully, 'Which one is it, sir?'

'The U-27 at the end.'

'The submarine?' The colossus took in the boat's simple lines – the short length, the small conning tower and bridge, the rusted steel casing that looked like it had seen better days, the empty deck gun turret – and the lines on his face became thoughtful. 'What's that old thing being used for?'

'Training drills.'

'Really?' He sparked one eye. 'You know, I've always wanted to have a look inside one of those.'

Stefan extended a convivial arm.

'Welcome aboard.'

The giant shook his head. 'Nah, don't like being shut in. Such a shame.' And as Zorko, who had tiptoed down, waited in horrified fascination, he added, 'Perhaps I could just poke my head in. No harm in that.'

'Good man!' said Stefan. 'Bring your barge around. You can fill her up at the same time.'

He waited as the barge turned a slow circle from the tug and attached a mooring line to the stern of the submarine. Then he stepped off the quay onto the first boat and jumped across the three intervening boats to join it. The men had already unrolled the length of hose that had serviced the tug. They threw the hose attached to a weighted rope across to Stefan who reeled it in and secured its end to an outboard valve. Once the tanks on the side of the hull were sucking in the fuel, Stefan opened the heavy iron hatch on top of the conning tower. Cold wet air wafted slowly skywards. The bunker man stepped across onto the deck and peered doubtfully into the abyss.

'You've got rats in there,' he said, wrinkling his nose. 'More than one. Boy rat, girl rat, a lot of lonely nights...' He straightened up. 'Thank you, sir, but no. No rats. I think I'll leave the submarine to you.'

The refueling took an hour. As the afternoon shadows lengthened and the burning sun lost some of its heat, Stefan paid a second visit to the harbor master.

'He's going to let us go,' he explained to Zorko on his return. 'But there's got to be a song and a dance first to impress the locals. Naturally.'

The sun set late on those summer evenings and something of twilight still painted the ripples in the harbor with amber as they cut the mooring ropes and separated the small submarine from the other three by pushing it off with a barge pole. It took some minutes of strenuous heaving, sometimes shoving with their feet, to dislodge thirty-odd meters of steel but, once they had established some momentum, the bow slid out from the vessel beside it and they could get to work on the stern.

When it was free, Zorko lowered his girth through the tower hatch, climbed down the ladder and made his way across the control room to the engine room. Stefan crouched at the wheel on the bridge with an ear cocked for any noise from below, scarcely breathing, listening for the first characteristic knock that indicated the operation of the diesel engines. Now he felt impatient and he held his jaw, biting his lip until he heard the explosion of one piston, then two, the rest joining in. The tower began to tremble. The first wake emerged from the propellers and he caught the whiff of exhaust. Without giving the engines time to warm up and with no consideration for their possible performance, he swung the helm to starboard and pointed it straight towards the main channel. He knew that once the pistons had established their strokes they could go from Pola to Athens and back, but at first he waited and listened as the boat surged and halted, heaved hopefully, paused again, knocked and shuddered. But the further they went the more robust the engines were sounding. Behind them, the quay looked deserted but the noise created by two diesel engines so late at night could not be easily ignored, and he was certain that behind curtained windows curious eyes observed them.

At the end of the bridge, two fishermen looked up. Stefan waved at them; they waved back. A clever fish jumped above the water and splashed back just beyond their lines and, while the fishermen waited for it to reappear, the submarine had already passed.

Before him, the tide was receding in rows of ripples as tight as ringlets. The bow drew them aside, ploughing through the dark water. Then the breeze hardened their edges and the submarine began to bump across them – liberating little knocks on the keel – and the wake washed a long triangle behind, black in the middle, white at the hypotenuses. Stefan sensed that the boat was glad to be seaborne. He experienced a surge of admiration for Zorko's skill and a happiness that, like the boat, he had not felt for a long time. The clunks from the engine room increased in frequency. Zorko was coaxing more speed from the diesels. The bow picked up the extra velocity and, like a knife, divided the waves, while above the brooding banks the moonless night was only vaguely brighter.

His Most Italian City

They had just reached the point past the Islet of Andrea in the center of the harbor where they could see their way out of the twisting foreshores to the sea when he heard the sound of another engine behind them. He swung around and caught sight of a jagged white beam; an Italian motorboat was approaching from around the northern channel, closing rapidly. The powerful boat roared through the night and created a considerable wash that splashed black against the wooded shore of the island, disturbing a cluster of evening gulls that soared shrieking into the air. At the wheel stood the harbor master and, with him, a man in uniform behind a machine gun pointed straight at them. A third man held a signal lamp trained on the bridge.

Hearing the pursuit, Zorko's huge head protruded through the conning tower. When he saw the motorboat the blood drained from his face.

'They're going to shoot us!'

'No, they're not.'

The words had scarcely left his mouth when the gun fired a round of shots over their bow.

'I told you.'

'Keep going!'

The islet behind them, they turned northwest amid a further round of fire. The motorboat then executed a complete circle around them, creating so much wash that the submarine rocked violently on its keel, pitching headlong into the trough as the water was displaced. Stefan was hit by a wave of surf that completely drenched him, shooting salt water up his nose and into his eyes. The water drained away from the conning tower until the deck was visible and the reflection of the signal lamp zigzagged crazily around it. Then, in a final cadenza, the officer fired straight up into the air, the boat leaned heavily into the turn back around the islet and spun away into the night.

Stefan waved broadly at the retreating silhouette.

'*Brava, Regia Marina!* A pleasure doing business with you!'

He must remember to properly thank his well-fed friend.

The evening settled around them. With the ease of their escape, he sank effortlessly into its calm velvet. In a further five minutes, he estimated, they would be out into the swell of the Adriatic and turning south down the coast. Already the heavier, rolling waves announced the approach to the harbor entrance and, as if to greet the sea, the bow heaved up and the stern relaxed into the trough. Some further nimble pitches tossed them lightly up and down, then, before his eyes, the mouth of the harbor expanded. Even the stars seemed to shine more brightly and the breeze off the water welcomed him. He had room to breathe and hope in his heart.

It was then that he heard the return of the motorboat and, in the pounding of its engines, a note of anger that hadn't been there before. And was it his imagination or had the trio swapped places? Was the man who had been behind the gun now at the wheel? With a wild roar, the boat completed a circuit of the island and once more decreased the distance between them, heading straight for the small submarine. Just as Stefan thought they would be rammed, the motorboat twisted hard to port, creating another wave that fell upon the submarine like surf and drenched him a second time upon the exposed bridge.

A waterfall cascaded into the tower, drowning Zorko, who had retreated inside when he thought he had the all clear.

'What's happening?' he yelled.

'They're trying to sink us! Hold her steady, we're nearly out.'

Within the shelter of the harbor, the submarine produced enough wash to upset a smaller boat but, once out into a rough sea, its stability was threatened by its own design. Despite the heavy keel, the ballast tanks squashed like saddle bags onto either side of the circular hull virtually guaranteed the submarine would roll in anything but a dead calm, and the furious naval officer chasing them clearly knew it.

His Most Italian City

But by now the black banks had fallen away and there was nothing before them but the horizon. Stefan looked around and saw the motorboat perform a figure eight as tightly as possible and surge back for a third swipe. The officer drove far over to starboard, coming as close to the submarine as he could. Stefan dragged the wheel hard to angle the boat into the anticipated wave, and received a face full of exhaust. A third huge breaker cascaded over the deck, which completely disappeared in the swell. They veered violently over its crest while once again the sea poured through the open hatch, filling the bilges and splashing about inside the dim ironwork.

Stefan leapt from the wheel and into the tower.

'I'm coming down!'

He tumbled urgently from the ladder and with a sinking heart Zorko watched him yank the engine clutch, disconnecting the diesel engines and allowing the electric motors to take over.

'Secure the hatches.' He hauled the wide handwheel operating one hydroplane to an angle of thirty degrees. 'And give me a hand!'

White with disbelief, Zorko nevertheless knew better than to argue. He fought with the second wheel then dragged himself into the conning tower, securing first the top hatch, then closing the main induction vent and next the hatch into the pressure hull. By the time he thudded down again onto the floor plates Stefan had opened the valves below the main ballast tanks and the air vents above them, and from below he heard torrents of water forcing the air out. It screamed up into the sky.

'Flood the forward tanks!'

Realizing the impossibility of their position, Zorko thought, 'I will go with the death I have some control over.' Winding, winding, winding…

The bow grew heavy and tilted forward. And after that, there was no time to think.

He climbed through the bulkhead into the tiny cramped corridor housing the diesel engines, stumbling robotically on into the electrical control room, hoping that the motors would perform as they should and at the same time frightened that they would overheat, or, worse, that the batteries would run out of charge and their attempted escape would end in a very dismal fashion. From both sides of the hull he heard water thundering into the tanks and felt the bow slip from under his feet. The boat reacted almost in surprise; it groaned, creaked and quaked in protest. Then familiar sensations reasserted themselves: the cascading flood, the push of the planes through the sea, forcing the boat down. In less than half a minute the conning tower and the retracted head of the periscope dipped below the surface just as Zorko heard the engines of the motorboat grind above their heads, venting their anger at the stars.

The boat went quickly down and too soon afterwards there came a glancing blow from the bow, vibrating up the hull towards them. They were flung forward then back against the front of the control room as the submarine veered up at a diminishing angle to the perpendicular and broke the surface like a dolphin. As if briefly uncertain, it floated upon the lapping waves, then, bow heavy, plunged once more to the bottom.

Stefan heaved his tangle of traumatized limbs from the wedge of wall and floor, staggered upwards, struggling to flood the aft tanks from the wheel at the back of the control room that now looked more like a slope than a wall. He had underestimated the effort required to reverse the heavy hydroplanes under these conditions and he wasted time pushing his weight into the wheel as their altering angle complicated the adjustment. Zorko had struggled from the engine room and was grunting at the other wheel, ramming his knee into the spokes. As they surfaced a second time, the propellers rose out of the water. Instead of working with the planes to force the boat down, they flailed impotently in the air until hauled back below. Then came grating shrieks from the hull as they skidded over rocks upon the silt, until finally they established an uneasy peace, bumping along the seabed.

Zorko thumped himself on the sternum and coughed his lungs out.

His Most Italian City

'Your angle was too steep,' he croaked.

'Error of judgment. I thought we were deeper.'

The impromptu dive had sprayed a barrage of bubbles on the surface and they heard the Italian patrol prowling back and forth through it, reaching a crescendo before fading away into the distance. As soon as it appeared that they were not returning, Stefan increased the upward angle of the hydroplanes as well as their modest speed, and they steered the submersible to the surface. When finally they raised the hatch into the clean night air, there was nothing to be seen but sea. The motorboat, having asserted its rights, had headed back to port. The exhaust from the diesel engines once again operating below them gradually expelled the last of the water from the tanks and there were no emotions left to feel except relief.

Zorko wiped a liter of sweat from his brow and it was on his lips to express the wish that Stefan never do that again, but the serenity of the night fell sweetly upon him and he let the heated words go.

Chapter Eighteen

They arrived in Split on July 13th 1920. It had taken thirty hours to sail there on the diesel engines alone and they had almost made it when the port engine overheated and had to be shut down. Maneuvering on the single shaft and starboard propeller was not the type of challenge they needed when they were both sleep-deprived, and, when finally they limped into Split at dawn on the second morning, they were too exhausted to do anything but melt into unconsciousness in the greasy old bunks of the boat, littered with mold and rat droppings. Four hours later they awoke to a hammer pounding on the hull and emerged bleary-eyed through the conning tower to find an irate harbor master, demanding to know what the hell they thought they were doing docking in Split. Hadn't they noticed the Italian warship in his harbor? hissed the man. A stolen Italian submarine was all he needed.

And if Stefan thought the damage caused by nationalism was confined only to Trieste, he was sadly mistaken. He shook his head at the battered Italian storefronts, the torn Yugoslav flags, the inhabitants warily eyeing him and Zorko. None of these towns was new. Split had been a notable settlement on this coast for two millennia, and the Emperor Diocletian, who achieved fame amongst Roman emperors by dying a natural death, had left his legacy in the huge Roman palace behind whose walls a portion of the old town was built. The stone was stark now, stripped of its glory and protective, as if it did not want to lose any more. It was clear to Stefan that modern Split was going the same way. He found it difficult to comprehend that these people of different races who had been neighbors for centuries could be so undone by the racial hatred whipped up in a fraction of that time.

When Stefan asked what was the cause of the present unrest the universal answer was, 'We're next.'

This referred to their fear that Italian irregular forces backed up by the military would behave as they had in Rijeka, at the base of Istria. Only last year, the Allied troops who occupied the town had stood back and allowed the decadent poet Gabriele D'Annunzio and his followers to walk in, fuelled by cocaine and alcohol, shouting 'death to all Croats.' Heading south, a similar thing had been tried in the Dalmatian towns of Zara and Trogir. Split looked likely to be next and the men and women were frightened.

Split had an Italian minority in the same way that Trieste had a Slovenian minority, but Italy claimed that any town or region that included an Italian- or Venetian-speaking population was unredeemed Italian territory. Irredentism, the fashionable word for this interpretation of foreign land as Italian, fueled myths of an empire. So it was that there had been trouble here two days before he arrived. Two Italians and one Croatian had been killed and the fascists were ripe for revenge.

Stefan slept that night in the stink of the old bunks in the moored boat, wondering why his thoughts kept returning home and why Nataša's face haunted his dreams. The next morning the news of the tragedy in Trieste came through by telegraph.

He left Zorko then for the agonizing two and a half day trip back on the dirty, crowded steamer filled with anonymous faces who, concerned with their own worries, were unable to read the torture in his. It seemed to him that the tangled archipelago of islands impeded their progress and the crossing of the exposed Gulf of Quarnero spelled the same doom for him as it had for thousands of sailors over thousands of years. The boat stopped an interminable number of times to load and unload people and goods. Eventually he came to believe that it would never arrive.

*****

That was always the defining characteristic of a fire in a city – the smell that lingered until it became part of the everyday normality until, when at last it faded away, people had become accustomed to it and could scarcely remember anything different. He caught the first whiff out at sea, well before the steamer docked and, from that distance, saw the smoke that in the hot, cloudy weather had not dissipated but still hung oppressively over the city like a gray shroud. He noticed trivial things that would remain in his memory when the important things had faded: the two-masted schooner at the docks, the man in a bow tie searching in a manila folder, the small girl standing beside a cleat as big as she was, a boy riding on the running board of a car. And when he went home searching for Nataša – for, of course, in his anxiety he went home before even looking at the burned-out Narodni Dom – she wasn't there. And the children weren't there. And the neighbors looked at him with strange pity, as if they'd known about his dreams.

He eventually found the children at her mother's house and she still wasn't there. And no one said anything, and he sensed that they were frightened of him.

'Where is she?' he asked.

He reached for his son but the little boy ran away and, when he searched and found him, the child was inconsolable.

And so his mother-in-law told him that Nataša had been at the Narodni Dom with the children in the early evening when the hotel was set on fire by the four hundred fascists stirred up by Francesco Giunta. And the police did nothing. The fascists had forced the doors to the ground floor of the building, pouring in petrol, lighting it, oblivious to the terrified people, the apartment dwellers who lived in the building, the guests in the restaurant, café and theatre, the workers in the gym. Nataša had grabbed the children and run with the crowd that surged out into the Piazza Caserma and, when she was safely outside, Luka was not with them. And so she left Evie and went back in to find her son. And because he hadn't been there, the pharmacist had gone to help and had perished with her. And afterwards – after the catcalls from the mob, the police who threw fuel into the fire, the fascists, the young, demented *squadristi* who joined the *carabinieri* in preventing the fire brigade from putting it out and who cheered '*Vinceremo! Trieste è la città Italianissima!*' – even as the surge of the flames grew and filled the night sky over the city – Evie had found Luka in the piazza, where he had been all along.

And he knew, because he was honest with everyone – and most honest with himself – that he had had no reason not to be with her on that night, except for the desire to steal something that was not his. He had sat through her funeral so wracked with guilt and shame that he was unable to allow himself the relief of tears when all around him were weeping. At the graveside, with Luka in his arms, he watched Nataša's distraught mother say farewell to her daughter, saw Evie, aged seven, throw her rose onto the coffin as it descended into the earth with its bouquet of flowers. And even the wrench of that final parting failed to extinguish the knowledge of the part he had played in her death, because he could not deceive himself.

The next day he went back into the city for no reason except that he had nothing to do and nowhere to go, and saw the devastated shell, open to the sky and the rain. And he kept on his mindless walk, trying to understand how this could have happened in a city that had lived in harmony with its multitude of races for so long.

Eventually, he became aware of a commotion in a side street and turned to discover Matej Banich blind drunk, tears coursing down his face, gulping back sobs, being led from a bar out onto the street by two bartenders who proceeded to dump him on the footpath.

Stefan crossed quickly to the other side of the street, but Banich had recognized him and was calling his name in a low drone that carried like the hum of a beehive.

'Stefan! Stefan Pirjevec!'

Wordlessly Stefan stood still and stared at him.

'I'm sorry,' wept Banich. 'I'm so sorry.'

There was nothing to say, so Stefan started walking again.

And Banich, the talker, the vast ego, finding himself ignored, became abusive.

'Damn you! Why don't you talk? She's dead and you say nothing.'

He commenced weeping again.

Stefan kept walking and Banich followed him unsteadily, lurching across the footpath, supporting himself on marble facades and street lamps.

'Where were you that night?'

The drunken tirade had attracted a small crowd and the pavement on which the bystanders gawped was damp from a night of rain. The rain had poured through the roof of the Narodni Dom and its gaping windows, resting upon the debris that had fallen from the upper stories: of cafés and gym equipment, art and furnishings, theatres and the blackened contents of the apartments. The sodden wreckage lay in piles without comprehension, as if it were the soul of an older Trieste that would never have allowed this to happen.

But the shocked city wanted a reprieve from the violence, and that competed with its compassion.

'One died?' asked a voice in the crowd. 'Only one?'

'No,' said another, 'There were two.'

'Only two, then.'

They were relieved. Buildings could be rebuilt, after all. The Slovenes had erected their National Hall well enough away from the grand public areas. Facing inland. You couldn't see the remains from the port. Still it was a shame. Perhaps this would be the end, the crowd hoped, and there would be no more destruction in the name of nationalism.

At the corner of the street a small girl handed her mother a flower. The preciousness of this insignificant gift was wholly bound up in love, and the lady smiled. For anyone else its beauty was transitory and by the next day it would have faded. Stefan walked on. A fresh blue sky enlivened the city but he could not bear to look at it because it shone on a day without her. The girl and her mother were going home to their sunny street, the spreading trees and the leaves that relieved the heat of summer. But it was his steps that flickered in their light and shadow, his the warm fumbling fingers in the pocket. His the key and his the expectations behind the slowly opening door, where she was not.

Finally Banich stopped, gut heaving. Any moment now, he would spew its contents into the gutter. He hoisted himself up pompously against a streetlight, the offended drunk.

'How dare you leave her alone!' he shrieked, though it twisted his face to do so. '*How dare you?* How dare you make her wait for you year after year like you're so special, and you didn't even win the war! Where's your navy now, Commander?'

He peered down at his rumpled suit, smirked a disapproving frown and pouted lewdly. 'Well, I'm not sorry for what we did, you loser.'

That brought the words to Stefan's lips.

'What are you talking about?'

Now Banich had his audience, but the bile was gurgling in his throat. He spat it out, yellow, onto the pavement.

'I'll bet you never wondered what she did while you were at sea.' He bent his head to a discerning angle and surveyed Stefan, who was disheveled and unshaven, wearing the clothes he'd slept in, with a superior smile. 'I can see you dressed up for her funeral. What would someone like you know about pleasing women?'

Then he vomited copiously into the gutter and staggered the way he had come, back into the bar, leaving Stefan as drawn and bloodless as if his heart had been ripped from his chest.

It often seemed to Stefan that his life had progressed logically until the day that he'd met Nataša and become himself. After she died the days merged into one another, the long afternoons into endless weeks and the months into years of blurred dimensions, and one day he would slip over the edge of the horizon where the dragons were and life would be over.

What tortured him most in the empty months was not knowing why she had chosen to be with him, or even if she had. Banich had loved her? Well, Banich had loved many women since they'd been young together, not forgetting a wife who agreed to put up with him for the respectability of marriage. What weight did the words of a drunk have? Banich, for all his city suavity, had a vicious streak to his ego that, even intoxicated, sought to self-justify. He could easily have flung the adulterous slurs on purpose, out of spite or jealousy, or to enjoy their impact.

But whatever his intentions, Banich had hit his mark and Stefan, who had not faltered in the face of Allied attack, the threat of death, capture and sinking, had commenced down the slippery slope of the suspicious mind. He would have washed away the dirt that smeared Nataša's memory with his tears if he'd been able to weep without imagining her with another man. He couldn't grieve, he couldn't rest. Banich had killed those, too. And he couldn't relate the drunken incident or ask anyone for the truth because the intimation of adultery would soil her.

Over and over he reviewed that final day when she had said those brief words about Banich. Had he overlooked some subtlety of meaning? Had her movements, the language of her body, been telling him that all was not right between them? It was true that he had gone to sea without ever considering what she did without him in the long lonely weeks stretching sometimes into months. But wasn't that what sailors had done since time immemorial? Should he hold himself responsible? For what? What precisely did Banich mean by 'what we did'? Nataša was her own woman. He knew she would defend the seafarer he was with her last breath, but had Banich, who read women so much better than he did, found a weak spot in her defenses? Some need of which he had not been aware?

'He's not that bad,' she had said.

What had she meant by that? *I have found he's good? I have found he's better than you? I can't tell you what I've found because you wouldn't understand?* At these times, her image would confront him and he'd hear Banich's words coming from her lips: "What would you know about pleasing women?" It wasn't that he hadn't understood the cruel accusation, but weren't seamen supposed to come home from sea and take their wives to bed? He'd thought she had been pleased.

He struggled to recall what she had been wearing that final day. White, wasn't it? But all the women wore white. Could he remember how she had arranged her hair? And was that lavender he had smelled when he had last kissed her? He just couldn't remember. Had he always been that forgetful?

Banich would remember. Yes, he was just the type who would. And what had transpired during that final week when he'd walked out and left her for his own thoughtless crusade? Had they seen each other then? Could it possibly be true that Matej Banich and not Stefan Pirjevec had been the last man to love her, the man to remember what she had worn, how she had smelt, what she had said and perhaps – just perhaps – to remember a great deal more?

He could not pursue the most innocent of human activities in those days. Could he eat, could he even breathe? The question almost became: could he live? Could he close his eyes in the sleep that would not come, only to see Matej's lips on her cheek, his hands in her hair, his gaze on her breasts and at the last to hear his name on her lips?

Ultimately, it was the implications that were more destructive than the words themselves: that he'd never really known this woman whom he cherished so much. That, all along, the love he had had for Nataša had really been about how he defined himself, and that the desperate drunk screaming his own grief on the footpath had been the one to really know her. Therefore, he could not define himself by her anymore. Therefore, Banich had destroyed the person he thought he was.

Stefan kept a small photograph of Nataša in his wallet and looked at it repeatedly, seeing her first as the beautiful girl whose acceptance of his unpoetic proposal had so amazed him, then as the wife who understood him without the need for words, the mother of his children, the face he dreamed of most during the weeks at sea, then as a charred corpse dragged from a fiery building. After these reminiscences, he would become distressed at the photo's dog-eared appearance, realize that he was making it worse, press the softened edges down flat, kiss her image over and over, and beg her forgiveness.

In the end, he had two choices: go back to sea or go insane. It was no choice, really.

For lack of officers he was needed, if for no other reason, so at the beginning of 1921, while the fascists continued to destroy symbols of Slavic culture from Trieste to Pola to Rijeka, he joined the Navy of the Kingdom of Serbs, Croats and Slovenes. Half the Slavic officers who had served with the Austrian navy had left rather than join the fledgling navy and the aging, paltry fleet assigned to it by the Allies. Austria and Hungary, land-locked as they were now, would never again need them. So he went to sea as he always had, while his daughter and son stayed with Nataša's mother. With his torture unresolved and looking to remain that way, he took it out on all and sundry until they believed him beyond redemption. From being a captain known for the quality of his seamanship, he gained the reputation of That Angry Man. The seamen of his new navy asked to be reassigned elsewhere, and the only people who would work with him were the young Slovenian men whom he felt unable to intimidate because they reminded him of his children.

His Most Italian City

They became accustomed to him in time: his taciturnity, the brooding silence that etched lines on his face. Sometimes they were even cocky with him, as young men will be, but he knew he had their absolute loyalty. They thought he controlled the sea. As if, when they were with him, it was he who spread out his hand and opened the fountains of the deep. But he did not deliberately dare the god's anger – those vindictive marine deities that were said by generations of sailors to feel affronted when man intruded on their element. Instead, he found relief in being completely out of a world that had so badly betrayed him. As the ballast tanks filled and the submarine left the realm he was expected to inhabit and entered the depths, it was the only quiet, respectful place that gave him any relief from the turmoil in his soul, that quenched the rage, that said, like Christ to the storm, 'Be still.'

Ultimately that was the contradiction and the great irony – he could only hear her by using the very thing that had led him to abandon her. He couldn't live with himself but he couldn't live without it.

The boys called him Captain, but, during the war, he had been one of the younger and more successful commanders of the U-27 class submarines, from the U-27 to the U-41, built by Austria when it became apparent that the war would not be a short one. After the fleet was disbanded he was given the command of an old torpedo boat in a bundle of salvaged leftovers from the Austrian fleet when the other Slavic captains had resigned in disgust – and he would have, too, if he'd had anywhere else to go, but what was left for him? Since Nataša's death his only solace had been to imagine himself once more sinking below the sea into the world that was not intended for men. It became the one place where he could hear her voice. But even for that he had to wait. Finally, in 1927, the Yugoslav Navy bought two new British *Hrabi*-class submarines and he was given command of the *Nebojša* with a compliment of forty-five mostly young, mostly Slovene sailors, and Zorko, of course, who had requested him. Zorko, faithful, unimaginative, as strong as an ox. Zorko stood by him, watching the faces of the boys the first time they slid beneath the waves change from excitement, to fear, to awe, which moved Stefan to a sense of responsibility that he thought had been wiped from his soul forever. So he became more careful, more skilled, more ready to prove his seamanship than he had been since his world had lost its moorings. He longed, oddly, to be their reassuring presence, and that surprised him.

With his young men to train he was fully occupied and almost happy. It was during these days of balmy employment that a sailor from Trieste first told him of the anti-Fascist resistance group of Slovene youths which plotted in hushed tones, the group that would soon become known as TIGR. Andrej, the wiry young Slovene with the logical head and controlled temper, had had more communication with the organizers of TIGR than any of them. His family had left Trieste for Ljubljana with a burning resentment against the racial violence they had experienced in their home city, but he himself frequently returned to partake in terrorist activities that would have horrified his parents had he told them. Andrej felt that an organized base for resistance would achieve more than individual anger, of which he had plenty, kept well under control.

Well, Stefan hadn't a lot of hope for the future and his ears had pricked up at once. The thoughts of vengeance that had plagued his days and haunted his nights finally found an outlet.

How much he wanted to fight fascism and how much was revenge against Banich he did not spend too much time contemplating. On the whole, he felt that the spirit of fascism was born, not made, and that in every schoolroom on earth one could conceivably find intolerance to those who were different. He felt he could better challenge the nationalism from which it had emerged. Over the millennia Dalmatia, the coast from Istria to Albania, with its splash of islands and the limestone hills behind, had seen countless comings and goings of tribes too numerous to name. This was the coast he now patrolled and, of all places to claim nationalistic rights, surely it was the most absurd. Yet, typically, Italian propaganda had been employed to achieve this. Slanging matches about which language to use had been going on for over half a century. He had even read arguments from foreign powers who favored Italy simply because they believed it would be better for business. This sort of crowd pleasing was nothing new but it didn't take a professor to calculate that, after a long series of Italian military blunders, organization and innovation must stand as the key features of Slavic resistance now and into the future. And the dispossessed young men from these towns, whom he was training and of whom he seemed to have attracted a disproportionate number, were ready for some sort of stunt. Of his crew of forty-five there were at least a dozen whom he came across in dark corners discussing retaliation.

Over his seven years in Kotor, Trieste had ceased to exist for him other than as the home of his children. That moment in the street with Banich had become frozen in time. Now, compelled by that same spirit of revenge he knew Nataša would not have approved of, he wrote to colleagues still living in the city concerning the activities of one Matej Banich, alias Matteo Brazzi, and gradually compiled what amounted to a compendium of fascist crimes against Slovenes and Croats.

He pulled out a fresh sheet of paper, a ruler and a pencil and drew a thick line down the center of the page. Then he wrote a heading at the top of each column: 'There' and 'Not There'. He divided the crimes between the columns and was not surprised to discover that Banich had been present on only a handful of occasions, out of dozens. Those in his second column were ambiguous: a record of shops looted (counter-signed, M. Brazzi), names of media outlets in regional towns to be targeted, rocks hurled at the Yugoslavian consulate, the home side of a soccer team all with their German and Slovene surnames changed to Italian, a poster in Banich's flowery style banning the use of the Slovenian language in public, a few articles in *Il Piccolo*.

But the more he studied the second column, the more he struggled to fit the vicious propaganda with the vain, opportunistic man he had known. Eventually he gave up and concluded that allowing one's name to be associated with crimes of that nature was enough of a crime in itself to fulfill his purpose.

So he threw Banich into the ring as a suitable candidate for an act of terrorism. Murder was not on his menu but he gained perverse satisfaction from the idea of frightening someone who couldn't fight back; and the notion of setting him back financially wasn't a bad idea, either. If he had been able to both navigate and man the submarine he would have set off on this strange adventure alone, for did he not feel responsible for the young men who sailed with him? But they were ripe for adventure. He hadn't had to ask them twice.

The small submarine from Pola had been refitted and used to train the young submariners. It sat in Tivat in the Bay of Kotor with the rest of the flotilla, a lonely relic of the glory days of Austrian, symbolic in its desolation, and appertaining to all the regrets of that small landlocked nation, its glory gone, its royal house entombed in the Kaisergruft in far-off Vienna. On his gloomy days, he even wondered whether the Yugoslav navy would decide to scrap it as the Italians had, call it obsolete, calculate how much money they could get for the metal or what use they could find for its parts. Occasionally he would stroll past it in the long evenings when he liked to be alone with his memories. Then he would clamber across the decks of the two submarines it was moored with, sit on its narrow deck and pat it affectionately when he thought no one was looking. At other times he resented it with the fiercest definition of that verb because his obsession with its salvation had cost him Nataša. In his maudlin moments, he even wondered how he had done it. The answer that came back to him was that, of course, the man who had committed that audacious act no longer existed. Like her, he was far away, in the time they used to belong to.

His Most Italian City

So, in April 1928, he had explained to his superior officer that he'd like to go to Trieste to see his children.

'Haven't you just returned from seeing them?' enquired the man.

'Six weeks ago.'

The captain looked skeptical.

'I thought I could take the old U-27 up,' continued Stefan before he could interrupt. 'And some of the boys, sir. Practice a few drills along the route.'

'All the way to Trieste and back? That'll take you a week.'

'Not that long.'

The officer regarded him. Even in uniform Stefan looked every inch the ancient mariner. Shrewd eyes, strong arms, watchful. A quiet voice rather than quietly spoken. The difference lay in the authority of the delivery.

The man had heard the story of the stolen submarine. He knew the officer before him had a reputation for pushing the boundaries, and he thought that in all likelihood he was capable of doing the same thing again, if not worse. He also knew about his wife. Revenge could be a patient enemy, waiting for years until the perfect opportunity. He had heard talk, as well, among the junior Slovene sailors, of organized resistance to the dictatorship that was pillaging their homeland. Youths who believed themselves immortal, like all young men. He was well aware that if he closed one route they would open another and the consequences of not allowing Stefan Pirjevec to lead his eager young crew into fascist territory could be much worse. He at least was not young, and he was no fool.

The captain gave a resigned sigh. 'And what else are you going to do, Pirjevec?'

Stefan didn't reply, and the two of them stood gauging each other's reactions like a couple of mastiffs until, without further parley, the officer turned on his heel in the direction of his office.

'Very well!' he snapped, his clipped tones echoing behind him up the corridor. 'I want *all of you* back in a week. And I don't want to know anything about it.'

*****

They came in during the earliest hours of the morning, a low black eel gliding silently on the electric motors. Stefan scouted around the hulls soaring over them, unable to see very much except the gray sky above, the harbor lights and the diffuse city glow beyond the old port. The mountain wall that surrounded Trieste and the homely white houses stretching up the hill behind the port he had seen, in any case, a thousand times.

Trieste was no longer the port of an empire and he didn't anticipate pushing through crowds of ships to find a berth. Yet it had a population to serve. It still imported goods, it had tugs and ferries and steamers, the *piroscafi* – which left for the coast of Istria, going as far south as Montenegro – and the *vaporetti,* the water buses. There were ships in plenty and piers to moor them.

But he had no intention of mooring within sight of the docks. He carefully brought the submarine to the base of the Audace Pier closest to the Piazza Unità d'Italia. Here he, Mirko and Andrej jumped from the deck onto the steps cut into the pier. Zorko and the other sailors reversed the boat back out and continued on to a meeting point two kilometers around the point, near the southern railway line. Over his shoulder Stefan carried a rucksack containing an incendiary bomb, a battery-operated detonator, a timer, a small blanket, a hammer and a flashlight.

The night breeze chilled his face. He smelled the familiar marine smells of salt water, diesel, coal and smoke, but, for all its impressive architecture, Trieste was a quiet city at night. In a thousand beds in a thousand apartments and houses, citizens were dreaming of love and life and money-making activities. During a hard day of acquisition they had bartered and sold, eaten and drunk and made love, and, for the sake of the city he had once loved, Stefan hesitated to disturb its slumber. And then he remembered fascism and how Trieste, of all places, had welcomed it, even as its message of intolerance towards ethnic minorities destroyed the multiculturalism he had thought defined the city. And he thought, well, to hell with it, and marched on.

In the shadow of the imposing buildings, they skirted the southern edge of the piazza and crossed into the narrower streets behind, stopping just before the Old Town commenced its climb up the hill. With a finger to his lips, Stefan motioned to Mirko and Andrej to follow him in silence until they arrived at a steel-framed Art Deco window within a stone façade, a double door and a plaque that read: BRAZZI M. Coffee trader.

Not a soul was about, but like a willful wraith a single puff of air twirled down the lane and curled a pile of leaves at their feet. Opening the rucksack, he took the blanket, folded it twice, pushed it against the rectangular pane of glass, then hit it with the hammer until the glass broke and pieces of it fell quietly onto the carpet inside. He shone the flashlight within, illuminating the peaceful interior, a mahogany desk and an easy chair, several upright Austrian chairs of polished wood with curved backs, books, files, a neglected coffee cup, an ashtray, curtains. To his left, about two meters away, a staircase disappeared into an upper story and at the rear another door connected with a loading bay outside.

Cautiously he inserted the detonator into the top of the bomb, setting the timer for ten minutes. Then he handed it to Andrej. With complete composure, the young man eased the bomb through the hole in the glass and laid it on the carpet. Then the three men ran towards the rendezvous point on the southern shore.

Mirko and Andrej sprinted beneath the soaring black buildings, watching for the place where they opened to the broad shore that they could sense just beyond their vision. Around the corners, on and off gutters, agile, careful, too exhilarated to be afraid. Stefan, jogging behind, kept their lithe figures in his sight until, at the end of one street, he paused to look back.

Margaret Walker

In four minutes, he estimated, he would see the fruits of revenge: a night illuminated by furious blasts and broiling clouds, fire and brimstone, flames like a furnace. Impatiently, he scanned the black sky. Three minutes. The city slept on. On the slopes of the Old Town a dog barked. Stefan remained, watching. Two minutes.

Then from the blur of a black lane a shadow emerged, a hat, a furtive figure crouched inside a coat.

Stefan jumped into a doorway but the figure had seen him.

'What are you doing?'

A strong voice in that sorcerous night. Unexpectedly assertive.

Stefan leapt from the doorway and started running.

'Hey, you there! Stop!'

The man continued to shout, gesturing with his arms towards the still-vacant street, when suddenly a crack of light shot into the night sky and Stefan heard the hiss of flames catching hold, muffled by distance. Far behind, glass shattered and the sound of a fire began to roar through the quiet city. As he ran, he twisted his head and looked back to see sparks erupting upwards. He heard cries of 'Fire!' and 'Police!'

'Over here!' yelled the man in response to the cries. 'Help! Help! Over here!'

When Mirko heard the commotion and saw the glow of flames building in the sky, he looked behind him and couldn't see the captain. Alerting Andrej, they returned the way they had come.

The stranger, meanwhile, had picked up his pace and continued briskly forward but, upon seeing the two young men catapulting towards Stefan, he wavered uncertainly. All too soon they were upon him. Each grabbed an arm and dragged him towards the shore with such velocity that he gasped and coughed and, after a few attempts, was unable to speak at all.

Two streets, one street, a block of apartments, then they ran across to the pier, where Zorko was waiting with the motors running, pulling and shoving the hapless man as they went. Then they all but tossed him down the conning tower, headfirst.

Stefan remained on the bridge to direct the helmsman, leaving his surprised guest doubled up on the floor plates of the control room, gasping harshly in the reeking air as the submarine pulled out from the pier.

With the crescendo of excitement and exercise, Mirko beside him was so exhilarated that he couldn't calm down.

'*O, povero Matteo Brazzi!*' he yelled. '*Che peccato! Che bastardo! O merda, merda, mille merde!*'

'Traitor!' replied Andrej prosaically.

'*Mamma mia!*'

Andrej shrugged.

'Serves the bastard right.'

'May he who did this never drink coffee again!' sang Mirko.

Zorko prodded the figure on the floor.

'Who's this, you two?'

'A journalist,' croaked the man.

'What, Mussolini?' mocked Zorko.

'*Il Popolo di Trieste.*' The fascist newspaper established by the dictator.

'Then we're in luck,' remarked Andrej. 'Two in one day.'

Behind him Stefan jumped down the ladder, followed by Danilo. Danilo closed the hatch and took the control-room helm.

'There's movement on the quay,' announced Stefan. 'Diving stations! Take her down to periscope depth.'

In the half-light, the journalist's face went rigid.

'What?'

Hurrying to their stations, the crew ignored him. He stood up.

'Let me out now!' he insisted urgently. 'Open that hatch.'

His voice was drowned out by the sound of water rushing into the ballast tanks. The bow tilted forward.

'Oh, shit.'

He bolted towards the ladder. Zorko put out a hand, but the man had begun to panic, struggling against Zorco in an effort to gain a foothold on the aluminum ladder and escape the enclosure, stretching his hands up to force the hatch. Zorko pulled him down onto the floor. In a second he was upright again, battling and thumping the huge man who was barring his path. So Zorko punched him once on the back of the head, and the man fell straight down at his feet and was still.

From the quay came a volley of shots and a single shrill crack from a bullet against the conning tower as it descended beneath the dark waters and the slim periscope alone headed out to sea. But distance is an odd measurement at night. The stars and the harbor confuse it and the Gulf of Trieste is shallow near the city. Submarines belong at Pola, which is a much more suitable harbor.

*****

The upshot of that dramatic night proved harder to investigate. Tivat lay in the Bay of Kotor, a waterway shaped like a squashed figure eight in Dalmatia's far south. A long way from Trieste, in another country now, and though, after the bombing, his young men felt amply recompensed for the risk they had taken, Stefan himself was left restless and idle. All he seemed to have achieved was a fire in a shop in the back streets of Trieste. The inevitable disappointment was the trouble with revenge. Many more things needed to be established before he acknowledged its deficiencies and achieved peace, but he kept his ears above water on whatever patrol he found himself, on the lookout for hints that all was not well in the life of his enemy. The weeks of excitement after the attack were buoyed up for him by the spirit of his men, but, having nursed bitterness for so long, he was actively looking for the remedy.

Early in July as the mountains soaring around the bay were verdant with oak, beech, and cypress, as the olives bore fruit and the summer heat beat down upon him, Stefan departed the submarine base to visit a friend in Kotor. It was here that he heard the first hint of the results of the bombing.

Ivan, like Zorko, was a marine mechanic. Ivan and Stefan liked each other's company and, following the multiple embraces typical of men in Yugoslavia, words seemed unnecessary. Ivan would get a quiet idea, Stefan would give the project his silent acknowledgement and like a torpedo they would shoot mutely away to pursue it together. Ivan had recently taken a trip to Pola to visit his son and, like father, like son, the two of them had been engrossed in a wordless conversation on the quay when the steamer from Trieste had struggled into the harbor belching more than just black smoke.

Ivan was immediately interested.

'Trouble?' he had bawled across the water to the captain.

'Boiler!' returned the man.

'Safety valve?'

'Probably.'

On the strength of this exchange, a dialogue was established between the captain, Ivan and the engineer regarding time, cost and parts, and somehow enough words escaped to give Ivan the impression that a person of interest had moved from Trieste to Cittanova in Istria. Over the intervening months this person had overloaded the captain's steamer with such a volume of crates, furniture, decorative sundries and the paraphernalia associated with coffee that a relationship had formed between the individual responsible and the trouble with his boiler by weight of association. The captain would be happy if he never saw the place again.

'Coffee?' mused Stefan back in Kotor.

'Cittanova,' said Ivan.

But how to be sure?

Summer was already well advanced and there's nothing like urgency to sharpen the appetite. When next Stefan wrote to his children it was the end of July and he proposed to them that in the middle of August they spend a week of their holidays at Cittanova mingling with the other tourists who flocked to that seaside resort in the hot summer months. Evie, now fifteen, and Luka, twelve, were delighted to be taken to the beach for once instead of the never-ending series of lakes and mountains their father dragged them to every summer holiday to get as far from the Italian flag as possible. So Stefan duly packed his swimsuit and promised to teach them how to sail, determined to find out, while mixing with the babel of Austrian, Italian and German tourists, whether or not Banich was indeed sheltering there.

To be frank, he didn't lose any sleep over the possibility of running into him. He figured he would slot that into his agenda if and when it occurred. He knew he was safe if he stayed close to the water because Banich, despite living on the coast his entire life, had never liked getting wet.

They took two rooms in a family villa near the Venetian Belvedere looking out to sea, a double room for Stefan and Luka and a tiny single room under the eaves with a skylight for Evie, who was not at an age where she wanted to share with two male relatives. At fifteen she had almost her mother's height and shared Nataša's thick dark hair, her beautifully symmetrical features and her interest in other people. She possessed, as well, her father's steady eyes, so that people tended to obey her without question even though at such a young age questioning was advisable. Stefan, who was sufficiently absent to notice the changes as she grew, regarded Evie's resemblance to Nataša as a blessing. Wistfully watching his beautiful daughter mature was proof that though his wife was gone she was not lost to him forever. He was enough of a father, however, to be alarmed at the sight of her in her new bathing suit, bought especially for the occasion. Resembling Nataša was one thing, turning into a desirable young woman was quite another.

His Most Italian City

'Did Grandma buy you that?' he asked, watching her swivel around in front of the mirror, admiring herself from all angles.

'No, Dad, you did,' she informed him smartly. 'Do you like it?'

Stefan accepted this rebuttal with stifled grace, realizing that, though he sent the bulk of his pay north each month, he had not until now stopped to consider what his mother-in-law did with the money. Clearly she had given his daughter a clothing allowance and this jaw-dropping fashion statement was the result. He hoped Evie had no conception of the effect it had.

'Yes,' he murmured. 'Very nice.'

Mercifully the bathing suit came with a matching cover-up and every morning Evie, dressed up and on display, along with Stefan and Luka, trailing along behind, explored the twisting streets of Cittanova, as centuries of families had done before them, ending up always at the *mandracio*, where Stefan hired a small sailboat for the first lesson of the day. The entrance to the internal port was long and narrow and they began by rowing through it and only when safely out engaging the boom and the sail. Then Evie, under instruction from her father, tacked haltingly north past the tiny chapel of Saint Anthony and around the bay to Carpignano. The hills baked under the summer sun that sparkled from the water like blue diamonds and, in the view they had of Cittanova from this distance, the town rested as peacefully beneath the wide sky as if it had been there forever. Then Luka wobbled back to the *mandracio* where Stefan took over. By their fourth or fifth lesson their sailing skills were much improved and, on their most daring trip yet, they journeyed right around the port, turned south and then sailed east into the Val di Torre, passing the quarries and the limestone furnaces. Finally, they sailed far out to sea, pretended they were pirates, then sailed all the way back again.

They wrote postcards to their grandmother and their friends. They told ghost stories at bedtime. They sat on the breakwater and watched the boats go in and out. They beat Stefan three to one playing soccer on the sporting fields of the Rivarella. They overheated while hiking in the hills, then marched home to dive straight into the water to cool down.

It all added to the appetite. They consumed a great deal of fish, tons of pasta, local fruit and berries, *al fresco* meals at the *Trovatore* in the *mandracio*, drank coffee and lemonade, and sampled the country wines and the famous Istrian olive oil. The only place they didn't visit was the Caffè Fascisti.

'What a silly name,' remarked Luka.

Stefan had to agree.

'But don't let the name put you off,' said their landlady. It was their last night and there remained only the next morning before the steamer returned them to Trieste. 'I believe the proprietor was under pressure from the Party in Trieste and – oh,' she paused for effect, 'our local bully, Giuseppe Monfalcon, who uses politics to make money.'

'Who runs this cafe?' Stefan asked her suspiciously.

'Oh, the mayor,' she replied, relieved that he had finally addressed a question to her instead of merely handing over his money and ignoring her like he usually did. She sent him a radiant smile.

The landlady had taken quite a shine to the widowed captain with his two clever children. It was not that long since she had lost her own husband and she had begun to provide bed, breakfast and dinner over the summer months to lay up money for the winter when she took in washing, ironing and mending, which didn't pay as well. She had made a quick approximation of Stefan's age and figured, allowing herself a generous margin for error, that they were within five years of each other. A wife five years older than her husband was quite respectable in the opinion of most husband-hunting widows. She was not sentimental about either Italy, Austria or Yugoslavia and didn't mind which country a potential husband came from. Her ambitions were not deterred, either, by noticing that Stefan seemed constantly to have something else on his mind, rarely venturing far from the sea and looking at every second pedestrian with a suspicion that she couldn't account for.

Well, seamen, she thought, *what did you expect?*

But when she started to dress better, add that magic ingredient to their dinner and beam with desperate rectitude every time she saw him, and he still didn't notice her, she was inclined to wish him gone as soon as possible out of sheer frustration. And now finally he had asked her a question of four words. She could have wept with relief.

'It's a very good café, sior,' she continued happily. 'You can't get better cooking anywhere. What Teresa Urizio doesn't know about cakes isn't worth knowing, and I am insanely jealous of her meringues.'

A married woman could be praised without threat.

Stefan stared at her.

'Why would you be jealous of a meringue?'

'It is the ambition of most women to make the perfect meringue,' the landlady replied tartly before plonking his dinner on the table before him and huffing back to the kitchen.

And so the holiday in Cittanova was winding to its end. Between swimming, rowing, sailing, hiking, eating and drinking, Evie and Luka had had a wonderful time. That night after dinner they informed their father that they were totally over lakes and mountains. They adored Cittanova and they expected to return next summer. And, on that theme, had he noticed how mild the weather was at Easter?

Stefan was taken aback to be dictated to by his children. He noted, moreover, that he had apparently displeased his landlady, although he wasn't sure how. So he booked an extra three nights, which seemed to pacify everyone and, as there had still been no sighting of Banich, he began to suspect that Ivan had been wrong.

They visited the Caffè Fascisti the following morning and Stefan's hackles were up the instant he walked into the exquisitely furnished cafe.

Margaret Walker

A week in this place and still no sighting of Banich, and yet here he could almost smell the man. So he was the mayor now, was he?

The cakes for the day were Black Forest gateau and cherry strudel. The young waitress, who looked only as old as Evie, served them coffee as good as any he had ever drunk and placed the three slices of cake delicately on bone china plates, accompanied by generous dollops of cream, and all the while he sensed Banich as acutely as if he had laid eyes on him. The finesse proclaimed the man. Beautiful parquet flooring, paneling of fragrant oak, with only the most delicate veil of lacquer – the scent of wood as if it had been milled yesterday. Two rows of tables strategically placed to give diners the illusion of privacy. They were shaded from prying eyes in the piazza by a half-curtain, machine lace, it is true, but high quality, although Stefan knew little about any lace. Delicately shaded lamps cast the perfect glow to relax parched lips and tempt appetites. Around the walls and over the lintel were decorations of exceptional art nouveau, officially outmoded now in favor of art deco, but Banich so stamped his creative authority on its use that one had to admit that the new was ungainly compared with the old. The menu had been printed on expensive vellum paper, and down at the very bottom in fine print rested the inscription, *Proprietor, Brazzi M.*

And then he knew.

Afterwards they stepped back into the piazza where the campanile soared into the blue sky and the sunlight blanched the old stone buildings. Ladies wore colorful dresses and cloche hats, men strolled in suits, children in holiday clothes ran and shouted. Oak, pine and salt breeze. Yet he saw and smelled none of it because the last piece of his jigsaw had fallen into place. He felt very calm, like the peace before the storm; but behind his peace waited a grinding resolve.

On their final afternoon but one Evie announced to her father and brother that she required some girl time. They must excuse her from their projected activities – she knew they wouldn't mind – she was just going to take herself off alone, do a little window shopping, write an entry in her diary, and probably sit at the end of the breakwater and draw a sketch of the town. Would she write a poem? Well, perhaps she might even do that. She just needed a little time to herself.

So, while Stefan and Luka threw themselves on their beds and slept, Evie brushed her hair, changed her clothes, smartened herself up, tripped lightly down the stairs and opened the front door onto the street. It was the hour of siesta. Most of the shops had closed until later in the afternoon and the myriad tourists, tired after enjoying the seaside in the heat of the day, had consumed a splendid holiday lunch and retired to rest. Later on some intended to visit the Bagno San Marco where they could listen to the orchestra, followed by dancing for those still young enough to have the energy. In the twilight between dinner and dancing, the band serenaded strolling couples on the waterfront and there was even a performance of *La Traviata* being staged by the town's opera society the following night.

In the afternoon hush Evie wandered alone into the broad piazza and took a desultory glance at a couple of shops, which were shut. At the far end, away from the park, several men appeared to be setting up market stalls. From an open window nearby a plaintive aria floated down to her, sung by a phantom voice, accompanied by a mandolin. The sad strains of a lost love stirred the chords of her heart. They made her think of her mother. But it is not in the interests of the young to remain sad forever. Evie blew a kiss in the direction of the solemn singer, smiled at her mother in heaven, and strolled on past the duomo and the campanile, entering the iron gates of the public garden and passing swiftly through onto the breakwater. Here she pulled out her travel diary, sat cross-legged and completed a rapid sketch of the port including the campanile, very prominently, lest her lack of artistic skill caused the actual town to be obfuscated. Just in case the leaning tower still did not identify Cittanova as she hoped it would – she had to convince her father and Luka – she wrote underneath it 'HOLIDAY IN CITTANOVA' and the date. It was the only entry in her book, but they weren't to know that.

Then she climbed carefully down from the breakwater onto the stretch of rock that passed for a beach. The tide never went out very far, but it had receded sufficiently for Evie to stroll along the rocky beach in front of its houses, beside the private sea walls and outhouses of the occupants looking out onto the Adriatic. At the very end near the pier she said a polite good afternoon to a courting couple who, but for her, would have had the vista all to themselves.

She climbed back up to the commencement of the pier, where she made a quick little sketch of the antique tower and the school then ducked back into the maze of winding streets, so different in their charming disorder from the purposeful tramways of Trieste. It was like getting lost in a fairy tale in which one might at any moment come face to face with a fire-breathing dragon, a witch on a broomstick, a maiden of bygone days and her gallant prince. Evie shivered with delight and roamed on.

And it was along one of these stone rivulets where, charging around the corner to see where it might lead her, she almost ran into that very white-faced man. He was there and gone in an instant and Evie quickly decided he must have been one of those war veterans she sometimes saw in Trieste, suffering from shellshock, though she'd never seen one quite so fashionably dressed. She admired the gold cufflink inlaid with mother-of-pearl as his hand shot to his mouth, noticed that his short moustache was superbly styled and his silk bow tie beneath the bulging Adam's apple was such a lovely rich rose that she almost stopped and asked him where he had bought it. But he was a bit old for her. Never mind. And he did look sick, poor man. Why walk around with your mouth hanging open if you weren't? The gold fillings in his back teeth were painfully obvious and not as good quality as the gold of his cuff link. Evie flashed him the briefest smile of sympathy then forgot all about him.

His Most Italian City

All good things must come to an end. On August 26th Evie and Luka reflected bleakly that school awaited them back in Trieste and hauled their suitcases from beneath their beds to begin the melancholy process of packing. Outside the sun was shining and the bells of the campanile rang out into the clear air. Indeed, they had been ringing joyfully since early that morning and Evie with all the romance of youth felt her heart lift and soar far away, as if she were a note from a chime and was winging her way to heaven to kiss her mother and return rejuvenated to the earth. As they lugged their cases downstairs to where Stefan was waiting impatiently to be off, the bells were joined by chimes from a second church. Where the two alighted on the same note, a great vibration arose and swelled the air so that it seemed to burst into life. Suddenly Evie was terribly sad to be leaving Cittanova, for it appeared to her that something exciting was happening of which she wanted to be a part.

Once in the hall her expectations were confirmed when their landlady greeted them with a blossoming smile that clearly had nothing to do with her father leaving. (Evie was very perceptive in matters of the heart.)

'What's going on?' she asked.

'The festival of our patron saint,' replied the woman joyfully, 'is in two days' time. You didn't notice the men setting up stalls in the piazza?'

'Well, yes I did,' answered Evie. 'I just didn't know what they were for.'

'It's a shame you can't stay, but I'm full. My family is coming down from Capodistria. Perhaps next year you can come for Saint Pelagio? The 28th and 29th of August. Now don't forget.'

Evie shot her father a smile of triumph.

'We'll be there.'

*****

Once back at the submarine base, Stefan took the incendiary bomb he had been saving from its hiding place beneath his bed and wrapped it up like a birthday present. When he had finished, the whole thing looked as if it had been made by a five-year-old child trying to impress and he grimaced, thinking he should have gotten Evie to do it. But the sister-in-law of the postmaster at Kotor who worked on Tuesdays and Wednesdays tidied it up for him, stifling an indulgent smirk, and affixed the large ceremonial bow he handed her to the top, right in the middle.

For a special friend, Stefan explained. She said she hoped the lady would like it, and Stefan smiled beneficently and thanked her for the help.

'Address?' she asked.

'M Brazzi. Caffè Fascisti, Piazza Umberto I, Cittanova, Italy,' replied Stefan.

So the woman wrote 'Signora M Brazzi. Caffè Fascisti, Piazza Umberto I, Cittanova, Italy' on the parcel and wished him luck.

Nema problema.

That sentiment was not entirely true, for Stefan still had one problem. What to do when he got him. As he would. He had no doubt about it. Just a bit more softening – he would let the incendiary bomb sink in – and then one little letter.

What was the point?

He knew the answer to that one. He would have no peace until he saw Brazzi again. Until he knew for sure. Then he could leave the wretched man alone.

Chapter Nineteen

The irony of his situation had not escaped Brazzi. He who rarely gave a thought to interests beyond his own comfort was being hunted because of the single selfless act in a lifetime of indulgence. Truly there was no justice in this world. Brazzi was drowning in self-pity. The dam had broken, the deluge was heading his way and there was no Noah to intercede for him.

After that first night, watching the pier from the window of the City of Trieste, he had been unable to sleep. From dusk until dawn as the weary hours rolled on, his head upon his pillow recalled a cocktail of his iniquities, and for none of them had he suffered any remorse except for this one desire nobly resisted, for which he had heartily congratulated himself afterwards and which he had termed an act of mercy. And for this he had been bombed and was being stalked by a superior mind. 'Unfair' didn't begin to describe it! Why, after seven months' residence in this nice little town he barely recognized himself, such a faux philanthropist he had become!

Nataša! What a beautiful woman she had been! A strong, beautiful woman. Her love could have made him someone for whom life meant more than just money and lust.

Brazzi knew that she had first met Stefan at one of the Saturday dances at the Slovenian hall in Barkovlje, north of the city. Brazzi had not been present that night, and he'd been dismayed to hear afterwards that the

Nataša he had so often admired had danced the night away with that peasant Stefan Pirjevec, a man who evidently regarded clothes as nothing more than an inconvenient naval requirement. Brazzi wasn't to know that, after her first keen summation, Nataša had barely registered what the cadet wore once they'd started dancing, and when Stefan dispensed with his collar and tie and slung his jacket over his shoulder the instant he left the hall to walk her home, she had been too star-struck to notice.

To Brazzi, the entire thing, and the speed of it, defied belief. How could the sensible Nataša have allowed herself to become so infatuated so quickly? Why let herself be possessed? Laughing at his jokes, sharing his gelato, wandering along the seafront with him like beauty and the beast. That climactic image of Stefan and Nataša all over each other as they walked up her parents' garden path! There couldn't have been too many surprises on her wedding night, he thought spitefully.

And all the while there he had been, the eternal outsider, watching them as hungrily as a werewolf behind the tree, waiting for the silver bullet to lay him human and bleeding in the dirt. Definitely, Stefan was responsible for Brazzi's promiscuity and its consequences and therefore, by default, his own bitter railings against Stefan after her death, his bombed office and Stefan's vengeful behavior that followed.

Yes, it was all his fault.

Every time he laid eyes on her Brazzi's well-developed voyeurism (for which he daily gave thanks) rallied like the call to arms he had evaded: in the piazza, in the shops, walking her daughter to school, sitting by the shore afterwards watching the boats go in and out of the harbor with Stefan's small son. Brazzi was blessed with excellent taste and Nataša's exquisitely symmetrical features haunted his sense of panache. She had been such a conundrum! In his considerable experience, women perfected by symmetry held within their breasts hearts of mathematical coldness. Yet she had been warm and friendly, very direct in her speech and more comfortable in male company, he suspected, than female. She was interested in men and liked to listen to them. Her gift to him had been to raise his awareness of the better part of himself, that spark of human sympathy he had occasionally felt for a wounded animal, a mutilated war veteran, a disabled child. The man he might have been if she had been his, which would have superseded the profanity that had rushed in to fill the void when he couldn't have her.

The spark that initially attracted him had been her rare talent for understanding men on their own terms. Stefan was at sea – thankfully, he was away a lot of the time – and in those early days of the Triestine marriage market there had been a time when Brazzi saw so much of Nataša that he even thought she might veer his way. That illusion had been exploded one glistening spring day in 1911 when the leaves seemed astonishingly green and the sea shimmered like the New Jerusalem, and Stefan had stepped completely out of character and bought her something beautiful. That small but perfect diamond, the pick of the crop, not set in garish yellow gold but its finer compound that held a delicate pink blush within its circlet, as if she had kissed it and made it holy. Brazzi shuddered to think of Stefan down on one knee and he rarely itemized the reasons why Nataša had ultimately rejected him for a seaman.

For Stefan was a man who needed to be understood without a lot of words, and it was no wonder he had married her. It had been as if she had acted as his interpreter for the few sentences he'd utter. Like poetry she could paraphrase them, like food for his soul she had enabled him to know himself. She had been exactly what Brazzi needed as well, and the curse of his life was that he had been given the capacity to approve their union from afar. It forced him to put aside his own interests. It made him very resentful.

They had moved to Pola after the marriage and, until their return, as the war was drawing to its close, her absence had quashed the worst of his acrimony. Inevitably, when he saw her again his feelings had stormed back in with such a vengeance that he felt he was once again living in that tormented, desperate world he had inhabited when first he had fallen in love with her. In four years, war had changed Stefan from a talented young officer to a focused commander, and its grueling separations had metamorphosed the marriage from limestone to marble in a way that the inexperienced Brazzi could never have understood. Now and forever, Stefan was a one-woman man.

Unlike Brazzi. This was the reason Brazzi had ended up in his current situation. Or had the syphilis been the fault of the war? And he hadn't even taken part! Back to his primary gripe: it wasn't fair.

He had long suspected the carrier. That blond Teuton with the big boobs he'd had when he was going through his breast-feeding stage, whose husband was a returned soldier and had brought the disease back from one squalid brothel or another. He'd heard that once the rash and that sore, as mild as it had been shameful, had disappeared he might even be lucky. Some people never went on to develop further symptoms. He could live out the remainder of his days without problems, without ever having to seek medical treatment. Perhaps, after all, he had misdiagnosed himself.

But after Angelica miscarried well into the middle of that first pregnancy, he had begun to suspect the truth. It was about a month before Nataša died and he had stopped pursuing his fanciful notion that only soldiers could become infected. He hadn't been a soldier, so he was safe, right? Well, there were many ways of deceiving yourself. That was the first myth, and here was the second: that he hadn't pursued his passion for Nataša to its conclusion because he genuinely loved her and didn't want to infect her.

They had met for the final time the week of the fire. The worst of this wretched world was that there always seemed to be a final time that you remembered more than the others, whose colors reflected the intensity of that day. She had been alone, for Stefan was away. 'At sea,' she had asserted overconfidently, as if there had been more to his absence than that. Brazzi hadn't asked. He knew Stefan didn't sail with the Regia

His Most Italian City

Marina and wondered what she could mean, but the minutes were ticking away and he pushed the question aside in favor of the importance of the moment. If ever there was a time to act, it was now. Her daughter was at school and the small boy was in the care of his grandmother while she had an appointment – the doctor, the dentist, he couldn't recall. She'd said she had an hour free, and they had agreed to meet for the coffee that he could only see as the last bridge before consummation. Coffee, always coffee. Trieste was famous for it. It was his living. Everybody drank it here. Coffee became the reason for talking, for celebrating, for relaxing. Almost the reason for being.

Well, the *demitasse* in the Piazza della Borsa was quickly dispensed with and then they had forty minutes. She might stretch it to sixty. He pushed open for her the heavy door into the street, watching the wartime dress she had altered to prevailing fashions flatten her breasts and diminish her hips. Even so, every curve of her body goaded him on.

'Shall we go for a walk?' he almost panted.

His hands shook and the walk was stilted. He was itching – no, aching – with desire for her. When he closed his eyes, he saw them already together. I will open them; I will let in the light. Like our slow steps on the pavement and the sun that hurries too quickly across the sky, I will see us as we ought to be. Not this eternal hedging. How much time would they have? He checked his watch, excusing the action by saying he was checking the mechanism. (It had been stopping.) There was just time. Should he take her home? Would Angelica be there? Not today, he remembered. She would be away until late evening. The timing seemed perfect. Yet you could hardly pull the wool over Nataša's eyes. Her, of all people.

She must have known the direction his thoughts were taking. He had looked into her eyes, on a level with his own, that dapple of green that streaked their brown irises, their unaffected interest that drew him in so that he couldn't imagine a world without her. It seemed that he would be only half the person he was if she weren't there. The sea on which he would be abandoned was broad and disengaging, and no one would care about him anymore. His need had becoming a living thing.

They stood at the corner. The gutter they would have to step over and the bulk of the stone buildings that rushed away before and behind them represented the two choices they would swiftly make. The ways they would go. Yes or no. And while he still hesitated, searching for the right words, she had said it for him.

'You know, Matej, I am going home now. Stefan won't be back for a week and I have friends from the country staying at the Narodni Dom.'

A spasm of unease flickered across Brazzi's hopeful features. The Narodni Dom! Giunta had often spoken about that eyesore. What to do, he demanded, about such an obvious threat to the glory of Italy? A Slavic shrine in an Italian city. What next? Tension was mounting and all the conflagration required was the spark. Brazzi had observed him apprehensively in those last days, arrogant, assured, attractive. A hard man to resist. 'Trieste has placed itself at the head of fascism' wrote Rino Alessi in *Il Piccolo*, and Giunta was making sure his words came true. Nataša could very well be in danger if she visited the Narodni Dom.

He reached a tender hand towards her and she stepped back. With the scallops of her white skirt she shook him off. Her calves in their patterned lisle twisted to escape him.

She had made up her mind. She was going. Thanks for the coffee and the chat. Nice to see you, but… a litany of homely things: the children, bath time, dinner, her overflowing sewing basket.

'Stefan's so hard on his clothes, Matej.'

There. He was less important than the mending.

'When exactly are you going to the Narodni Dom?' he had asked her, fumbling with words, trying to get her to stay.

'Not tonight.'

His Most Italian City

No further information. He had been dismissed. All his build up, the hopes, his certainty, her beauty, his need. Belittled. Of no account. Give the man the brush-off by telling him she has to look after the children.

Brazzi knew a lot about women. Nataša was as clear as a bell. She knew what he wanted and had rejected him. He felt ashamed and too quickly his shame turned to anger. What sort of fool had he been? Living on daydreams. He was not one-tenth the man her husband was and she wouldn't have him. Perhaps, he felt, she even pitied him. And her pity would be the cruelest cut of all.

Fury arose in him for even thinking she would betray Stefan, and he was even angrier because he hated denying himself what he wanted. So he let her go resentfully, like a school boy, detecting her scent even as the meters grew between them – peach, blood orange, chardonnay, fermented citrus, sauerkraut – and, by the time his acerbic musings concluded and he tried to locate her again, she was gone. The crowd had closed over her. Even the dust on the hot footpath had erased the imprint of her shoe.

Well done to Brazzi, who was not the hero after all! Not a war hero, not even a moral hero, afterwards consoling himself by fabricating the myth that he had stopped himself infecting her out of love. And it was half true. He really had loved her. He just loved himself more. Too much to demean himself by warning her of the gloating fascist eyes on the building where her friends were staying.

Moodiness quickly overcame him and on the evening of the fire he had not been anyone's hero, either. He had not heeded Giunta's call to rally in the Piazza Unità on July 13th, neither had he supported the numerous attacks on Slavic businesses in the city which culminated in the Narodni Dom, their prize that violent evening. He was not the fascist hero burning the symbol of Slavic barbarism in an Italian city, nor one of the two who ignited the building with petrol then jumped from its windows into the street, neither was he the police who stood by and let it burn, or the *carabinieri* who had stopped the fire brigade from dousing the flames. Not even the Slovene turned fascist who, if he truly loved Nataša, could have been there to help the apartment dwellers, whose friend she was, escape from the inferno. No, he had been at home with a sulky Angelica, who demanded to know which other woman was responsible for his bad mood this time.

And then, quite unexpectedly, he had met Stefan on the street the day after Nataša's funeral.

He had to be spiteful. He couldn't just let the man walk away without justifying his jealousy, without that little present for his ego, without inflicting that satisfying wound. And, of course, he had to support the myth that by that time had assumed monolithic proportions.

Damn these men who wouldn't talk! Brazzi couldn't cope with being ignored. At the ravaged face that regarded him silently the alcoholic accusations flew thick and fast from his lips. Neglect, abandonment, selfish disregard. Still no response, so Brazzi moved it up a gear. Adultery – yes, we did it and it's your fault, not mine. Your fault she was lonely, your fault she betrayed you, your fault she's dead. Did you think you knew her? Well, think again, dockyard laborer. Make sure you back the winners next time.

And, with that, he drank himself blind.

Brazzi had never seen Stefan again. He made no enquiries. For all he knew the man had thrown himself into the harbor.

Eight years and one month passed. And then in August 1928 Brazzi had seen Nataša on the street leading to the markets in Cittanova. The shock had so nearly demolished him that he could barely remain upright. She had even smiled at him with so much of her old familiar sympathy that he seemed in his longing to have been struck in the chest by his own heart. For a while after that he had doubted his sanity until he remembered stories he'd heard about loving revenants. Yes, clearly that was it.

There were so many things that she could have returned to him for. His guilt that final time for thinking only of his sexual frustration. His dismay at his own churlishness. His desperate grief at her death. The problem with alcohol that that had sparked. His deep desire to be understood by her. His pleasure at the whole man she had made him feel he was. His loneliness without her. She was the succor for his soul, the balm for his moody marriage, the tenderness he needed, the loving spirit that was missing from his life.

But after that had come that evil can of soup, addressed to his wife. Only one guess who that was from. Brazzi felt dismally threatened by a man who could intimidate someone as insignificant as Angelica. He was actually surprised that Stefan would act that way. Truly inhuman. Next time Brazzi felt like being spiteful he must consider the consequences. The man's brain had been turned. Not just audacious. Forbidding. What could it mean, addressing it to Angelica? As he'd looked at the obscene birthday present, he had begun to shake. Carefully hustling the bomb home to make sure that his sad little wife could never see it, he had shoved it into the drawer in the hall table. Yes, Nataša in her celestial sphere had clearly known that Stefan was likely to behave in this scheming and indecent manner. She had come back to warn him, to bring comfort in turmoil, to encourage him to gird up his loins like a man and not give way to threats.

But soon after came the letter. *Meet me at ten o'clock at the inlet.*

'Dear Nataša,' enquired Brazzi of the heavenly realms, 'what should I do?'

Quick as a flash the answer had come to him: reschedule your meeting to the City of Trieste where you will have a good view and plenty of company. Then you will be in a more secure position to make a decision. The solution was so sensible. He felt as if Nataša had been standing at his elbow.

Brazzi turned to the mirror and saw a man admiring his look of strangled affection like an opium addict. Perhaps he was going mad, and wasn't dementia one of the symptoms of third-stage syphilis?

'Matteo?'

At the quiet voice, Brazzi looked to see Angelica watching him from the bedroom door. Although only four in the afternoon by the oak standing-clock in the hall, the winter darkness had entered the house and the sprawling acacia tree in the yard reduced what light remained to gray streaks so that night seemed already to clutch them in its embrace. Angelica had removed her dress and girdle and, stockings discarded as well, stood in the doorway dressed only in her slip and a woolen dressing gown.

'You were talking to yourself.' Wide-eyed, pale-skinned, curly brown hair cut short to the nape of her neck, she waited quietly, regarding his vulnerability in the deep hush of the hour with the shyness of the neglected lover. 'You were talking about Nataša.'

It was far too late for deceit or even subterfuge and, in any case, Brazzi had given up the fight. Too tired, too sick. It all seemed so useless.

'You couldn't have married her anyway. Wasn't I enough for you?'

'Nataša's dead,' Brazzi answered her wearily, for her ghost had departed. 'And there's an end to it.'

He had removed his collar and silk tie and sat on the bed in his shirt and unbuttoned waistcoat. Angelica left the doorway. She came and sat beside him, opening the top of her gown. Taking his hand, she slipped it into the warmth within, watching the glint of his signet ring as the hand disappeared. And he left it there, which surprised her because she had never played her part as the spurned wife with any degree of aplomb. Over the eight years of their marriage there had been so many rejections that she had almost given up trying. But the hand remained on her breast until she felt the nipple harden and her breath quicken.

'Matteo,' she whispered, 'give me a baby.'

His mind was on anything else but that and it was on his lips to brush her aside, but the drowsy hush of his afternoon, into which she had wandered, made him pause, put aside his irritation at her interruption. Even this brief encouragement gave her heart, she, who expected so little.

His Most Italian City

She began to speak again, but he took his warmed hand from her breast and put two fingers upon her lips to silence her. She took the hand, even though her hopefulness embarrassed him, and slid it back to where it had been. He kissed her and pulled her down beside him so that they landed on the silk eiderdown in a soft thuff of feathers.

His fear of Monfalcon had certainly been life-affirming! He would do this for Angelica and then he would go. She need never know the truth and, by the time she had her next miscarriage, he'd be gone. Never would he have to negotiate again with the ghastly old sinner unless he bullied his victims from the grave, and Brazzi did not believe that even Monfalcon had the means to do that, unless he was dead already.

One night hiding in the City of Trieste and he would be off to Pola on the morning steamer – no more Cittanova, no more Monfalcon and *addio, Angelica* as well. Just let Stefan Pirjevec try and find him then!

And just as Angelica's hands began roaming further afield and he thought he might get something out of this without putting in too much effort himself, her eye fell on the half-packed overnight bag next to the bed.

The moment died. Angelica sat up and pushed her slip back down over her thighs.

'What's that?' she asked.

The small crocodile-skin case was neatly packed, and her husband had given it some thought, since it was clearly not the work of a moment. Angelica saw a checkbook, a folded shirt, underwear, socks, a bottle of cologne, a small wad of money.

'It's nothing,' he said quickly. 'I'm going away for a couple of days, that's all.'

'Without telling me?'

Angelica eyed the money with hurt curiosity but without envy. He was generous towards her; money had never been an issue between them. But such a small amount? How can you travel without money?

'Where are you going?'

'Trieste,' he fumbled – via Pola, but he wouldn't tell her that. He reached over her and snapped the two sides of the bag together.

'I'd like to go to Trieste,' she said eagerly. 'Can I come, too?'

Brazzi jerked his head back, experiencing a wave of nausea, and a thick lump of fear that hammered at the back of his brain. Or was it the syphilis finally catching up with him? He groped forward to the edge of the bed and put his head between his knees.

'It's not far enough,' he garbled. 'He'll be back.'

Angelica shook her head and her curls bounced.

'I don't understand, Matteo. Who'll be back?'

Brazzi staggered to his feet, fumbling to replace his collar and tie, his waistcoat, close the open trousers which hung by their braces. Angelica watched him and the loneliness of the night ahead crept into her soul.

'I can't give you what you want, Angelica,' said her husband brutally, shoving his shirt into his trousers, grabbing the bag, searching the floor for evidence of his guilt. 'Go to the doctor. He'll tell you why you can't have a baby.'

'But if you know something...' she begged. He headed for the door and she didn't even attempt to run after him but sat in the resignation tinged with despair she had felt so frequently whenever they were together. 'Why can't you tell me? Matteo, I'm thirty-four. I don't have much time left.' She hesitated, trying to articulate the little about men that she had gleaned over the years. 'Do you have... is there some... some problem with...'

He looked at her in horror.

'No!'

Then why?

So as the last of the light faded down the lane upon which his feet would shortly tread, he threw the words at her over his shoulder, 'Because you have syphilis which you caught from me before we were married. You should have waited until you walked down the aisle. You might have known me better by then.'

And he left.

Twilight made rapid strides. From the park a great flock of small birds – perhaps a thousand – rose into the air. As the wind rushed in, they whirled round and round in the gray sky. The tight winding streets had darkened perceptibly and only the feeble glow from candles within its houses made any sense of the thick gloom that was closing in around Brazzi. It was like struggling through a frigid cavern from whose roof hung stalactites and whose dark recesses held demons that might fly out to attack without warning. Somewhere along the way he took a wrong turn and instead of the freedom of the port he discovered himself crumpled at the bottom of a steep flight of stones steps, looking as if he needed to climb out of a crypt. As he hurried away his breathlessness increased, that suggestion of sickness still clutched his head, along with an overall sense of doom he could not put his finger on. With a final turn, he discovered himself not at the City of Trieste at all but at the *mandracio*, with the grove of trees on its southern shore to his right. Certain that all eyes behind all doors were turned upon him, but too sick to care, he followed the murmur of the sea and, as the wind rose in his hair, at length discovered himself blown, or so it seemed, to the Riva Nazario Sauro at whose far end lay the hotel, looming black above the night sky.

Breathing more and more unsteadily, he staggered towards it and thumped at the rear door, pausing for a handful of seconds before rushing around to the front and scratching timidly there, well aware that just across the lane was the Micatovich house where the sight of him was likely to provoke feelings that were far from friendly. He lost his nerve and ran around to the back again, only to see the door inch closed before him.

'Morato!' he hissed, wedging the point of his shoe into the diminishing chink of light. 'Morato!'

And to his astonishment, Andrea Morato himself opened the door, reached out an arm and dragged him inside.

'You look like a rat in a trap,' declared that large gentleman comfortably. 'Rushing between doors like that. Just when I'd almost opened the front one to let you in, you rushed around to the back again.'

'I *am* a rat,' wheezed Brazzi slumping onto the wall behind him and arresting his thumping heart with a hand placed over his chest. His overnight bag dropped to the floor. 'I'm done for. Monfalcon's going to shoot me. You have to shelter me, Andrea. Just until morning, then I'm leaving. I'm out of here.'

'Shoot you?' chuckled Morato. 'He's had that old pistol for years and I've never seen him use it.'

Brazzi's breath came in short rasps. It was becoming difficult to talk.

'You weren't there to see him bully that old man like I was.'

'Ah, it's probably that hand of his. Being labeled a coward when he's not. It's made him bitter, that's for sure. I've seen him take it out on people, too. Plenty of soldiers would be happy just to have survived with three fingers and to hell with the accusations of cowardice. Was the pistol loaded?'

'How would I know?'

Morato paused. To a prosperous man in a pleasant town, there was little that could account for Brazzi's melodrama.

'Are you sure you're not just having a couple of bad days, Matteo? You weren't yourself last night and, you see, nothing came of all that worrying. Now you don't want to rush off like this just as you're settling into the town. The café's been a great success. Many people admire you, you know. It won't look good, you walking out like this. You don't want to take Giuseppe as seriously as you are.'

'You're on his side now, are you?' wheezed Brazzi peevishly. 'You know, he drinks too much.'

'Well, would you begrudge a man a drink in his condition?'

Morato's practical compassion only provoked a further cartload of complaints.

'Why? Does it hurt? Is he bedridden? Look, forget about him. What about me? It isn't only Giuseppe...' Brazzi hesitated. Should he tell him? Could the hotelier be trusted? 'Well, you see...'

'Yes?' Two bushy eyebrows rose expectantly.

He had already told Monfalcon, of course. Morato would have to find out sooner or later. Or would he?

'There was something else about last night...'

He stopped, suddenly unable to decide whom he could trust and, just as he made the decision to provided Morato with an edited version, dizziness washed over him like a waterfall and his furtive gasps failed to supply his chest with air. He clutched one hand to his head and straightened up as far as he could go in an effort to fill his chest, thrusting his other hand above himself. From the restaurant came the muffled chatter of overnight visitors enjoying a drink at the bar; warmth and light poured from a doorway, the smell of varnish on oak.

'Are you all right?' Morato hovered over him and it seemed to Brazzi that he heard his voice come from very far away. 'Matteo? Matteo?'

He picked up Brazzi's bag, put a palm beneath his shoulder and steered him heavily along the corridor and up a staircase. 'You're overwrought.' He shook his head. 'Cittanova doesn't normally have this effect on people. Come into my room and lie down. No one will disturb you there, not even Monfalcon, and when you're feeling better you can tell me all about it.'

'Can't lie down,' gasped Brazzi. 'Can't breathe.'

'Stay quiet then, if you can. I'll get you an extra pillow. Prop you up.'

They had reached a plain door opening upon an equally sparse room. A small fire smoldered in the hearth. Morato turned down the ample bed and sat Brazzi on it, before searching his wardrobe and returning with a large feathered-stuffed pillow and a knitted woolen bedspread, which he rolled into a firm wad. He removed Brazzi's shoes, his tie and his collar, then propped him against the head of the bed and shoved both the pillow and the bedspread behind his back so that Brazzi was almost sitting upright. Then he pulled the blankets up. Brazzi lay in his suit, the silk rose still drooping from his buttonhole, oblivious to all aid, as white and stark as an onion.

Morato regarded him with fatherly disapproval.

'You're not fat like me, Matteo. You want to take some regular exercise. It would help that chest of yours. You shouldn't collapse in a heap just because some old rascal points a pistol at you. Weak constitution.' He waved a finger three times towards the still figure on the bed. 'Eat, drink, sleep. I'll send Ida up with a tray.' He closed the door.

Chapter Twenty

Now that he had come this far, Stefan was beginning to deliberate about his plans for Banich once he found him: why he had wanted him? Here he was on the final stage of his journey of revenge and he realized that the journey itself had been enough.

When he had last seen Banich's face, it had been as grief-stricken as his own but not embittered. As brutally honest as he could be, Stefan knew that, in essence, the fault lay with himself, and what would a confrontation with Banich achieve now? Over the eight years since Nataša had died his emotions had metamorphosed from burning revenge to the thud of a hull that had finally run aground.

Stefan fought no fight with truth. He knew that if he had been there that night Nataša would not have died, and that had nothing to do with Banich. The legions of fascists who had killed her might wage their war with the swagger of the bully: intimidate, rampage, get their kicks without ever going into battle. He had no illusions that he was fighting a real enemy. To his young crew it was all very simple: punish those who were guilty of ethnic cleansing, redeem their land, get money for the fight.

Stefan had a very small cabin, more like a cupboard, which held a narrow bunk and a single shelf. For privacy there was a curtain, but he never closed it. He never shut the boys out when they needed him. On the shelf lay a wooden box, polished and lined with felt, and in it he carried the old dog-eared photograph of Nataša that he had transferred from his wallet. Next to it lay the engagement ring with the small diamond he had given her along with her wedding ring.

He sat on the edge of the bunk and opened the box. Reverently he laid a finger upon the delicate gold wedding ring, and for the first time he was aware of the contrast it presented beside his broad finger, smeared with oil, perfumed by diesel. He regretted the dirt and the impurity when laid beside her relics, which time had kept so holy. He felt unable to express the mystery he sensed when he touched her rings: that he felt she was so close and yet she had gone. Stefan did not dispute the right of time to march on, though he often wondered about its nature for if Nataša belonged only to his past he would be a sad case indeed. Were his the desultory reflections of the widower who at twilight pulls out the drawer in which his wife's memories are preserved in camphor and rosemary? Who, having completed his solitary meal, washes his few dishes and leaves the kitchen spotless, folding his memories away again with his handkerchiefs, and says, 'This is my shrine to her'? Is that all he was doing now?

When he touched the rings, he thought that she was in his present, not his past. At that moment, his belief that she was close to him was so acute that he felt he could reach out and touch her. How much more would he have to endure before they met again? How many circumstances would change for him? How much life had yet to be lived?

A call from the helm distracted him and his thoughts returned immediately to the present. He closed the box. Replaced it on its shelf. Made his way to the bridge. Solved the minor problem that had summoned him there, relieved the seamen on watch. He watched the flat black coast pass by him as the seamen disappeared into the tower, and for a few minutes he was alone. He felt the roll of the boat, heard the night wind picking up – and then he's waiting for her again, the girl in the apricot chemise, wondering how to begin. She's suddenly shy – she's never seen him without his shirt before – and they still have confetti in their hair.

His Most Italian City

And in a heartbeat behind him on the bridge, that certainty.

'*Tukaj si, Nataša.*'

And then she was gone – and in her place, peace.

Swiftly fled his sarcasm, his bitterness, the desire to wound. They dropped from him as the breeze caresses the horizon and blows away the gathering storm. Though it had seemed unending, his burden scraped and bowed and was obsequious in its departure, as if it were sorry to have caused him distress.

Stefan stepped into the conning tower.

'Danilo!' he said to the helmsman who eased inwards to make room for him. 'Bring Giovanni up to the bridge.'

There came noises of creaks and shuffling from below, mechanical grunts, thud, knock, knock, thud, and a hesitant step mounted the rungs of the ladder, not confident of the steep ascent. Stefan mounted the bridge again, Danilo leaned back to let him pass then resumed his station, and finally a dark head and two shoulders in a brown suit emerged. Accentuated by the encroaching darkness, the light of the bare bulb below pulsed up the tower in a thick orange glow. Giovanni looked like he had arisen from the mouth of a furnace. With a weary push and an expectant face, he stepped up onto the half circle of bridge beside Stefan. Above them the night sky stretched over the sea, as omnipresent as it had always been, the final glimmer of sunset just fading away at its westernmost reach.

Giovanni felt that he had been released from purgatory and was soon to wing his way to heaven with the latest batch of celestial deliveries that day. He breathed deeply of the life-giving air until he felt lightheaded. The diesel engines were throbbing again and he had the sense of moving forward, leaving behind the toxic waste from the boat like a wake in the air while before him the breeze was clear and streamed past his ears, playing with his hair, his thick fringe which, untamed, blew backwards. He filled his lungs, wiped away the greasy sweat that had accumulated in the laugh lines around his eyes. He shivered in the cold and it was wonderful.

A wave whipped up by the mischievous wind pitched the bow over its crest and the captain shifted his weight, letting it rest back where it had been, absorbed in his own world, as if he were part of the sea itself. Standing wordlessly together they could have been anywhere, in any time and, as Giovanni clutched the railing with both hands, he considered what Mirko had said about the quiet figure beside him. And it dawned upon him like a sunray that the captain was in love and that he, Giovanni, had not recognized it. Neither the regret he had witnessed nor the focused revenge the captain seemed bent upon had, until now, spoken of a hurt that could only have come from his heart. It amazed him that the knowledge had been allowed to escape, and that he was its recipient.

So he refashioned his attitude to his confinement – the violence that had brought him aboard this strange vessel and made him a part of its ambiguous mission – and he pondered his involvement in its conclusion with something like wonder. He waited, watching the still silhouette flushed by the glow from the conning tower and, just as he thought the captain was too far gone into eternity ever to speak again, Stefan suddenly said, 'You know the man I want?'

Giovanni started at the voice, husky and accented, but he nodded in response.

'You know where he lives?'

'Yes.'

'Did Mirko warn you I would ask?'

'Yes. You could try the café in the piazza. The mayor lives in one of the streets behind it heading towards the *rivarella* in the south, but I don't know the exact house. I would have to ask my parents.'

Stefan remained thoughtful.

'All right,' he said.

His Most Italian City

Venus had come to keep them company in the remains of the day. As the earth passed into a new night, the first in its own history, the archaic planet hovered soundlessly above, where it had always been. Giovanni gazed at its beauty and searched his conscience. How could he save both himself and a man he had never met, already damned by hearsay? Should Brazzi or Banich, or whoever he was, be condemned without a trial? What justice was possible in the present dictatorship? Giovanni searched his brain, but the workable solution did not present itself.

In a few hours they would moor again at the end of the pier at Cittanova and in the darkness Giovanni would feel the pulse of the old town and sense the quiet, rhythmic breathing that marked its sleep. Beneath the sky, now brightened only by blushing constellations and a new moon, he could scarcely discern the Istrian coast, yet away in that darkness lay its patchwork of towns, shimmering as softly as glow-worms in a cave. Lit only by candles, oil lamps, wood and vine prunings, and with the passing hours even these would vanish until the only light left would be the lighthouses and the harbor lights that ran on kerosene.

Below the conning tower he heard a wave wash over the deck, felt the boat slip into its trough, smelled fresh brine and dimly discerned a line of railing. Ropes of metal wire were strung from the bow to the bridge and onwards to the stern. It was all very boat-like, and he suddenly had the ridiculous notion that he was not on a submarine at all but a tugboat with a prominent cabin that might drop below the waves without warning to startle the fish. It would have little portholes of glass, unbreakable under the greatest pressure, and the fish, once they had recovered, would join him happily in whatever educational material he had prepared for them that day, their blank googly eyes assuming a human intelligence and regarding him expectantly.

Dear fish, thought Giovanni.

Chapter Twenty-One

After she had collected the shreds of her future and pasted them together into something resembling existence, after the anger and the indictment, the grief and the despair, Angelica got dressed and left the house. The sound of the sea crashing against the rocks was ever present, the breeze nipped sharply and, as it gained strength, she heard the waves pounding like surf. Through the stone arches cut into the wall, the street was littered with salt spray, and so dark as to be almost unnavigable.

It suited her to be hidden. Slowly she faltered towards Teresa and Emilio's house, feeling her way from dwelling to dwelling, and there, bereft and betrayed, she sobbed the whole shameful story out upon Teresa's generous bosom until she could sob no more. Realizing that they had spread out the welcome mat for at least the remainder of the evening, Emilio laid another place at the table.

'Serves him right if he never lays eyes on you again!' soothed Teresa violently. 'Throwing away the most beautiful lady in Cittanova. Ungrateful, underhand, sick, scheming! Don't cry any more, sweetheart, they can cure it now.'

It. Angelica burst into a renewed fit of weeping.

'I'll take you to the doctor's myself, first thing in the morning. Then we'll go to the duomo, see Father about an annulment and start a Novena to make sure you get it. Then we'll pray to Saint Pelagio. I know he was only thirteen when he was martyred and boys that age aren't always sympathetic to women, but if he can't look kindly on a dear heart like yours then he doesn't deserve the town he's got.' Then, having organized Earth and Heaven, Teresa continued encouragingly, 'There's plenty of nice farmers who would love a pretty wife like you. You'll get your baby, you just see if you don't. Thirty-four's young these days. Look at Euphemia Munda, still popping them out at forty-seven, although granted that was Bruno.'

And when this encouragement failed to soothe, as well it might, Teresa poured two glasses of Emilio's best Dalmatian Prošek and sat down beside Angelica so that they could lose awareness together, Prošek bring renowned, as everybody knew, for the speed at which it went to one's head.

'You know what we could do while you're waiting?' she began, struck by a sudden inspiration. 'We could run that café of his. That would be a good way to meet men. Caffè Fascisti! Of all the ridiculous names. We'll change it tomorrow. What should we call it, Emilio?'

'Caffè Cittanova?' suggested her husband.

'Not bad.' Teresa peered quizzically through the ruby liquid in her glass. 'I had thought of the Caffè Trieste to remind Angelica of her home but we already have a City of Trieste. Can't double up, I suppose.' She pursed her lips. 'But he's getting too fat, that Sior Morato, to run up and down stairs. And I don't know why he was at the café today with Sior Monfalcon. He's a bad influence, that one, looking like he hasn't got long for this world. I'd be saying my prayers if I was him.'

The quiet afternoon had become a fitful evening. Teresa shivered and listened to the wind rattling the shutters. A cracked tile on the roof awaited repair and a chill current of air curled into the room. She moved her chair closer to the range, pulling Angelica across with her.

'There'll be snow on the hills before Christmas. Last year was so mild, we barely got any even in January.

'Do you know what I heard on the way home from the market this afternoon?' Another idea! Wonderful Prošek! 'Poor Sior Micatovich has had a ransom demand for the life of his only son, Giovanni. You remember, the teacher who moved to Florence? Fancy that! Apparently he has been missing since last night when he went for a walk after dinner.'

'Who told you?' asked Emilio.

'Mercedes,' replied Teresa. 'You know, whose husband works down at the quarry? He told her when he came home from work.'

'And who told him?'

'Ah, the kids were all talking about it after school, so Mercedes said. They said it was a big secret so we must try not to spread it about.'

She stared into the flames dancing up the chimney, feeling their pleasant warmth without, warmed by the wine within. 'You know Sior Brazzi and Sior Monfalcon were hard at it, and Sior Morato. I don't know what they were talking about but your husband, Angelica, certainly drew the short straw. Monfalcon knocked the stuffing out of him. I didn't think you could bully Sior Brazzi, but Sior Monfalcon managed to do it. Talk about the three little pigs! One fat, one thin and the other… Well, we know all about him.'

Teresa drained her glass and lurched up. Over on the bench lay the large piece of tuna she had bought for dinner. She abandoned the fire and took up her knife, dividing the dark pink flesh into three pieces instead of two, deeming that she did well to restrain her appetite in the cause of compassion. Then she peeled another potato. The range was only half enclosed, and on the side across from the open fire lay a small oven and beside it a hot plate. On the other side, the flames roared up the chimney. A piece of glowing charcoal spilled out and rolled into the grate. Teresa scooped it up and reloaded it.

Legend had it that many years ago a poor widow was burned to death in this very kitchen, her voluminous skirts caught by the flames, and that she haunted the room on just such dark and windy nights as this one, slapping at her dress until the Second Coming to extinguish the flames. The occasional companionship of this pathetic specter did not bother Teresa, who possessed so much strident sympathy that Emilio had even caught her on the occasional midnight striking a wet rag into the air to help the widow, who remained invisible to everyone but her.

Teresa stood poised with the tuna in her hand.

'Angelica, do you know where your husband has gone?'

'Trieste,' gulped Angelica, red-eyed and tipsy. 'He said Trieste.'

'Well, he won't get out tonight.' Teresa dipped the fish energetically in egg and flour. 'I wonder where he's staying.'

'Why is he leaving so abruptly?' asked Emilio.

'He said… He said, "He'll be back",' gulped Angelica.

Teresa turned sharply. A cloud of flour burst into the air.

'"He'll be back?" Who'll be back?'

'I don't know! He was talking to himself. He sounded frightened.'

Teresa plopped the fish into the pan. Its edges quickly became beige and the rich smell drifted across the room. Teresa chopped lemons and capers.

Angelica finished her glass of Prošek and Emilio, fearing further squalls of tears heading his way, topped it up. Angelica did not wish to offend her host and, perhaps fearing further tears herself – for there comes a time when even the most persistent weeper has wept enough – obliged him by drinking it. Now she sat back in her chair, her head lolling in time with the splattering tuna, her curls falling over her forehead.

'Don't sleep yet, sweetheart!' chided Teresa. 'You'll feel better once you've eaten.'

She laid a loaf of bread upon the table for mopping up the juices and prized from their jar a few capsicum slices pickled in autumn, to garnish the fish; then a spoonful of sauerkraut and a potato landed on each plate. She placed the trio of plates on the table and Angelica aroused herself sufficiently to work up an appetite. The wine had calmed her and her thoughts drifted off into less painful places.

'I suppose it could have been Nataša's husband,' she mused, playing with her knife and fork dreamily.

'What? What's that?' Teresa started up from her mopping, bread in hand.

'Matteo was always falling in love. It was foolishness to marry him, but I was…' She stopped and blushed.

'Every baby's nine months but the first.'

'Pietro was ten, Emilio.'

The wind made impetuous attempts to overhear the conversation. It rattled the door. Angelica swished it away.

'I knew he was in love with Nataša,' she continued. 'But she was married with two children. I just thought he'd get over it… that it would pass once he was married with a child of his own. But he'd grown up with her husband and she'd been in his life for a long time. And then Nataša was killed in the troubles in Trieste the year we were married. And her husband… I don't know what happened to him.

'But this afternoon, Matteo was talking about Nataša. And, you know, he's never mentioned her since. Not once. He was upset when she died but I just thought… after all these years…' She shrugged. 'And then today he suddenly said, "He'll be back."'

Emilio had hurried through his meal. The trouble with conversations of this nature was that they invariably ended with action of some sort. Very soon, departure. He would place a bet on it.

'What do you know about this husband?' he asked.

'Not a lot, really. He was in the navy during the war. A commander or something… I don't know.' She twirled her cutlery in the air as a thought struck her. 'Matteo would know, of course! But he was so frightened after the fire.'

'Fire?'

'Oh, didn't they tell you?' Angelica continued recklessly. The room revolved around her. It brought the tuna back to life and she chased it across her plate – 'There! Got you!' – made strident cuts into the pink flesh with her knife, chewed contentedly. Teresa could hardly hear what Angelica was saying as she talked through her food. 'That's why we came here. Matteo said I wasn't to tell. Someone burned down his office in Trieste. And there was no note, no warning, no threat, no one claiming responsibility.' She glanced behind her as if her words had been overheard. 'It was rather eerie, if you want the truth, Teresa. And Emilio. Sorry. Just saw you over there. It was as if someone had set out to scare him. And he doesn't think I know, but he's so careless. He leaves his things all over the house. Well, someone sent him a can of soup through the mail, a can of soup with a hat – just recently.'

'Soup with a hat?' asked Teresa.

'No, I don't think it *was* soup.'

'It was a bomb,' said Emilio. 'The hat contained the detonator.'

'Yes, I wondered why a can of soup needed a hat,' lisped Angelica blithely. 'Except that it was addressed to me at the café, not him. Matteo just shoved it beneath the hall table.'

Teresa threw up her hands in delighted horror.

'Why would anyone send you such a thing?'

To which the prosaic Emilio replied, 'As a reminder.'

But his answer was too much for the ladies. Teresa jumped from her chair and bolted the front door. Angelica's delicate complexion paled to a mid-winter white.

'Of what?'

'The original act, no doubt. Do you know that a similar device was used to start the fire?'

'The police said so.' Poor, suppressed Angelica. Without makeup she had lost even the look of the painted doll that had supported her. 'Oh dear, oh dear! What will we do? He'll set fire to the café next and there are those three old ladies living in the apartment above it.'

'Ransom demands are very effective,' observed Emilio dryly. 'Give us some money or we'll burn your café down.'

'There are those words again.' Teresa stopped short, the bolt in her hand. 'A ransom demand. What does a ransom demand look like?'

'It means they're asking for money.'

'Yes, I know what it means! I asked what it looks like.'

'A letter,' replied Emilio. 'Usually.'

Teresa was not the fainting type, but at his words she turned as white as Angelica. She fell abruptly into her chair and sat frozen before her fish, looking as if she would collapse on the spot and finally leave Emilio to eat his dinner in peace. But the hour had come. He had virtually cleaned his plate anyway and he was always right about these things. Forward planning, very wise. Up they would leap, and quite shortly.

'I took a letter to Sior Micatovich,' gasped his wife. 'From Siuri Monfalcon and Brazzi only this afternoon. I was on my way home from the café and they said not to delay myself but find, you know, little what's-his-name who's always hanging around the pier, and pay him to do it. And I didn't think. I was in a hurry to get to the markets before they finished and I just did as I was told. They told me it was an invoice, although what they could have been invoicing the old man for, I can't imagine.' She swiveled around to Emilio. 'Do you think…? Could it be…?'

Then she stopped talking entirely. An alarming occurrence. Emilio was forced to finish her sentence for her, which didn't happen very often.

'That that was your ransom demand?'

'It wasn't *my* ransom demand,' Teresa whispered. 'But only think, if it was, doesn't that mean that Siuri Monfalcon and Brazzi have kidnapped Giovanni?'

'Monfalcon's not up to kidnapping anyone.'

'Neither is Matteo,' piped up Angelica.

'Well, he might have.'

'But he didn't.'

Emilio rested his knife and fork on his empty plate. 'Are you sure?'

'I'm not trying to excuse him,' Angelica volunteered. 'But he isn't very physical. He pleaded a rheumatic heart during the war, but I don't believe he's got one.'

'He certainly doesn't have a heart,' agreed Teresa.

'But it might be like him to exploit someone else's misfortune?' suggested her husband.

'Yes,' replied Angelica, head down. 'I expect so.'

'How would we find out?'

'We can't, but we can tell old Zan that he's being robbed by a couple of crooks. They'd be after money, of course.'

Angelica sat perplexed.

'I don't know why Matteo would want more money. He's got plenty in the bank, plus his emergency money in the safe at the café.'

'Sior Monfalcon's a greedy man,' nodded Teresa.

She reached for her coat. Emilio rose after her. He would have risen before her but he had his bet to consider. Angelica remained at the table and worried.

'What if the man with the bomb's out there?'

Emilio handed Angelica her coat of fine red wool, put on his own coarse jacket, shiny at the elbows through much wear.

'You don't want to find out alone. Come on, let's go.'

Teresa knotted a scarf around her head and followed them. At the door lay a small kerosene lamp with a handle. Emilio lit a match and watched as the light flared beneath the glass, then he unbolted the door and the strange party of three tumbled out into the dark street.

The Urizio house was one of a row of semi-detached houses, two-storied and straight-fronted, having, as well, two attic windows at their very tops. The door opened directly onto the street that, at this time of the year, was lined with wintry trees whose bare branches threw warning shadows across the road, as if the trio's errand had already assumed an air of mystery and pursuit. Behind them the road swept on into the dense black of the countryside. Teresa looked cautiously over her shoulder.

There is a train of thought that recommends talking as a good antidote to nerves. Though guilt still clutched at her larynx, Teresa dismissed it with purpose and continued, 'It can't be much past seven. You know, Emilio. I just had a thought, I'll bet it's that husband who's captured poor Giovanni Micatovich.'

'It's not,' replied Emilio. He set his shoulders and trudged on through the cold night with Teresa struggling to keep up with him. 'More likely it was he who sent Sior Brazzi the bomb.'

'Why?'

'Because that's what I'd do in his place.'

'I would never lay eyes on another man, Emilio! I'm shocked you would even think so.'

'But surely the can of soup is the same stuff that blew up his office?' slurred Angelica dropping further and further behind.

Teresa took her hand.

'Don't dally, sweetheart.'

'Then that suggests it's the same man,' said Emilio.

'*Santo cielo!*' Angelica stopped short and clasped both hands to her mouth. '"He'll be back." That's what Matteo said. "He'll be back." He's found out where we live.'

'*Who?*' asked Teresa and Emilio together.

Angelica looked blankly around, almost surprised to find herself the center of attention.

'Why, Stefan, of course. Nataša's husband. It must have been him who blew up Matteo's office.'

'Eight years after her death, just for being in love with his wife? Unlikely, Angelica,' concluded sensible Emilio. 'Bombing is a political act and your husband is a declared fascist. What sort of activities has he been involved with in the years since then that might have prompted it?'

'I don't know,' moaned Angelica. To her left a shooting star sailed over the black bay. 'I didn't know very much about him when I married him. He's got a mother somewhere he won't let me meet – I don't know why. A cousin he won't talk to.'

'Yes, but what does he do?'

'Do? Nothing? Goes to his office, goes out, comes home.'

'What are his views on Mussolini?'

'Who?'

'The prime minister.'

'Oh, that small politician? The one who talks a lot and smiles at crowds? People generally like him, I think, and we did see him once. But Matteo frightens so easily. I don't believe we stayed at the rally.' She fingered her collar. 'No, we didn't.'

'Why was he frightened?' asked Emilio.

'I don't know. I don't know anything about politics.'

They were passing the cemetery of Saint Agatha. Cold mist rose from above the old wall. Teresa and Emilio hurried quickly past and while Angelica trailed along at the end of Teresa's arm she gazed with moonstruck eyes at the galaxy sweeping the heavens.

'I'm going to wish on that star way up there,' she murmured, 'that Matteo drives away tonight and I never see him again.'

'There are two cars in Cittanova,' answered Emilio, 'one in Torre and another on the Venier estate. The monastery has one, too. But the roads are in a disgraceful condition. He'll never get out that way.'

'I'll try a different star,' said Angelica.

Before her, the houses began to close in around the old town. The road narrowed. Rather than pass through the piazza they made a detour to the corner of the *mandracio,* where the long flat fishing vessels rocked on their moorings in the night breeze. Then they hurried through the darkened

School Street and into the Corso, then through Fish Shop Lane and around to the back of the tall old Micatovich house. From within came light and movement. Emilio mounted the single step and knocked heavily upon the door until a creak and a shuffle declared it about to open. A slit of light, a surge of warm air. Teresa shoved her foot in.

'Sior Micatovich,' she announced, 'I've come to tell you that I sent the ransom demand.'

Chapter Twenty-Two

Euphemia Munda was a reliable woman. She had promised Sior Micatovich that she would send her son Bruno to his home the minute he stepped through her front door, and that was what she intended to do. But it was nearly nine and there was, as yet, no sign of him.

He's tired, sore and well fed, she thought. *And he's sleeping it off.*

It was the only explanation for his delay. But it grieved her that she had been unable to fulfill the promise she'd made to the old man.

Bruno did not share his mother's concerns. After his day behind the wheelbarrow, he had eaten the large dinner that was set before him in the farmhouse kitchen, then, exhausted from the manual labor, he had fallen asleep at the kitchen table before he could even begin the journey home. Knowing that Bruno, even awake, had his own agenda, Martin Picolich left him there, his wife cleaned the kitchen and his son Dominic, watching the heavy face turn blank and drop out of consciousness, cursed his luck. There was no option now but to wait for Bruno to wake up, and this only happened when it had been dark for some hours and the breeze was murmuring along the trees lining the road back to town.

True to form, the night and the wind had the usual pleasurable effect on Bruno's nerves. At last he opened his eyes, twitched his nose and, knowing at once that the breeze would be stronger by the water, he rose wordlessly, shot out the door refreshed and rejuvenated and made straight for Cittanova as fast as his legs would carry him. Hot on his heels trotted a weary Dominic Picolich.

'Bruno, wait! Wait! *Wait!!*'

The country road from Buie wound through a mosaic of thriving olive groves, winter-pruned vines, ploughed fields of red earth, chubby forests without leaves in winter, and tall pine groves above soft and verdant grass. The land sloped to the sea and was dotted with small farms.

With his father's money in his pocket, Dominic could think of far more pleasurable pursuits than following what he thought of as the town's liability three kilometers into town in the cold, and three back. He had a good mind to give up and find somewhere warm and convivial to spend the cash, instead of roaming this cold, dark, isolated road. Much to his chagrin, the ghostly journey seemed to be invigorating Bruno, who saw no reason to go home and was apparently heading for the port as quickly as he could, knowing that at this hour he'd have it all to himself.

Silence lay upon the land. The boys hurried through a countryside as dotted with dwellings and chapels as a treasure map, houses and barns of rough-cut stone, seemingly falling down for centuries yet still upright. Dominic, chasing Bruno, navigated the familiar route by their black shapes against a night sky only barely lighter. They were as familiar to him as his face and he put not a foot wrong, recognizing here a modest shrine, there the protruding bulk of a Venetian manor established when feudalism ruled Europe. The grain had yet to be sown; bare fields ended at a ridge of whispering pines, and beyond them was the sea.

Lapped by the tide, the town reposed like the ancient island it had once been. From this height the small sweeping beam of the lighthouse could be clearly seen; to its right shone the harbor light on the pier and, further along, was the lamp at the entrance to the *mandracio*. The scene represented such a statement of calm existence that Dominic felt that even should the sea rise up and cover the town, it would remain beneath the waves just as it was at this instant of time, going about its life untroubled.

His Most Italian City

'Bruno, wait for me. Bruno!'

By now they were approaching the outskirts of Cittanova. Dominic puffed fifty meters behind, disgusted that a fixture like Bruno could move with such surprising speed when he felt like it. He jogged on past the first straggling houses, the road to Parenzo and, on his left, the waters of the lake rippling in the night breeze, the tall pines surrounding it soaring into the sky. In summer this road was flanked by deciduous trees, in autumn their greens changed from golden to red. By now they were in mourning, their glory gone, as stark as many-fingered hands begging to the sky. Up ahead he saw the chapel and the walled cemetery of Saint Agatha. Dominic shivered with cold and superstition and wished himself home in bed but, before he could act on this, Bruno shot up a side street and Dominic lost him.

Making up his mind on the spur of the moment as he usually did, he abandoned Bruno (as Bruno had abandoned him, he reasoned) and decided to go straight to Bruno's home, and pay his mother before temptation got the better of him. Let her worry about wherever Bruno was heading. Bruno was not Dominic's responsibility, after all. With a bit of luck, Bruno had gone straight home but, having observed his widening stride and ecstatic body language as the wind rose, then that furtive duck around the corner, Dominic doubted it.

Sure enough, when chilled, windswept and grumpy he at length knocked on the flat-fronted door of the Mundas' simple dwelling, Euphemia's worn features fell at the sight of him. She had been hoping that the haphazard thumping at her door would be her twelfth child (though Bruno neither knocked nor thumped).

Dominic extended a sweaty bunch of notes towards her.

'That's from my father,' he grunted. If Dominic could have said the same thing in one syllable he would have.

'Thank you, Dominic,' sighed Euphemia. 'Ah…' (*Here it comes*, thought Dominic.) 'Is Bruno with you?'

Dominic did not tell Euphemia that she should have known that was a dumb question. Instead he stepped back to expose the barren gray shoreline beyond the row of small houses to make it quite obvious to the unfortunate woman that no Bruno was about.

Then, eager to get his onerous task over with, he added, 'Bruno said something about Giovanni Micatovich being on the pier with some guy called Zorko.'

'*What?*' gasped Euphemia.

'Dunno,' replied Dominic and started for home.

Euphemia stood in her doorway, perplexed and frightened, but, after twelve children, she was not about to take attitude from a sixteen year old.

'Dominic!' she called smartly to the retreating figure. Dominic slunk to a halt. 'I'll have to look for Bruno. He might be in danger. You need to stay and help me. Go and tell Sior Micatovich what you've just told me.'

Telling himself he was the biggest loser for not spending the money and taking off while he had the chance, Dominic did as he was told.

*****

Bruno, for his part, had long since forgotten Dominic's existence. Humming a repetitive little melody beneath his breath, he had veered right into New Street off the road from Buie and passed through the groves on either side, briskly navigating their short length until he reached the shore of the *mandracio* and its rows of moored fishing boats. The wind whispered through the pines. The waves crashed against the rocks to the south. Bruno breathed deeply and felt exhilarated.

By ducking down Boatyard Lane and out the other end, he avoided his home near the loading docks – not an easy maneuver in the dark, although Euphemia often said that Bruno had cat's eyes. At the end of the lane the old houses that overshadowed him towered three stories high and the narrow spaces in between were frigid and black. Bruno dashed forward until he located his favorite place, closeted in gloom, from which he could see without being seen. A short distance in front of him lay the commencement of the pier and the hotel, City of Trieste.

Here a smile of pure pleasure disrupted his passive features. It was back! Moving slowly across the entrance to the port created by the breakwater and the pier was the black boat that had so interested him last night, when the Bora blew and the whole town had stayed safely indoors except him. Beneath the revolving beam from the lighthouse, its sleek deck moved with stealthy grace and its bow created two waves of shiny surf that washed back and outwards like mountains of obsidian capped with snow. A solid band of froth emerged from the propellers and spun out behind its stern, caught yellow here and there, and shooting a tail of spray into the air. Bruno, watching entranced from his shadows, thought it was the most wonderful thing he had ever seen.

The wind whipped through his hair and the surf came crashing over the breakwater. The stern boulders that protected it were too black to see, but he could hear the roar of the waves. Before his eyes, the boat glided on and disappeared around the far end of the pier, reemerging on the other side at exactly the spot where the steamer unloaded its passengers. Bruno stepped cautiously from his hiding place and moved towards the commencement of the pier to get a better look. But the pier swept away from him, broad and flat, with no discernible hiding places and Bruno, being well acquainted with that fact, hesitated to go any further in case he was seen. He slipped carefully behind the bulk of the hotel and around the front of the customs house, until he reached the half dozen stairs descending to the shore and perched precipitously on the last one so that the small rising tide did not wet his boots. Then, by poking his nose just above the stone wall, he had a limited view of the boat, but limited was better than nothing.

Bruno could not bear the company of people for too long. It often made him so anxious that he longed to scream, and sometimes he did. In addition, he felt secure with his routine and, if fate was going to throw any alterations his way, he needed to know in advance. Within his sanctuary he felt safe as long as he believed people could not see him but, as he peered with cautious excitement above the stone quay, he observed a man walking on the low deck with a rope in his hands. It was a very low deck indeed, so low that it resembled the water it lay upon, but Bruno could make out what he thought was a small cabin rising in the middle of the deck. In all it looked black. As black as a sea bird soaring from a rock on which a schooner might hole herself and sink.

The sight of the man heaving the mooring line over one of the cleats agitated those nasty little insects Bruno was sure crawled around inside him. He laid a hand on his belly and compressed a finger on either side of his nose. Little habits he had to calm himself. He felt upset that the man had spoiled his boat – Bruno thought of it as his boat – and decided with that immediacy which was in a class of its own that he needed to Go Home, Now. Fortunately, home was the line of fishermen's houses on the shore of the *mandracio*, so Bruno hurried up the stairs and hot-footed it out of there as fast as he could.

*****

Long before they had reached the sweep of the breakwater and the pier beyond it, they had cut the diesel engines and sailed in silently on the electric motors. Slowly, carefully, as warily as a cat, the captain directed the helmsman to approach the pier, then stepped down onto the deck and secured the mooring lines to the cleat. For those knowing little about submarines, it appeared to be nothing more than a boat. It was only the more curious observer who, seeing its shape appear vaguely out of the blackness, would realize that the conning tower was not a cabin, the periscope was not a fishing rod and the turret forward of the tower had once contained a gun.

Climbing one step at a time up the ladder of the conning tower and through the hatch to the bridge, Zorko went before Giovanni, with Mirko and Andrej immediately after him. Once into the clean night air, they turned and jumped down onto the deck, then, as the boat lay so low in the water, they scrambled up a meter of stone encrusted with barnacles to join the captain who was already on the pier. At the harbor light, Mirko clasped his hands together and from them Andrej sprang up the ladder. In a second they were plunged into darkness as the flame was extinguished.

*****

The sight of his front door wide open did little to assuage Bruno's mounting anxiety, but he barged through and closed it firmly behind him, after which he calmed down somewhat. But here was his mother, hurrying towards him all dressed up to go out and look for him. Her anxiety melted into relief.

'Black boat on pier!' announced Bruno without greeting her.

'The steamer is white, Bruno,' corrected Euphemia.

Bruno shook his head. 'Black boat on pier!'

Revelation dawned on Euphemia's face.

'Did you see this black boat last night, too, Bruno?' she gasped.

'Yes!' barked Bruno before pushing past her to the main room of the house that served as kitchen, dining room, lounge and bedroom.

Having just battled the ire of Dominic at this late hour, Euphemia was in no mood to put up with bad manners from Bruno.

'Stop!' she commanded. Single words had a good effect on Bruno. Bruno stopped. 'You must tell Sior Micatovich right away. Say "black boat on the pier" to Sior Micatovich. Go! Good boy, Bruno!'

She shoved him out the door.

Thwarted in his attempts to shield himself from unwanted company by going home, Bruno crept along the shore and down the lane, barely holding his mounting anxiety at bay. Keeping as far away from his boat as he could, he made it to his well-off neighbor's unseen and in under a minute.

On his way he passed a figure even more furtive and anxious than he was. Bruno ignored him. He had been told to do one job and it was not part of his own rules for himself to do anything else.

*****

Eat, drink, sleep. Brazzi had obeyed Morato's advice except the sleep, and he couldn't sleep because he couldn't breathe. A common asthma attack! This is what came of exercise. Matteo Brazzi swore he would never take any again.

The attack had rendered it impossible for him to return to the café and retrieve his money. After Morato had left, Brazzi floated in a realm without pleasure save for the hope that sometime soon he might be able to breathe again. He had heard the serving girl Ida enter and deposit a tray by his bed but couldn't recall her departure. As disassociated from his body as a ghost, he inspected a single star through the window and had an ethereal notion that a savory smell was wafting towards him. It occurred to him that perhaps he had passed away next to a bowl of soup and would float off to join the star in a heaven where there would be neither bombs nor guns nor fascism, and he would reap a justified reward for looking after himself so well.

The first shred of normality appeared as the campanile chimed a quarter past nine. He inhaled gently and discovered that by thinking calmly he could slow down the great gulps of air he had been forced to swallow and that his chest had, over the several hours he had lain in Morato's bed, relaxed a little. He no longer felt that a rope was being tightened around his ribs. He pulled at his watch chain, slid his watch from his pocket and nearly died again when he saw the time. Nearly half past nine. Well, that might be good after all, for surely Monfalcon would have gone by now. He could take his overnight bag, fill it with the cash and return to the hotel. Get a proper night's sleep before his departure in the morning.

His Most Italian City

He stood up slowly, registered the dizziness associated with the effort, held his head up, put his hat on and, sucking in some air, told himself that he would be all right once he got going. Slowly he negotiated the stairs and, at the bottom, walked in a measured tread to the restaurant, where he found Morato negotiating with a customer about a room.

'I won't be long,' said Brazzi in a subdued voice that didn't sound like his at all.

Morato hastily excused himself to the customer and hurried out.

'Where are you going?' he asked with concern.

'I won't be long,' repeated the new Brazzi.

'Say that again.' Morato cupped his ear. 'I can't hear you.'

'*Ciao*,' murmured Brazzi and waved.

'That night air won't be good for your chest!'

But Brazzi had already staggered outside and the minute he hit the cold air he began to cough. *Won't be long, won't be long*, he reassured himself. Cough, cough, cough. Just get the money. At some stage during the catastrophe, he realized that Morato had removed his collar and tie, and undone the top buttons of his shirt. Brazzi had not successfully put himself back together and now, as he crept through the black streets gasping and coughing, he looked like an airplane had used him for a runway.

His hat lay askew, he had used his immaculate handkerchief to blow his nose, his suit looked as slept-in as it was, his tie had assumed complete asymmetry, his collar button had broken and the stiff collar itself had shuffled up his neck. One shoelace was undone, two fingernails were cracked and three strands of hair coated with Brilliantine flopped like buzzards in a blizzard upon his forehead. And little did he know that the fine silk rose that had adorned his buttonhole had been accidentally pilfered by Ida, who hadn't realized that fashionable men wore artificial flowers and didn't know what it was doing there.

But – wonder of wonders! – amidst the adversity mounting around him he discovered the key to the safe securely in his pocket, where he had laid it. And, with that last shred of hope, Brazzi put his blinkers back on. He could again be focused. All would be well.

He crept into the deserted piazza and entered the café.

Chapter Twenty-Three

The clock in the hall read half past nine, the campanile had boomed twice, but no one had told Silvana to go to bed. She sat in the formal front room of her grandparents' house surrounded by more family members than she saw at Christmas dinner: Nono, smokeless for once, with Gilda at his feet. Beside him, Nona turned the heel of a sock on four needles to take her mind off her son. Next there was her father in his precisely pinstriped suit and her mother, too worried about her brother to chide Silvana for sitting in polite company in her school dress. Beside them, in the straight-backed mahogany chair, sat her mother's cousin, Giorgio, who had hurried into town from his rural estate at the dreadful news about Giovanni, which he'd heard from his estate manager. Next to him was Auntie Agatha, her cousins Marina and Gemma, and, finally, Nono Zambon, her father's father, widowed and white, who had not been well for some time but insisted on being present to share the family crisis. In the sole corner of the room not abundant with relatives sat the local mechanic, Emilio Urizio, his wife Teresa, restrained and sorrowful, and beside them Angelica Brazzi, who from time to time wiped away gentle tears with an embroidered handkerchief. They had arrived at the front door some time ago bearing an extraordinary story about Angelica's husband himself having written the ransom letter. A naive Teresa, now scarlet with remorse, said she had enlisted the delivery boy, and vowed she would 'never, ever commit such a guileless crime again – God help me – and if I had only known the contents of that vile letter I would have called out the *polizia* that instant rather than cause the poor white hairs of Sior Micatovich to grow any whiter by acting in haste, for Signor Brazzi is out to swindle you, the despicable villain!'

Sadly, their arrival did not answer the question of where Giovanni actually was, and general gloom and consternation still reigned. On the table in the center of the room lay two plates of cakes and savories which everyone was too upset to eat, and a bottle of wine slowly being consumed by Angelica.

Giorgio, the son of Zan's long-dead brother, had taken the lead in the move towards action.

'I don't like it,' he growled. 'Missing sons! Ransom notes! You haven't been very successful in covering it up, Zan. Anyone could have exploited you. What proof do we have that the perpetrators, if such there were, sent this letter?'

'I took a letter from Siuri Monfalcon and Brazzi,' lamented Teresa.

'A boy brought it,' said Zan wilting under his nephew's scorn.

'I gave it to the boy.'

'You didn't know what was in it?' demanded Giorgio.

'No, sior,' said Teresa.

'Whom do you suspect?' asked Romano, who was more guarded in his distress.

'Whom do you think? I suspect this Brazzi, and now it appears that we have proof.'

'I don't like him,' Zan said miserably. 'I never liked him, but I didn't want to say so.'

'You could have said so,' replied Romano kindly.

'But I didn't.'

'When these men arrive here suddenly,' continued Giorgio, who felt it was his job to rally the conversation, 'they're always running away from something.

His Most Italian City

'What did the constable suggest, Romano? That we just sit here until half past ten, or whatever ridiculous time it was, then roll up at the pier as if we're going for a midnight swim? We accuse Brazzi of complicity and he denies it?'

'We don't know where he is,' Romano replied.

Angelica stood up with the bottle in her hand.

'I know where he'll be,' she said, laying it resolutely on the table. 'He's got…'

But her courage failed her and, just as all eyes were turned her way, Gilda's ears pricked up and there came a knock at the door. Zan began to rise.

'Let me get it, Zan,' offered Romano.

Zan flopped down again, patting his jacket pocket for his tobacco pouch, but the soft silk was flat and he recalled desolately that he had left the tobacco on his bedside table because Dolores disapproved of smoking. Gilda barked and bounded into the hall and down the steps, returning in half a minute with Romano and a pimply youth in work pants that he was growing out of. A scowl of apprehension soiled his face at appearing in a room of such well-dressed people. He made his way directly to the corner where Emilio Urizio sat with his wife, and stood in their more comfortable company without speaking.

'Dominic Picolich!' began Teresa, covering three functions: introduction, enquiry and accusation. 'What have you got to say for yourself?'

'Zorko was on the pier,' mumbled Dominic, wishing himself anywhere but here. 'With,' he indicated Zan with a flick of his head, 'his son.'

Zan's heart leapt into his throat and Giorgio jumped to his feet.

'How do you know this, Dominic?' he demanded.

'Bruno Munda told us.'

'Bruno? Are you certain?'

'No,' mumbled Dominic.

'And who is this Zorko?'

Dominic shrugged and glowered at the assembled crowd as if they should know, not him. He had scarcely showed them what he thought of them disrupting his evening when there came a second knock on the lower door, made by a hand that lacked Dominic's sullen attitude but which also lacked the co-ordination to knock correctly. It had been perhaps made with a palm instead of a knuckle.

Gilda barked again, and this time Zan, very tired, rose with the mixture of hope and urgency that Dominic's news had prompted and shuffled down to the door. He opened it a fraction, just enough to prevent the frosty air from overpowering the warmth in the hall, and cautiously poked his worried head around the crack.

There stood Bruno, large and anxious.

'Ah, yes, Bruno?' mumbled Zan at the sight of the boy. 'Come in out of the cold.'

Bruno did not seem to notice the temperature at all but waited where he was, neither moving nor accepting Zan's offer, clad only in his shirt, trousers and a sweater.

'Black boat on pier!' he announced with his head averted.

'There is a black boat on the pier?' queried Zan.

'Black boat on pier!' repeated Bruno before turning to leave, his duty done.

'Bruno, wait a moment!' cried Zan, snatching his hat and coat from the stand behind him. The boy stood blank and immobile. 'Can you show me the black boat on the pier?'

'Yes!' replied Bruno in his usual peremptory tone.

'Well then, show me the black boat on the pier and then I want you to go straight home to bed.'

'Home to bed,' repeated Bruno.

'Home to bed,' said Zan.

His Most Italian City

He took Bruno's hand, patted it to reassure the boy, and walked with him into the kitchen to the window that overlooked the port. Cautiously he opened first the window then the shutter and peered out. The night was impenetrable. The garden below the window gaped like a black pit and he could not see the gate beyond it that passed through the sea wall. Far across the port, only the beam from the lighthouse intruded into the darkness.

Beside him Bruno had begun to tug at his hand.

'Home to bed,' said Bruno. He shuffled his feet. 'Home to bed!'

'Yes,' Zan told him. 'First boat, then bed.'

At the top of the stairs he donned the hat and coat, and led Bruno back down into the lane. After a strict injunction to be silent, he asked the boy to lead him to the black boat. Behind them, in the house, he heard further talk. He could not have been the only one to hear Bruno's knock, and they would be wondering why he had not returned. Presently, perhaps, they would rise and follow him.

Well, he couldn't worry about them now. All he could think of was his son.

They got as far as the end of the lane, about five meters. Straight in front of them stood the City of Trieste and at the back of the hotel, a little to his right, he saw a troupe of five men standing at the broadest end of the pier where it continued along the Riva Nazario Sauro. The beam from the lighthouse only lit up the sea in front of it, and did not enable Zan to distinguish between the men. He only knew they were there because they contrasted with the thicker darkness of the lane. He froze back against the wall of the last house, dragging Bruno behind him so that they were facing the entry to the dogleg that commenced the Corso Victor Emanuele. The cold stone dug into his back; the smell of the lane rose into his nostrils, damp earth and dog's piss. From the port came the sharp salt tang of the sea.

As he watched, the men walked down the dogleg towards Zan's hiding place as if they would pass it, peering from side to side, their wary footsteps muffled. With both joy and a cold dismay, Zan recognized the erect head and square shoulders of his son. More than this he could not make out. Despite Bruno's bulk by his side, he squashed the two of them into the cold stone. As much as he tried to consider the feelings of the youth, he was unable to take his eyes off Giovanni. The fleeting beam from the lighthouse raised Giovanni's features a fraction above black before they vanished again.

Zan waited until the group had passed through the dogleg a mere ten meters, twice as far as he had come. But when they reached the entrance to Fish Shop Lane they paused.

For what could they be waiting?

Behind a shutter a candle flickered. Zan saw his warm breath turning white before his eyes and the longer they waited, the more it resembled a signal flare, signaling 'Here I am!'. Surely his hiding place must be obvious? He endeavored to stop breathing, covering his mouth with his hand. Across the lane Giovanni seemed to be exchanging words with the figure beside him, his head bent to catch the whispered reply. Twice Giovanni appeared to be listening, then he pointed along the lane and the other head nodded.

Close behind him Zan heard a door slam loudly and Gilda bark.

They have finally realized I have not come back, thought Zan.

'Did anyone see Zan leave?'

'Yes, he answered that last knock at the door. But where has he gone?'

Maria will be worrying, continued Zan to himself. *First her son disappears and now her husband.*

He looked behind him and saw the light flare in the lower windows. How far away from the house were he and Bruno now? Half a dozen steps? And that strange group was so close. How could he warn his family to restrain their movements so as not to compromise Giovanni's safety?

His Most Italian City

Wait, wait, not yet! A glance at the doorway. Zan was finding it harder to remain composed and, behind him, he felt Bruno begin to squirm. Zan eased a hand onto the boy's wriggling chest, trying to hold him back, to reassure him, when he was the one who really needed reassurance. But eighteen-year-old boys are very strong and when Bruno wanted something enough he possessed hidden reserves of strength, so that the struggle seemed certain to end badly.

All at once Zan heard, 'Home to bed!' and, to his horror, Bruno simply prized Zan's hand from his arm without difficulty and ran from his hiding place directly in front of the men.

As quick as a sword thrust a big man in front pushed forward and grabbed Bruno by the shoulder. Bruno, though solid and strong, frightened easily and this exacerbated the co-ordination difficulties that made most townspeople label him a large, clumsy lump. He twisted and turned in Zorko's grasp of cold steel – Zorko had him with both hands now – shaking his head and yelling, 'Home to bed! Home to bed!' as loudly as he could. Then he began to scream.

A candle appeared in a window above them, then another and another down the lane. Questioning shouts, among them Giorgio's sharp voice, Romano's restrained tones, Maria telling Silvana to stay in the house. Doors opened, footsteps hastened onto the cobbles and out of the shadows stepped Zan, saying in the same self-effacing manner he used when asking Maria to pass the salt, 'Let him go, please.'

To complete the effect he turned to his son and said, 'Ah, Giovanni, there you are.'

A crowd had formed, overcoats hiding sleep attire, several men holding kerosene lamps. By their light, Zan noted his son's disheveled appearance, his strained face and pinched features, the suit that the prim little tailor in Florence had taken such pains with, creased and stained.

A man who by his terse authority appeared to be their leader grunted a command to the big man, who released Bruno. Bruno catapulted into the crowd in the direction of his home, barging through the men and women who were too preoccupied by the commotion to move. A group that had emerged from the City of Trieste were knocked to one side, among them Andrea Morato.

'What's happening?' he demanded as Bruno's agitated figure departed pell-mell down the dark street. He straightened his coat. 'I thought the Turks had arrived.'

'I'm not a Turk, Signor Morato,' said Zan.

'Then what's the matter with Bruno?'

'He's gone home. He's all right.'

Morato cast his gaze upon the strange group. The lamps held aloft by fishermen and store owners wavered golden light upon orange in uncertain streaks. The over-large man from whose grasp Bruno had fled had taken his stand at the back from where, presumably, he could observe the proceedings. Two young men stood in front of him wearing uniforms of heavy drill – belted, proud, unapologetic. One wore a cap upon his dark head. At the very front, closer to the lamps and therefore more distinctly lit, stood the leader of the group, a man in early middle age. Despite the cold that whitened his breath, he wore no coat and stood without shivering, as if he had other things more pressing on his mind and considerations of temperature would have to wait.

And then Morato's eye alighted on Giovanni, who had distanced himself from the four strangers to stand beside his father. Morato drew back and, to mask his culpability, added a false confidence to his words. 'Who are these men?'

'They're looking for Signor Brazzi.' This from Giovanni.

At the sound of his voice – and surely it was years since he had heard it? – Zan felt such gratitude that it was as if his heart had just now learned how to sing.

'Why, Signor Brazzi was at the hotel with me,' continued Morato guardedly. 'But he went out, and not so long ago, either.'

'Where?'

'He didn't say.'

Quickly Morato scanned the crowd and, not finding Brazzi, moved to withdraw.

Angelica had joined the others and now stood, hiccoughing quietly, staring at Stefan who, finding himself the focus of the crowd's attention, waited with frustration for someone to reach the decision that would free him. She had only ever seen him once or twice and knew him as the naval man whose wife Matteo had been in love with. Matteo who had betrayed her. So she lifted her voice, and this time everybody listened.

'I know where he is.'

At once Stefan turned his eyes upon her and, under their piercing mandate, Angelica reversed until she bounced off Teresa's soft thighs.

'He's… he's gone to the café to collect his money, St…Stefan,' she stammered. 'He had some with him but he keeps a whole lot more locked in the safe below the till.' The men marched off. 'Stridently,' considered Angelica, who wasn't given to description but thought that after alcohol an adjective was appropriate. 'That is, I think he has,' she added.

Her moment of reprisal over, she began to sway. And it was a terrible thing she had done, really, betraying someone whom she had sworn to have and to hold, for better or for worse.

'That was him?' Teresa's excitement was bubbling over. She grabbed Angelica's hand, fearful of what she might miss if she let it go. 'That was the husband with the bomb?'

Angelica was too agitated to reply.

'Oh, do you think I've done the right thing, Teresa?'

'Yes, I do.'

'But what will they do to him?'

'Do you care?'

'Yes.' Angelica chewed her rosy lips. 'I don't know.'

'Come on, then! Let's follow them.'

'Oh no, Teresa! Poor Matteo!'

'"Poor Matteo," rubbish! What about poor Angelica?'

'Yes, you're quite right.'

'We'll watch from around the corner of the piazza.'

'Just until we find out if he's safe.'

They started off after the men and when at last they saw them disappear into the Caffè Fascisti, they took up their stand in the shadow of the final house, as cold as two storks on an iceberg.

Chapter Twenty-Four

In the deserted piazza the entrance bell above the door assumed tremendous volume, powerful enough, he thought, to summon every policeman from up and down the coast. Stefan put his hand up to deaden it, but it seemed to echo even against his palm. He opened the door. Thin white starlight pushed into the interior. A chill wind lifted the lace curtains. Emilio raised the lamp and they all followed in a line behind Stefan: Romano, Mirko, Zorko and Andrej, then Giovanni and, lastly, Zan. Within the café the scents of cinnamon and cocoa hung as reminders of the day. Pristine cloths covered the tables. Just visible beneath them were the curved legs of the chairs.

His heart felt light now, he was happy; in these final moments he was only curious. He was certain that the wife who had reacted to him with such alarm had had more than enough reason to brave whatever she thought him capable of in order to betray her husband.

He hurried now. Two rapid steps, no room for any more, and a curious lurch into the unknown as if from the top of a cliff. Should he be nervous to see again this tangible link to Nataša? But with the knowledge of her presence, the rupture between his soul and mind had healed and he was calm. They were meeting him together. The long room, the quiet tables, the suggestion of lamplight dimmed the slanders and sorrows of so long ago. Their shadows passed by and went on their way, and the sea wind no longer cut him so keenly. Like Banich, they had lost their power to hurt, and the solitary hours would not be lonely.

*****

The safe was closed, the key was in his pocket; Brazzi had the bag full of notes in his hands when he saw the men broaching the impenetrable darkness of the piazza. Black, gray, night surrounded the drifting ghosts and an amber light glowed between them. He crept into the darkest corner and from the floor watched the troop of legs enter his café. Tall legs, some shorter, men of several heights, he thought. A quiet dusting of gossamer on gray wool, then blue cloth trousers. Sea boots, cork soles, well worn, peeked out from beneath them. The trousers crossed towards him, a belt, a shirt, he couldn't see any higher. He heard two more thumps behind and other boots landed with purpose on his fine floor, then he spied more working clothes. He saw a lamp, metal bearings, some rust to show its age, a looped handle. A broad palm and a thumb held it firmly. He smelt kerosene and saw that the lamp was hot. He thought it must be raising the temperature of the room but its warmth didn't reach him.

Someone went 'Humph!" He knew what that meant – he had not yet been found. *They think they have come for nothing.* He remained very still. He believed that, covered in his dark corner, he could not be seen. He was not yet at the point of terror. But his breathing betrayed him. The stiller he stayed the more he panted and his heart began to thump in his chest. *Curse this quiet hour when all sounds carry!* Even his thoughts seemed to shout across the room and he was sure that they could sense the fear of the hunted, smell his stale stink.

Brazzi clutched his overnight bag and shrank back under the shadow of the counter.

'There he is!' shouted Romano.

His clothes were crumpled and awry. He had lost the last shreds of his self-possession. Later he might resurrect himself – when this bad dream was over – so, ultimately, it didn't matter who saw him like this. He was leaving. Who cared? – well, he didn't – there was only one person he cared about and that was himself. For the rest, he was apparently the mayor, and under that title he held a certain degree of authority. He pushed himself up on his hands until his face appeared, blotched by the lamps, below his poster that read 'Devotion to Italy.'

Plastering a smile across his face and gasping a little, he enquired, 'Can I help you, signori?'

Stefan peered across the counter, probably as confidently as he had always done, and was surprised to see fear in the face below him.

'You!' gasped Brazzi.

'Told you he knew him,' whispered Mirko to Giovanni.

'Gospod Banich!' returned Stefan. Now that the moment was upon him, doubt washed away. He knew exactly what to say. 'You've looked better.'

Brazzi shrunk, as if he were melting.

'I never touched her!' He pointed a trembling finger at Stefan. 'She wouldn't let me.'

In the eight years since Matteo Brazzi had last seen Stefan Pirjevec, his dress had not changed but much else had. Grief and care had carved furrows into the face that had once been untroubled. Hope had fled. Endurance had taken its place. Only Stefan's eyes, their focused regard, at best encouraging, at worst intimidating, reminded Brazzi of the vigorous young man he had been. It was more than possible to conclude that time had been kinder to Matteo Brazzi, Best Dressed Man in Trieste, who had slain his competition in the ditches along his way.

Heads turned.

'Banich?' asked Teresa.

'Banich?' asked Zan.

'Banich?' quivered Brazzi. 'Never heard of him.'

He endeavored to resume his customary posture of superiority, and every time he tried, he wheezed. He splattered heavy mucus into his hands and had nowhere to wipe it. He swiped his palms on the hard floor and put two shiny hands in the air – that felt better – filled his lungs. Realizing that his hands resembled a declaration of surrender, he abandoned the attempt and put one down, left the other up in order to expand his lungs and only succeeded in looking as if he were drowning. So he gave up and shooed the unmanageable appendages into the air.

'Go away and leave me alone!'

'We had an appointment.'

'Did we?' Brazzi struggled to his knees, still wheezing. 'I don't recall, although your memory was always better than mine.' Cough, cough. 'I believe I may have been more pleasantly engaged. Ask my friends here.'

'Your friends don't know you like I do, Banich.'

'Are you threatening me? What do you want? Money? Here, take it.' He shoved the stuffed overnight case towards them. It was immediately snatched by Andrej, who upended it on the floor, sifting and sorting through items of an intimate nature: underpants, socks, vests, a razor, talcum powder, cologne, the detritus of a disordered person who still liked to dress well.

Brazzi sniffed as if he had been stripped naked.

'Do you mind?'

Andrej repacked the bag, now at least half full with notes.

'Thanks for financing the resistance movement,' Andrej quipped, before adding darkly, 'You're lucky that's the only prize I'm taking.'

'You smell,' replied Brazzi as the bag disappeared over a young shoulder.

Who were these people? He saw a tall, overweight man of about his own age who shoved past him with disinclination, as if he wasn't worth the effort. Two boys, equally contemptuous, examined Brazzi with the superiority of those with a higher cause. The one with his bag turned to Stefan.

'What will we do with him, Captain?'

His Most Italian City

'We'll let the fascists deal with him,' Stefan answered.

The lamp swung on its handle and its glow discolored Brazzi's recoiling face.

'He doesn't seem to like that idea,' observed the boy drily. He bent his head down until their eyes met. 'Now's your chance to justify your actions, you genuine fascist hero.'

'I've got nothing to say to you,' wheezed Brazzi.

'Italy will live to regret its association with fascism. But you mightn't.'

Brazzi ignored him. He wheezed at Stefan, 'So you're a partisan now, are you? I always wondered what happened to you.'

'No, you didn't.'

Brazzi watched a line of sugar ants, idly examined a crumb on the parquet floor, and his attention wandered off. He saw the lamp, felt the cold, drowsed into mindfulness, that space where he could at least breathe. Nothing else mattered.

'Well, perhaps you're right and I didn't. Right now I really don't care.'

Andrej started from his spot as if ignited.

'*You don't care!*' he broke in hotly. 'You've sold your soul to Italy, you miserable little shit. We should kill him right now, Captain.' He gave Brazzi a brutal kick in the ribs. '*Traitor!*' He kicked him again. Brazzi began to whimper.

'Call your dog off,' he pleaded.

'Take the money and go, Andrej,' said Stefan quietly.

'Justice is more important than money.'

Andrej stood for an instant as if trying to control himself, then abruptly he heaved a chair above his head and smashed it against the counter. The delicate lacquered curves exploded below the joint, exposing the pink wood beneath.

Stefan observed the agonized action without flinching and, as Andrej raised the carcass to strike again, he extended a hand.

'Don't waste yourself on him.'

Don't do what I did – unsaid, but understood.

A gentle rustle on the stairs distracted them. They turned to see Fräulein Müller the elder in voluminous nightgown and shawl, carrying a candle. A broad linen nightcap resplendent with drawn threadwork and insertions of Flemish lace almost obscured her elderly face, and her long-sighted gaze shot straight to Matteo Brazzi slumped in his pose of suffering.

'What was that noise?' she lisped softly, given the hour and her state of undress. 'Why, Signor Brazzi, whatever are you doing on the floor?'

Romano stepped forward.

'Forgive the intrusion, fräulein,' he replied courteously. 'You have been deceived. When I find out who this man really is, I will inform you.'

Fräulein Müller hastily departed to give her sisters the shocking news. The faint light of the Austrian candle traipsed its way up the stairs and the door closed shut.

'What are you going to do with him?' asked Romano.

'I've got what I came for,' Stefan replied.

Brazzi propped himself up on an unsteady hand.

'I'll leave you in peace. I'll go back to Trieste with Angelica.'

'It was your wife who told us you were here.'

Dead silence, save for the edge of his wheezing. Chest rising and falling, scrape, collapse. Emilio let the lamp drop to his hip. Its light fell and no one could see Brazzi's face. Brazzi was thankful for that mercy. He had not responded to the accusations leveled against him. He showed no inclination to measure his suffering against that which he had caused. He could not see beyond his present needs.

'Goodbye, Banich,' said Stefan, and, to Romano, 'You can have him.'

'We don't want him.'

Stefan watched Andrej struggling to master his anger, saw the townspeople hoping that he would make a decision that would free them.

His Most Italian City

So he said, 'We'll get rid of him for you.' He saw their relief and noted Andrej's spark of interest. He nodded to Brazzi. 'You want to go to Trieste, Banich? You can get there yourself.' To those assembled in the room, 'We'll dump him down the coast, but it won't be in Italy.'

And now Zan saw that Brazzi had known all along what Silvana's monster was. He watched the blood drain from the face on the floor, to be replaced by a crawling horror that warped his features, stretched his mouth, humbled him as nothing else had done.

'Oh, no, no, no, no,' Brazzi raised his hands. 'Not in that thing… You can't… I can't… I'll die.'

'No, you won't,' said Stefan.

He nodded to Zorko who hauled Brazzi to his feet; then he followed them, Mirko and Andrej out into the night.

In this life there were different kinds of peace. For him there was always the sea upon whose unchanging waves he never failed to find tranquility. In the depths he heard Nataša's voice. Stefan no longer desired revenge. He had his life. He had his children. He acknowledged that Banich had been partly right. Though he was never intentionally neglectful, without consulting Nataša's opinion about being so often alone he had expected that she would wait for him. He had married her knowing that she liked to listen to men and that Banich appreciated this. Could he bear the thought of someone else loving her, and could he judge that love by the virtue of the lover? What would Nataša have said? It all lay in the realm of conjecture and he put conjecture aside as an impediment to peace.

Giovanni stood by the door, watching the captain dissolve into the piazza and turn down the dark Corso, then he kissed his father.

'I won't be long.'

Between the shadowed buildings a black shape flew across the night sky. A dog barked. A cat went hunting down the lane. Below the Venetian Belvedere, the south wind was pounding the sea into surf. But such small tides the Adriatic has! The townsfolk had taken their candles to bed without fear and were listening to the waves in their sleep. To the west, the black port stretched between the pier and the breakwater and no one could see beyond it.

Giovanni ran to the end of the piazza through the trees to the port. As the lighthouse shone spasmodically, he saw Mirko and Andrej running up the pier and tagging each other. Half its length behind him, emerging from the shadow of the houses, he could just discern the figures of the captain and Zorko, who supported between them a pile of disheveled humanity. A strange exit for a fallen man. Strangest of all, as the men disappeared below the level of the pier, the harbor light once more gleamed upon its pedestal.

The boat pulled out on the far side, leaving behind the town and the rocks and the wind. Again Giovanni heard that bell, muffled by distance. Then the faraway black shape headed towards the open sea and silently slid below it.

Chapter Twenty-Five

There is a road that stretches into the hills, its path of beaten earth tramped flat by generations of feet, of men and women, of donkeys and oxen. Carts keep to the center, for the edges have fallen away somewhat and if two wish to pass then one must wait for the other. Here and there the remains of an old wall overgrown with thorny shrubs can be seen and, beside one of these, a single tree grows optimistically. Perhaps it is trying to attract another tree to increase the available shade, for the landscape is sparse and the vegetation short, no more than waist height. Looking back, the road leads down to the Adriatic. The hills rise up and the sea is always visible behind them as a line of shimmering blue.

This road leads from Cittanova to Torre, and Giovanni takes it the day before he returns to the University of Florence. On the path he meets three girls and a donkey. The donkey is burdened with a wicker basket on either side and two of the girls bear bunches of flowers, which they have taken from the baskets as decorations, as if someone is about to take their photo.

But the December days are short. Soon the sun will sink below the Adriatic, and Giovanni has to see all the old sights before the long twilight dissolves into dark. He greets the girls, who smile back at him, then he passes on.

Since his return Silvana has persistently quizzed him about his adventure, but he tells her he can't remember much, and her grandfather adds that the boat was too far away for him to see in the dark. Silvana is not impressed and has written a story for her school teacher called 'My Uncle and the Black Submarine of Cittanova.' Silvana is not normally an imaginative child and, as she has been deprived of the details she needs, she is forced to employ considerable technical license.

*****

Signor Matteo Brazzi runs a small café in Trieste. It is tucked up a street leading off the Grand Canal that can scarcely be seen for all the masts.

This situation suits Signor Brazzi. To have betrayed one's country, one's dictator, one's wife and one's benefactors in the cause of oneself is no minor sin, and Signor Brazzi sighs when he realizes he will be looking over his shoulder for the remainder of his days. A stiff neck is a light a penalty, and many would be glad to see him depart this life in a more imaginative way.

He is careful not to draw attention to himself, for he never knows who might know his history. Of course, he has his regulars, those who have remained faithful throughout his rise and fall, for though he is down he has avoided turning himself into the victim this time. His self-pity will only go so far and he has his standards to maintain.

His glory days are behind him now and he no longer imports coffee but instead purchases the best beans from a merchant he knew back then. He takes them home lovingly and grinds them fresh for each cup, as he has always done. Perhaps a medium-sized family or half a dozen businessmen on their way to the tram could slide carefully into his narrow shop but scarcely more than that, and often Signor Brazzi will sit there all by himself reflecting on the days when Trieste was the port of an empire. He may have a copy of *Il Piccolo* before him or he may not. Politics, he acknowledges, was not a good choice.

Signor Brazzi struggles to imagine a world without coffee and so he has gone back to the one thing that truly gives him pleasure. You may visit him if you choose, traveller, but his café can only be found by word of mouth, so be careful who you talk to.

THE END

About the Author

Margaret Walker

Margaret Walker is a casual teacher. She has a Bachelor of Science degree from the University of Sydney and a Diploma in Education.

Between 1999 and 2001, she had six short stories published in Australia and the UK, and plunged head first into novel writing. *His Most Italian City* is her fifth novel but the first to be published, as she had a troubling tendency with the first four to give up after three rejections and start another one.

Her epiphany came in 2016 when she graduated with a Diploma in Professional Communication and actually learned a few things about editing and publishing. An understanding of the industry dispelled much of its mystique, and becoming a published author no longer seemed like the impossible dream.

Margaret likes history, research and day dreaming. She has her husband to thank for developing an interest in modern languages. She is presently translating a book of Partisan poetry, bought in a second-hand book store in Croatia, for her next novel about the Yugoslav Partisans.

It is true that you should be careful what you wish for. Margaret's adoption papers read: Nationality of mother, Yugoslavian. After forty years of research punctuated by adoption reunions (yes, there were several) she discovered that her mother came from Istria where the novel is set. She spoke Venetian, German, Italian and English but flew on a Yugoslav passport and, even today, opinions as to whether she was Yugoslavian or Italian divide the family.

Claims have been made for the pro-Italian towns in Istria that 'we were gentle people between the wars. There was not crime then as we know it today.' However, we know from the Slovenian writer Boris Pahor that the fascists were burning and destroying Slavic culture from Trieste to Split at this time.

It was to investigate this apparent dichotomy that *His Most Italian City* was written.

If You Enjoyed This Book Visit

The California Run

by

Mark A. Rimmer

New York, 1850. Two clipper ships depart on a race around Cape Horn to the boomtown of San Francisco, where the first to arrive will gain the largest profits and also win a $50,000 wager for her owner.

Sapphire is a veteran ship with an experienced crew. Achilles is a new-build with a crimped, mostly unwilling crew. Inside Achilles' forecastle space reside an unruly gang of British sailors whose only goal is to reach the gold fields, a group of contrarily reluctant Swedish immigrants whose only desire is to return to New York and the luckless Englishman, Harry Jenkins, who has somehow managed to get himself crimped by the equally as deceitful Sarah Doyle, and must now spend the entire voyage working as a common sailor down in Achilles' forecastle while Sarah enjoys all the rich comforts of the aft passenger saloon.

Despite having such a clear advantage, Sapphire's owner has also placed a saboteur, Gideon, aboard Achilles with instructions to impede her in any way possible. Gideon sets to with enthusiasm and before she even reaches Cape Horn Achilles' chief mate and captain have both been murdered. Her inexperienced 2nd Mate, Nate Cooper, suddenly finds himself in command of Achilles and, with the help of the late captain's niece, Emma, who herself is the only experienced navigator remaining on board, they must somehow regain control over this diverse crew of misfits and encourage them onwards and around the Horn.

PENMORE PRESS
www.penmorepress.com

A CHERRY BLOSSOM IN WINTER
BY
RON SINGERTON

As the 20th century dawns, Japan is a rising power at odds with determinedly expanding Russia. In Moscow and St. Petersburg, aristocrats advance their political interests and have affairs as factory workers starve. Young Alexei Brusilov, son of an ambassador, accompanies his father to Japan and there falls in love with the daughter of a Japanese war hero. Despite threats and warnings, he pursues this forbidden romance, delighted to discover that Kimi-san returns his affection, until disaster overtakes them.

Amid the rising storm of revolution at home, Alexei returns to St. Petersburg to become a naval officer. A deadly rivalry with another cadet, a dangerous family secret, and friendships with revolutionaries imperil his career – and his life. Years later, Alexei finds himself aboard ship as the rusting and badly out of date Russian fleet is sent half way around the world to fight a modern and determined Japanese Navy. Will Alexei live to see his love again, or die under the blazing guns of the fast moving enemy cruisers?

"This is a sweeping work about the clash between Western and Eastern cultures, pretended morality, and grand passions struggling against heavily ritualized matrimony.... The author's observations about Russian society and his grasp of its good and bad points would likely have gained an approving nod from Tolstoy. This is first-rate storytelling!" —John Danielski, author of The King's Scarlet and Blue Water Scarlet Tide

PENMORE PRESS
www.penmorepress.com

Close to the Sun
by
Donald Michael Platt

WWII Fighter pilots, Air war over Europe. German Fighter aces, American Fighter Aces, War in Europe . Air War over Russia. German politics during WWII.

Close to the Sun follows the lives of fighter pilots during the Second World War. As a boy, Hank Milroy from Wyoming idealized the gallant exploits of WWI fighter aces. Karl, Fürst von Pfalz-Teuffelreich, aspires to surpass his father's 49 Luftsiegen. Seth Braham falls in love with flying during an air show at San Francisco's Chrissy Field. The young men encounter friends, rivals, and exceptional women. Braxton Mobley, the hotshot, wants to outscore every man in the air force. Texas tomboy Catherine "Winty" McCabe is as good a flyer as any man. Princess Maria-Xenia, a stateless White Russian, works for the Abwehr, German Intelligence. Elfriede Wohlman is a frontline nurse with a dangerous secret. Miriam Keramopoulos is the girl from Brooklyn with a voice that will take her places.

Once the United States enter the war, Hank, Brax, and Seth experience the exhilaration of aerial combat and acedom during the unromantic reality of combat losses, tedious bomber escort, strafing runs, and the firebombing of entire cities. As one of the hated aristocrats, Karl is in as much danger from Nazis as he is from enemy fighter pilots, as he and his colleagues desperately try to stem the overwhelming tide as the war turns against Germany. Callous political decisions, disastrous mistakes, and horrific atrocities they witness at the end of WWII put a dark spin on all their dreams of glory.

PENMORE PRESS
www.penmorepress.com

Historical fiction and nonfiction
Paperback available for order on line
and as Ebook with all major distributers

HEAVEN CRIES

BY

STEPHAN SILVA

Heaven Cries is a compelling story.

Captain Artemio Battaglia, a young World War II pilot, who when repulsed by the brutality of Mussolini's fascist state, joins a partisan band to fight the Nazi death squads that were terrorizing Italian citizens. Nicolas Gage, author of bestselling *Eleni* praised ***Heaven Cries*** for reminding *"us of the true spring waters of freedom: hope, kindness, courage, and love. In the dark light of recent events, this history is particularly relevant."*

Now available at Amazon, Barnes&Nobel, iBooks, and Kobo.

PENMORE PRESS
www.penmorepress.com

Penmore Press

Challenging, Intriguing, Adventurous, Historical and Imaginative

www.penmorepress.com